Anitbeet Productions Presents

Hood Boy:

I AM WHAT I AM

by LeRoy Payton

Hood Boy: I Am What I Am

By LeRoy Payton

Published by Anitbeet Productions

Copyright © 2016 by LeRoy Payton

ISBN **978-0-9969666-6-5**

Printed in the U.S.A

www.anitbeetproductions.net

At a very young age, Slim discovers an uncompromising, but self-sufficient lifestyle he feels he's essentially built for. Fast money in the dope game consumes him with its sense of freedom and control. As sweet as the game is to him, it comes with challenges that tests his commitment to what he claims to be.

Slim's biggest and most challenging test comes when he's betrayed by the life he puts his heart into. It's a tragedy that causes him to question his commitment to who he claims to be. At a devastating point in his life when his love for his family conflicts with his love for the game, he struggles to remain faithful to a lifestyle which proves to be maliciously cold. One pivotal decision will reveal his character.

Hood Boy: I Am What I Am I **by LeRoy Payton**

LeRoy

Chapters:

Chapter 1: Wild Child

On the night of February 27, 1980 in St. Louis, Missouri, a child forced his existence into the world after only being in his mother's womb for seven and a half months. A strong will to survive was already present within this four-pound, premature infant's body. His mother prayed with desperation as she watched him fight for his life. It was critical, and his chances of survival were slim, at the very best. That was how the professionals perceived it. Despite their professional perception, however, his mother did not allow herself to consider any chance of a potential loss.

Jenah spent three weeks watching her son, Jevon Johnson, in an incubator with his tiny body attached to life preserving devices. He was making very little progress, and the expenses to keep her baby alive grew by the day. Money was the last thing on her mind, though. Nothing was more valuable than the survival of her baby. A lifetime of debt meant nothing to her, as she was willing to relinquish every dime she had to save her son's life.

This was a very difficult time for Jenah. Her husband of three years had recently been sentenced to five years in the penitentiary for drug trafficking. Despite his uncompromising lifestyle, he gave her the excitement she was looking for, which ultimately led to him becoming her everything. She hadn't spoken with her immediate family in over three years. Her commitment to the rugged man who was now her husband led to them disowning her. Because of their disapproval of her relationship, Jenah was left to make a difficult choice. She was deeply affected by the charm of a street nigga, who made her feel like a queen. She decided to fully commit to him, hoping that her prominent family would come to see him as her innocent eyes did. They never gave him a chance, though. The only person she had to support her in any time of need was her dear friend, Angie.

After three weeks had gone by, Jenah's hopes were turned into relief causing her to thank God in some of the most emotional ways. She jumped up and down with joy, hugging and kissing everyone who was involved in her son's progress. The devices were removed from his body as it was developing and functioning on its own. Though he was still fragile, she felt a miracle in the making.

Jenah didn't understand how the abrupt delivery came about. This was her second pregnancy, and she was a healthy, twenty-five-year-old Black woman. Her doctor told her that the premature birth could have come from stress. She was secretly stressing over the absence of her husband. However, she disregarded the doctor's notions and concluded that her son was ready to make his presence. She thought of it as an early sign of what would turn out to be a bold, stubborn and an aggressive child.

"Slim," Jenah softly whispered as she sat next to his little bed. Jenah called her miracle baby Slim, as she thought of the hardest three weeks of her life. It was a name that represented his survival chances, and how precious life is. Jenah couldn't take her eyes off Slim, nor could she bare to be away from him. She was relieved, and that relief allowed her to relax. It's was then that the long, distressed days began to catch up with her. She attempted to fight off the sleep, but after a few nods, she became consumed by her weariness.

Jenah had only been asleep for a short while before she was abruptly awakened by a doctor. She was being lifted from her chair, and became resistant as her conscious came. She turned to Slim, who was violently shaking. Before she could come to his aid, she was forcefully escorted from the room by two doctors. She kicked and screamed to get to her baby, but the strong arms of the doctors prevented her.

"What's wrong wit my baby," Jenah cried as the doctors released her into the hall.

"Please wait here," one of the doctors said before they rushed back into the room.

"God, please don't take my baby away from me," Jenah pleaded as she ran to the large, glass window.

From the window, Jenah could see into the room. Slim was lost in the crowd of doctors and nurses, who were performing their duties. From their facial expressions, she could tell that things were serious.

"Noooo!" Jenah cried out as she continued to slap the glass. Jenah's joy was demolished as tears of fading hope ran down her face. She helplessly watched the commotion until it became unbearable. Her stomach was in knots, and her knees were weak. She began to slowly slide down the glass with her eyes closed. When she came to the floor, she sat curled in a ball as she clutched her stomach.

Jenah had been rocking back and forth on the floor for about ten minutes when things in the room became quiet. It was a quietness that scared her. She jumped up from the floor and seen that the doctors and nurses were stepping away from Slim's bed. The sight of him laying still took her breath as she ran into the room.

"Is my baby okay," Jenah asked as she ran into the arms of a doctor.

"He's okay. Please, come with me into the hall, and I'll explain his condition to you," the doctor calmly spoke.

"What condition?"

"Please, come with me."

Jenah wasn't trying to hear anything the doctor had to say just yet. She stood on her toes and looked over his shoulders to her baby Slim. Seeing his little stomach going up and down gave her an instant relief. A young nurse standing over him gave her a promising smile.

"He's fine," the nurse assured Jenah.

"Thank God," Jenah said with a distressed smile. She then allowed the doctor to lead her into the hall by her hand.

"Mrs. Johnson, your son just had a minor seizure," the doctor began to calmly speak. Jenah dropped her head and shook it in disbelief as she covered her mouth. When she looked back up to the doctor, he began to explain the nature of Slim's seizures. She listened attentively as she kept her eyes on her precious baby.

"This is very common in your son's type of situation. As he gets older, the seizures are most likely to go away," the doctor concluded.

"So, when will I be able to take him home?"

"I would like to keep him a little while longer to verify my predictions."

"Can I go see him, now?" Jenah eagerly asked.

"Sure. But only for a moment. I would like to begin immediately with some formal testing."

After a few days of running tests, the doctor gave Jenah the approval to take Slim home. He gave her simple instructions to deal with his seizures. She excitedly rushed to the phone and called Angie. She was staying at her house, babysitting her two-year-old son, Marcel.

At home with Slim, Jenah had everything prepared for his arrival. She gently laid him in his plush cradle, and stood over him with a smile. He was peacefully sleeping. Jenah could hear the phone ringing in the other room as she was hoping that it was her husband. She hadn't spoken with him in over five weeks. Angie relayed their messages as she remained by Slim's bedside. When she looked over to the door, Angie was coming into the room with the phone.

"It's Donnell." Jenah's face lit up with a glow as she took the phone.

"Hey baby," she sweetly spoke.

"What's up, sweetheart? You sound nice."

"I'm jus glad to be at home wit the baby. He doin' real good, and he jus so quiet."

"I never thought for one minute that he wouldn't pull through. He got the blood of a survivor flowin' through his veins, and the eyes of an Angel lookin' over him. Wit that, he could never lose."

"No, he can't. And I'll always be by his side," Jenah promisingly expressed.

"I know you will. But ay, I don't have long to talk. I jus wanted to touch bases wit'chu. Get that money from Angie, and take care of everything that'chu need to take care of wit it. We'll talk more later on tonight. But in the meantime, I want'chu to get some rest. Can you do that for me?"

"Yeeeah, I can do that," Jenah sweetly answered.

"I love you. Put Angie back on."

"I love you too." When Jenah gave Angie the phone, she left the room. She was familiar with the nature of their conversations. Her husband took care of her and their kids with drug money he made in the penitentiary. It was Angie, who he had paying a guard to smuggle his drugs in. He never included Jenah in any of the business that went on with him in the penitentiary, or when he was in the streets.

Donnell spent three years in the penitentiary before he was released on parole. Jenah was there early that morning to bring him home. When they got there, he was impressed with the upgrades she made.

"I like what'chu did wit' the place," Donnell said as he looked around the living room.

"Thank you, but wait 'til you see the bedroom," Jenah seductively whispered as she approached Donnell.

"I knew you was gon keep it togetha for me." Donnell wrapped his arms around Jenah's waist and cupped the bottom of her ass with his big hands. She submitted herself to him as she wrapped her arms around his neck. Their passionate kissing began as they stared deep into each other's eyes with strong desires. There were no guards watching over them, so the absence of boundaries excited them further.

"You got me ready to disregard everything and deal wit'chu right now," Donnell said as he gave Jenah's ass a hard squeeze.

"Whatever you wanna do, baby."

"We gon get to that. Right now, I want'chu to do yo' thing for me in the kitchen while I spend some time wit' my sons."

Jenah kissed Donnell's lips before she led him to the room where their children were. She purposely twisted her hips, proudly showing him that she'd kept herself together.

When Jenah and Donnell got to the room where their children were, they stood hugged up in the doorway unnoticed. Angie laid at the head of the bed while Slim and Marcel laid at the foot of it. They were in their pajamas watching cartoons.

"What's up?"

Slim and Marcel turned around at the same time as they heard their father's voice.

"S'up," Slim lazily spoke before he turned back to the cartoons. Unlike Slim, Marcel was very enthused to see their father. He jumped from the bed and ran towards him with his arms up. They were very familiar with their father from their once a week visit to the penitentiary. Now at the age of three, Slim had grown out of the seizures. Even though he was very quiet and distant at times, he had a stubborn attitude with a violent temper. His mother figured that it was from how he was born. To deal with him, she allowed him to have his way. When his disturbing tantrums occurred, she would restrain him and calmly talk to him until he was calm. His father had no idea of the other side of him.

"What's up Jevon? Come and see what's up wit'cho ol'dude," Donnell said as he put Marcel down.

"Baby, please leave that crazy boy alone while he quiet," Jenah pleaded with Donnell.

Donnell looked at Jenah with confusion before he headed over to Slim.

"Okay. Don't say I didn't tell you," Jenah said before she left the room.

"What's up? You chillin'," Donnell asked as he sat next to Slim.

Slim nodded his head up and down as he kept his eyes on the cartoons.

"Tell yo' daddy how you cussed me out this mornin'," Angie said as she tapped Slim with her foot. Slim twisted his face at Angie as he pushed her foot away from him.

"Damn. What's that all about?" Donnell asked with a look of confusion.

"That lil' boy is somethin' else. Soon as he don't get his way, he act a fool."

"What'chu mean?" Donnell demanded details.

It was then when Angie realized that she spoke out of turn. From Donnell's relentless expression, she knew that he wasn't going to let up. She took a deep breath and blew it out before she told him about that morning's incident. She even included extra information as she got carried away.

"So," Slim said as he slid from the bed. He then headed towards the door with his face twisted at Angie.

"C'mere, boy," Donnell barked at Slim. Slim stopped in the doorway and turned to his approaching father. "All this lil' shit yo' mama been allowin' you to do finna come to a stop," Donnell said as he kneeled down to Slim. "You hear me?"

Slim stared into his father's face without a blink from his eye. He then shrugged his shoulders as he turned to leave. After only a step, he was snatched back into place.

"You can show yo' ass if you want to! I guarantee you yo' mama won't be able to save you," Donnell said as he got into Slim's face.

Slim slipped away from his father's grasp. He ran into the kitchen and wrapped his skinny arms around his mother's leg. She was over the stove, and looked down to him as she knew what the problem was.

"What'chu do to my baby," Jenah asked as Donnell came into the kitchen.

"Why you ain't tell me this boy been showin' his ass like that?" Donnell calmly asked with disappointment.

"It ain't nothin' I can't handle."

"I ain't questionin' yo' abilities, but c'mon sweetheart, we 'pose to be togetha. But I'm here now, and that's how I want us to deal wit' things."

Jenah shook her head up and down as she turned back to her cooking. She wondered how her husband was going to react to Slim's tantrums.

"Baby, go over there 'fore you get popped by this hot grease," Jenah said as she looked down to Slim.

Slim looked up to his mother, wondering if he'd still have her wrapped around his finger with his father being there with his dominate presence. After a moment, he slowly unwrapped his arms from around her leg. He then sat in the hall just outside of the kitchen.

"This food'll be done in a lil' bit," Jenah said as she looked to her husband, then back to the stove.

"It's srnellin', and lookin' good," Donnell softly spoke as he hugged Jenah from behind.

"You jus' go have a seat and let me cater to you."

"I like how that sound."

While Jenah and Donnell ate, he gave her some relieving news. He proudly told her that he was through with the street life, and how his family was his main priority. He was going to invest the $75,000 he accumulated in the dope game into real estate. He was also going to do construction work with his uncle, who was a successful, independent contractor. Finally, Jenah was going to have the type of family life her husband always promised her. Her worries of the streets taking him away from her were put to rest. The exciting news took her appetite. The only thing she wanted to consume was her husband as she welcomed him into their new life with her passionate love making. On the way to their room, their anxiousness left no room for them to notice Slim. He was still sitting in the hall with his jealous frown.

Jenah and Donnell came into their room hot, and ready to get loose. Their lips were locked together, and their hands were all over each other. During the presexual activities, he managed to close the door behind him with his foot. Making their way to the bed, they stripped each other like excited children on christmas.

At the bed, Jenah pushed Donnell onto it as she moistened her lips. She was preparing them for his hard dick that was aimed at her. Her voluptuous titties hung from her body as she slowly crawled onto the bed. Getting herself in position to welcome her husband home with some fire head, she was over him on her elbows and knees.

"Do yo' thing baby," Donnell smoothly said as he removed strands of hair from Jenah's face. Just as Jenah was about to do her thing, a loud crash shook the house. Following the crash, Angie's shouts and rumbling came.

"What the fuck is goin' on down there," Donnell asked as he sat up. Jenah already knew what time it was. She quickly jumped from the bed and grabbed her robe. She fixed it on her naked body as she rushed downstairs. When Jenah got downstairs where everyone was, it looked like a tornado came through. The t.v. that was still on laid face down on the floor. Sunlight lit up the room from windows where curtains had been snatched away. Clothes were everywhere, and hung from drawers that were ajar.

"Girl, get this lil' rnonsta away from me," Angie shouted as Jenah rushed into the room.

Slim had a yellow, plastic bat in his hand. As soon as Angie released him, he smacked her across the face with it Just as he was about to swing it at her again, his mother snatched him up. Jenah wrapped Slim's upper body in her arms as she sat on the bed. He was standing between her legs that restrained his lower body. This was the routine she used when he began to wild out. Still holding the bat, he cussed and squirmed. His mother had him completely subdued as she softly talked in his ear.

"What the fuck is goin' on in here," Donnell asked as he became shocked by the disaster. His attention was then snatched by Jenah, who had Slim wrapped up like a snake. "Let his ass go," he ordered as he snatched the bat from Slim.

"He need to calm down first," Jenah cried out.

"Let his ass go," Donnell repeated himself with a more aggressive tone.

As soon as Jenah released Slim, it was like watching a tazmania devil spinning towards Angie. She was standing in the doorway with Marcel. Seeing him coming with that devilish expression, she closed the door.

Slim was pulling and kicking on the door when his father began to whip him with the bat.

"That's not gon work," Jenah informed. Donnell ignored Jenah and seen for himself that whipping Slim was ineffective. With every strike, he only became more furious. He took a few whips across his hand before he got a hold to the bat. His father snatched it away from him and sent him crashing to the floor. His head hit the floor with a loud thump, but not even that could calm him. He jumped back to his feet with a fat knot on his forehead. He shot back towards his father, who was coming towards him.

"This not gon work!" Jenah cried out as she jumped between Slim and his father. Jenah wrapped Slim in her arms and rubbed the knot on his head with her back to her husband.

"You right," Donnell said as he snatched Slim from his mother.

"Where you takin' him?" Jenah asked as she followed her husband.

Donnell ignored Jenah as he continued down the hall with Slim dangling from his arms. She followed him with her questions that fell on deaf ears. When he got to the empty room at the end of the hall, he put Slim inside and left him there.

"How the hell you let this boy get like this," Donnell furiously asked as he held onto the door handle.

"Why do it have to be from somethin' I did, or didn't do?" Jenah asked, trying to open her husband's mind to other reasons. On the other side of the door, Slim pulled on the knob as he cried out for his mother. When he got no response, he began to curse and kick on the door. He was feeling like his mother abandoned him.

"Well, this how it's gon' be. Every time he show his ass, I'ma whup his ass and lock him in this room!"

It would be the isolation that would create Slim's control issues with a strong desire for liberation; free from bondage or restraint.

"That's not right," Jenah spoke. Intuitively.

"I don't wanna lock my son up like he some kinda wild animal. But I'm not finna have him tearin' up shit around the house. Now, if you have another idea other than what'chu been doin', I'm all ears."

Jenah stared at her husband as she had no idea of what to do with their troubled son. They only hoped that his disturbing behavior was a phase.

Chapter 2: Dysfunctional

Years pass by with Slim at the age of five, and his behavior has shown no progress. His parents concluded that it wasn't a phase. They didn't know what else to do, except to lock him in his room. His room had been relocated to the basement. In the room he had previously, he managed to find ways to escape. His father moved his room when he kicked a hole in the wall to get out through the next room. With his room in the basement, there was no escaping. Concrete walls secured him with a thick, wooden door that held a pad lock. He was fed in that room, and there was a bathroom in the basement which made it convenient.

Slim's mother tried to work as a school teacher, but his behavior demanded too much of her attention. He recently had been expelled from school for pushing a boy down a flight of steps creating a domino effect, causing other students to fall.

As a qualified teacher, Slim's mother took it upon herself to school him during his absences. To her surprise, he was a bright child, who loved to learn. It was one of the times where she found him completely adorable. Then there were the times he spent with his two-year-old sister, Jayla. He was gentle with her, and showed a soft side that was shocking. Jayla's first words were, Von-Von. It was a sign of a tight bond that would become stronger as they grew older. It was the exact opposite with his big brother, who he constantly fought with.

Slim had been confined to his room since until dinner time. His mother stopped her restraining routine some time ago as it became ineffective. He would only pretend to be calm until he was released. But no matter what he did, she could never bring herself to severely discipline him. She would only drag him to his room and lock him inside with his TV. It was something she fought with her husband about letting him have. Over time, he learned not to tear up the things he enjoyed. It showed that he had a comprehensive mind.

"What's up lil' boy? Are you ready to come outta this room?"

Slim ignored his mother as she stood in the doorway. He laid at the foot of his bed, curled under a blanket as he watched TV.

"You hear me talkin' to you?"

"Nope," Slim mumbled.

"Nope, you don't wanna come upstairs and eat, or nope, you don't hear me talkin' to you," Jenah asked as she sat next to him.

"Leave me alone!" Slim shouted.

"I'm the one who should be mad!"

"So!"

"I ain't tell yo' daddy that'chu was fightin' yo' brotha this mornin'." Jenah looked at him for a response as she knew why he didn't want to go upstairs. After a moment, he shrugged his shoulders.

"Don't act like you don't care, 'cause I can still go tell him."

"No, you ain't," Slim said with a smile as he laid his head in his mother's lap.

Jenah shook her head from side to side as she stared into his sleepy, brown eyes. "I'm not playin' wit'chu lil' boy! I ain't gon have you fightin' wit'cho brotha," she said as she squeezed his cheeks causing his lips stuck out.

"I'm sorry mama," Slim managed to say.

"Okay. Let's go up here and eat," Jenah suggested before she kissed his forehead.

After the peaceful dinner, Jenah ran him a hot bath without any hassle to get him in the tub. When he came from the bathroom, she called him into the living room where she was going to French braid his hair. She preferred braiding his hair instead of going through the hassle of getting him to sit still in the barber's chair.

"Sit down right here," Jenah said as she directed him between her legs.

"Mama don't be tryin'a do it all tight," Slim whined.

"Boy, sit down!"

"Why I'm gettin' my hair braided," Slim asked, knowing that he only got it done on special occasions.

"I'm takin' you to yo' new school in the mornin'."

"I wanna stay here and let'chu be my teacher."

"Baby, you have to go to a real school. And if you act up, I'm not gon' get'chu that bike for Christmas," Jenah said as a tactic that would hopefully encourage him to behave accordingly.

"Mama, please! I'ma be good!"

"Boy, turn around 'fore I mess yo' head up!"

Slim immediately complied as he was trying to show his mother that he could cooperate.

"If you have a problem at school, go to your teacher, or come home and talk to me about it. Do you understand me?"

"I will," Slim said as he had sincere intentions to stay out of trouble.

Slim's mother was finished with his hair in no time. His two French braids were neatly done and dangled pass his shoulders. Along with his long, pretty hair that caused people to mistake him as a girl, it was his sleepy eyes and his slurry speech that he was teased about. Being teased is part of the reason why he stayed in trouble.

Because of Slim's behavior problems, he was placed in a special class where there were only a handful of students. Jenah was familiar with the behavior disorder class that he was being placed in. He could only return to regular classes if his behavior improved. She knew that it was a long shot, but she still left him with some encouraging words.

When Jenah came home from dropping Slim off at his new school, she ran into Angie. She was sitting on her porch with her head down. It was cold outside, and from her posture, she could tell that something was wrong.

"Girl, how long you been sittin' out here?" Jenah asked as she came up the steps.

"Not long," Angie mumbled as she kept her head down.

"What's wrong wit'chu?"

Angie shook her head from side to side as she slowly rose her head.

Jenah became shocked as she noticed Angie's swollen lip. "What the hell happened to you?"

"That jealous-ass nigga put his hands on me," Angie bitterly replied. "I'm alright though. I just put my stuff in the car and left his ass. I didn't know nowhere else to go, but here."

"Angie, you know you are more than welcomed to stay here."

"What Donnell gon say?" Angie asked.

"Girl, don't be silly. C'mon."

After Jenah helped Angie get her things into the house, she brought her a bag of ice that was wrapped in a towel. It was natural for her to comfort her dear friend. With no doubt in her mind, she knew that she would do the same thing if the shoe was on the other foot.

"Now, talk to me," Jenah said as she sat next to Angie. "What happened?"

"It ain't nothin' to talk about. I just ain't finna let him control me."

"Girl, what'chu do?"

"Bein' me, and doin' what makes me happy."

"And lemme guess, he don't approve of what it is that makes you happy."

Angie shrugged her shoulders as she looked to the floor.

"Well, you'll always be my girl. And I don't care what'chu do. He ain't got no right to be puttin' his hands on you."

"I love you, Jenah. And here, this for the house," Angie replied before she went into her purse. Angie pulled a thick roll of money from her purse and peeled $200 from it for Jenah. Jenah was used to seeing her with money, so she thought nothing of it. She refused to accept it, considering that she had always been there for her. It was Angie's stubbornness that made her end up taking it.

That evening when Donnell came in from work, he ran into Angie. He instantly became stunned as he noticed her fat lip. "Damn girl! What happened to you?"

Before Angie could respond, Jenah came into the living room and intervened. She took her husband to the kitchen and explained Angie's situation.

"It's just 'til she finds her a place," Jenah finished telling her husband.

"It's cool. She's like family," Donnell said as he was still processing everything.

"You sure?" Jenah asked as she noticed the perplexed look on her husband's face.

"It's just that, I been knowing Lil' Charles for years, and he ain't the type to do things for no reason."

"I don't care what she did! He ain't got no business puttin' his hands on her," Jenah defended Angie.

"I got just as much love for Angie as you do. But c'mon baby, let's not be naive about this," Donnell stated before he left the kitchen.

Giving it no thought, Jenah shrugged her shoulders as she continued to prepare dinner.

During the next two weeks, Slim managed to keep himself out of trouble. A few minor incidents happened at school that had him agitated, but he came home and talked to his mother like she encouraged him to.

Angie didn't spend a lot of time around the house. She was in the house long enough to shower, change her clothes, and grab a small bite to eat. Jenah didn't suspect a thing from her behavior, but her husband was all about the best interest of his family decided to do some investigating. When he came in from work, he had some shocking news to reveal to his naive wife.

"Where the hell Angie at?" Donnell asked as he came into the kitchen.

"I don't know. I haven't seen her since the other day," Jenah replied as she turned from the stove. "What's wrong?"

"She needs to come and get her shit and find somewhere else to live! I caught up with Lil' Charles, and he told me about how she gettin' down in the streets. She out there prostitutin' and smokin' that shit!"

"What?!" Jenah exclaimed feeling shocked. Donnell's words echoed repeatedly in Jenah's head as it felt like she'd been punched in her stomach. She dropped the spatula to the floor and grabbed onto the counter as she held her stomach.

"That's why she been movin' like that," Donnell continued on. "But all that runnin' in and outta here finna come to a stop!"

"Wait a minute! We can't just abandon her. We need to help her." Jenah tried to reason with her husband.

"She don't want no help. She out there enjoyin' herself. And that's cool, but we got kids to think about. Ain't no tellin' what else she doin' out there."

"I do think about the kids, and I'll never put them in harm's way. But Angie is like family, and I don't see how you can just you're your back on her so easily."

"Let me tell you how," Donnell argued as he stepped closer to Jenah. "It's 'cause I put my kids first."

"I'm really not understandin' how you can become somethin' that'chu once despised.

"What the hell is that 'pose to mean?" Donnell frowned.

"My family condemned you 'cause of the way you was, " Jenah began her defense for her best friend.

"Don't compare what I did to the shit she out there doin'," Donnell interrupted Jenah.

"I'm not comparin' you with her. I'm just tryin' to point out, despite what she is doin', she is still a good person. And that's why I stayed wit'chu, despite what'chu did. I left my family for you, and it hurts me to see you treat Angie like this," Jenah cried.

Donnell took a few seconds to swallow Jenah's words. "I got love for Angie, but as a man, I can't always let what I feel dictate what I do.

I have to make logical decisions that are in the best interest of this family. I left the streets alone, 'cause it contradicts my commitment as a family man. Now, what makes you think that I'ma allow somebody else to bring it to the house? Love ain't got nothin' to do wit it."

"You right," Jenah said as she turned back to her cooking.

After dinner, Jenah received a phone call that added to her stress. "Hello," she wearily answered.

"May I speak with a Mr. or Mrs. Johnson?" a woman politely asked.

"This is she."

"It's Ms. Harris, Jevon's teacher. I'm calling in regard to his behavior at school today. He was sent home with a three-day suspension notice."

"What!"

"I take it that you didn't receive it."

"No, I did not. What happened?" Jenah dreadfully asked.

"Well, there were a series of incidents that came to Jevon punching one of his classmates in the face."

"Ms. Harris, I am so sorry for this!"

"I'm hoping Jevon's behavior can improve before it leads to him being expelled."

"I will see to it that Jevon is further disciplined," Jenah said in a promising tone.

When Jenah got off the phone with Slim's teacher, she leaned against the counter and dropped her head. She knew that her baby boy had a behavior problem and it was only a matter of time before it got him into trouble. She looked up quickly as she thought about how her husband was going to respond. The thought of his harsh discipline made her stomach bubble as perspiration formed on her forehead. She hung her head once again as she came up with a deceitful solution. Jenah wasn't going to tell her husband about Slim's suspension. She was going to keep it to herself, and deal with Slim in her own way. Her husband was always off to work before their children went to school, and was always back after them.

After cleaning the kitchen, Slim's mother found him in his room. He was curled on his bed, watching TV

"Where that damn note at?" she asked as she popped his head.

"Mama, quit hittin' me," Slim whined as he frowned his face.

"Shut up 'fore I got get'cho daddy," Slim's mother said as she popped him again. "I don't care about'chu bein' mad," she added as she pushed his head with her finger.

Slim fell to the bed, and remained there with his face twisted.

"Get'cho butt up and get that paper yo' teacher sent'chu home wit!"

"I lost it," Slim lied.

"You betta find it 'fore yo' daddy do." Jenah warned her son.

"He not," Slim assured his mother.

"What happened to you comin' home and talkin' to me?"

"Mama, I promise, I was tryin' to be good," Slim said as he sat up.

"Baby, what did we talk about?" Jenah softly asked as she sat next to him. "You have to think about things, and what'll happen if you get in trouble. You have to start bein' a big boy, 'cause mama won't always be able to save you."

"I'm sorry, mama," Slim cried as he threw his arms around her. Jenah held back her tears as she returned the embrace. It was the sweet side of him that melted her heart as she knew that her baby was special.

"It's time for you to go to bed, 'cause you still gettin' up in the mornin'. And I will make some school work for you to do, so don't think you gon' watch cartoons all day," Jenah said as she turned his TV off.

"Mama," Slim called for her when she got to the door.

"What, baby?"

"Can I still have my bike?" Slim asked with his charming eyes.

"Boy, I am not thinkin' about no damn bike!"

Slim watched his mother leave his room with a smile on his face.

That next morning, Jenah was in the living room watching soap operas. Slim was stretched out on the floor doing math problems she made for him. Jayla was stretched out next to him, listening attentively as he explained the math to her. Even though her two-year-old mind wasn't fully comprehensive, his desire to teach her would eventually become progressive.

Jenah turned her attention to the door knob as someone was twisting it from the outside. Seeing that the door was locked, they began to knock. She had a good idea of who it was as she went for the door.

"Girl, what the hell?" Jenah sneered as she held the door open. She cut herself off, because of her children being present. "Come in here, 'cause we need to talk!"

Angie had a blank expression as she followed Jenah to the kitchen. Slim twisted his face at her as he never grew to like her.

"What the hell is goin' on wit'chu?" Jenah asked as she spun around to Angie.

"I guess you heard, huh," Angie nonchalantly spoke.

"Why you let me find out like this? And why you actin' so settle about it?" Jenah was fuming.

"I'm sorry you had to find out like this. Jenah, I love you, and I care about what'chu think. I ain't tell you, 'cause I didn't want'chu to turn on me like everybody else did," Angie explained.

"Girl, stop it! You know betta than that! I'm pissed off, but I'll never turn my back on you. We been through too much together."

"Thank you," Angie said as a smile appeared on her face. "And I'm so settle about this 'cause this is what I wanna do. It's my choice and I don't have a problem wit gettin' down for a few hunnid and goin' to blow my brains out."

Jenah couldn't help laughing a little. She shook her head in disbelief as she realized that there was nothing she could do to pull Angie back.

"I'm not gon' pretend to like how you gettin' down, and I'm not gon' hold it against you. You still my girl, and I just want'chu to take care of yo'self."

"Love you too," Angie sweetly said as she hugged her dear friend. Their embrace was brief, but it was one that confirmed the depths of their relationship.

"Like I said, you still my girl, but Donnell don't want'chu around while you doin' what'chu do. I have to respect that, so please, don't put me in an awkward position," Jenah said sternly.

Angie chuckled as she shook her head from side to side. "I understand, and I'll never intentionally put'chu in a position that'll have you into it wit'cho man," she spoke with sincerity. "I actually came to get my stuff, give you some money, and somehow tell you what was goin' on wit' me. I guess things just worked out."

"I'm glad we talked. Now, just 'cause you out there hoein', that don't mean that we have to be strangers," Jenah said with a laugh.

"Girl, please! I don't have this out nowhere. I'm professional wit' mines," Angie smirked with a sassy attitude as she slapped her ass.

"But we can still get together sometime. Help me wit' my stuff, so I can show you my place."

In the neighborhood, Jenah came to see that Angie lived in an apartment with a lot of nice things. It was her sanctuary where she never brought her tricks. For the time being, she was a beautiful woman with a sensual figure. Being that, Jenah wasn't surprised to know that men would pay top dollar to sleep with her. From the looks of everything, she appeared to be at the top of her game. Jenah had no idea that someone who smoked crack with the occupation as a prostitute could live so comfortably. She left Angie's apartment fascinated with that discovery.

Over the next few weeks, Jenah didn't see Angie at all. They only talked over the phone. Their conversations were usually interrupted by the popular demand for Angie's services. She was hot. It was now the weekend, and they planned on going out to a lounge.

"Damn baby! You lookin' good," Donnell complimented his wife as he noticed her at her finest. "Where you finna go?"

"To Jessie's wit' Angie," Jenah blushed as she went for her car keys.

"Nah, I don't want'chu nowhere around her," Donnell said as he sat up and grabbed Jenah's keys.

"Donnell," Jenah said as she stood over him with her hands on her hips. "What is yo' problem?"

"Nah What is yo' problem? I'm not finna allow you to be around her, knowing what type of shit she be into," Donnell snarled with authority.

"What'chu mean allow me!? Don't talk to me like that. And whatever she do is her business!"

"Nah! Whatever she do or has already done becomes my business when you runnin' around wit' her! You can't be that fuckin' naive!"

"You just worried about what other people gon' think! Well guess what? I don't! And I don't appreciate how you treatin' me like a child," Jenah said as she became more frustrated.

"Check this out," Donnell calmly said as he rose from the bed. Jenah took a step back with her hands on her hips as her husband got into her face. She just knew that he wasn't about to put his hands on her. "I'm not tryin'a argue and debate "

"Then don't! Just gimme my keys," Jenah interrupted.

"I ain't givin' you shit! And you ain't finna hang around that bitch," Donnell shouted as he pointed his finger in Jenah's face.

"Who the hell…? "

Donnell cut Jenah off as he slapped her across the mouth with the back of his hand. She stumbled backwards and fell to one knee. She slowly looked up to him in shock as she held her bloody mouth. He had never put his hands on her. But there were never any clashes that tested his tolerance.

"I can't believe you just put'cho fuckin' hands on me," Jenah cried as she ran and locked herself in the bathroom.

Over the next few days, Jenah only spoke to her husband when it was necessary. She did it with no eye contact and in a mumble. The connection between them was broken. She even slept in a separate room, feeling betrayed, violated and confused. For the first time in her marriage, she was completely unhappy. She yearned for his apology, and for him to throw himself to her for forgiveness. It never happened. Jenah continued to do the "good wifey" things, which consisted of cooking, cleaning, and caring for the children. She spent most of her time with them. They could sense her sadness, especially Slim.

After three days of solitude, Jenah came to find her husband in bed. He would usually be gone to work. She thought about leaving him asleep, but she wasn't a spiteful or a vindictive woman.

When Jenah woke her husband, she found out that he took a few days off from work. Despite the tension between them, he thanked her for being courteous. Not only was it the most he said to her in days, it was the nicest. It brightened her day as she became hopeful that they could reconcile during his off days. She was going to even take the first steps towards reconciling by cooking a big breakfast for them.

After cooking, Jenah softly sung love songs while she set the table. She heard the phone ringing in the other room and dropped everything she was doing before it woke her husband.

When Jenah got to their room, it was too late. Her husband was sitting up on the bed with the phone to his ear. From his facial expressions, she could tell that it wasn't a pleasant phone call.

"I'm on my way," Donnell angrily said before he slammed the phone to the receiver. While Donnell got dressed, he explained the nature of the phone call to Jenah.

"Let me go get him," Jenah begged, hoping to take control.

"I'ma deal wit' this! I don't know how long that boy been showin' his ass at that school, but I'm finna put a stop to it," Donnell said before he stormed off. Jenah went into the kitchen and sat at the table with a long face. She stared at the big breakfast she prepared. Her appetite was dead, and she had a gut feeling that reconciliation with her husband was also dead.

At the school, Slim's teacher explained more of the incident to his father. He sabotaged the entire class, including the teacher. It began when his teacher instructed him to read aloud. He was initially proud to show off his reading skills. As he began to read, a few boys started to laugh at his slurry speech. It's what set him off. However, his father found his behavior unacceptable. He became more furious when he was told that he was being expelled from the school. He was also informed about his recent suspension. Having no knowledge of that was humiliating. It was his wife's deceptive conduct that pushed him past furious.

"Take yo' ass to that room," Donnell barked at him as he slammed the door behind him.

Slim sorrowfully looked at his mother as he continued on. He wanted her to save him, but he knew that it was now out of her hands.

"What happened?" Jenah asked as she jumped up from the couch.

"The same shit that's been happenin'! Why you ain't tell me about that boy gettin' suspended?"

"I talked to him, and I felt like I had it under control."

"You 'pose to let me know about shit like that! He needs to be disciplined!"

"What's beatin' him half to death and lockin' him in that room doin'?" Jenah yelled back at her husband.

"Don't question me on how I discipline him! That's my fuckin' son too! And I won't have him showin' his ass like that just like I won't have you undermining me," Donnell declared as he snatched his belt off. He then stormed away.

Jenah took a deep breath and slowly exhaled as she sat on the couch. She shook her head in disbelief as she felt her marriage drifting further apart.

"Take them damn clothes off," Jenah heard Donnell bark at Slim. Moments later, she could hear the thick belt slapping across Slim's skin. His loud cries followed. She looked up and covered her mouth as Jayla ran to her crying. Slim's cries were unbearable. No mother could ignore the tormenting cries of their baby. The thought of his frail, tender body filled her head as she stood up. She couldn't take it anymore. She furiously ran to his room as if she were about to save his life.

When Jenah got to Slim's room, the sight of him brought tears to her eyes. He was completely naked, laying on his stomach as he gripped his sheets. His father held him to the bed by the back of his neck, even though he showed no signs of struggling. He laid motionless with his hoarse cries.

"That's enough!" Jenah cried out as she charged her husband. Donnell was just about to give Slim another lick when Jenah crashed into him. Her 5'7, thick figure took him from his feet. They both went down, and was on the floor exchanging blows. He was the first to get to his feet. His opened hand caught her face a few times before she grabbed onto his shirt. He stumbled as she pulled herself up. It gave her the opportunity to catch him with a few whips across his face. He took a few more of them before he got a hold of her. He tossed her across the room as if she was a rag doll. She bounced off the wall and came charging back towards him. He weaved her windmill swinging arms before he was able to slam her to the floor. He sat on her chest and held her wrist to the floor while they chased their breath.

"You need to get'cho head right 'fore I seriously hurt'chu!"

"Get off me!" Jenah cried as she squirmed. Donnell had Jenah completely subdued. After a moment, she laid still.

"Don't make me hurt'chu," Donnell warned as he rose from Jenah's chest. Jenah quickly jumped to her feet while Donnell stood a few feet away from her. For a moment, they stared at each other as they anticipated each other's next move. She broke the eye contact as her glare shifted to Slim. He was laying on his side, curled into a ball. Disregarding the hostile eyes of her husband, she rushed to comfort her baby. She wrapped his naked body in his blanket and held him in her arms as she sat on his bed.

"We ain't finish wit' this shit. You need to come to some type of understanding of where yo' place is," Donnell said as he stood over Jenah and Slim.

"I have no understanding of how you treat me, and beat my baby half to death," Jenah cried.

"When he show his ass, I'ma discipline him the way I see fit! And if you keep undermining what 'pose to be coherent, we gon' always have problems," Donnell said before he left the room.

Within the next few weeks, the distance between Jenah and her husband grew wider. She felt completely lost in her own home. Every night, she cried herself to sleep from the reality of the dead passion in her marriage. It was a passion that was once her everything, and caused her to leave her family. She couldn't help thinking about their warnings. They told her that her husband would end up hurting her.

He was from the slums, and it was his thoughts, perceptions and actions they wanted to protect her from. Their children were the only reason she was sticking around.

It took a lot of courage for Jenah to confront her husband in another attempt to reconcile. When he came in from work, he ate, showered, and went to the room they once shared. She found him laying in the bed, looking at sports.

"We really need to talk," Jenah softly said as she sat on the bed.

Donnell looked at Jenah for a few seconds, then back to the TV.

"It's a few things that we need to talk about. Jevon, the distance between us, and how you been treatin' me. Now, I apologize for the part I played in this mess. I excluded you from what was goin' on wit Jevon, 'cause it hurts me to see how you discipline him. I feel like it tells him, that's how problems are to be handled."

"And what'chu think the shit'chu doin' tellin' him?"

"I understand and I apologized, and I'm aware of the importance of creating a united front. That's why we need to talk."

"I'm listening."

"We been goin' through this wit' Jevon for a while now, and I don't see him gettin' any betta. I think we should consider gettin' him some professional help."

"Ain't nothin' wrong wit' that boy. I went through the same shit when I was his age, and I'm aiight."

"If you call puttin' yo' hands on me alright, maybe you should get some professional help too," Jenah said as she managed to keep her cool.

"Is that 'pose to be funny," Donnell asked with a slight twist in his face.

"I don't think me walkin' around bruised up is funny. You have an anger problem just like Jevon, and nobody should be subjected to it," Jenah said as she became frustrated from her husband's stubbornness.

"You subject yo'self to shit as a result of lyin' and keepin' shit from me!"

"I'm yo' wife! Nothin' I do should make you wanna put'cho hands on me, and I won't accept it!"

"And I won't accept the shit'chu doin'!"

"As yo' wife, I respect yo' opinion, but I will not be controlled by you," Jenah said as she tried to collect herself.

"I ain't tryin'a control you, but I will put my foot down when it's necessary!"

"I didn't come in here to fight wit… "

"Then don't! Just play yo role like you been doin and everything'll be aiight," Donnell interrupted.

"My role," Jenah said as she jumped up from the bed. "I'm not'cho fuckin' puppet, and I don't have to take this shit from you," she angrily said as she stormed from the room in tears.

Jenah left the house feeling that she'd lost her dignity with trying to reconcile with her husband. She seen him as irrational and uncompromising.

Jenah didn't come back home until late that night. She went to the only person she could go to for consolation. She and Angie talked for hours as she became pissy-drunk. For that reason, Angie made sure she got home safely.

Inside the house, Jenah stumbled to the bathroom where she fell to her knees over the toilet. After she wiped her mouth, she came out into the hall and ran into her husband. It was as if she'd encountered a fire breathing dragon.

"Where the hell you been?" Donnell barked in Jenah's face.

"I needed to get away from you," Jenah bluntly spoke as she wobbled back and forth.

"You been drinkin'! And I bet'chu you was wit that bitch Angie!"

"I ain't got time for this. I just wanna lay down," Jenah slurred as she brushed past her husband.

"What's yo' fuckin' problem?" Donnell asked as he snatched Jenah back towards him.

Jenah lost her balance, and fell to the floor on her hands and knees. "You my fuckin' problem," she cried as she pounded the floor with her fist.

"Get'cho ass up," Donnell said as he stood Jenah up. He held onto her arms to keep her from wobbling. "You need to listen to me! Yo' place is here wit'cho family! You need to get that through yo' head 'fore you find yo'self out there wit that bitch!"

"You got some fuckin' nerves! I took care of this house when you was runnin' the streets, and when you left me! I ain't goin' nowhere, and I'ma do whatever I wanna do," Jenah screamed in her husband's face as she snatched herself away from him.

As Jenah turned to walk away from her husband, he pushed the back of her head with excessive force. She stumbled into the living room and crashed to the floor. She bounced from the floor and charged him like a raging bull.

"I'm tired of this shit," Jenah cried as she swung wildly at her husband.

Donnell took a few blows before he got a hold of Jenah. He had her by her throat as he slapped her face with the back of his hand. She fell to the floor and brought him along with her. He was on top of her, still holding her throat as he slapped her face. During the strangulation, she managed to plant her sharp claws in his face. She opened his face and left flesh hanging when she scraped it. Blood instantly gushed as he became more furious. His whips across her face turned into blows as his grasp around her neck became tighter. Her pretty face began to swell as blood oozed from the sharp cuts made by his fist. She was sadly no match for him. Her fighting and struggling came to a stop as she began to gasp for breath. Seeing that, he released his grasp and rose from her chest.

Donnell stood a few feet away from Jenah, who remained on the floor. She laid in a curl, coughing and holding her throat. After a moment, she slowly got to her feet from one knee. She stood chasing her breath while he anticipated her charge. But it was the door she ran to. When she got to it, she stopped and turned to him.

"Fuck you I quit," Jenah cried as she took off her wedding band and threw it at Donnell. She then ran off into the night with a broken spirit.

When Angie got to her apartment from Jenah's house, she sat on the couch and fixed herself a nice hit. Just as she was about to put the flame to the end of the glass pipe, someone started beating on her door.

"Now, who the hell is this," Angie asked herself as she sat the lighter and pipe on the table.

Angie knew that it wasn't none of her tricks at the door. She wasn't the type of woman who eats and shits in the same place. For that reason, she answered the door with her pistol.

"What the hell?" Angie began to say as she swung the door open. Angie's breath was taken away by the disturbing sight of her dearest friend, Jenah. She was leaning against the wall as if it was her only support to standing. Her swollen and bloody face almost made her unrecognizable. She stared at her in shock for a moment before she came to her senses. She helped her into the apartment and eased her onto the couch.

"Oh my god!" Angie cried as she stood over Jenah. "I'm sorry! I'll be right back," she said as she rushed off to get some things to nurture her wounds.

When Angie came back to the living room, she came to a stop as she was stunned by what she was seeing. Jenah had the glass pipe and the lighter she left on the table. She slowly brought the pipe to her swollen lips with the lighter behind it. With one strike, an instant flame jumped from the lighter. She pulled on the pipe as she watched the flame gravitate towards it. She took a hard pull as the crack crackled. After the long and hard pull, she inhaled deeply and slowly blew the funky crack smoke into the air. She then slumped into the couch. It's where her new passion began.

Chapter 3: The Connections
(7 years later)

While Slim was waiting on his bus, he noticed a familiar boy approaching him. J-Will was not someone he was happy to see. Over the summer when he was coming from the store with Jayla, he exchanged some hostile words with J- Will and his homeboys. J-Will admired his courage and allowed him to leave untouched. It was then when one of his ignorant homeboys hit Jayla with a rock that was intended for him. The sound of Jayla's cries infuriated him as he was ready to fight.

The sight of pistols was the only reason he backed down. "What's up cuz? Don't I know you?" J-Will asked with certainty.

"Nah… You don't know me."

"Yes, I do. I stopped the homeboys from gettin' on you that day."

"You niggas ain't scare me," Slim said as he twisted his face at J-Will.

"Cuz… This how I get down. I don't do no fightin'," J-Will said as he pulled a .380 from his coat pocket.

Slim took a step back as he looked at the pistol, then back to J-Will.

"I ain't got no problem wit'chu," J-Will said as he put his pistol away. "We thought 'chu was somebody else."

"Aiight… But when I see that nigga who hit my sister, we gotta get down."

"His name Red, and he go to school wit us. Matta fact… here he come now. Y'all can get down in the bathroom at school. And I put that on the hood… I ain't gon let no mu-fucka jump in it," J-Will promisingly spoke as he twisted his fingers into gang signs.

Slim confusingly stared at J-Will as he found his support odd.

Red was running towards them just as their small, yellow bus was pulling up. He gave no attention to Slim, who had his hostile eyes on him. He was too busy with giving J-Will a friendly greeting. J-Will ignored him as he got onto the bus. Slim was quite sure that there was a problem between them as he could sense the hostility in J-Will's silence.

"Ay, cuz! Come back here," J-Will said as Slim got onto the bus.

Red's eyebrows went up as he became aware of who Slim was. "Cuz! That's the nigga we was finna jump down on that day," he said as he twisted his face at him.

Before Red knew it, Slim lunged towards him. There was nothing he could do as he sat slumped in the seat. But Slim was snatched up before he could release his blows.

"Wait 'til we get to school. It's a way y'all can get down without 'chu gettin' suspended," J-Will said as he sat Slim in the seat. Getting suspended was the last thing Slim needed. He was just starting this new school, and he was not trying to meet his father's fury. He nodded his head up and down as he relaxed in the seat.

On their way to school, Red continuously punched his palm with his fist, talking about what he was going to do to Slim. Slim sat quiet and relaxed. He had confidence in abilities that were obtained through experience. The boys' bathroom was very spacious. Slim came in and envisioned it as a boxing ring. Red was already there with J-Will and a handful of other boys. Red was still running his mouth as he took off his coat.

"C'mon cuz… Let's beat this nigga ass and take his Starter coat," Red said as he looked to J-Will, then back to Slim.

"Nah nigga! Y'all finna get down one on one," J-Will said as he twisted his face at Red. "And ain't no mu-fucka gon get in it," he added with aggression as he looked around at the audience.

J-Will was a big, dark skinned, sixteen-year-old eighth grader. His long French braids that ran down the sides of his head made him look like a tarantula. He intimidated the audience as they fell back to the walls.

"Handle yo' business," J-Will said before he lit a cigarette. Slim nodded his head up and down as he let his coat fall to the floor.

"I could handle this," Red confidently claimed.

Slim came towards Red with his chin tucked, guards up, and his face twisted. He then planted himself and watched Red rush towards him. He swung twice, missing Slim's face by inches. He was desperately trying to make his wild combos connect, but Slim bobbed and weaved them as he kept his guards up. Red threw a wild right hook that missed Slim by afar. It was one that took his balance. Slim was aware, and able to take advantage of this inexperienced clown. Slim's combination consisted of two, swift jabs to Red's face. He connected his jabs with a fierce, right hook to his chin. He stepped into it as he brought his weight. Red became discombobulated as he stumbled towards J-Will. J-Will pushed him back towards Slim, who met him with a left and right jab. This time, he connected his jabs with an uppercut to Red's chin. It stretched him out flat on his back. It was over.

Slim grabbed his dick as he looked around at the audience with his face twisted. It was an arrogant gesture that invited anyone to step up. No one moved but J-Will. He went and stood over Red.

"Nigga, quit playin' games wit' me and get my money together," J-Will ordered as he kneeled down to Red's face. He then turned to Slim. "Cuz, you good. Ain't nobody else talkin' 'bout shit."

Slim shrugged his shoulders as he turned to leave. J-Will thumped his cigarette into the stall as he followed him.

"I'ma catch up wit'chu at lunch," J-Will said as he came to Slim's side.

Slim looked at J-Will with uncertainty, then back ahead as he continued on.

Coming into his new class, Slim already knew the routine. Considered to be a sixth grader, he was still in the B.D. class. His new classmates consisted of six boys and one girl.

"Are you Jevon Johnson," the teacher kindly asked as he approached her desk.

Slim shook his head up and down as he sat in a chair that was next to the teacher's desk.

"I've been expecting you. I'm Ms. Holiday. Welcome to class. I already have your things in your desk, and the assignment schedule is on the board. If you have any questions, you are always welcomed to my desk."

Slim was taken by Ms. Holiday's kindness. He was used to getting old and grumpy teachers, who abused their perfume. She was a beautiful, young black woman. She looked out of place as she sat behind her large, oak desk. He gave her a slight smile as he rose from the chair and looked for his desk.

"This yo' seat right here," the girl sweetly said as she pointed to the desk next to hers.

Slim had never frozen up when he saw a pretty girl. But this girl was heavenly beautiful. As he came for his seat, he couldn't take his eyes off of her. She had a pretty, honey-brown skin complexion with long, jet black hair that was in a ponytail. Her bangs laid perfectly across her head as they drew attention to her brown, cat eyes. She had a thick face with a button nose and plump lips. She gracefully chewed her gum, and blushed as she was aware of the mesmerized state she had him in.

"Thank you," Slim managed to say as he took his seat.

"I'm Angel," she softly spoke.

A smile appeared on Slim's face as he thought that Angel was a perfect name for what he believed to be heavenly beautiful. Before he could respond, Ms. Holiday called for her to take the attendance to the office. Slim watched as Angel rose from her desk. She was five feet with a developed figure and a gracious catwalk. Before she left the class, she turned and found his eyes still on her. She gave a little laugh as she continued to the office. He listened to her popping her gum as it echoed in the empty hall and gradually faded.

"What the hell is she doin' in this class?" Slim asked himself as he pulled his assignment out. Slim could hear gum popping in the hall as it gradually became louder. When he looked up from his assignment, Angel was coming into the class as she continued to snap her gum.

"Angelica Reed," Ms. Holiday said as she was irritated. Angel gave Ms. Holiday a guilty smile as she stopped popping her gum. When she took her seat, she gave her attention to Slim, who was doing his assignment. She began to check him out becoming intrigued by him. Slim was neatly dressed standing at 5'6 and had a skinny build. His bushy afro was evenly patted down on his big head. His sleepy eyes had sharp corners with long lashes that hid his brown eyes. He had full lips that naturally parted with his face relaxed. They revealed his perfect, four front teeth. He sat in a slump with his creased jeans sagging. They were neatly cuffed over his black boots. His boots matched his thick sweater. It was cuffed at the bottom with a fresh, white t-shirt coming from under it. He could feel Angel's analytical eyes on him as he continued to do his assignment.

"Why you start smilin' when I told you my name?" Angel asked as she began to play with her gum.

"'Cause, I like yo' name. I think it fit'chu," Slim softly spoke with no modesty.

"You don't even know me," Angel blushed.

"I jus know what I see." Slim replied in bold honesty.

"You shouldn't be lookin' at me like that."

"You gotta change how you look then."

"I'ma always look like this, so you just gotta deal wit it."

"I can deal wit that," Slim stated as he looked Angel up and Down..

"That don't mean I'm givin' you permission to," Angel said as she rolled her head at Slim.

"I wouldn't be in this class if I worried about permission," Slim said before he turned back to his assignment.

Angel shook her head from side to side with a smile before she continued to do her assignment. Up until lunch, there were only glances between them. Slim's held admiration while hers held uncertainty. In the cafeteria, Slim noticed that no one was really in the lunch line. It was an unpopular thing to eat the unpleasant meals. Majority of everyone ate from the vendor machines. He had no money as he wished. His father took his weekly allowances for being expelled from his last school. But he was hungry, so he continued on towards the lunch line with no shame, or concern about the popularity.

"Hold on cuz! I can't let'chu eat that shit," J-Will said as he stepped in front of Slim.

"I ain't trippin'. I'm hungry."

"Aiight. Get'chu somethin' from the machines," J-Will said as he pulled a wad of money from his pocket.

"I'm cool," Slim said as he looked at the money, then back to J-Will.

"You don't owe me shit back for this. I'm tryin'a fuck wit'chu, and I wanna see you eat good on the strength of that," J-Will spoke with sincerity.

Slim wasn't used to receiving generosity from his peers. But it was evident to him that J-Will admired him. For that reason, he accepted the five one dollar bills.

"When you get'cho shit, come to the table," J-Will said before he turned to leave.

At the vendor machine, Slim stood observing its many items

"Do you need some help figurin' out what'chu want?" a soft voice whispered in Slim's ear. It was the sweet smell that told him who it was.

"I already know what I want," Slim said as he turned to the gracious smile of Angel.

Angel blushed at Slim's remark while he looked her up and down again. He then made his selection and moved to the next vendor.

"Can I have one of yo' dollas?" Angel sweetly asked.

"Won't cho boyfriend get jealous?" Slim asked as he was fishing for information.

Angel knew what Slim was doing. She gave a little laugh before she responded. "I don't have one."

"We gotta fix that," Slim smirked before he gave Angel a dollar.

"Thank you. And we'll see about that," Angel said before she turned to leave. Angel didn't really need Slim's dollar. She only wanted to see if her sweet charm was affective on him.

J-Will was at a table that was in the corner of the cafeteria. He was there with two of his homeboys, who looked to be his age. They were all dressed in navy blue and bright orange. The S.D. & K.C. stitching on their hats and jerseys symbolized the gang they represented. Slim was aware of the Six Duce and Kitchen Crip gang that dwelled in the neighborhood he grew up in. His cousin Nut was also a Six Duce from another hood.

When Slim sat at the table, J-Will introduced his homeboys, Seven and Bo-Duce. They already knew about Slim as the news about his victorious morning got around the school.

"This the hood table, and you good over here," J-Will said, welcoming Slim to the circle.

"It's all good," Slim said as he began to eat his snacks. Just then, J-Will shifted his eyes to two boys that came to the table. He acted as if he was expecting them as he put his hands in his lap. "What's good?"

"Let us get two for fifteen," one of the boys asked.

"C'mon, nigga. You know how I play it," J-Will said with a frown.

"It's all good," the boy said as he dropped $20 on the table.

"Cuz, grab that for me, and give him this," J-Will said as he held something out to Slim under the table.

It was two fat sacks of dark green weed that Slim passed to the boy. He then continued to eat his snacks.

During lunch, Slim was quiet and observant as he sat. He was one of the last ones to return to class after lunch. He felt cooler than the clouds as he floated in. Angel had just pulled her assignment out and looked at him as if she was surprised. He sat slumped in his desk, not caring about what assignment they were supposed to be doing. He pulled a random book from his desk and made it look as though he was doing his work. There was no way he was about to ignore his newly discovered feeling with school work.

"That's the wrong book," Angel softly whispered to Slim in a teasing manner.

"I ain't trippin'.

"You was doin' yo' work this mornin'. What happened?"

"I'ma do it. I just don't feel like doin' it right now."

"Can I ask you anotha question?"

"What's up?"

"Do you always talk like that wit'cho eyes lookin' like that?" Angel asked, trying to expose what was obvious from another angle.

"Why? You like me?"

"Do you like me?" Angel asked as she rolled her head at Slim.

"Yeah. I like you. If I didn't, I wouldn't have let you trick me outta my dollar."

"I didn't trick you," Angel retorted with a smile as she began to play with her ponytail.

"That's cool, but you still didn't answer my question."

"Why you like me?" Angel asked, continuing to avoid Slim's question.

"I haven't really tried to figure it out yet. I just know I like you," Slim softly spoke.

"Well… I like you, 'cause you gave me your dollar," Angel said before she turned back to her assignment.

For a moment, Slim stared at Angel with a puzzled expression. He then figured out what she meant. She liked him, because her charm was effective on him. He nodded with a smile as he took a silent vow to be submissive to her charming ways.

During the rest of the school day, Slim enjoyed his high and scribbled on paper while Angel was seeing how far she could get with him on her charm. He threw her trash away, picked up the pencils she intentionally dropped, and answered some of her silliest questions. Tolerating her playfulness and graciousness was a pleasure as he found her adorable. By the end of the day, she was convinced that he genuinely liked her. After coming to that conclusion, she had something for him.

"Call me later on," Angel said as she sat a piece of paper on Slim's desk.

"I can do that," Slim replied with a smile. "And here go my number," he said before he wrote it down.

When Slim got on his bus after school, Red was sitting in the front seat. He turned his swollen face towards the window when Slim walked pass. He continued on to the back of the bus where he found J-Will. He was counting small stacks of money on the back seat. Slim sat across from him and watched as he seemed to be free and in control with his lifestyle.

"Here. This twenty dollars for holdin' me down," J-Will said as he gave Slim a wad of small bills.

Slim accepted it as he felt like he deserved it.

"I seen you talkin' to Angel. What's up wit that?"

"Yeah, we talkin'," Slim stated as he hid his excitement behind his coolness.

"I fuck wit' her sister, Teri. She'll be back to school tomorrow, and I'ma try to put somethin' together. But ay, come up to my house in the mornin'. I live on the next block, on the right pass the alley."

When Slim got home, he raided the refrigerator for something to eat before he did his chores. He then went to his room.

Slim's room was still in the basement. The padlock still hung from his door, and was a reminder of his isolation. It had been almost a year since he'd been locked in his room. He was growing out of the violent tantrums. With minor incidents, his father would take his video game, TV and radio, and give him extra chores with no allowance. When his tantrums did occur, his father would only subdue him and lock him in his naked room. The beatings stopped shortly after his mother went astray.

Slim laid on his bed and stared at the ceiling as he thought about his adventurous day with Angel being the high-light of it. Her sweet gracious appeal touched him in a place he had never felt before. Sleep took over him with her being his last thought.

"Von Von, wake up," Jayla said as she continued to shake him.

When Slim opened his eyes, Jayla was standing over him with her hands on her hips.

"Why you was smilin' in yo' sleep?"

His smile reappeared on as he realized where it came from.

"What'chu was dreamin' about?" Jayla quizzed.

"I don't know what'chu talkin' 'bout, Jay," Slim said with a laugh.

"You was dreamin' about a girl," Jayla smirked with certainty.

"Why you botherin' me?"

"Because I can," Jayla teased as she pushed her big brother.

"Aiight. Don't make me get up," Slim playfully threatened.

"You ain't gon do nothin'," Jayla sneered as she pushed Slim again. "You gotta get up anyway, 'cause daddy told me to come and get'chu. We finna eat."

"Here I come."

"So, do you like yo' new school?" Jayla continued to question Slim.

"Yeah. I'll tell you about it later," Slim said with a smile. Jayla returned a smile to Slim before she left his room.

When Slim came to the kitchen, his father, brother and sister were already at the table. They were eating a dinner their father prepared. He was a rare single father, who did everything for his children. He was an inheritor of the prosperous, Johnson & Johnson Construction Co., and he owned real estate. With that, he was able to provide for his children with no problem.

"How was yo' day at school?" Slim's father asked.

"It was good," Slim simply replied without going into detail.

Dinner went on peacefully with Marcel blabbing on about his accomplishments.

After dinner, Slim was helping Jayla with the dishes when his father gave him his video game back. She was so excited, she made him go hook it up while she finished the dishes. When she came to his room, he'd just finished setting everything up to the TV.

"I'm finna kick yo' butt," Jayla said as she sat on the bed next to Slim.

Slim's room was their little sanctuary. They did everything down there, from homework to play fighting. She would sometimes bring their girl cousins down and have him play music while they made up dance routines. His only company was his cousin, Nut. He was only a few months older than Nut, but Nut was a lot bigger. Nut was just as wild as he was. When they were together, they terrorized and sabotaged anything that stood in their way. For the reason of them being unbearable together, they were recently kept separate.

"Why you don't never let me win?" Jayla whined as she pushed Slim with her shoulder.

Slim laughed at Jayla as he continued to demolish her.

"You make me sick," Jayla frustratingly said as she slammed the controller onto the bed.

"I think you had enough anyway. Plus, I need to use the phone. Can you go get it for me?"

Jayla stared at Slim with a puzzled expression before she came to a conclusion. "Von Von, I knew you had a girlfriend!" she squealed excitedly as she pushed him. "Do she go to yo' new school? Is she pretty? Von Von, what's her name?"

"She the prettiest girl in school, and her name Angel."

Jayla had never seen Slim light up over a girl. She stared at him with a smile before she rose from the bed. "Angel, Angel, Aaaaangel," she sang and danced as she left the room. She came back moments later with the phone and sat next to him. She stared at him with a smile filled with curiosity and anticipation as he went into his pocket. When he pulled Angel's number out, the money he got from J-Will came with it.

"Von Von, where you get all that money from," Jayla excitedly asked.

"This ain't nothin'."

"Well, if it ain't nothin', gimme two dollars so I can buy stuff at school," Jayla asked with charm as she held her hand out.

After Slim gave Jayla two dollars, she politely thanked him. She then watched as he dialed Angel's number and put the phone to his ear.

"Can I speak to Angel?" Slim asked when a woman answered.

"Angel, some lil' boy want'chu on the phone," the woman yelled as she took the phone from her ear.

"I got it, mama," Angel said as she picked up another phone. "Who is this?" she asked as if she wasn't expecting a call.

"This, Slim."

"I like Jevon betta, so that's what I'm callin' you."

"I ain't got no problem wit' that."

"Hi, Angel," Jayla yelled towards the phone.

"Who was that?" Angel asked.

"That's Jay, my lil' sister."

"Tell her I said hi," Angel said with a smile.

"That ain't gon' be enough for her. I'ma let'chu tell her yo'self while I go to the bathroom," Slim said before he gave Jayla the phone. Jayla took the phone with a big smile and greeted Angel with friendliness. It's where they would begin to make a connection. Slim returned to his room just as their father was calling for Jayla from the top of the steps. As she came from his room, she gave him the phone with a mischievous smile. She then hurried away.

"What'chu and Jay was talkin' 'bout?" Slim asked as he sat on his bed and kicked his shoes off.

"Why you was smilin' in yo' slee?" Angel asked in return with a laugh.

"I was dreamin' 'bout this girl."

"And?" Angel demanded more information.

"I can't tell you, 'cause she might get jealous," Slim teased.

"Jevon, stop playin' wit me, 'cause Jay already told me that'chu don't have a girlfriend!"

"I could've told you that, and anything else you wanna know 'bout me."

"So, you ain't got no secrets?"

"Yeah. But I can share 'em wit'chu, if you share yours wit me."

"You must really like me!"

"You should've figured that out by all that crazy stuff I was lettin' you make me do at school."

"So, you was lettin' me?"

"Yeah. And you should feel special, 'cause I ain't never let no girl make me do all that crazy stuff you had me doin'."

"Can you keep it like that?" Angel softly asked for Slim's faithfulness.

"I can, and I want to."

"Jevon, how old is you?" Angel asked as she was intrigued by his maturity.

"I'll be thirteen next month on the twenty-seventh."

"I turned thirteen last month on the seventeenth. I'm older than you, so that mean, you gotta listen to me," Angel teased.

"I ain't got no problem wit' that."

"So, you gon just let me run all over you, huh?"

"You wouldn't do that. Yo' name Angel."

"You think you got me figured out?"

"I figured out that I like you. I just can't figure out why you in the bad class."

Angel gave a cute little laugh before she responded. "To make a long story short, when I was little, my grandma told me that I was a real angel. So, I grew up thinkin' I had the authority to tell people what they can, and can't do. And that's how I ended up in the bad class. But I'll be out next year," she proudly ended her story.

"I think you is a real angel."

"Thank you, and I know why you in the bad class. I heard about what'chu did to that boy this mornin'." Angel sneered.

"He did somethin' to Jay. But what's up? Am I gon' see you tomorrow?"

"I come to school every day. And you betta come too, 'cause I wanna braid yo' nappy head. I could do it on the steps at lunch time."

"That's cool," Slim said as Angel's sweet thoughtfulness made him think about his mother.

Slim's mother had been in and out of his life since he was five years old. The neglect made him bitter towards her, as he had no understanding of how she could just up and leave him. He took it hard, because of the significant bond they shared. When she came around, she would braid his hair and spend some time with her children. As her crack addiction worsened, she became more unreliable. It's when his father had his hair cut. He became so bitter with his mother, he went to his room when she came around. It was because he knew that she would leave him disappointed again. It had been over a year since the last time they saw or heard from her.

"Jevon, why you so quiet?" Angel softly asked.

"Can I kiss you tomorrow?"

"What?" Angel asked in shock.

"Angel, baby, let me use the phone," her mother interrupted.

"Okay. Gimme a second to say bye."

"Thank you," Angel's mother said before she hung up the phone.

"Bye, Jevon. I'll see you in the mornin'," Angel said sweetly.

"Bye. And I won't let'chu get away from answerin' my question."

"I won't try to get away from it."

Chapter 4: First Love

When Slim got to J-Will's house the next morning, a woman on the other side of the front door told him to go to the basement door. An older dude resembling J-Will was coming from the basement steps when he got there. He came to know him as J-Will's big brother, G-Will.

When Slim came into the basement, J-Will had him wait in the living room area while he finished getting himself together. He left him smoking on a blunt and watching cartoons.

After getting himself together, J-Will came into the living room area. He was carrying a shoe box and smoking on a blunt. He sat the box on the table and sat on the couch across from Slim.

"I told you, I'm tryin'a fuck wit'chu," J-Will said as he removed the lid from the box.

"What's up," Slim asked as he remained in his slump.

"You wanna get this money wit' me?"

"Holla at me. What's up?"

"I'm kinda hot at school, and I ain't tryin' to go back to juvee for shit. Plus, I'm still on probation. You hella laid back, and I dig that. I wanna let'chu do yo' thing, and have mu-fuckas hollerin' at'chu."

Slim nodded his head with understanding as he pulled on his blunt.

"These ounces, and I could easily bag up twenty dimes from 'em. But I just bag up fifteen to kill any competition. Just bring in a slump." Slim continued to use his cool composed assistance as he sat in the middle of the action. He had never seen so much money come and go through his hands. It aroused something deep inside of him as a connection was made. Even though he kept his cool composure, J-Will could see the hunger in his eyes.

"C'mon. Let's go put somethin' in the air 'fore the bell ring," J-Will said as he rose from the table.

Slim had an idea of what J-Will was talking about, but he didn't ask questions. He just went along with them as he was about to find out.

When they got to the boys' bathroom, J-Will split a blunt open with his fingernails and dumped the tobacco in the toilet. Seven and Bo-Duce stood on the wall, talking about some girls they planned on getting with. Slim was leaning on the wall, anticipating what was about to happen next.

"What's up, cuz? You smoke?" J-Will asked as he filled the blunt with weed.

"I ain't never smoked, but I'll hit it a few times," Slim nonchalantly spoke.

J-Will shook his head up and down while Seven and Bo-Duce immediately stopped talking. It was Slim's first time smoking weed, and they wanted to be entertained by the occasion.

After J-Will licked the blunt to a seal, he pulled on one end while he lit the other end. Smoke came from his nose as he continued to pull on the blunt. The thick, skunk smelling smoke clouded over his head as he made smoking weed look appealing. After pulling on it a few more times, he passed it to Slim.

Slim took the blunt and held it between his fingers as if he was a natural. He took a light pull as he watched the cherry glow on the tip. When he inhaled, he could feel the weed smoke as it thumped his chest. He took another light pull as smoke came from his nose. Seven and Bo-Duce encouraged him to hit it harder while J-Will leaned against the wall with his arms folded across his chest. He blew the ashes from the blunt as he twisted his face at Seven and Bo-Duce. He was accepting their challenge. He took a long, hard pull from the blunt as the cherry became alarmingly bright. J-Will shook his head from side to side while Seven and Bo-Duce stood by with their anticipating smiles. When Slim deeply inhaled the weed smoke, there was no thump. It hit his chest like a sledge hammer and took his cool composure. His body became bent as he choked, feeling like he was about to cough up his lungs. Water filled his eyes and eventually ran down his face. Despite the dizzy stupor he was in, he held on to the blunt. When he finally gained his composure, he discovered an emancipating sensation within his mind and body. He was high.

"Damn!" Slim exclaimed as he wiped the water from his eyes. He then pulled on the blunt again.

After school, Slim went back to J-Will's house where he was told how much weed he would be given to sell as well as the cut of the profits he would receive. J-Will then showed Slim how to bag the weed, and told him about the weed game. When they were done, he gave him thirty dime sacks, the equivalent of two ounces.

Before Slim and J-Will were about to leave, ,J-Will went into his room and came back out with a S.D. hat.

"I think this'll fit'chu perfect," J-Will said as he held the hat out to Slim.

Slim knew that with accepting the hat, he was becoming Six Duce. J-Will had an influence on him as he appeared to be free and in control within his lifestyle. It was a lifestyle that fascinated Slim as he had a strong desire for freedom and control that came with self-sufficiency. He accepted the hat and became Six Duce seeing it as a part of the lifestyle he was introduced to.

After Slim accepted the hat, he and J-Will clapped hands twice and connected their index fingers to make a "c". It was the hood clap.

Red didn't come to school, and Slim would never see him again. While at school, Slim and J-Will ran into Angel and her sister. They were standing around the lockers with a few girls. It was obvious of who Angel's sister was. Teri was an eighth grader, who was only taller and thinner than her little sister. They all turned to Slim and J-Will as they were approaching them.

"What's up?" Slim greeted Angel with his coolness.

"Hi, Jevon," Angel replied with a smile. She then introduced him to everyone. Slim ignored the introduction as he kept his eyes on Angel's lips. They were enticing as the cherry lip gloss made them look extra juicy.

"I'm still waitin' on you to answer my question," Slim smoothly spoke with a relentless desire for Angel in his eyes.

"Jevon, stop," Angel whined as she shifted her eyes around the audience.

"I don't care about them lookin'," Slim said as he stepped closer to Angel. "But I'm still waiting on you."

Slim made Angel feel special by not being ashamed to publicly show his affection for her.

"I still haven't made my mind up anyway," Angel teased.

"Made yo' mind up about what," Teri intervened. "You bet'not be tryin'a play wit' my sista head," she said as she stepped in between Slim and Angel.

"Nah, I ain't tryin'a do that." Slim replied defensively.

"He cool. Let them do they thing," J-Will said as he pulled Teri away.

Slim and Angel watched J-Will and Teri leave with her entourage. They then turned back to each other.

"You hungry?"

"No, but thank you for askin'," Angel responded with a smile. Slim and Angel then turned to two boys who were approaching them.

"J-Will told me to holla at'chu," one of the boys said.

"What'chu tryin' to do," Slim asked as he put his hands into his coat pockets.

"We got twenty."

After looking from left to right, Slim took the money and gave the boy two dime sacks. He watched them hurry away before he turned back to Angel.

"So, is that why you come to school?" Angel asked as she was disappointed. "And how you 'pose to do yo' work like that?"

"Nah, and I'ma do my work," Slim said as he was touched by Angel's concern.

"You betta! Or I ain't never gon' answer yo' question," Angel retorted as she rolled her eyes. "Now c'mon, 'cause the bell finna ring," she said with authority as she led the way.

During class, Slim kept his word to Angel. He sat slumped in his desk while he did his assignments. However, he couldn't help interacting with her. He kept asking her to help him with his assignments, even though he didn't need help. When she noticed him admiring her as she explained the assignment, she caught on to his sweet deception. She found it charming as they had a laugh together.

At lunch time, Slim was mesmerized as he watched Angel gracefully make her request at the vendor machine.

"Jevon, c'mon! Put some money in the thing," Angel whined, breaking him from his trance.

"My bad. I just like lookin' at'chu."

"I like lookin' at'chu too. And how you not scared to say what most boys'll be scared to say, or act like they too tough to say."

"Believe it or not, but I ain't never been like this wit' a girl, so I don't know how to be scared," Slim spoke with sincerity.

"I believe you," Angel softly said as she stepped closer to Slim.

Slim and Angel stared into each other's eyes where they discovered a strong chemistry. It literally brought them closer together. Lost in the hot moment, they disregarded the public's eye as they were about to share their first kiss.

"Y'all bet'not," Teri interrupted.

Snapping out of their oblivious trance, Slim and Angel turned to Teri with smiles. She shook her head in disbelief before she continued on.

Before Slim and Angel went to the steps, he stopped at the hood table and told J-Will where he was going to be. The steps were just outside of the cafeteria. As soon as he sat between Angel's legs, a boy came to see him for some weed. He was followed by two girls, who also wanted to buy some sacks.

Angel had already began to eat her snacks when Slim finally got to his. They sat quietly as they processed their newly discovered chemistry.

"I'ma give you six braids to the back," Angel said as she removed Slim's hat.

"That's cool," Slim said as he continued to eat.

As Angel began to do Slim's hair, she sang softly. Her sweet voice and gentle touch was a mesmerizing combination.

"What is you doin' to me?!" Slim exclaimed.

"I'm sorry! I'm not tryin' to hurt'chu on purpose!"

"You aint hurtin' me. I just like how you combin' my hair and singin' to me."

"Boy," Angel said as she adjusted Slim's head back in place.

"Where you learn how to sing like that?"

"I don't know. But I been singin' in the choir ever since I was eight. And I go to church wit' my grandma every Sunday," Angel proudly said.

"See? You is a real angel!"

Angel laughed with Slim as she continued to do his hair. He then sat quietly as he was captivated by her sweet voice and her gentle touch. They were only interrupted a few times by the request of the fire weed he had.

Just as Angel was finishing Slim's hair, J-Will came with the homeboys along with Teri and her entourage. He came to get Slim to smoke with them before the bell rung. Angel had to relieve herself, so after checking out her work and giving it her approval, she left with Teri and her entourage.

In the boys' bathroom, Slim made more weed sells. With only being half way through the school day, he'd become a known pusher by the weed heads. Shortly after he got to class, a boy stood in the hall and waved for him. It was in the boys' bathroom where he made his last transactions. He made exactly $300 from the two ounces.

On Slim's way back to class from the bathroom, he ran into Angel. She was coming towards him, snapping her gum.

"Where you finna go?" Slim asked.

"To answer a question," Angel answered with a smile.

"I'll see you when you get back," Slim said as he passed Angel.

"Jevon, don't play wit me," Angel whined.

When Slim turned around, Angel was standing in the middle of the hall with her hands on her hips. Along with being high as a kite, the excitement from the money caused him to forget. After a moment, the confusion left his face as he remembered about the question. A smile appeared on his face as he approached her.

"My bad. I thought…"

"Jus c'mon," Angel interrupted.

Angel took Slim to the far end of the school on the top floor. It was in a corner that hid them from everyone. They could only be seen if someone came up the steps, or around the corner.

"This a good place to answer a question," Slim said as he stepped to Angel.

"So, ask me," Angel sweetly said as she batted her eyelashes at Slim.

Slim grabbed Angel's hands and backed her against the wall. When they got there, she wrapped her arms around his neck.

His arms gently secured her as his hands squeezed her booty. As he lifted her to her toes, they gazed into each other's eyes and became captured by their chemistry. Their lips uncontrollably met with a modest kiss.

"I like yo' lips. They taste like gummy bears," Slim softly spoke.

A cute giggle escaped Angel's lips as she thought what he said was the sweetest thing she had ever heard.

The chemistry between them quickly erased the sweet humor as their facial expression became tender. Within their young eyes, they expressed the same amount of passion and desire for each other. Their lips were attracted together like magnets. Their kisses were still modest as they were savoring the moment. It was the chemistry that forced them into a passionate kiss. Their eyes closed slowly as they became lost in each other's embrace. His gentle squeeze brought intensity between their lips while it remained graceful.

After breaking their kiss, Angel gave Slim a peck on his lips. Silently chasing their breath, they stared into each other's eyes with satisfaction. It was a perfect first kiss.

"Can I have my gum back?" Angel softly asked.

"I swallowed it."

"Why?"

"'Cause I want'chu to always be a part of me."

"Do you mean that?"

"I wouldn't lie to you," Slim said as he desperately wanted to take away Angel's uncertainty.

"I believe you," Angel said as she laid her head on Slim's chest.

Slim dropped his head to Angel's neck, and lovingly inhaled the sweet smell of her. He rubbed his nose across her neck and included his soft kisses. They stayed wrapped up until the bell rung for regular classes to change. They would return to their secret place every day where they would let the chemistry between them grow stronger.

After school, J-Will was in his usual seat when Slim got onto the bus. He sat across from him and counted out the money he owed him.

"We gon do the same thing tomorrow," J-Will said as he took the money from Slim.

"I'm wit'chu," Slim said as he slumped into the seat.

"I holla'd at Teri, too. She snapped out on me and said Angel ain't goin' for no shit like that."

"Shit like what?" Slim asked as he sat up from his slump.

"I told you I was gon' try to put somethin' together. They live around the corner from the school, and I'm skippin' wit' Teri next week. I was tryin' to take you wit' me, so you could do yo' thing wit Angel."

"Nigga, you trippin'! You ain't have to do no shit like that!"

"Cuz, my bad. I thought… "

"Don't think for me! Let me do my own thing wit' Angel," Slim cut J-Will off with a sharp tone.

J-Will understandingly shook his head as he realized that Angel wasn't an ordinary girl to Slim.

Later on that night, Slim took the phone down to his room where he was going to call Angel. He was desperately hoping that J-Will didn't ruin things with his stupidity.

"What'chu doin'?" Slim asked when Angel answered.

"I'm confused. And I'm tryin' to figure out why you have J-Will ask my sister that. Jevon, I thought'chu was different from other boys."

Slim could hear the hurt and the disappointment in Angel's soft voice. A strong desire to console her immediately took over him as he wanted to give her reassurance.

"Angel, I don't need nobody to speak for me, especially when it come to you. I don't know where he got that idea from, but I checked him, and told him to stay outta my business. When I told you that I wouldn't lie to you, I meant that," Slim spoke in a soothing tone.

Angel took a moment to process Slim's words. "Jevon, I believe you," she softly spoke. Angel put a smile on Slim's face as he was relieved. Their connection was stronger than he realized. He remained silent with his smile as he acknowledged it.

"Why you smilin'?"

"How you know I was smilin'?" Slim surprisingly asked.

"I can feel it."

"I'm feelin' us, and that's why I'm smilin'."

"So, tell me… have you ever done it?"

It took Slim a few seconds to figure out what Angel was asking him. "Nah… I ain't never done it."

"Then, why you was squeezin' my booty like that?" Angel asked with a laugh.

"'Cause, I like it."

"And I like how you was holdin' me when we kissed."

"So, what about'chu…? Have you ever done it?" Slim quizzed.

"Jevon, you not 'pose to ask a girl that!" Angel exclaimed. "But since we don't have secrets, I can tell you that I have never done it… I'm Angel."

"I coulda figured that out. But what's up? Sing somethin' for me."

"No, 'cause you gon go to sleep on me," Angel whined. Just as Slim was about to try convincing Angel to sing, a call came in for his father. It's when they said their sweet good-byes.

Over the next few weeks, Slim's love grew intensely for two things; money and Angel. Every school morning, he bagged up thirty dime sacks in J-Will's basement. After giving J-Will his cut, he brought $150 home almost every day. He had $1,700 under his mattress that was wrapped in rubber bands. Other than a gift he bought for Angel, he was basically stacking his money. He wanted a heavier money flow, which meant that he had to come from under J-Will's wings.

Slim talked with Angel on the phone every night. Some nights, they fell asleep together. At school, they visited their secret place. Their embrace became tighter as their kisses became more passionate. Ms. Holiday knew what was going on between them. Their scheduled departures from class made it obvious. She never confronted them though. She enjoyed watching their young love as they laughed, teased and tutored each other with passion in their eyes. They were the highlight of the school.

When Slim came to school on Valentine's Day, Angel was waiting on him in their usual spot. She leaned against the lockers with her hands behind her back. Her smile was brighter than ever. He told J-Will that he would see him at lunch as he continued on towards her.

"Happy Valentine's Day," Angel sweetly said as she brought a red envelope from behind her back.

"Happy Valentine's Day to you too," Slim said as he took the card. He kept his eyes on Angel's glowing face.

"Open it," Angel whined as she gave Slim a light push. When Slim opened the card, he was captured by a familiar, sweet smell. He took the card from its envelope and lovingly inhaled it as he kept his eyes on Angel. It was the sweet smell of the body spray she wore. It made him think about his hugs with her. He looked back to the card that read: *To My Special One.* Under the cursive words was a single rose in a clear, heart shaped vase. When he opened the card, his eyes were taken by her lip prints. They were in red lip stick. He then shifted his eyes to her pretty handwriting. It read: *First Love, I seen it in your eyes, and it caused me to blush. I heard it in your voice, and then came the crush. When I felt it in your touch, I was sure of what it was. I found my soul mate… My very first love. Your Angel*

When Slim finished reading the poem, there was a smile on his face as he looked up to Angel. For a moment, he stared at her until he found the correct words.

"I like the card, and I love you too. It's like you took the words right outta my mouth, 'cause I feel the same way about'chu," Slim said as he wrapped his arms around Angel.

After the affectionate embrace, Slim went into his back pocket. He pulled out a red velvet, rectangular box and gave it to Angel.

"What is it?" Angel asked anxiously.

"Open it. It's somethin' that'll always remind you of us." Slim watched Angel with a smile as she carefully opened the box. Her eyes widened as she blinked continuously. She was astonished. An 18k gold, Figaro necklace glistened from the box with an 18k gold, heart pendant.

"Let me put it on you." Angel remained in awe as Slim gently put the thin necklace around her neck. "It looks good on you."

"Jevon, I love it. Thank you," Angel softly spoke. "I ain't never takin' it off!"

"I don't want'chu to," Slim said as he stepped closer to Angel. Everything and everyone became irrelevant to Slim and Angel as they submitted to their passion. They met each other's gentle embrace with their passionate kissing. Not even the bell or the audience that found them admirable could restrain them. This was no puppy love.

"Okay… That's enough! Stop that and get to class," a teacher said as she became a witness to the public display of affection.

Still wrapped up, Slim's and Angel's lips came apart with guilty smiles as they watched the teacher continue on.

The night before Slim's thirteenth birthday, he was laying across his bed, talking with Angel.

"So what'chu bringin' me to school tomorrow?" Slim asked, still trying to get Angel to open up about his birthday present.

"I'm not goin' to school tomorrow, and you not either," Angel whispered.

"Straight up!"

"I'ma be waitin' on you when you get off yo' bus."

"Aiight," Slim said as he became quiet.

"Don't be gettin' all quiet now," Angel said with a laugh.

"I'm just thinkin' "

"You betta be thinkin' about me!"

"You know I am."

"Well, I'm finna go to bed. I love you, and I'll see yo' big head self in the mornin'."

"Love you too."

The next morning, Angel was exactly where she said she would be when Slim got off his bus. She greeted him by telling him "Happy Birthday" and then gave him a kiss. They then waited a short while before they slipped away. On their way to her house, they casually talked as if they didn't have a care in the world. She lived in a two-story brick house with a big porch.

"Why you srnilin'?" Angel asked as she walked up the steps with Slim.

"Angel, huh?"

"Shut up," Angel said as she pushed Slim. "This is my house," she proudly said as she opened the door.

When Slim came into the nicely decorated house, Angel took his hat and coat.

"I'm finna cook us somethin'. I want'chu to stay in here and watch TV or somethin'."

"I'ma miss you," Slim said as he stepped closer to Angel.

"Go on ," Angel said as she pushed Slim towards the couch.

Angel watched Slim as he went and made himself comfortable on the couch. He sat in a slump with the remote and flipped to cartoons.

"I'm good," Slim said with a laugh as he looked to Angel. Angel rolled her eyes at Slim before she left him alone.

Slim had been watching cartoons for about fifteen minutes when he captured the aroma of Angel's cooking. It led him to her. He stood unnoticed in the doorway of the kitchen and watched her. She was over the stove, softly singing in her pajamas. After a moment, he shook his head from side to side and approached her.

"You got it smellin' hella good," Slim whispered in Angel's ear as he hugged her from behind.

"I thought I told you to stay in there," Angel whined.

"I miss you," Slim said as he began to kiss Angel's neck.

"Jevon, stop," Angel whined as she twisted her body to him. "Stop 'fore I stick you wit this hot fork!"

Slim stood back and looked at Angel with his bottom lip out. "Now, go on back in there," Angel ordered as she pointed to the living room with the fork.

Slim slowly turned and headed towards the door with his head down. When he got there, he stopped and turned to Angel with a sad look.

"Go on," Angel told him again with a laugh as she stood with her hands on her hips.

When Angel came into the living room, she was carrying a plate full of food and a glass of orange juice. She placed the glass on the table and sat next to Slim. He sat up from his slump and stretched his neck towards the plate. There were four pancakes, four sausages, four strips of crispy bacon, and a pile of scrambled eggs. When he reached towards the plate, she pulled it away from him.

"Stop," Angel said as she slapped Slim's hand. "I'm feedin' you today."

"That's cool too," Slim said as he sat back with a smile. Angel held the plate in the palm of her hand as she prepared a bite for Slim. She cut a piece of the pancake and sausage before she forked them together with some eggs. She smiled as she saw he was satisfied with her cooking by the expression on his face. She got just as much pleasure out of feeding him as he did by getting fed. She even held the glass to his mouth while he sipped the juice. When they were done eating, he gratefully thanked her.

"You don't have to thank me," Angel said as she collected the dishes. "I'm just makin' you feel how you make me feel."

Angel took the dishes to the kitchen and came back to find Slim more relaxed. He fell back into his slump and had his shoes off.

"I see you made yo'self at home."

"You make me feel at home." Slim told her.

"I wanna watch a movie that I think you'll like."

"That's cool."

After starting the movie that was already set in the VCR, Angel cuddled on the couch with Slim. They watched a movie about a player, who unexpectedly found love. He struggled to abandon his old ways that contradicted the monogamous commitment he accepted. It wasn't until she left him that caused him to get his act together. After his reformation, she took him back.

During the movie, Slim and Angel debated, laughed, and kissed when the romantic moments in the movie touched them.

"I liked that movie," Slim said as the credits began to run.

"I knew you would," Angel said as she laid her head in Slim's lap. She stared up at him with a tender look as she caressed his face. "Jevon, do you really love me?" she softly asked.

"Angel, that's like askin' me, do I really need oxygen. I can't see myself bein' wit'out chu. I'm in love wit'chu," Slim spoke in a soothing tone before he kissed her lips.

"I'm in love wit'chu too, and I'm ready to show you my room," Angel whispered.

When Slim and Angel got to her room, hfelt like he stepped into heaven. Everything was decorated in sky blue and white. The sunlight beamed through the white curtains and created a glow. The furniture sunk into sky-blue carpet, where he felt like he was standing on clouds. A sky-blue blanket covered her queen-sized bed. Sky-blue and white stuffed animals were at the head of it. They were organized as if they were about to take a picture. When Slim heard the door close, he turned around to Angel.

"I like yo' room."

"I like you," Angel said as she stood on her toes, initiating the passionate kissing.

When their lips came apart, Angel backed Slim to her bed. It would be where they made love for the first time in their young lives.

"What's up cuz? You still ain't tell me why you ain't come to school yesterday," J-Will said as he let Slim into the basement.

"C'mon, nigga. You know how I play it," Slim said as he continued on to the living room area.

J-Will was on one of the couches breaking down an ounce of crack. He was breaking it into all dimes. He took a liking towards Slim. It was Slim's cool composure and relentlessness towards getting money. He came to know J-Will as the big homie. He was a small-time crack pusher. The hunger for money could be seen in his eyes as ,it flowed through his voice when he spoke.

"What's up, cuz," G-Will spoke without taking his eyes from the table.

"What's up," Slim replied as he sat across from G-Will.

"You already know what it is wit' me. When I get my feet right in the game, I'ma fuck wit'chu."

Slim shook his head up and down as he continued to watch G-Will do his thing. Just like every school morning, J-Will came with the shoe box, ready to do business with Slim. But this morning was different. Slim was ready to come from under J-Will's wings and do his own thing.

"This a hunnid and fifty. I'm tryin' to do my own thing, but I'ma still re-up wit'chu every mornin'," Slim said as he sat the money on the table.

J-Will looked over to Slim with confusion as he never seen this coming.

"Cuz, that's cool. But if we gon do it like that, I'ma need a hunnid for every ounce."

"That's cool. I'll have yo' other fifty before lunch."

J-Will shook his head up and down as he gave Slim two ounces.

While Slim bagged his weed, things were oddly quiet. He and J-Will was so wrapped up in what they were doing, they lost track of the time.

"Cuz, we missed our bus," Slim said as he became aware of the time.

"Y'all cool. I'll drop y'all off," G-Will said as he came from one of the rooms.

Slim and J-Will collected their things from the table and followed G-Will. When they got to the door, J-Will stopped Slim.

"Ay cuz, hold this burner for me. They been trippin' off me at school. You laid back, and they don't fuck wit'chu."

"I got'chu," Slim said as he took the pistol and zipped it into his coat pocket. "But we need to find a locker to stash it in, 'cause I ain't tryin' to walk around like this at school."

"I'ma do that," J-Will said before he and Slim continued to G-Will's car.

When Slim and J-Will got to school, they got out of G-Will's car with a thick cloud of funky weed smoke. They went their separate ways when they got inside. The halls were quiet and empty, reminding Slim that he was late. As he approached his class, he searched for an excuse, but nothing satisfying came to his mind. When he stepped into his class, it was chaotic without Ms. Holiday present. He was relieved, and quickly took his seat while Angel frowned at him.

"Why you late?" Angel asked.

"Where Ms. Holiday?"

"She ain't here yet. And you smell like too much of that stuff!"

Just as Slim was about to lean over and try to steal a kiss from Angel, Ms. Holiday showed up. She stood in the doorway with her face frowned. Her presence alone brought order in the class.

"I am very disappointed," Ms. Holiday furiously spoke. "I could hear this class a mile away! And I know you all haven't been smoking in here!"

Slim's heart dropped to his stomach as Ms. Holiday looked around with her nose in the air.

"You all can cancel free day Friday! Now, get them assignments out and start working," she ordered before she headed towards her desk.

Everyone immediately complied, especially Slim.

"Gimme yo' coat," Angel angrily whispered as she leaned over to Slim. Angel knew that Slim kept his weed in his coat pocket, and by her being Angel, she was most likely not to be searched. Slim thought for a few seconds before he looked for Ms. Holiday. She was in one of the file cabinets with her back to the class. He carefully took his coat off and gave it to his angry girlfriend. He watched her put it on before he looked back to the teacher. She was still in the file cabinet. When he looked back to Angel, she was slowly removing her hand from his coat pocket as she shockingly stared at him.

At lunch time, Slim and Angel stood outside of the cafeteria. They were quietly arguing about why he had the pistol in his coat pocket. She was scared, thinking that he brought it to shoot someone. For that reason, she kept his coat on, and refused to give it to him.

"I don't care what'chu say. I'm not givin' you this coat 'til you get on yo' bus," Angel said as she folded her arms across her chest.

"Angel, that's cool. And I promise you, you'll never catch me wit it again," Slim spoke with sincerity. "Now, can you quit trippin' wit me?"

Slim always won Angel over with his promises, but this time, she wasn't letting him off so easily. This was a time when they were really supposed to be sharing each other's affectionate company. Losing their virginity to one another was an occasion that united their mind, body and soul. Instead, that focus was stolen by his poor decision making skills. She rolled her eyes at him, then shifted them to someone who was approaching them.

"What's up, Slim? Let me spend this fifty wit'chu," a familiar boy said.

"I'm on somethin' else right now. I'ma catch up wit'chu later."

"Aiight."

Slim watched the boy leave before he turned back to Angel.

"Jevon, I'm scared, and I want'chu to stop sellin' this stuff."

Slim could see the fear in Angel's eyes as distress flowed through her voice.

"Angel, you know I'll do anything for you, but… " Slim suddenly froze up as Angel shifted her eyes to someone who was approaching them. She looked shocked and terrified. When he turned around, he dropped his head and shook it in disbelief. A detective woman was approaching Slim and Angel with two policemen and the principal. The principal pointed him out to the detective woman as they continue to approach them. "Turn around and put your hands up against the locker," one of the policemen ordered.

"You too young lady," the detective woman ordered Angel. Slim could see the fright in Angel's face as the search began. Her tears were unbearable for him to look at. He dropped his head and shook it from side to side. He was clean, but the two ounces of weed and the pistol was found on her. As soon as he heard the handcuffs clicking, he rose his head and acted with no thought or hesitation.

"That's my coat. And that's my stuff. She ain't know it was in there," Slim calmly said as he stepped to the detective.

The detective didn't hesitate to turn her attention to Slim as she let Angel go. "He is the one I got the information on. Along with that, he's admitting ownership to the marijuana and gun. Arrest him and read him his rights."

Slim was submissive while the policeman did his job. As he was being taken away, he could hear Angel's hysterical cries. They were broken as they came from the depths of her soul.

Chapter 5: Jammed Up

At the Juvenile Detention Center, Slim was processed before he was placed into a small, cold cubical. He was offered a phone call, but he refused it. He was still processing what just happened to him. He laid on the cold steel with his hands behind his head. The detective's words about someone giving information stayed in his head. He wasn't aware of anyone who envied him. Everyone appeared to admire him and his cool swag. He had no idea of who snitched on him. The only comfort he got was knowing that Angel was free. Her hysterical cries sadden him as they were a reflection of how deeply he affected her. He sat up on the bed as he thought about how his absence was going to affect Jayla. Not once did he think about the upcoming consequences from the authorities and his father.

"Take those braids out of your head," a man said after tapping on the glass.

"What?" Slim asked as he twisted his face at the man.

The man twisted his face back at Slim as he unlocked the door. He then came into the room. He was 6 foot 6, dark-skinned, and wore a tight t-shirt that emphasized his muscular build.

"I'm Mr. B," he spoke with a deep voice as he stood over Slim. "I will personally cut them fuckin' braids outta your head if you don't have 'em out by the time I get back!"

Slim stared up at Mr. B, returning the same frown.

"Try me," Mr. B challenged before he turned to leave.

Slim sat with a defiant twist in his face, but couldn't ignore Mr. B's threat. He imagined him cutting his hair while he restrained him with his muscular build. He knew that it was possible. After a moment, he began to slowly undo his French braids.

Just as Slim was undoing his last French braid, Mr. B came back for him. He took him to a shower room where a procedural shower took place. He stayed in the same room, watching him shower with his arms folded across his chest.

After the quick and uncomfortable shower, Mr. B had underclothes and a blue uniform laid out for Slim. Blue slip on shoes came with it. While he got dressed, reality sunk in deeper. He knew that he wasn't going home anytime soon. When he was dressed, Mr. B had him pick up a bundle and follow him. The bundle consisted of his bedding, a face towel and a toothbrush.

Mr. B took Slim to a unit that was the size of a basketball court. Three boys sat on stools in front of the glass room. They were watching a TV that sat on the inside of it. A skinny white man that came from the bubble was expecting Slim. He gave him a room number and told him to sit in front of the TV after he dropped his bundle off.

As soon as Slim opened the door that led to the rooms, he was taken by the noise level. Rooms on each side of the hall were filled with thugs from all over the city. This was the confinement area that was better known as "the hole". It's where he would be until the morning. The boys yelled out their hoods while they beat and kicked on the doors. Gang signs went up with disrespectful and hostile words between rivaling gangs. Slim continued on, holding his dick as he looked straight ahead with a slight twist in his face.

After Slim put his bundle away, he came back to sit in front of the TV with the other new arrivals. They were laughing and joking with each other as if losing their freedom meant nothing.

"Ay cuz, where you from?" one of the boys asked Slim.

"Nigga, do I look friendly to you?" Slim responded with hostility.

Slim was in no mood to make friends. He stared at the boy with his face twisted, hoping that he responded with any kind of aggression. He was looking for someone to take his frustration and anger out on. The boy saw that he was ready to get ignorant and turned his playfulness back to the other boys.

Slim stared at the TV, wrapped up in his mixed thoughts and feelings. He didn't even move to go eat the horrible dinner that came. He remained in his thoughts as he was trying to get a grasp on reality.

By the next morning, Slim had already accepted the reality of him being jammed up. It was what it was with him, and he was prepared to deal with what lied ahead of him. He didn't get any sleep. Besides him not being sleepy, the noise level made it impossible. He laid in his bed and listened to rapping, war stories and hostile arguments while pounding on the doors vibrated through the concrete. When things finally became quiet, his door was being buzzed open for breakfast. Shortly after breakfast, he was being transferred to Unit-H.

Unit-H was the roughest unit in the detention center. It's where the juveniles with the dangerous felony charges were housed. When Slim came onto the unit, all eyes were on him. The boys were all dressed in red uniforms, and sat against the side and the back wall. They were all older and bigger than him, but he wasn't intimidated. He held his dick with his face slightly twisted as he made his way to the bubble.

At the bubble, Slim was given a room number. He was then told to drop his bundle off and sit under his number. It was on the back wall.

"Ms. Wells' class, line up," one of the staff members yelled as he came from the bubble.

When the boys got up from their stools, they did it with a lot of commotion. Slim was in Mr. Todd's class, so he remained on his stool.

"Hold the noise level down," the other staff member yelled as he came from the bubble. "Y'all asses will go back on lock down!"

"Fuck a lock down!" one of the boys said with his voice disguised.

"Ms. Wells' class, lock down," staff yelled as they stood together.

"Cuz, you betta take yo' weight," one of the boys said as he frowned at the back of the line.

"You got me fucked up, blood," the boy at the end of the line responded with hostility.

"Lock down," staff aggressively repeated themselves. Ms. Wells' class slowly complied as more of them became furious from the stupidity. On the way to their rooms, hostile words were being exchanged. One of the staff members followed them while the other one buzzed their doors from the bubble. Just as the atmosphere predicted, fights broke out in the hall.

"Break it up," one of the staff yelled as he ran from the bubble and into the hall.

Mr. Todd's class was left unattended as if they were trustworthy. A fight broke out on the side wall. Two boys were jumping on another boy. They quickly had him on the floor and was stumping his head to the concrete. A boy from the back wall jumped up from his stool to assist his overwhelmed homeboy. Another boy was right behind him. When he caught up with him, he snatched him from his feet by his collar and slammed his head to the floor. It sounded like a pumpkin being smashed against the ground. Blood instantly began to color the white floor as the boy laid motionless. His assailant was a big, dark-skinned boy, who looked like he was too old to be at the detention center. He calmly walked back to his stool, looking for someone else to be victimized. He caught eye contact with the youngest thug on the unit and twisted his fingers into gang signs at him. Slim didn't hesitate to hit him back up with the same gang signs. They represented the same gang, but was from different hoods.

More staff quickly stormed onto the unit where more brutal fights had ignited. The boys began to fight with the staff as they tried to gain control. Mr. B was there. He handled two and three boys at the same time, subduing them with his python arms. After a short while, the staff gained control and hauled the ruthless teenagers off to the hole. They then turned their attention to the boy who laid unconscious in a puddle of blood. Slim and a few more observers were ordered to their rooms. He then made his bed and finally went to sleep.

It had been two days, and Unit-H was still on lock down. They were fed in their rooms, and let out individually to take showers. Slim was familiar with isolation, so he was able to adjust.

Shortly after lunch on the third day of lock down, Slim was called to the bubble and told that he had a visitor. He figured that it was his father and dreaded it.

Mr. B took Slim downstairs on an elevator. He then led him down a hall before they stopped at a door. He was expecting his furious father on the other side of the door, but he was surprised. He came to find the detective woman who arrested him. She was accompanied by a sharply dressed white man, who was also a detective. They both were in the interrogation room.

When Slim stepped into the small room, the detectives rose from the table and left their folders there. He stood in confusion as he looked back and forth to them.

"I'm sure you remember me. I'm Detective Swanson, and this is Detective Allen," she kindly spoke.

"Yeah I remember you. Why you wanna see me? What? You finna let me go?"

"Anything is possible with your cooperation. I would like for you to have a seat, and maybe we can have a helpful conversation."

Of course, freedom interested Slim's naive mind. After a few seconds, he sat at the table while Mr. B left him alone with the detectives. Detective Swanson sat across from him while Detective. Allen remained standing.

"Would you like a soda and a snack?" Det. Swanson kindly asked.

"I'm cool," Slim replied as he was only interested in how he could be freed.

"Well, I would like to first commend you on the responsibility you took. I admire how you stepped up and didn't let your girlfriend go down. It shows that you are an honorable person."

Slim ignored Det. Swanson's praise as it meant nothing to him.

"I want you to be aware of the seriousness in the charges that you are facing. You were in possession of narcotics in a drug-free zone with a loaded gun. You can be certified as an adult and face a lot of jail time," Det. Swanson informed as a tactic to scare Slim. "But if you give us your cooperation, I can make this all go away for you," she added in a promising tone.

Slim confusingly stared at Det. Swanson as Det. Allen approached the table.

"Let's start with you telling us where you were last Friday night," Det. Allen calmly spoke.

"I was at home talkin' wit' my girl on the phone," Slim said with no hesitation.

Det. Swanson shook her head up and down as if Slim's answer coincided with another. She then went into her folder. "You know this boy, right," she asked with certainty as she slid Slim a picture.

As soon as Slim seen the picture, his face became twisted in confusion. It was a picture of Red.

"Nah, I don't know him," he said as he slid the picture back to Det. Swanson.

"We know about the fight you had with him," Det. Allen said.

"Like I said, I don't know him."

Things in the small room were about to come to a head as Det. Allen went into his folder. "The gun that was in your possession did this to Redman Wallace," he said as he slid Slim a picture. Slim was instantly taken by the gruesome picture of Red. His face was unrecognizable with three bullet holes that disfigured it.

"I ain't do this," he said as he swiped the picture from the table.

"We just want to know who you got the gun from," Det. Swanson calmly said. "I promise to get you out of here if you cooperate with us. Think about your family and your girlfriend who misses you."

Slim slumped into the chair as he put the pieces together. He came to the conclusion that J-Will killed Red over the money he owed him. He then became furious at J-Will for asking him to hold the hot pistol. Despite his contemptuous state of mind, turning his ignorant homeboy over to the authorities never crossed his mind. Even if it meant he would be reunited with his family and his precious Angel.

"Jevon, is there something you would like to tell me?" Det. Swanson softly asked.

"Yeah… I got the gun from a crack head."

The detectives could read the rebelliousness in Slim's posture as it flowed through his tone. It's when they lost their calm and generous tactic.

"That's bullshit," Det. Swanson said as she slapped the table and stood up. "You give me a name, or I will see to it that you are prosecuted to the fullest extent of the law," she threatened as she pointed her finger in Slim's face.

"And be charged with accessory to murder," Det. Allen jumped in.

"I ain't did shit, and I don't know shit," Slim yelled back at the detectives as he stood up.

"Sit down," Det. Allen ordered.

"I ain't gotta talk to y'all! Send me back to my room!"

"Is everything alright in here?" Mr. B asked as he came into the room.

The detectives looked at Slim with fury as they shook their head in disbelief.

"We're done with him," Det. Swanson said in a more settle tone.

"Young street punk," Det. Allen said as he pounded the table with his fist.

Slim twisted his face at the detectives as he started to leave.

"And one more thing," Det. Swanson said as Slim got to the door. "What you are committed to, and so called being loyal to, it holds deception that will eventually catch up with you."

Slim shrugged his shoulders as Det. Swanson's insightful words went over his head. His mind was too inexperienced and under developed in regard to the street life, so he wasn't able to grasp the concept of her words. He continued on with Mr. B as he gave them no thought.

The weekend quickly arrived and Slim's unit was still on lock down. That Saturday night, he was called for a visit. A few more boys were called, so he was quite sure that it was his father.

The visiting room was small and crowded. Everyone sat in tight rows. Slim stepped in and looked around before he noticed Jayla. She was running towards him with a weak smile.

"Von Von, I miss you!" Jayla cried as she threw her arms around him.

"I miss you too, Jay," Slim said as he hugged and kissed her.

"Please have a seat," a lady politely said.

Jayla took Slim to their father and brother. They stood up with weak smiles and hugged him before they all sat down.

Slim was anticipating his father's fury, but he only got questions in regard to his well-being.

"A public defender came to the house the other day. He said you have a hearin' scheduled for Monday," Slim's father said as he became more serious. "It's just a hearin' to schedule a court date. He said you'll most likely be here until then. These people tryin' to come down hard on you, so I went and got'chu a lawyer. Two detectives came to the house, too. They said that gun you got caught wit' was used in a murder. I told 'em you was at the house on that phone the night they said it happened."

"They came to see me. I told 'em where I was, and I got that gun from a crack head."

Slim's father shook his head from side to side as he knew that he was withholding information. He also knew that snitching could jeopardize the safety of his family, so he moved on.

"And that weed…Why is you sellin' that shit?" Slim's father asked as he began to release his fury. "You don't need no money! I take damn good care of y'all! All you need to do is take yo ass to school and focus on yo school work," he barked with no concern of his tone.

Slim's father drew attention with his furious tone, but the staff didn't intervene. They were actually supportive, and wished to see more of the parents take an aggressive approach towards the out of control juveniles.

"We gon' deal wit' this when all this is settled," Slim's father said in a more settle tone. "You just keep yo' ass outta trouble, and we'll be here every weekend to check on you."

During the rest of the visit, Slim talked with Jayla and Marcel. He was surprised by Marcel's brotherly concerns. He encouraged him to keep his head up and stay out of trouble. Jayla kept her arms wrapped around him during the whole visit. He'd never been away from her since the day she was born.

When it was time for them to go, she didn't understand having to leave without him. She cried when realized he wasn't coming home with her.

Slim's unit was still on lock down when he went to his hearing. Just as he expected, he was detained until his court date. It was in one month. His mind was conditioned for it, so he wasn't too upset.

One of the three boys who was a new arrival with Slim got good news at his hearing. He was being released later on that day. The four of them were in a small holding room, waiting to be taken back to their unit. They were all upset except for the boy who was getting released. He circled the room, punching the palm of his hand as he talked about what he was going to do when he got out. He was irritating Slim as it seemed like he was getting closer to him with every circle he made.

"Nigga, quit doin' that," Slim said as he twisted his face at the boy.

The boy was too wrapped up in his excitement to hear Slim. Slim became angrier, taking it that the boy ignored him.

Slim came from the wall with a fierce right hook to the boys' face as he was approaching him. The boy didn't know what was going on as he was being attacked with quick blows. He was shaken up as he stumbled towards the door and fell on the floor. Slim was right there with him, stumping him to the floor. The only refuge the boy had was to curl into a ball. His excitement was now cries for help. He remained in a ball when Slim took his place back on the wall.

"What the hell is goin' on in here?" Mr. B asked as he swung the door open. The boy fell out into the hall and jumped to his feet.

"I don't know what's wrong wit' him," he cried as he pointed to Slim.

From the holding room, Slim was taken straight to the hole. It's where he would spend his next ten days.

When Slim's time in the hole was up, he went back to Unit-H. They were finally off lock down, and back to the normal functions. Everyone was quietly seated under their numbers as they waited for school call.

After Slim got his number from the bubble, he dropped his bundle off and sat under his number. As he looked around, he noticed a lot of new faces. Amongst those new faces was his homeboy, Seven. He was happy to see a familiar face. They nodded at each other with slight smiles. Slim was anxious to talk with him so he can find out what was going on with Angel. They were in different classes, so he wouldn't be able to talk with him until gym time.

After lunch, Slim was in the gym with his class before Seven came in with his. He was sitting on the steps, watching the boys play basketball.

"What's up, cuz?" Seven dully spoke as he did the hood clap with Slim.

"What's up?" Slim curiously asked, noticing the sadness in Seven's tone.

Seven shook his head from side to side as he sat next to Slim.

"Damn, nigga! What's up?"

"Cuz, the homeboy J-Will got knocked," Seven sorrowfully informed.

"What?!" Slim shrieked. His heart began to pound in his chest.

"Yeah. Some cats jumped down on him when he was comin' from Teri's house. They hit him up seventeen times and closed his casket."

"Y'all know who did it?"

"Nah. But me, Bo and some of the other homeboys went through every cat hood over there and jumped down on 'em," Seven spoke with aggression. "That's why I'm in here now. But I just got caught up on some curfew bullshit. My PO gon' let me out tomorrow."

Slim fell silent with Seven as he was torn by the loss of the homeboy who introduced him to the streets.

"Cuz, what's up wit'cho situation though?" Seven broke the silence.

"These people tryin' to hang me for this shit," Slim said after a few seconds. He then told Seven about the interrogation, and the conclusion he came to about J-Will killing Red.

"That's some real shit how you didn't fold under that pressure. And the homeboy did ask me about a locker to stash that burna in." Slim shook his head up and down, feeling better knowing that J-Will didn't ignore his concern about the pistol.

"What's up wit' Angel?" he asked after a moment.

"Cuz, she lost it, and nobody couldn't calm her down. Her mama had to come and get her. And that was the last time I seen her," Seven reluctantly informed.

Slim dropped his head as he realized that Angel was affected deeper than he imagined.

The next day, Seven was released just as he expected. When Slim went to court, it was rescheduled for two months. After that, he spent majority of his time in the hole for fighting. Everything and everyone irritated him. When he finally went to court, he was sentenced to an 18 to 36 month program in Divisional Youth Service.

Chapter 6: The Development

Slim was in the hole when the people from the boys' home came for him. Two white men walked on each side of him to a car that was parked in front of the detention center. He walked freely as the bright sun twisted his face. It was a beautiful spring day, and he couldn't ignore the thought of running off into it. It was the big, athletic white men that erased those thoughts. He knew that they would snatch him up before he picked up any speed.

When they got to the car, one of the men opened the back door and climbed in after Slim. As the car pulled away from the curb, he stared out of the window at the functions of the free world.

"I'm Phil, and that's Stan," the man next to Slim kindly introduced himself and the driver. "As you know, you are going to an eighteen to thirty-six month program. Most guys come and complete the program in the mandatory eighteen months. It's very possible. Just cooperate and allow the program to assist you with becoming a better person. I just wanted to give you a heads up. When we arrive at the cabin, you will go through an orientation that gives you the functions of the program," he said before he left Slim to look out of the window.

All Slim wanted was to get this over and done with, so he could get back to his Angel.

The drive from the city was a long hour and thirty minutes. Slim was intrigued by the unfamiliar place as he took everything in. They turned onto a narrow road from the main street. The density of the trees gave no visual on either side of the road. It took them ten minutes to get pass the trees. The road curved as it went up and down hills before it brought them to the camp.

The camp was like a small town. Six cabins were spaciously lined on the left with beautiful landscaping. On the right side of the road, there was an administration building followed by a small school. A cafeteria came next, followed by a medical building which completed the block. A recreational building and a ball field covered the entire next block. It was used for soccer, softball, flag football, and had a quarter mile track course that outlined it. A group of boys enjoyed the weather while they practiced softball.

Stan stopped the car in front of the last cabin. "This is where you will reside," he said before he and Phil got out of the car.

When Slim got out of the car, Phil and Stan were already heading towards the cabin. When they got to the door, they stopped and waited on him. He was standing outside of the car, continuing to look around. He almost felt free. After a moment, he headed towards the cabin.

The two-story cabin opened up to a spacious dining room on the left, and a spacious living room on the right. A kitchen was beyond the dining room with an arched entrance.

The cabin was comfortably furnished with a fire place. In the living room, five white boys were lounging on the couches with a staff member. They were watching a TV that played from an entertainment center.

When the group noticed Slim come in with the staff, they turned the TV off and adjusted their posture.

"This is Jevon Johnson, our newest addition to the group," Stan introduced him before he sat down. "Shawn, would you like to begin with the orientation?"

"Sure," Shawn gladly said as he took the floor. Shawn introduced himself with friendliness followed by the other boys. They were all older and bigger than Slim.

"We're about to begin orientation where you'll be familiarized with the functions of the program. Doing so, it may take a while. Would you like to use the restroom before we begin?" Shan asked Slim.

"I'm cool," Slim replied blandly as he sat slumped on the couch.

"I will begin with telling you the objective of the program. It's designed to help us identify with ourselves and others. It's an ability that allows us to be more comprehensive. With that ability, we can make better decisions for ourselves.

"We have group meetings Monday through Friday where we discuss several topics in regard to that objective. I'll tell you more about group meetings as I familiarize you with our daily functions," Shawn informed before he paused. "We operate on a tight schedule with impeccable organization. Organization helps establish stability. With stability, we can focus more on our objectives."

Slim stared at Shawn as he didn't have a clue of what he was talking about.

"On weekdays, we begin our day at six a.m. Within an hour, we take care of our basic hygiene. We then come down to the day room and watch TV until we are called for breakfast. After breakfast, we go directly to school, which is year-round. We go to lunch from school, then back until three o'clock. At that time, we come back to the cabin and have personal time in the dorm. During that time, we can either nap, socialize, read, write, iron, look at TV, listen to music or shower. We have female staff working with us, so we are not allowed in anything less than a tank-top and basket• ball shorts. When our two-hour personal time is over, we prepare for dinner. After dinner, we come back to the cabin and have our group meeting. There is no specific time frame for group meetings. They are very captivating, and sometimes last until our bedtime, which is nine forty-five. In other cases when group meetings last the usual two hours, we have the rest of the day to ourselves. During that time, we cook and eat our personal things that our family can bring. We also watch movies, or do other activities at the group's discretion. Visiting days are Fridays and Saturdays from six to nine in the evenings. Your family can bring your personal food and clothes at those times. Prior to your arrival, administration sent your family an information package, so they are aware of such things. Regular phone call days are Sundays after dinner. In your case, you will be allowed to have a special one after group meeting tonight."

Shawn took a breath and let the other boys intervene. They talked about the year-round sport events before Shawn took the floor again.

"You will be assigned to an advocate who will work personally with you as your mentor. Her name is Crissy, and she'll be in on the next shift. There are four levels that we must obtain to complete the program. However, we all must do the required eighteen months. No one has ever done the maximum thirty-six. As of now, you have no level. You will be on a thirty-day observation by the staff before they decide to give you your first level. On level two, you will have more privileges such as, more phone time and off campus trips with the group. We go out to eat, to the movies, skating, amusement parks, and other fun stuff or educational activities. On level three, you will be able to go off campus with your advocate. With level four, your home plan begins, and you'll spend every weekend at home," Shawn proudly said before he paused.

Slim figured that Shawn must be on level four from how he was glowing.

"We basically do everything as a group," Shawn continued. "We govern each other and address negativity in a circle. It's where we stand in a circle and give positive alternatives to the negative behavior. When a group member becomes a threat to himself or others, he will be restrained by the group on staff's call." Slim twisted his face at Shawn before he looked around at the group. What he said about addressing negativity sounded like snitching to him. He wasn't about to do no snitching, and he most definitely wasn't going to let them restrain him.

"Do you have any questions?" Shawn asked.

"Nah. But when can I take a shower?"

"With no questions, I guess that brings this orientation to an end. I would just like to welcome you to the group once again," Shawn spoke with friendliness. "It's our personal time now, and in your section of the dorm, there's a care package on your bed," he added before he looked to the staff.

The staff led the group up to the dorm in a single file line. The spacious dorm had six sections where the boys slept with their personal things. Each section had a twin-sized bed, a dresser, and a desk with a night lamp attached to it. There was also a living room area with couches and an entertainment center. A big desk that the staff used sat next to the entrance of the dorm. From there, they had a clear view of the dorm.

Slim's section was in the far right corner upon entering the dorm. It's where he found the care package. Everything was brand new. He had cosmetics, underclothes, and sweats.

He stripped down to his basketball shorts and tank-top before he headed to the shower. A huge bathroom was connected to the dorm. Four sink bowls sat in the counter with a big glass mirror that covered the wall behind it. The bathroom included four showers with tinted glass doors, four stalls, and two private toilets. It was the group's responsibility to keep the bathroom clean along with the entire cabin. They did a thorough cleaning every Sunday before they had the rest of that day to themselves.

Slim took almost an hour in the shower. After putting his hair in a ponytail, he came from the bathroom. He was a little surprised when he came out. A young lady sat on the desk while an older white man sat in the chair next to it. He figured that she must be Crissy.

Crissy looked like a teenager. She was 4'9 with a petite figure. Her bleach blonde hair wasn't quite long enough for the ponytail she tried to put it in. Strands of hair fell to the sides of her face. She would occasionally push them behind her big ears with her fingers. Her blue eyes matched the short-sleeved blouse she wore. She had a baby nose with small, plump lips. Her lemon sized breasts sat up as though they were just beginning to develop. Whatever feminine fragrance she wore, it had the whole dorm smelling fruity.

Slim thought Crissy was funny looking, but cute.

"And you must be Jevon," Crissy sweetly said with her squeaky voice.

Slim stopped and shook his head up and down as he was still taking Crissy in.

"I'm your advocate, Crissy. And this is James," she politely introduced herself and her coworker. "When you get yourself situated, I would like to talk with you."

"Aiight," Slim said before he continued to his room.

Slim didn't have much to organize in his section. After getting dressed, he went over to Crissy. His eyes couldn't help being attracted to her ass as she led him over to the living room area. It was small and plump. Her blue jeans gave it a little room to jiggle. She was too short to sit on the couch without her feet dangling. She sat in a curl on one end while he sat in a slump on the other end.

"Do you have any questions about orientation, or your new environment?" Crissy asked.

"Nah. I ain't got no questions," Slim said as he kept his eyes on the TV.

"That's new to me. Usually when guys come in, they have lots of questions. I guess you understand everything so far."

"I wouldn't say that."

"So, what is it that you don't understand?"

"I really ain't tryin' to understand none of this shit. I'm just tryin' to do what I'm 'pose to do so I can go home."

"Please don't use that word."

"My bad," Slim said as he looked to Crissy, then back to the TV.

"Does that mean that you're sorry?" Crissy curiously asked as she pushed a strand of hair behind her ear.

"Somethin' like that."

"I'm not hip to the slang talk, but I think I understand. And I accept your apology, if that's what it is. Just don't do it again, or I'll have to call a circle on you," Crissy humorously threatened as she shook her finger at Slim.

Slim shrugged his shoulders as he looked at Crissy with a nonchalant expression.

"Well, let me just say, an understanding is one of the basic steps to success. Do you understand that?"

"Not really."

"Everything has its reasons and ways of functioning. Understanding the reasons and ways of how things function gives you insight. With that insight, you'll have a better chance to succeed at anything you put your mind to."

"That sound good, but I think you gon' have to break that down to me some more."

"I will be more than happy to. And I will always be here to assist you in the program with your development," Crissy said with a smile. "But right now, I would like for you to prepare yourself for dinner. We'll talk more later."

After dinner, the group had a meeting where sacrifices was the topic. A person's sincerity was pointed out by the sacrifices they made. Slim found himself confronted with a personal issue within the topic. He thought about him sacrificing his freedom to save Angel. It was something that pointed out his sincerity in regard to how he felt about her. The group also learned how sacrifices can help bring acknowledgment to who has their best interest. It was to give them insight on who to embrace.

While the boys in the group opened up and shared personal information, Slim quietly sat in a slump as he was captivated. It's where he would begin to be receptive to the knowledge as his mind is hungry for the intellectual development.

After the hour and forty-five minute group meeting, it was personal time, and Slim's time to make a phone call. He had one person on his mind. Shawn took him to the phone in the dining room while the rest of the group cooked and prepared to watch a movie. When they got to the phone, Shawn pulled a piece of paper out and began dialing numbers.

"You trippin'! It's my time to use this phone," Slim said as he clicked the phone off.

Shawn gave Slim a dumbfounded look as he remembered that he forgot to tell him something. "I'm sorry, but I forgot to tell you about the phone policies. Someone always have to be aware of the lower level phone calls. It's a safety precaution. I'm a level four, and it's one of my responsibilities."

"That's cool, but I just wanna call my girl and let her know what's up wit' me."

"I understand, but we are only allowed to call immediate family," Shawn said as he showed Slim a piece of paper with the approved numbers on it.

Slim looked around before he responded. "Ain't nobody over here but us. I need to talk to my girl hella bad! I ain't gon be long, and I ain't gon say nothin' about it."

It could of been the desperation in Slim's tone, or that Shawn could relate to him as a new arrival, but he looked as if he was considering it.

"Dude, you have to promise me that you will keep this between us. I can lose my level for this, and I'm supposed to go home next month," Shawn said in a whisper.

"Part of the reason I'm in here is 'cause I didn't snitch on my homeboy, so you ain't gotta worry about me sayin' somethin' about this."

Shawn shook his head up and down as he took Slim's words as trusting ones. He then dialed Angel's number as Slim called it out to him.

When Slim put the phone to his ear, his heart thumped hard and fast as he was excited. He was finally about to hear the sweet voice of his Angel. He planned on telling her how much he loved and missed her, and how he was going to do everything he could to get back to her. He relied on his promise to console her as it always did.

Slim's excitement was turned into a hurtful disappointment as his face became twisted. A computerized operator came onto the line. She called out Angel's number and said that it was no longer in service.

With the disappointing and discouraging discovery, Slim dropped his head and held the phone down to his side. He figured that Angel must've moved, and that made him feel like she was lost forever.

Shawn could sense Slim's sadness, so he gave him a minute before he spoke "Would you like to call your family?" Slim shook his head up and down as he looked to Shawn. Slim had just missed his father, so he talked with Jayla.

She excitedly told him that they were corning to see him that weekend. She could sense his sadness from his lack of enthusiasm. It led him to tell her about his disconnection with Angel. Knowing how he felt about her, she deeply sympathized with him.

That weekend, Slim's father came to see him with Jayla and Marcel. He had trouble with finding the place, so when they finally arrived, they only had an hour to visit. His father brought him clothes, and a lot of groceries. He encouraged him to utilize the program to better himself. For majority of the visit, he talked with Jayla and Marcel. She kept her arms around him as if he was her teddy bear. She encouraged him to stay out of trouble, and even made him promise to do so. In return, he made her promise to not cry when it was time for her to leave him. She left with a smile as she was anxious to see him again. His father would come every other weekend to visit him with his brother and sister. He was so caught up with enjoying his visit, he didn't notice Crissy observing him with a smile.

There were a lot of things that Slim didn't like about the program, but he knew that it was something that he had to deal with. The boys in the group were all friendly with him. He couldn't relate to any of them, so he stayed to himself. At school, he did his assignments, and in group meetings he paid attention. He missed his Angel, and sadly thought about her every day. At the same time, he was developing a crush for Crissy, who was always sweet and polite to him.

After four weeks in the program, Slim got his first one on one time with his advocate. The rest of the group was in the dorm having personal time while they were in the day room. Crissy sat in a curl on one end of the couch while he sat slumped in the middle of it.

"We had a staff meeting today, and you were the main topic," Crissy said with a smile before she took a spoon of her ice cream.

"Straight up?" Slim queried before he sipped his juice.

"Aren't you excited and curious to know why you was the main topic?"

"I ain't excited, but I am a lil' curious."

Crissy stared at Slim with a puzzled expression for a moment. "You are very mysterious and quiet. We are familiar with- no offense- your troubled history. We were all expecting for you to be a handful, but we were all surprised from what we have observed. You are very well behaved, and you are doing a tremendous job in school. From what we have observed, we decided to give you your first level."

"That's cool," Slim said with no enthusiasm. "So, when am I gon' get my next one?"

"Well, in order for you to get your next level, we must see some participation from you."

"Participation," Slim repeated as he looked at Crissy with confusion.

"Jevon, participation means, calling circles and addressing negativity. It also means, opening up in group meetings with sharing your thoughts, feelings and perceptions, Crissy explained as she sat her ice cream on the table.

"You trippin'! I ain't never gon call circles," Slim firmly stated. That's snitchin' to me. And whatever you said I don't share in group meetin' is my business."

"Jevon, you are in an environment where another person's actions can affect the progress towards your objective. Making them aware of it with giving them a positive alternative is a way for you to create stability in your environment. With that stability, you can focus more on your objective."

"That sound good, but I still ain't callin' no circles."

"I will always encourage you to look at it with another perspective. Now, as for as you opening up in group meetings, it's for the staff to identify with you. With you being identifiable, we can understand you and begin dealing with your issues. So, in order for you to advance in the program, you must open up," Crissy desperately tried to get through to Slim.

"That's bullshit," Slim angrily said as he jumped up from the couch. "I been stayin' outta trouble, thinkin' I was doin' what was right, and you mu-fuckas tellin' me that ain't enough!"

"Jevon, I'm sorry! I didn't mean to upset you," Crissy sorrowfully expressed as she stood in front of him. "I want to help you! But you have to open your mind," she said as she gently grabbed his wrist. Slim stared into Crissy's eyes as they appeared to be sincere, but he was reluctant to accept her. He remembered a group meeting where he learned how generosity was used as a manipulating tactic. He also remembered how the detectives tried to use their generosity.

"I'm goin' back upstairs," Slim finally said as he broke away from Crissy.

"Jevon!"

Slim ignored Crissy's squeaky call as he continued on.

Two months passed and Slim was still in a defiant state of mind. It still didn't stop Crissy from trying to get through to him. She didn't want to upset him, so she used indirect approaches. Her professional tactics were always unsuccessful. It made him more intriguing to her as she became persistent. She noticed that the only time he opened up was when he was with Jayla. She finally found an entry that night after his visit when she had him in the day room for one on one time.

"Your sister is cute. How old is she?"

"Eleven," Slim answered after a few seconds.

"I'm the only child, but I've always wanted a little sister to do fun things with," Crissy said before she looked away with a longing expression. "I think it's what makes the relationship special. Please, tell me you have fun with her."

"I do, and we do everything together."

"Like what?" Crissy asked with disbelief. Crissy knew that Jayla was special to Slim. It was quite obvious to her analytical eyes. Her questioning his relationship with her was to get him defensive. He didn't even think about the group meeting they had where they talked about how a defensive person becomes open. He spilled everything from how they talk, to how they play fight.

"That's nice. Do you have that same relationship with your brother?"

"We just started gettin' along when I left. He used to always be snitchin' on me. That's one of the reasons I don't call circles."

"He always seem to be happy to see you. Maybe he just wants to see you do better. What do you think?"

"I don't know what be goin' on in his head," Slim said as he shrugged his shoulders.

"Have you ever asked him?" Crissy quizzed Slim.

"For what?"

"To get an understanding. With that understanding comes the opportunity to gain control and alleviate conflict. Now, to get that understanding, you must open up and communicate," Crissy said as she brushed the lining of Slim's hair with her finger.

A smile appeared on Slim's face as he realized that Crissy cunningly worked the program on him. At the same time, he was able to grasp the insight. He was impressed. "You think you got some game, don't chu?"

"Does that mean that I got through to you?" Crissy asked with a smile.

"Yeah. You got me, and I understand where you comin' from."

"So, does that mean that you are going to call circles?" Crissy excitedly asked.

"C'mon now, yo' lil' game ain't that strong," Slim said with a laugh.

"I won't push it. I guess we can take it one step at a time. But, I would like to ask you a personal question, if you don't mind."

"What's up," Slim asked as he looked Crissy up and down.

"Where is your mother?"

"I lost her," Slim said after a moment.

"I'm sorry to hear that," Crissy sorrowfully expressed. Slim shrugged his shoulders as he continued to eat his snacks.

As time went on, Crissy became more familiar with Slim as he opened up. He participated in group meetings, and from that development, he earned his second level. He even became very active with the boys in the group. They socialized, played games, and he even played on the team when sport events came up. He still became distant at times. During some of those times, he would think about Angel. Those times became shorter as his crush on Crissy became stronger.

After Slim's sixteenth month in the program, he was given his third level. It was a gesture to encourage him. But to earn his fourth level, he needed to show leadership and address negativity in a circle.

One weekend when Slim's family came to visit him, he noticed that Jayla was developing a womanly figure. She was now thirteen, but her figure made her appear much older. He and Jayla always talked openly, so he didn't have to use the slick tactics he learned to get her to open up. She was shy when he first asked her about boys. He was then relieved to find out that she was only interested in her school work. It led her to tell him that she was being advanced a grade. It touched him when she gave him some of the credit. It was how he always helped her with her homework and his persistency to teach her when she was only two years old. She would be one grade behind him. They were excited as they talked about going to school together. She also surprised him with learning how to French braid. He was very satisfied with her neat work, and she would do his hair every time she visited.

Crissy came in on her off day to take Slim on another off-campus trip. It was his fifth one with her. When he got into her car, she was frustratingly rambling through her purse.

"Don't tell me you left the money again," Slim said with a laugh as he found Crissy's dramatic behavior amusing.

"I can be such an air head at times," Crissy said as she continued to ramble through her purse. "We'll just have to make a quick stop by my apartment. We're going to see a horror movie," she said before she pulled off.

It finally hit Slim. Not only did Crissy know about his crush on her, she was trying to seduce him. He sat quietly as he began to put the pieces together. This was Crissy's second time claiming that she left her money and took Slim to her apartment. He figured that she was testing him. Then, there were the horror movies that she always wanted to see. It's where she snuggled up against him as she appeared to be frightened. He was quite sure she felt his hands on her goodies when she became hysterical from the horrific scenes. There were also times when she was touchy with him with her hugs and kisses. As he thought about it, she was only loose with him when they were alone. He no longer felt that it was all a part of her free-spirit.

On the way to Crissy's apartment, she was unusually quiet. She looked at Slim as she knew that he was putting the pieces together. He shook his head up and down as he returned her smile. When she pulled into the parking lot of her apartment complex, she parked and turned the car off.

"The theatre is so far across town, so by the time we get there, it'll almost be time for me to take you back. I was thinking, we can watch a movie here. That way, you'll still have your time away, and you can make yourself comfortable however you please," Crissy said with a careless attitude.

"That's cool," Slim said, knowing that the convenience wasn't coincidental.

Slim kept his cool as Crissy led him into her apartment. "Please, make yourself comfortable. There are some things in the kitchen that I think you may enjoy," Crissy said as she locked the door behind herself. "I'll just be a minute."

Slim shook his head up and down as he watched Crissy disappear into a hall. He then rubbed his hands together as he headed to the kitchen.

In the kitchen, Slim found another one of Crissy's hints. She had a lot of his favorite things. He saw it as no coincidence, considering that she was allergic to some of them. She was expecting for him to be there. With that additional discovery, eating was the last thing on his mind. He went back into the living room and waited on her. He slumped on the couch and turned the TV on with no interest in what he was watching.

"I'm back. I just wanted to change into something comfortable to lounge in," Crissy said as she came from the hall.

When Slim turned around, he was astonished by Crissy. She was bare feet, showing off her pedicured toes. They were painted light pink, looking like little pieces of candy. Pink cotton shorts fitted her tightly as they rode up her thighs. They showed off her curves and made her lips obviously visible. The rim of her shorts was inches from her bellybutton that her halter top exposed. Her nipples made little buttons on her shirt as her breasts modestly bounced. When she walked pass him, his eyes followed her without a blink. Her plump ass jiggled with no restraint as her cheeks peeked from the bottom of her shorts.

"What would you like to watch?" Crissy asked as she slightly bent at the entertainment center.

"I like what I'm watchin' now," Slim explicitly replied as he slid to the edge of the couch.

When Crissy turned around, she could see the hunger in Slim's lustrous eyes. "What is this about?" she asked as she looked to the TV, then back to him.

"I don't know, but I gotta feelin' that I'm 'bout to find out."

"If this is what you want to be entertained by, it's fine with me," Crissy said as she came and curled next to Slim.

Slim kept his eyes on Crissy as she made herself comfortable.

"Why are you looking at me like that?" Crissy softly asked. Slim slid closer to Crissy before he smoothly responded.

"Let's stop playin' these lil' games. I know what it is wit'chu, just like you know what it is wit' me. Now let's utilize this time for the real reason you brought me here."

"I love it when you talk to me that way."

"I ain't tryin' to talk no more. You always told me, you gotta open up to get a understandin'. So, I'm tryin' to get'chu open to get things more clear."

"I like the sound of that," Crissy softly said as she saddled into Slim's lap.

Slim helped Crissy onto his lap as he gripped the bottom of her ass. When she was positioned, she kissed and sucked on his lips as she caressed his face. He slid his hands under her shorts and gripped her hot, naked ass. She didn't have any panties on, and knowing that she was prepared to give him some pussy aroused him further. She could feel his passion as he participated in the kissing, and how he lovingly squeezed her ass.

"Let's go to my bedroom where I can make myself more accessible for you," Crissy said with a sluttish attitude.

In Crissy's bedroom, she fulfilled Slim's fantasies. She opened his fifteen-year-old mind with her amazing and raunchy sexual performance.

After a quick shower, Slim found Crissy in her bedroom getting dressed. As he began to do the same, she approached him with a serious expression. She grabbed his hand and led him to her bed where they both sat.

"Jevon, when I first met you, I did whatever I had to do to get you to open up. However, I've always had your best interest at heart," Crissy admitted. "In the process of me getting to know you, I found myself admiring you beyond my control. I'm not trying to justify what just happened between us. I'm only trying to tell you that you are very special."

"Aiight. Now, where you goin' wit' this?"

"I've watched you grow into a very intellectual young man, and I hope you use the development towards something positive. You have a delightful presence that I enjoy. Unfortunately, life throws us curves that we must turn with. If not, we lose who we are."

"Crissy, what'chu tryin' to tell me?" Slim dreadfully asked.

"I brought you here to share myself with you before I said good-bye," Crissy said as she caressed Slim's face.

Slim dropped his head and shook it in disbelief.

"Jevon, don't be sad," Crissy said as she gently lifted his head.

"I'm good. I gotta turn wit' the curves, right?" Slim replied with a slight smile.

"I'm so proud of you. I'm going to miss you, but I will always keep you in my thoughts and prayers," Crissy softly spoke before she kissed Slim's cheek.

When Crissy dropped Slim off at the cabin, it was his last time seeing her. Within the program, he remained the same. He still didn't call circles, and for that reason, he never earned his fourth level. He was the first ever to do the maximum thirty-six months in the program.

When he went home on that spring day of May, he was sixteen years old. Even though he received an unsuccessful discharge, he developed some intellect that was to his advantage. How he was going to use that intellect was yet to be determined. The positive opportunities lied ahead of him just as well as the self-sufficient street life he made a strong connection with.

Chapter 7: Changes

On Slim's way home with his father, he asked him to think about doing construction work for his company during the summer. He told him about the good money he would be making along with the valuable experience he would obtain. At 5'10 and 180 lbs. with a solid muscular build, he was very capable.

When Slim arrived at home with his father, he noticed a big difference in the house. Everything had been upgraded. The furniture that was once in the living room now occupied a big section of the basement. It was comfortably put together. His father gave him the responsibility to keep that area clean. It was basically his personal space.

At the door of his room, Slim noticed that the padlock and latch had been removed. Fresh paint on the door made it look as if it was never there. His days of isolation were a thing of the past.

When Slim stepped into his room, he dropped his bags and looked around. Everything was exactly how he left it, except for his bed. Someone made it up. It was obvious that someone had been keeping his room intact. He could smell traces of air freshener that still lingered in the air. It led him to think about the money he kept stashed under his mattress.

Slim walked over to his bed and kneeled down at the foot of it. His face was full of uncertainty as he slid his hand between the mattresses. He swayed his arms from side to side until he discovered his three rolls of money. He gathered them together with a smile and pulled them towards him. As he was pulling, his hand ran over something that aroused his curiosity. He let go of the money and began to feel what he made out to be an envelope. He then remembered. It was the card that Angel gave him on Valentine's Day over three years ago.

Slim sat on his bed and pulled the card from its envelope. It still held the sweet, mesmerizing scent of Angel. His mind was instantly flooded with memories as he held the card to his nose. He was taken back to his hugs with her, where he would lovingly inhale her aroma. He then remembered her broken cries when he was taken away from her. He shook his head from side to side and began reading the poem she wrote to him.

When Slim finished reading the poem, he held the card in his lap, wondering if Angel still felt something for him. He chuckled at that thought as he deemed it to be silly. It's been over three years, and he figured that she moved on with her life, forgetting all about him.

"Von-Von!" Jayla excitedly called for him as she ran down the steps. Slim had just put the card back under his mattress when Jayla ran into his room.

"I missed you," Jayla said as she tackled Slim with a bear hug.

Slim and Jayla fell onto the bed with her continuing to kiss his face.

"I missed you too, Jay," Slim said, returning the affection.

"I'm so glad you finally home," Jayla happily spoke as she and Slim sat up on the bed.

"Yeah, me too," Slim said as he put his arm around Jayla and pulled her closer to him.

"I been comin' down here cleanin' yo' room, and I been playin' the game."

"I don't care how long you been practicin', you already know what's up," Slim said with a laugh.

"C'mon then! I'm finna kick yo' butt," Jayla said with assertiveness as she pushed Slim's forehead with her finger. "C'mon," she ordered as she forced a controller into his hands.

"Aiight," Slim warned.

Jayla blew Slim's warning off as they began to play the video game. He wasn't really surprised to see that she'd become better. She demolished him two games in a row, and taunted him while doing so.

"Von, what's up? Why you lettin' her shine on you like that?" Marcel asked with a laugh as he stepped into the room.

"He ain't lettin' me do nothin'," Jayla said as she beat Slim once again.

"I taught her everything she know, so it's all good," Slim said as he sat the controller down. "What's up though?"

"I'm good, glad you home," Marcel said as he clapped hands with Slim and pulled him in for a hug.

Now at the age of eighteen, Marcel has graduated from high-school with a basketball scholarship to attend a university in Florida. He would be going away in the fall. In the meantime, he worked at their father's construction company. He and Slim's relationship grew into a more brotherly connection over the years.

"Well, let me go up here and help the ol' dude in the kitchen," Marcel said before he left the room.

Their father was preparing a big welcome home dinner for Slim.

"Von Von, let's put'cho stuff up," Jayla said as she began to unpack his things.

While they were putting his things away, Slim noticed that Jayla was strangely quiet. "What'chu got on yo' mind, Jay?"

Jayla remained quiet for a moment before she responded. "I don't know if I should tell you, but mama 'pose to come and eat wit us. Daddy wanted it to be a surprise, but I don't think it'll be a good surprise. I'm sorry if I'm wrong," she said as she sat on the bed.

"You ain't never wrong when you tryin' to look out for me," Slim stated as he sat next to Jayla.

"She probably don't come anyway 'cause every time we waited on her to go see you in that place, she never showed up."

"It's cool. I understand how shame can hold people back from doin' things they really wanna do. Let's just give her some time. She'll come around," Slim assured his sister.

Jayla was stunned by Slim's new perceptive as she stared at him with a smile. It was a tremendous change from his bitter attitude towards their mother. It was the program that gave him insight on his mother's issues. He figured that it was pressure that exposed her weakness and made her embrace the destructive habit for consolation. He had no idea of what that pressure was, but he sympathized with his lost mother. He shared his insight with Jayla to give her a better understanding.

Just as Jayla suspected, their mother didn't show up for the special dinner. What was supposed to be a surprise was never mentioned. Slim enjoyed the dinner with his family as they all laughed and talked together.

Chapter 8: The Reintroduction

After the special dinner, Slim went to the basement with Jayla.

"I like it down here," Slim said as he grabbed the remote and slumped on the couch.

"That don't mean you can bring yo' lil' girlfriends down here," Jayla teased as she sat next to Slim.

"I ain't tryin' to do the girlfriend thing, so whoever I bring down here ain't gon stay long."

"I don't wanna hear that," Jayla said as she pushed Slim with her face twisted in disgust.

"I didn't mean it like that," Slim said with a laugh.

"Did you ever catch up wit' Angel?"

Slim shook his head from side to side as he continued to flip through the channels.

Sensing that Angel was a sensitive subject, Jayla changed it with a brighter attitude. "I'm so glad that school is almost over! Auntie Keda lettin' Fe-Fe spend the summa over here."

Jayla and Fe-Fe were close cousins. They resembled each other, and was always mistaken for sisters. Fe-Fe was a year older than Jayla, and had a sassy attitude. She thought she was grown since the day she learned how to walk and talk. She was also the ring leader of "The Fast Ass Clic". It included Jayla and three more of their cousins. Her big brother Nut gave them that name as he seen them all as young divas.

"What's up wit' Nut," Slim asked.

"Bein' a Nut! Them police people kicked in Auntie Keda house and locked him up. They said he shot three people," Jayla informed.

"Damn," Slim said as he thought about the jam Nut was in.

"So, what's been goin' on around here?"

"You mean out there," Jayla confusingly asked as she looked to the window, then back to Slim.

"Yeah."

"Von-Von, why you wanna know what's goin' on out there?"

"I just wanna be aware of my surroundings," Slim simply replied.

Jayla took a few seconds to respond. "It's been quiet for the last few weeks, but it was crazy before that. I was goin' to my friend Meka's house one mornin' before school, and them police people smashed into this one house wit' one of them things. They had a lot of the Six Deuce boys sittin' on the curb wit' plastic handcuffs on. Then them people started bringin' all kinda stuff from that house. They had all these white bricks, big army guns, money, and black trash bags full of stuff."

Slim shook his head in disbelief as he thought about the scene.

"Well, I'm finna go get my stuff ready for school and get in the tub 'fore I go to bed," Jayla said as she rose from the couch.

"Do you still wear yo' Big Bird pajamas?" Slim teased.

"Shut up, Von-Von! I used to like my jammies!

"Wake me up 'fore you leave in the mornin'."

"It's gon be early," Jayla said before she left his room.

After Jayla left, Slim continued to channel surf. He caught a commercial where money was falling from the sky. It made him think about his stash.

Slim closed the door behind himself before he went over to his bed. When he got his money out, he sat on his bed and pulled the rubber bands from the rolls. He then organized the money by the digits and began counting. It took him five minutes to carefully count the money twice. Each time, he counted $1,900. The love still existed as he was reintroduced to the feeling of control and freedom that came with self-sufficiency.

Just as Slim asked, Jayla came to wake him before she went off to school. He was wide awake when she knocked on his door. His body was accustomed to getting up at 6a.m. He laid in his bed, listening to everyone moving around as they prepared to start their day "I'm good. Come in," Slim answered Jayla's knocks.

"I'm finna go to my friend Meka's house 'fore we go catch our bus. I'll see you later, and I made them leave you some food up there, too."

"Right on, Jay. You need some money?

"I don't need none, but I always like to have some extra money," Jayla said as she came further into the room. "Why? You gon' gimme some?"

"Yeah. Look in my top drawer. I put it in there for you last night."

Jayla was already going into Slim's top drawer before he finished his sentence. "Von-Von, all this mines? Where you get all this from?" she excitedly asked as she grabbed the roll of money.

"That's yours, Jay. It's four hundred, and that been down here ever since I left."

"Why you ain't tell me?"

"I wasn't thinkin' 'bout no money," Slim said with a laugh.

"Well, I'ma jus take some, and leave the rest in here for when I want some mo'. Thank you!"

When Jayla left, Slim got up and took care of his usual morning business. After he ate, he went into his room and brought his video game out to the living room area. He hooked it up to the big screen. The old game quickly became boring. For a while, he blasted the stereo while he sat slumped on the couch. It reminded him of how he used to chill at J-Will's house before school. It led him to think about G-Will as he wondered if he still lived up the street. With not too much thought, he got dressed and was out of the house. His intentions were to go and show his condolences. He had no idea that he was about to be reintroduced to a lifestyle he fell deeply in love with.

Slim noticed some people sitting on the porch steps next to where J-Will used to live. It was obvious to him that they were all junkies. They looked at him with a desperate craving in their eyes as he walked up the steps. One of the ladies nodded her head at him. He knew that she was asking him if he had some dope. He shook his head from side to side, leaving them all disappointed.

When Slim got to the backyard, there was a car parked there. It had a black, nylon cover over it. Chrome spokes with two inch tires peeked from the bottom of the cover. He figured that someone still lived there.

At the basement door, Slim knocked several times and got no answer. After a moment, he knocked again, and still got no answer. He figured that no one was home, so he turned to leave. When Slim got to the head of the gangway, he was stunned by who he seen as he came to a stop. The dude he knew over three years ago as a relentless hustla was getting out of a black Benz. The up-to-date convertible was sitting on shiny, chrome blades. His ears, neck, wrist, and pinkie fingers were all glistening with diamonds and gold as the sun hit him.

What was most amazing, was his grill. The sun twisted his face and revealed his mouth full of diamonds and golds. It was G-Will, and he was hood rich. When G-Will noticed someone standing at the head of his gangway, he grabbed onto the pistol that was tucked on his waist. Slim folded his arms across his chest, giving him a chance to figure out who he was. As he got closer, a big smile appeared on his face as he removed his hand from his pistol.

"Slim. My nigga back," G-Will excitedly said as he did the hood clap with him and pulled him in for a hug.

"What's up? I see you got'cho feet right," Slim said as he took a step back.

"C'mon, nigga You know you seen it comin'. And I 'memba what I told you back in the game. I got'chu! Let's step in right quick. I need to take care of somethin'," G-Will said as he led the way.

When they got into the basement, Slim seen that it had been extravagantly upgraded. The only thing that remained the same was the smell of weed. He sat on one of the couches while G-Will made a phone call. It was a brief one, where he told someone that he was ready. He then went into a vent that ran across the ceiling of the basement. He pulled out a quarter key of cocaine that was heavily wrapped in plastic. When he put the vent back together, he went into one of the rooms. He came back with a shopping bag and sat on the couch across from Slim.

"Cuz, you was gone for hellas on that shit," G-Will said as he began to roll a blunt. "I heard about everything, and I like how you played it. Plus, the homeboy Seven told me how you didn't fold when them people came to see you about that burna. I told J-Will to get rid of that mu-fucka after he did that shit. But that was some real shit on yo' end."

"It's all good. I was fucked up behind what happened to my nigga though."

"My ol' bird overdosed on that tar after that. I was fucked up behind that too, but I had to keep it together. I went ahead and bought the house, but I don't be here for real. If I ain't on the move, I'm at my county spot wit' my main girl and my two lil' girls," G-Will said before he lit the blunt.

"I'm sorry to hear 'bout'cho ol' bird, but I'm glad you kept it togetha."

G-Will shook his head up and down as he pulled on the blunt. After a few more pulls, he passed it to Slim. They both then turned their attention to a girl who was coming down the steps. After noticing her, G-Will gave his attention to his beeper. The girl took off her light blue, designer shades as she approached the couches. Her black curly hair was shorter than an inch. Waves of hair made her lining. She had a pecan complexion with a fairly cute face. It was her sex appeal that was most attractive. She was 5'7 with a thick and curvaceous figure. Her light blue sun dress complimented it excellently. Her B-cup sized breasts sat up nicely as the dress allowed her juicy ass to jiggle. She wore light blue stilettos that showed off her pedicured toes while lace wrapped her thick legs. She came and stood over G-Will with her hands on her hips.

"Do what'chu do, and I'ma catch up wit'chu later," G-Will said without taking his eyes from his beeper.

The girl stood over G-Will for a few more seconds before she rolled her eyes at him. She then grabbed the shopping bag and left.

By the time the entertaining girl was gone, Slim was reintroduced to that emancipating feeling within his mind and body.

"That was my bitch, Nikki Pooh," G-Will said as he looked up to Slim. "I'ma introduce you to her later on in the game. I told you, I was gon' fuck wit'chu when I got my feet right. I seen that'chu was built for this shit when you was doin' yo' thing wit' the weed. But when I heard how you held it down when you was jammed up, I told myself that I was gon' make sure that'chu was cool when you got out. I wanna put'chu in the game, but I wanna put some shit in yo' ear first. I want'chu to think about it, and get back at me."

Slim shook his head up and down as he passed G-Will the blunt. "The whole objective in the game is to get money. Wit doin' that, you gotta knock off anything, or any mu-fucka that get in yo' way," G-Will said before he pulled on the blunt. He then continued on to tell Slim about the game.

While G-Will gave Slim the game, he occasionally shook his head up and down as he absorbed it all.

"Plus, them people swept through here and jammed up a lot of the homeboys. It ain't nobody holdin' the hood down. It's a spot next doe where you can post up and do yo' thing. It's cool, 'cause them people know it ain't nothin' but crackheads over there. Ol' girl Sharon'll let'chu get that control over there, too. You could just break her off a fifty a day. That ain't shit, 'cause the money gon' be comin' so fuckin' fast!"

"I'ma think about that."

"Here go my beepa numba," G-Will said as he began to write it down. "Put two at the end of yo' numba so I'll know it's you. When you get at me, just let me know that'chu tryin'a eat, or somethin' like that."

Along with his beeper number, G-Will gave Slim $1,000 and an ounce of weed. It was a welcome back gesture. Slim accepted it as he felt the love.

"Let's go get somethin' to eat right quick," G-Will said as he rose from the couch.

Slim followed G-Will outside as he was anxious to ride in his Benz. "Check this out," G-Will said as he walked over to the car that was parked in the backyard. "Gimme three grand, and this yours," he said as he snatched the cover from the car.

Slim grabbed his dick as he became excited. It was a dark blue, two door, T-top, '85 Cutlass Supreme. It was in mint condition. It sat twelve inches from the ground with low profile tires that wrapped chrome, 100 spokes. Chrome pipes came from behind the back tires as they matched the trimming.

After circling the car a few times, G-Will let Slim in on the driver's side. The suede interior matched the paint job with a wood grain steering wheel. When G-Will started the car, he had Slim to press on the gas. He gripped the steering wheel as the powerful 350 rocked the car with its pipes roaring. G-Will then turned on the phenomenal stereo system. Tweeters in the dash and the four 6x9's that were lined in the back window created a perfect sound with the four twelve inch woofers that were in the trunk.

Slim didn't even think about not knowing how to drive. He only thought about the freedom that came with having a car as it fascinated him.

G-Will shook his head up and down as he turned the music down. "Check this out," he said as he began to dismantle a piece of the dash. "I could stash foe ounces and my burna in there. I just wanted to point that out to you."

Slim shook his head up and down as he thought the stash was conveniently clever.

"I'ma hold this for you," G-Will said as he turned the car off.

When Slim and G-Will came into the Chinese restaurant, two girls were at one of the tables, waiting on their order. They were stunned by G-Will, and Slim could see it in their eyes. It was as if they didn't see him. He was just an ordinary dude with an ordinary appearance. He wasn't jealous, but he did have a desire for the charismatic appearance.

At the service window, a lady kindly asked Slim and G-Will for their order. After G-Will placed his order, Slim was still staring up at the menu. When he finally placed his order, he slightly bent to one side and reached into his sagging pocket. He was high and tripping.

He pushed his pants further down as he was trying to grab his money. The girls at the table started laughing at him.

"I got'chu," G-Will said as he went into his pocket. Slim shook his head up and down before he went over to the giggling girls.

"Why y'all laughin' at me?" he asked as he sat across from them.

"You look like you was about to put on a show for us," the cute, chocolate girl said with a laugh.

"I was trippin' But what's up though? If y'all lookin' to be entertained, we could do that togetha."

"That's cool, but what's up wit' him," the chocolate girl asked as she looked to G-Will, then back to Slim.

"You see what it is."

G-Will had just paid for their order, and was coming to the table. "What's up, hornie? Which one of them you got'cho eyes on?" he asked as he sat next to Slim.

"I like her. She got some pretty lips."

Slim had his eyes on the girl with a reddish-brown skin complexion. Her lips were exotically beautiful with cherry lip gloss that made them look extra luscious. Her top lip had a natural curl to it while her plump bottom lip lingered in the opposite direction. Her hair matched her skin complexion. It fell to her shoulders and curled outwardly. Her sleepy, brown eyes had curly lashes with her eyebrows perfectly lined in a slight arch.

"I'm Slim," he said as he sat up to the table. "What's yo' name?"

"Kandi. My name Kandi," she said with an egotistical attitude.

"You mean, like candy you take home and have yo' way wit, or candy you put on display and don't touch?"

Just as Kandi was about to respond, the lady called her order out. She took that as an opportunity to put Slim in suspense. He took it as an opportunity to get a better look at her. Kandi had a sexy, pigeon-toed catwalk with a graceful twist in her hips. Her 5'7, fairly thick figure was alluring. She wore a sleeveless blouse that emphasized her C-cup sized breasts and her small waist. Her denim blue jeans fitted tightly and showed off her curves. They were cuffed pass her ankles. She wore blue sandals that showed off her fresh pedicure. When she stopped at the service window, her loose ass bounced as she stood leaning on one hip.

Slim shook his head from side to side as he left G-Will talking with the other girl.

"I'm feelin' you," he said as he leaned next to Kandi. "You ain't gotta answer my question yet. We could just keep each other company, and you can get back at me when you get'cho thoughts togetha.

"I got my thoughts togetha," Kandi assured Slim as she grabbed her order.

"That's cool, too. I'm just tryin' to get'chu to share 'em wit' me. I got some too, and if you give me the opportunity to get 'em out, I think you'll be impressed."

"So, you think," Kandi spoke with doubt.

"Get wit' me, and I'll show you!" Slim continued to press.

Kandi stopped and looked Slim up and down with her forehead wrinkled. She was wondering where he got his cocky attitude from. It was intriguing, because it didn't match his appearance. He could read her question, but was far from intimidated.

"What's up," Slim asked as he took a step closer to Kandi.

"Ay homie. Get the order. It's all good," G-Will called over to Slim.

Slim shook his head up and down before he turned to get their orders.

When Slim came back to the table, Kandi and the other girl were by the door whispering. The other girl looked like she was trying to convince Kandi of something. Kandi wasn't trying to hear it. Her face was full of disapproval.

"What's up wit them?"

"I got Shay ready to do whatever, but Kandi actin' like her shit too sweet," G-Will said as he looked over to them. "Y'all need to hurry up! My shit gettin' cold!"

Shay looked to G-Will, then back to Kandi and said a few more words. "We ready," she finally said.

When they got back to G-Will's house, they all ate while rap music played at a low tone. The TV was on, but the volume was off while music videos played. Shay sat close to G-Will, whispering in his ear while he ate with a nonchalant expression. Slim and Kandi sat on the couch across from them. He sat in the middle while she sat on the other end.

Slim appeared to be focusing on his food, but he was analyzing Kandi. She sat at the edge of the couch and modestly at her food. She was agitated and upset with Shay. He knew that he had to get her to relax before he pursued anything with her. When he finished eating, he rolled a blunt.

"Can you fire this up while I put my shit back togetha," Slim kindly asked as he held out the blunt to Kandi.

Kandi was reluctant to take the blunt. She stared at Slim with her face slightly twisted. When she finally took it, he started to wrap his weed up. When he looked back over to her, she had her sexy lips wrapped around the blunt as she lit the other end of it. As soon as she noticed his infatuated eyes on her lips, she took the blunt from her mouth. She continued to light it as she held it over her lap.

"Here," Kandi said as she held the blunt out to Slim.

"Don't we 'pose to be entertainin' each other?"

"Don't start wit me!"

"I'm sayin' We gotta start somewhere to get an understandin', Slim said before he pulled on the blunt.

"I don't know if I wanna get an understandin' wit'chu."

"I thought'chu already had yo' thoughts togetha," Slim said as he passed Kandi the blunt.

"Don't play word games wit' me."

"I ain't tryin'a play no games wit'chu," Slim said as he rested his arm on the back of the couch.

Kandi looked back to Slim's arm, then back to him with her face twisted.

"If I'm makin' you feel uncomfortable, I can go sit over there," Slim said as he pointed to the far end of the basement. "I know how to do sign language," he added with a smile.

Kandi involuntarily laughed in the process of inhaling the weed smoke. It choked her as she began to cough.

"You aiight? You need me to give you CPR," Slim asked as he patted Kandi's back. "'Cause you know I'll love to do that!"

"Boy, you is too silly," Kandi said with a laugh as she gained her composure. "And if you made me feel uncomfortable, I wouldn't be here."

It was a break-through for Slim. He finally got Kandi to relax. She sat back on the couch where his arm still rested behind her.

"Ay homie You can use the other room," G-Will said as he tossed a condom onto the table. He then continued on to one of the rooms with Shay.

Kandi immediately jumped back into her hostile attitude as she slid to the edge of the couch. She twisted her face at G-Will, then turned to Slim. He looked to the floor and shook his head in disbelief.

"I hope you don't think I'm finna do somethin' wit'chu!"

"You already know that I'm feelin' you, so I can't say that it ain't on my mind."

"I don't even know you!"

"I don't know you neitha, so that's one thing we got in common. Now, I don't know no betta way for us to become more familiar other than us gettin' loose."

"You might as well save all that smooth talkin' game, 'cause I am not finna do nothin' wit'chu," Kandi firmly stated.

"It's all good. I ain't trippin'," Slim said as he removed his arm from behind Kandi and slid in to a slump.

"I know you don't call yo'self bein' mad!"

"Nah I ain't mad. I am kinda disappointed though. You gotta nigga feelin' like a lil' kid in a candy store wit' out enough money to get what he want. It's all good though. I ain't trippin'," Slim said before he pulled on the blunt.

He then passed it to Kandi.

Kandi was surprised to see that Slim passed her his blunt after she rejected him. The average dude would become hostile when their pursuit became unsuccessful. It painted a picture of his cool composed character. She was impressed as a smile appeared on her face.

"I don't care how much money you got, 'cause my candy ain't for sale," Kandi clarified. "I think I might spoil yo' appetite anyway," she added with a laugh.

"I just wanna taste," Slim said as he turned his body towards Kandi and rested his arm behind her.

"That's all it'll take," Kandi claimed with sassiness. Slim shifted his eyes to Kandi's lips, then back to her eyes.

"Lemme see," he softly spoke as he inched towards her.

Kandi showed no signs of disapproval, so Slim continued on as he moistened his lips. He gently pressed his lips against her bottom lip. He then slid his lips up to her top lip with the tip of his tongue out. As he took her top lip between his lips, he gave it a gently squeeze as he pulled with his kiss.

"I'm in love wit'cho lips. They hella sweet, but they didn't spoil my appetite. They only made me want some mo' Kandi," Slim said before he kissed her lips again.

"That wasn't nothin' but a kiss," Kandi blushed.

"I know. And I know it get sweeter than that. So, what's up? Can I get anotha taste?"

"A taste, huh?"

"Yeah. That's all I want." Slim whispered as he eyed her.

"I think I can manage that."

Slim shook his head up and down as he grabbed the condom from the table. He then led Kandi to the room and closed the door behind them.

When Slim turned around, Kandi was sitting on the edge of the bed. She was undoing her pants. He stood and watch as she kept her seductive eyes on him. When she came out of her pants and panties, she brought the heels of her feet to the edge of the bed. Reddish-brown fuzz on her pelvis certified her as a true redbone.

Slim ripped the condom open with his teeth as he came towards Kandi. His sweat pants and boxers were already around his knees by the time he got between her thighs. He was fully aroused, so it only took him a second to wrap it up. When he tried to push her to the bed, his hand met resistance.

"You said you just wanna taste," Kandi said as she pushed Slim's hand away. "So, you gotta get it like this."

"Damn! What kinda games you playin'?"

"I'm just givin' you what'chu asked for. A taste! Now, if you want it, get it how I'm givin' it to you."

"That's cool, too," Slim said as he began to examine Kandi's awkward position.

Slim couldn't get nothing but an inch inside of Kandi. He got another inch in when he bent his knees. It put strain on his knees, but he was working with it. His strokes were limited to very short ones. However, he found pleasure as her tight' insides flushed her hot juices. She moaned softly as she bit her bottom lip, but she fought the urges to give him more.

Slim wanted to force Kandi to the bed and give her more, but those thoughts vanished when he felt that tingling sensation. It had only been three minutes, and he was already shooting. His strained knees became weak as he stumbled from her insides. If it wasn't for the wall that caught him, he would've crashed to the floor. She had that *good.*

Slim leaned against the wall, slightly bent as he held his clothes up to his knees. He held his head down, shaking it in disbelief as he was embarrassed and humiliated. On top of him only lasting three minutes, it was only from a piece of Kandi.

"You alright?" Kandi softly asked.

Without looking up, Slim waved his hand at Kandi.

"I ain't gon tell nobody," Kandi teased. It took Slim a short moment to gain his composure. Kandi was standing next to him, reapplying her lip gloss. She had that look on her face like she knew she had that good.

"I ain't done wit'chu!"

"I know. But I'ma have to leave you wit' my numba, and we could get togetha some other time," Kandi said before she left the room.

As soon as Kandi came from the room, she was snatched up by a furious Shay. Slim stood in confusion as he watched them head towards the door. When he looked over to the living room area, G-Will was slumped on the couch. He was smoking on a blunt, and talking on his phone. He then looked for Kandi as he heard the door slam. She was gone.

"What's up, homie? You good?" G-Will asked. "What was that all about?"

"Shit. She just got to actin' like a nigga owed her somethin'."

Slim looked to the door, then back to G-Will as he realized that his opportunity to redeem himself was gone.

"But ay, let me drop you off. I need to make a move."

Chapter 9: The Game

When G-Will dropped Slim off at home, Jayla was just walking up the steps from school. She stopped and stared at him as he got out of the car. He could see the scrutiny in her eyes as he approached her.

"Von-Von, you been smokin' weed! And who was that boy who just dropped you off?"

"That was my homeboy," Slim said as he stood in front of Jayla. "But what'chu know 'bout smokin' weed," he surprisingly asked.

"I wasn't born yesterday. Plus, they be smokin' that stuff at my school."

"And what about'chu?"

"Unh-unh. I wouldn't be able to do my work!"

"How you know if you wouldn't be able to do yo' work if you ain't never smoked it?"

"I didn't say I never smoked it," Jayla said with a guilty smile.

"So, you do smoke it," Slim confusingly asked.

"No, I don't."

"Jay, quit playin' word games wit' me!"

Jayla laughed at her frustrated brother as she sat on the steps. He sat next to her with his face full of curiosity.

"I only did it one time. It was me, Fe-Fe, April and The Twins," Jayla admitted. "Fe-Fe stole it from Auntie Keda.

"Straight up! Auntie Keda!"

"Yup... But I didn't like it though. I kept laughin' and that's how Auntie Keda found out. I was scared, but she ain't do nothin'. She just made us clean up her whole house. Fe-Fe and 'nem was mad at me," Jayla said before she laughed.

"So, what other secret you keepin' from me?"

"Von-Von, if you tryin' to ask me about boys, we already talked about that," Jayla said as she nudged him.

"Good! 'Cause, boys only be trippin' off of one thing."

"And what about'chu? Are you one of those boys who misuse girls?"

"Nah. I don't misuse girls. They gon know what's up wit' me from the jump. That way, they won't be surprised or disappointed."

"So, you think you a playa, huh?"

"If I thought I was, I wouldn't be. I am what I am, and I'ma be jus that," Slim said with a more serious tone.

"Von-Von, is we still talkin' about'chu bein' a playa, or is you tryin' to say somethin' else?"

"We talkin' 'bout me doin' what makes me what I am." Slim responded arrogantly.

"And what's that?" Jayla asked in return.

"Jay, I jus came home, and I'm still processin' a lot of things. But'chu know I'ma always let'chu know what's up wit' me."

"Well, I hope whatever it is that makes you what you are don't end up hurtin' you, or the people who care about'chu."

"You know I ain't tryin' to see you hurtin'. But when we accept people for what they are, we know what to expect from 'em. Like wit mama. It is what it is wit' her, and I learned to accept that. Wit' acceptin' that and knowin' what to expect, I won't be hurt or disappointed by somethin' she do, or don't do. I love her, but certain things just outta my control."

"I understand that, but I shouldn't have to learn how to accept somethin' that could end up hurtin' or disappointin' me, I don't know how to prepare myself for that possibility. I love you, and I always will. I just hope love is enough to keep you from makin' decisions that could end up hurtin' you, or the people who care about'chu," Jayla expressed with deep concerns before she went into the house.

Slim remained on the porch as he thought about Jayla's touching words. He was confronted with one of the hardest issues that came with the game. His strong desire for the self-sufficient lifestyle was conflicting with what he ultimately loved. He had a challenging decision to make.

During the weekend, Slim spent majority of his time in his personal space. He was trying to figure out a way to tell Jayla about his decision. She allowed him to have his space as she knew that he was contemplating something. By Sunday night, he realized that there was no easy way to let her down. He decided to open up to her that night she came to check on him before she went to bed.

"What's up, Jay? Sit down wit' me for a minute." After a moment, Jayla sat next to Slim with a disappointed expression. It was the seriousness in his tone that told her that she was about to receive some unpleasant news.

"I know I haven't been sayin' much to you in the last few days. I just been thinkin' 'bout what'chu said to me the other day wit some other things. You know I love you, and I care about'cho feelin's. Please, don't question that."

"Don't gimme reasons to!"

"Wit' everything we been through, I would never expect for you to feel like I don't care about how you feel."

"Don't throw that at me! 'Cause, if it meant somethin' to you, you wouldn't be talkin' to me like this."

"I do care 'bout how you feel. That's why I'm tryin' to get an understandin' wit'chu," Slim said as he sat up from his slump.

"I understand! You care more about what'chu wanna do more than how it'll effect the people who care about'chu. That's selfish, and I thought that place made you smarter," Jayla frustratingly said as she wiped a tear from her eye. "You didn't learn nothin'! You ain't been home a week, and you already makin' stupid decisions! All them times I cried for you to come home was for nothin'. It's sad to say, but I felt betta when you was in that place compared to how I feel now," she cried as she rose from the couch.

"Wait a minute, Jay," Slim said as he grabbed her hand.

"Let me go," Jayla mumbled through her tears as she snatched her hand away from Slim. "I'm tired of waitin' on you to stop doin' stupid stuff! I don't care no mo'," she cried as she stormed off.

Slim slumped into the couch as he was torn by Jayla's reaction. But not even her chastise could erase his passion and desire for the self-sufficient lifestyle. When he thought about his father, he decided to cross that bridge when he got there.

The next morning, Slim sat on the front porch with the cordless phone in his lap. He was waiting on G-Will to return his page. He smoked on a blunt as he was prepared to embrace the essentials that made him built for the game.

Almost thirty minutes had gone by and G-Will still hadn't returned Slim's page. He was quite sure that he dialed the right numbers. When he picked up the phone to check its ringer, a call came in. It was G-Will.

"I'm hungry. How long it's gon take you to fix me a plate?"

"Come through. I got one for you now," G-Will said before he clicked his phone off.

Inside of G-Will's basement, Slim found him slumped on the couch, smoking on a blunt. When he sat across from him, he sat up to the table. A plate was on the table with four and a half ounces of crack. Black 9's sat on each side of the plate with safety pins and a box of sandwich bags.

"You ready to get this money?"

"I was born ready," Slim calmly replied.

"Aiight. Lemme put'chu on point right quick," G-Will said as he grabbed one of the safety pins. "This four and a half zips, and I'ma put'chu in the game wit' this. I do not fuck wit this hard shit. I push quarter thangs soft. I'ma continue to drop these four and a halves on you for twenty-five hundred. I'ma give you time to get'cho shit togetha, but I'm tryin' to drop quarter thangs on you. That's nine ounces for forty-five hundred."

Slim understandingly shook his head up and down before G-Will continued on.

"These ounces on twenty-eight grams, and I'm finna break this one down to four quarters. I'ma cut twenty, twenty pieces from each quarter. I'm finna give you the game, so keep yo' eyes on me."

Slim paid close attention to G-Will as he began to break the dope down. He then broke an ounce and a half down just a G-Will showed him. In the process of them breaking and bagging the dope, they smoked blunts of their own while talking about the game.

"You know what'chu doin' wit that?" G-Will asked as he looked to one of the pistols, then back to Slim.

Slim picked up the pistol and cocked it as he watched a bullet jump into the chamber. He'd never fired a pistol, but he knew how to hold them. It was one of the many things J-Will taught him.

"That's yours, and you can't do yo' thing wit'out it." G-Will told him.

"I'm already knowin' what time it is."

"You know I stay on the move, so I'ma introduce you to the homeboy, Pooch. I'ma take you to yo' spot after that."

Pooch lived in the hood at his mama's house. He was a chubby, brown skinned older dude with a mouth full of solid golds. He sold weed, guns and pit-bulls from the basement. He had three sisters, who ran an illegal beauty salon and a day care center on the third floor of the house. In the backyard, vicious pit-bulls were on locks and thick chains. Cars and trucks that all sat on chrome made the backyard look like a car lot. They all belonged to Pooch.

With the introduction, G-Will proudly mentioned Slim's honorable character as a street nigga. Pooch embraced him, and offered his assistance with anything he needed. Slim accepted the welcoming as they smoked on a blunt that Pooch stuffed with weed.

With the purpose of the introduction being met, G-Will left with Slim to show him his spot. When G-Will brought Slim to the house where he was going to be doing his thing, they came through the front door with their pistols out. Slim was instantly taken by the foul smell and frowned. It was the funky smell of crack that lingered in the humid air. Two men were sitting on a couch. They looked up at them, but didn't appear to be alarmed by their bold entry. They looked at them with a sick hunger in their eyes, hoping that they came with some dope.

"Where Sharon?" G-Will asked.

Before G-Will could get an answer, a woman came into the living room. Slim remembered her from the other day. Traces of her once before beauty could be seen, but was overshadowed by the works of her destructive habit.

"What's up Sharon? I know it's been dry around here lately, but that's finna change. This my homeboy, Slim. He know how to play it," G-Will said as he looked to him, then back to her.

Sharon's face lit up with joy as G-Will gave her some relieving news. "It's all good."

"I'ma holla at'chu in a minute. Lemme just see what's goin' on around here," Slim said.

Sharon stayed in the living room while Slim did his inspection with G-Will. In the basement, a white woman sat alone on one of the couches. The fancy attire she wore made her look out of place. Slim saw that she was a high-class junkie. She was being harbored by the two men upstairs. They had her money, but not all of it. After spending $200 with Slim, he and G-Will continued the inspection.

On the second floor, Slim noticed that it was the most decent part of the house. There was also a room with feminine decor. After completing the inspection, he and G-Will came back down to the living room.

"I got it from here."

"Do yo' thing. You know how to reach me," G-Will said as he did the hood clap with Slim.

Slim took Sharon into the kitchen. He sat his dope and his pistol on the counter before he took a seat. He was about to get an understanding with her, and create some organization. That organization would create stability. With stability, he could focus more on his main objective. Getting money.

"Who else stay here wit'chu?"

"It's just me. Everybody else just my company," Sharon said as she sat at the table.

"Lemme do my thing how I want to, and I'ma make sure you cool on the dope. I'm tryin' to make the livin' room my space and run the traffic through the basement door. That's where I want'chu to catch it and bring the money up to me."

"I like that idea, and I can handle that."

"Wit' all due respect, I don't like how yo' company be posted in the front of the house. I'm tryin' to stop anything that'll draw attention."

"I understand, and I want'chu to do whatever you need to do to make yo'self feel comfortable."

Slim shook his head up and down as he went into his bag of rocks. He gave Sharon eight of them. His generosity came from her being submissive to his controlling ways.

"I think I'ma like you," Sharon said as she happily gathered the rocks. "I got a hundred I wanna spend wit'chu too."

After giving Sharon six more rocks for her $100, he went into the living room. He respectfully made it known to the two men that they were no longer allowed in the living room, or in front of the house. He also made it known to them that they had to use the basement door. He was the new man of the house, and Sharon stood next to him while he demonstrated it. The men understandingly accepted it before they both spent $100 with him.

When Sharon went into the basement with the two men, Slim sat his things on the table and opened a window. He then sat on the arm of the couch and fired a blunt. From there, he could see who came and went. From that spot, he could watch the traffic move as he took advantage of the crack drought.

Slim had been sitting on the arm of the couch for about twenty minutes when two ladies came up the steps. Despite their jazzy appearance, he could tell from their facial features that they were junkies. He got up and met them at the door with his pistol in his hand.

"What's up?" Slim asked. He had the door cracked showing only half of his body.

"Who is you?" one of the women asked.

"Nah? Who is y'all?"

"I'm Vee, and this Angie. We lookin' for Sharon."

"She downstairs doin' what she do. And if y'all tryin' to do somethin', y'all gotta use the basement door and go through her."

"Baby, that's cool, but I ain't no regular bitch that be comin' through. I spend big money, and I would like to deal wit'chu directly," Vee said with a sassy attitude.

"Big money, huh? Well, check this out. I'll see you when you come through, but'chu still gotta use the basement door," Slim said before he allowed the ladies to come in.

While Angie only spent $100, Vee spent $250. They were very well satisfied with what he gave them, and joyfully expressed it.

"Well, lemme go down here and holla at my girl, and I'll be over to see you again tonight," Vee said.

"I'll be here. I'm Slim."

As Vee and Angie were heading towards the basement, Angie turned to Slim with a peculiar expression. It then turned to a smile as she looked him up and down. He chuckled and shook his head from side to side as he thought that she was flirting with him.

Just like G-Will said, Slim was seeing fast money. He ran through his first package in three days. He counted $6,850 from it. Getting money was an addiction to him, and G-Will was quick to feed him. G-Will stayed on the move, so Slim only saw him when it was time for him to re-up. Slim had money on his mind, so socializing was the last thing on his things to do list anyway.

Slim's daily routine was getting up in the morning and going to the dope house. He would go home when Jayla got out of school. He was still trying to get an understanding with her, but she was relentless with her attitude. However, she did apologize for telling him that she didn't care. Despite her attitude, he noticed that she kept taking the money he put in his top drawer for her.

After Slim showed his face around the house, he left out again. He would even creep from the house late at night and early in the morning from the basement door. Every time he walked pass G-Will's house, he was reminded of the car that fascinated him. He was anxious to learn how to drive, so he convinced Sharon to teach him with her little car. It was his generous offer of five rock with every lesson that made convincing her easy. After a few long nights, his driving skills were good enough where she felt comfortable with renting her car to him. He was ready.

After a month of relentless hustlin', Slim crept back into his father's house around one o'clock in the morning. He came home to count his money as he was ready to get his car and blow some money on himself. He was unsure of how much he had. The numbers became blurry after $10,000. He would only count out what he needed to re-up with, and leave the rest wrapped in rubber bands. Within a month, he ran through four of the four and a half packages not including the one he had for only a day and a half.

Slim held his mattress up to make sure he got everything. He shook his head from side to side as he realized, he had more rolls of money than he expected. He scraped the money onto the floor before he organized it by the digits on his bed. Stacks of money covered a quarter of his twin sized bed while he sat in the middle. He took a deep breath and blew it out before he began to count it.

Just as Slim picked up a stack of money, he heard his door creak open. He quickly turned his head and became stuck with his eyes on his father. His father leaned in the doorway, rubbing his chin as he made an observation. As a former street nigga, he could tell that his son was a serious and relentless hustler. That conclusion would dictate his approach.

"So, this why you been creepin' in and outta the house while you was thinkin' I was sleep," Slim's father calmly said.

Slim was speechless as he was expecting a furious tone from his father.

"I guess the opportunity I gave you to work at the company wasn't good enough."

"I really didn't think too much about it," Slim honestly admitted.

"Well, you old enough to make yo' own decisions, so I ain't finna try to control you. I can only advise you at this point. But before I do that. Let's get one thing straight," Slim's father said as he took a step towards him.

"It's a respect thing now, so I'm comin' to you man to man. This is my house, and I don't want no guns or dope up in here. You keep that shit in the streets. Do I make myself clear?"

Slim understandingly shook his head up and down.

"Like I said, I can't do nothin' but advise you at this point. Now, I want'chu to listen to me, 'cause I know more about the game than you think I do."

Slim's eyebrows went up as his father sat across from him. He put the stack of money down as he turned to face him.

"First things first: While you choosin' this lifestyle, I advise you to sit some money to the side for a lawyer." Slim paid close attention as his father's approach was interesting.

"I used to be in the game, and I was in the joint when you was born. I was still doin' my thing, but that time away gave me the opportunity to see what was really important to me and put things into perspective. Hopefully, it won't come to that point for you to get' cho head right. I was blessed with the comprehension that made me realize my family was the most important thing to me. I'm tellin' you, no amount of money is worth jeopardizin' somethin' you can't get back when you lose it.

"When I came home, the game was over for me. I always had goals in the game, so when I stepped away, I was able to feed my family in a way where I wasn't jeopardizin' my presence. So while you out there gettin' money, remember that'chu in the game. And every game has an endin' to it. I advise you to stack this money towards somethin' you can live comfortably off of that don't jeopardize you, or what's most important to you."

Slim shook his head up and down as he understood the value in his father's insight. At the same time, he was shocked by the discovery of him being a former street nigga. He had only known him as a hard working family man, but he was the son of a hustler.

"Now, in the meantime, while you choosin' to be in the game, are you prepared to play it how it go? I mean, are you prepared to put that iron on a nigga if he get in yo' way? 'Cause if you not prepared to play it how it go on all levels, you won't survive! The game is more than what meets the eye. It's cold! And if you don't have the comprehension that'll make you immune to the cold game, you gon' fumble and freeze up. Now, just by lookin' at this lil' money you got stacked up, I can tell that'chu know somethin' about the game. I wouldn't recommend this lifestyle for you, and it's hard for me to accept. But I can't do nothin' but advise you. I just hope you value my experienced perceptions and take heed in my advice."

"I appreciate how you sat down wit' me and put me on point wit' how I'm livin' I'll always value yo' experience and respect it by openin' my ears and comin' to you for advice," Slim humbly spoke.

"Well, as long as you know what time it is, I'ma fall back and let'chu do you. But I'ma always be here."

Slim shook his head up and down as he looked at his money, then back at his father.

"How much money is this anyway?" Slim's father asked as he began to flip through the stacks.

"I ain't sure. I was just 'bout to count it, though."

"It look like a lil' bit over twenty grand," Slim's father estimated. "Well, I gotta get up in the rnornin' and go to the office. If you go out tonight, make sho you lock that door behind you."

Slim shook his head up and down as he watched his father leave. He then sat for a moment as he thought about his father's approach. There was no more creeping around. A slight smile appeared on his face as he got back to his money. Just as Slim's father estimated, he had a little over $20,000. It was $21,750 to be exact.

Slim's anxiousness prevented him from getting a good night's sleep. He woke up from his light sleep around 9AM and was ready to begin his day. His father and brother were off to work, so the commotion in the kitchen made him curious. He put the blunt he rolled behind his ear and headed upstairs.

On Slim's way upstairs, he caught the aroma of breakfast food with girls chattering. It was Jayla, Fe-Fe, and a dark chocolate girl. They were cooking and eating. The girl with the rich, dark chocolate complexion snatched his attention as he came into the kitchen. She stood five feet, and had a well-developed figure that her morning clothes showed off. Her dark-brown stretch pants showed the thickness in her thighs as they revealed her curves. They blended in with her skin complexion. giving the impression that she was naked down there. She wore a small, white t-shirt that was tied in a knot just above her bellybutton. It made her voluptuous titties noticeable as they sat up and close together. She had a round, cute face with slanted eyes, a button nose and plump lips. Her jet-black hair was in a stringy ponytail that came down to the middle of her back. Slim had no idea of who this hot girl was.

"Where mines at?" Slim asked as he approached the small buffet.

"You bet'not put'cho greedy hands on nothin'! You betta fix you some cereal," Jayla said as she rolled her eyes at Slim.

"You can have some of mines," the chocolate girl sweetly said as she offered Slim her plate.

"I do want some of yours. It look hot too. What's yo' name?"

"Meka," the chocolate girl blushed.

"Jevon, stop lookin' at her like that! And girl, get outta his face," Jayla ordered.

"I'ma holla at'chu," Slim said as he took Meka's plate.

"No, you not," Jayla protested.

Slim ignored Jayla as he headed over to the table. Fe-Fe was sitting there with a smile. "What's up? You trippin' wit me too?"

"We good. And we'll be even betta when you fire that blunt up."

"I got'chu," Slim said as he began to eat. "What's up wit Nut?"

"He just went to court last month, and if them witnesses don't show up again, they gotta let him go."

Slim shook his head up and down, continuing to eat as he thought about how it was going to be when he and Nut were reunited.

"Y'all gon be off the chain when y'all get back together," Fe-Fe said with a laugh.

"You already know," Slim said as he grabbed the phone. Slim paged G-Will and got a call back in less than five minutes. While he talked with him, Jayla shook her head from side to side. She was leaning on the counter with Meka, telling her that she didn't want her getting involved with him. When he got off the phone, he winked his eye at Meka and went to his room.

After a quick shower, Slim was in his room checking himself out. "Come in," he answered the knocks on his door.

"You is not cute," Jayla said as she came into the room.

"Meka think I am," Slim teased.

"Jevon, I ain't playin'! You betta leave her alone. She ain't over here for you to be nasty wit," Jayla said as she got into his face.

"I ain't finna talk to you 'bout that," Slim said with a laugh.

"It ain't nothin' to talk about! You just betta leave her alone!"

"Why you come down here trippin' wit me?"

Jayla stared at Slim for a moment with her face twisted. "'Cause, you still doin' stupid stuff. Don't chu think daddy gon' know what'chu doin' when he see you wit' a car? Stupid!"

Slim gave a little laugh at Jayla's feisty concern before he sat her down. He told her about the conversation he had with their father, and she was just as surprised as he was.

"So, do that mean you gon' move out," Jayla sadly asked.

"Nah, I ain't gon leave you," Slim said as he put his arm around Jayla.

"And what about school? Is you still goin' wit me?"

"I promise you, I'm still goin' to school wit'chu," Slim spoke with sincerity.

"I still don't like what'chu doin'," Jayla said as she removed Slim's arm from around her. "And where you finna go?"

"To the plaza. Them new J's came out, and I'ma buy us some."

"I don't want 'em," Jayla said as she folded her arms across her chest.

"I put some mo' money in that drawer," Slim said with a smile, letting Jayla know that he knew she was putting on a front.

"So!"

"Aiight, Jay. Can you gimme a minute? I'll be right behind you."

"You ain't gotta follow me," Jayla said as she pushed Slim. When Jayla was gone, Slim put $11,750 in his pockets. He then stuffed his dope in his pants along with his pistol. He intended on honoring his father's wishes by not bringing his dope, or his pistol back into the house.

After getting his car and blowing over $10,000 on himself, Slim came back home. Jayla, Fe-Fe and Meka were astonished by his new appearance. An 18K gold Turkish hung from his neck with a three inch, 18K gold anchor pendant. He had an 18K gold nugget watch on his wrist with the matching bracelet on his other wrist. His 14K gold, dollar sign pinkie symbolized his objective. On his other pinkie, his 14K gold playboy bunny symbolized that he was anti-monogamous. What was most astonishing was his grill. His four front teeth held solid golds with crushed diamonds.

Jayla and Fe-Fe met Slim as he got out of his car and bombarded him with crazy questions. Meka stood on the porch, holding her astonishment inside. His mouth was still numb from the dental work, so he wasn't trying to talk much. He handed out bags to them from his back seat and his trunk before they all took them inside.

When they got to Slim's room, Fe-Fe rambled through the bags for her shoes while Jayla pretended to be unexcited. He made her crack when he gave her a gold charm bracelet. She sweetly thanked him and gave him a hug. She then volunteered to put his things away with the intentions of getting to her shoes. Before he left the house, he put his numbers on the refrigerator.

When Slim came from the house, Meka was still standing on the porch. Her face lit up as soon as she seen him.

"I like yo' grill," Meka softly spoke.

"I like you," Slim said as he came to Meka.

"Jay don't want me messin' wit'chu."

"What'chu wanna do?" Slim asked in return

"I wanna see what's up wit'chu, but I don't want Jay to be mad at me. That's my best friend."

"I wanna see what's up wit'chu too, so I guess we gon' have to get down on the low." Slim suggested.

"I'm down wit that."

"Aiight, I'ma catch up wit'chu," Slim said before he turned to leave.

When Slim got to his car, his father was pulling up with Marcel behind him. He knew they were going to have something to say about his new appearance. He leaned against the passenger side of his car and waited on them. They approached him with their observing eyes, but showed no surprise. His father stood in front of him while Marcel checked out his car.

"Now, this don't make no sense," Slim's father finally said. Slim shrugged his shoulders with a slight smile that revealed his diamonds and golds. That gave his father a surprise. He bowed his head and shook it in disbelief. After a moment, he looked up at his son.

"Lemme see yo' keys."

While Slim's father gave his car a thorough inspection, he talked with Marcel on the sidewalk. Slim started to tell him about what was going on with him, but their father already told him. Marcel didn't express his opposition, he only encouraged his little brother to keep his head up. He then encouraged him to read the driver's book that he was going to give him.

"You gotta nice ride," Slim's father said as he tossed him his keys. "I got'cho title. I'ma get'cho plates in my name 'til you get a legitimate source of gettin' money. That way, them people can't take it. You cool wit' that?"

"That's cool." Slim agreed

"Aiight. Keep yo' head up out here," Slim's father said before he went into the house with Marcel.

Chapter 10: Utilize & Secure

When Slim got to Sharon's house, she was sitting on the porch steps. She looked agitated. He figured that she was waiting on him.

"I ain't gon' even ask where you been at," Sharon said, looking Slim up and down as he came up the steps. "C'mon, 'cause you been missin' all this money."

Slim hated missing money and not being there to provide. He knew how consistency played a major role in stability. He didn't trust Sharon enough to leave her with his dope. He needed some trustworthy assistance. Inside the house, Sharon gave Slim $300 that was from a white girl she had in the basement. He had her send the abundant spending girl up to him. It was then when he began to build his personal clientele by giving his beeper number out. He would give it to those who spent no less than $100. It would partially take care of the problem that came from his absence. He still had to find a solution to deal with the less prominent, who made up a significant amount of his money.

Later on that day, Slim heard arguing in front of the house. When he looked out of the window, a red Chevy Caprice was speeding off. He then turned his attention to a girl coming up the steps with her face twisted. She had her arms full of bags with more of them on the sidewalk. He thought she was a junkie coming to try and sell him stuff, but he seen otherwise as she got closer.

The girl had a pretty, but evil looking face. It was her sharp eyebrows that helped give her the evil look. She had light brown eyes that matched her skin complexion. Her black hair shined as it was pulled into a long ponytail. Two strands spiraled loosely down the sides of her face. Her 5'7, petite figure was in designer clothes that showed her every curve. With her petite figure, she had an extra plump ass that did her skirt no justice. Her perky breasts bounced as she stomped up the steps. Slim could tell that she was classy, but hood at the same. She wore sandals that showed off her French pedicure. It was freshly done with her nails. She wore a little jewelry, but it was the tiny diamond in her nose that stood out the most. It sparkled as it complimented her pretty face.

Slim had no idea of who this high maintenance diva was as he went for the door.

"What's up? Who is you?" Slim asked, looking the girl up and down with his forehead wrinkled.

The girl stared at Slim with one side of her top lip curled before she responded. "It ain't none of yo' business who I am," she said with hostility before she attempted to barge pass him.

"It is my business, 'cause this my spot," Slim calmly said as he blocked the entrance.

"Nigga, who the fuck is you?" the girl yelled in Slim's face.

"Who the fuck is you?" Slim asked as he pushed the girl from his face.

The girl stumbled down the steps and grabbed onto the rail before she could fall to the ground. Her nice things were all over the ground. She ignored them as she shot back towards Slim. He weaved her fierce jabs before he got a hold of her. His intentions were to put her against the door and calm her down. But the door was open, so when he spun her around, they fell into the house. Her head hit the floor with him on top of her.

"You trippin'! You betta calm the fuck down," Slim said with aggression as he shook the girl.

"Nigga, get the fuck off me! This my mama house!"

"You shoulda told me that at the door," Slim said as he released the girl and got to his feet.

"I don't owe you no fuckin' explanation," the girl said as she quickly got to her feet.

"Just go get'cho shit. I ain't tryin' to be trippin' wit'chu."

The girl stared at Slim with her face twisted as he sat on the arm of the couch. She still had her fist clenched as she though was ready to fight. He was trying to ignore her as he began to split a blunt with his fingernails. After a minute, she looked around for her sandal that came off during the tussle.

"You got me fucked up," the girl said before she went for her things.

Slim sat on the arm of the couch as he watched the girl take several trips for her things. He noticed that she had a lot of expensive items. They spilled from the black bags and onto the living room floor as she frustratingly dropped them. He then realized that the nice room upstairs was hers. After her last trip, she slammed the door behind her as she continued on. Within minutes, she came back with Sharon, who wasn't expecting her arrival.

"Slim, what'chu do to her?" Sharon asked.

"We just had a lil' misunderstandin'. I ain't trippin'," Slim said as he turned to Sharon and her daughter.

"This my daughter, and if y'all can get pass that lil' misunderstandin', I think y'all will get along real good." Sharon replied.

Slim was about to express his willingness, but Sharon's daughter intervened with her hostility.

"Please! I don't know who he think he is," Sharon's daughter said as she began to gather her things.

Sharon helped her daughter take her belongings to her room, and would tell her all about Slim.

Slim remained on the arm of the couch where he continued to smoke his blunt. He knew that he had to eliminate the hostility with Sharon's daughter. Otherwise, it would conflict with his objective. As he thought about it, he felt like his game was strong enough to utilize his new company once the hostility was gone. It would take care of the problem that came with his absence.

It wasn't until later on that night when Sharon's daughter came back into the living room. Slim was slumped on the couch, looking at the TV. The volume was off while B.G.'s latest CD played at a low tone.

"Can you sell me a sack?" Sharon's daughter impolitely asked as she stood over Slim.

"I don't sell weed, but… "

"You ol' caught up ass nigga! Fuck yo' weed!"

"If you woulda let me finish, I was finna say, you can roll you somethin'. I ain't caught up on this shit," Slim calmly responded.

"Well, you shoulda said that."

"You right. But what's yo' name? I don't wanna offend you by callin' you, ay girl, if I'm tryin' to get'cho attention."

"My name Peach. If you can't call me that, you won't be gettin' no attention from me," she said as she sat across from Slim and began rolling her blunt.

Slim disregarded what he was about to say to Peach and turned his attention to Sharon. She came to spend $30 with him. After giving her two rocks, he collected his things from the table.

"Slim, can you stick around tonight?" Sharon asked. "I got some company comin' over."

"I'll be here. I'm just finna go get somethin' to eat."

"Mama, can you make him bring us somethin' back?" Peach asked as she looked to Slim, then back to Sharon.

"I don't wan't nothin'. Now, why don't chu quit actin' bitchy and go wit' him or whatever. I told you, he ain't caught up on that stupid shit," Sharon said before she left.

Peach rolled her eyes at Sharon before she turned to Slim. "Where you finna go get somethin' to eat from?"

"I ain't made my mind up yet, but I was gon' ask you if you wanted somethin'. Roll wit' me and help me make my mind up."

"Let me get my purse," Peach said after a moment.

On the way to the fast-food restaurant, Slim rode with his pistol on his lap while the music beat at a low tone. He kept his eyes in the rear-view mirror as he was watching the streets. With his attentiveness, he kept his cool composure as he sat in a slump. He caught Peach checking him out a few times as she quietly smoked her blunt. Each time he caught her, she twisted her face at him and rolled her eyes as she mumbled something under her breath. He didn't know if she was holding a grudge, or if it was more behind her feisty attitude.

Natural Bridge & Kings-Highway was a crowded area. It was one of the popular strips where everyone hung out. Mostly every car sat on chrome while music blasted from every direction. Within the socializing, there was weed smoking, drinking, and explicit activities taking place. In the midst of everything, the jackers were lurking for a come up.

When Slim pulled onto the fast-food lot, he sat up to the steering wheel and gripped his pistol. He surveyed the night with his face slightly twisted. Other than being alert, the scene excited him as he felt like his shit was the hardest.

"You so stupid! I ain't never gettin' in the car wit'chu. Why you tryin' to show off wit'cho nappy head?" Peach said as she twisted her face at Slim.

Slim looked at Peach with uncertainty as it sounded like she liked him. It wouldn't surprise him, but he was more focused on getting a peaceful understanding with her. He turned his music down as he pulled next to the menu and placed his order.

"What'chu finna get?" Slim asked as he looked over to Peach.

"Why you pull so far from the thing? I can't even see it!" Peach rolled her eyes at Slim before she put her blunt into the ashtray.

"S'cuse me," she impolitely said as she stretched her body over him to observe the menu.

Slim couldn't ignore what was in his face. He gazed up and down Peach's body as he found it amazing. Her breasts hung from her chest as her skirt slid up another inch. Her lower back arched as it ran into her plump ass. He could see where her ass cheeks met as her skirt pressed them together. He thought about sliding his hand up her thigh and squeezing her ass as he tightened his face. He almost laughed as he thought about her slapping him behind that. He then caught a whiff of the feminine powder she wore to absorb the sweat from her breasts. It was sweet and modest. She was placing her order when he looked at her and shook his head from side to side. He found himself bringing his nose closer to her as the sweet smell was tantalizing.

"Don't be smellin' me," Peach said as she pushed Slim back into the seat.

A guilty smile appeared on Slim's face as he pulled up to the service window.

"I shoulda slapped you! Wit'cho creepy ass," Peach said as she held some money out to Slim.

"I got'chu." Slim said, refusing her money.

"I don't know why you tryin' to be all nice to me."

Slim paid the girl in the service window before he responded. "It ain't nothin'. I jus don't like all that hostility around me."

"Well, you need to apologize for slammin' me on that floor and makin' me hit my head!"

"My bad. I ain't try to hurt'chu. On some real shit, I was just tryin' to get an understandin' wit'chu. I hate that it went that far. I ain't never put my hands on a girl, and I ain't tryin' to start wit'chu. Can you accept my apology?"

Peach could feel the sincerity in Slim's compassion as a slight smile forced its way onto her face. She rolled her eyes at him as she turned her head away.

"So, I guess that mean you gon' stop bein' feisty wit' me," Slim asked as he leaned over to Peach.

"Just get our stuff," Peach said as she gently pushed Slim towards the service window.

"She could wait. I wanna get an understandin' wit'chu before anything."

"We cool," Peach said after a moment.

Slim shook his head up and down as he turned to get their orders.

Sharon was in the living room waiting on Slim when he came back with Peach. After dealing with her, he sat down to eat. He ate with no modesty while Peach sat across from him with her food. Now that the hostility was gone, he was ready to make his approach towards utilizing her.

When Slim finished his food, he rolled a blunt while Peach sipped on a wine cooler. Along with the wine coolers that she got for herself, she got him a half pint of Hennessy. Before he took a sip from the hot cognac, he lit the blunt. He then sat next to her in a slump. She stared down at him as she was in suspense.

"I like how we came to an understandin'. I feel like it was the right thing to do since we gon be around each other. I'm serious 'bout what's goin' on wit' me, and around me. That played a part in me wantin' to get an understandin' wit'chu," Slim explained before he pulled on the blunt. He then passed it to Peach.

"Is you tellin' me, you only bein' nice to me for convenient purposes?"

"Wit' what I'm doin' around here, I gotta do what's convenient for me. But that don't mean that I'm not a good nigga outside of this. If I woulda met'chu under other circumstances, you'll see the same characteristics as for as me bein' humble and generous. Now, that don't mean that I'ma sucka, but that's besides the point."

"So, what is the point?"

"The point is, I'm serious 'bout what's goin' on wit me, and around me like I just said. Wit' that bein' the point, I came to realize that I need some assistance around here."

"What kinda assistance?" Peach asked as she passed Slim the blunt.

Slim took a sip from his drink and pulled on the blunt before he answered. "I can't be in two places at one time, so I need somebody to hold it down for me when I'm gone."

"S'cuse me if I'm jumpin' to conclusions, but how you gon jus up and trust me wit'cho stuff?" Peach asked with a smile as she was flattered. "I mean. What if I ran off wit'cho stuff?"

"Like I said, I ain't no sucka. I'm hella comprehensive, and that makes me a good judge of character."

"So, you been watchin' me?"

"It only comes from me bein' serious 'bout what's goin' on wit me, and around me."

Peach made a sassy noise under her breath as if she was disappointed that it wasn't her sexiness that had Slim watching her. "It ain't all about me trustin' you personally. I can only say that I trust that'chu got common sense. For one, look at'chu. You hella high maintenance, and you take pride in yo' classy appearance. I know what it takes to maintain that. So, I know you wouldn't run off wit some bullshit and kill resources that's helpin' you maintain somethin' you take pride in. That's common sense," Slim said before he pulled on the blunt.

Peach shook her head up and down with a smile as she was impressed by Slim's intellect. "I guess you are a good judge of character. So, what exactly do you need me to do?"

"You see how I got shit organized. I just need you to post up and get money. What'chu know about the game though?"

"I'm familiar wit' the basics, and what's what."

"That's cool. I'ma give you an ounce to do yo' thing wit. I just want eight hundred back from every ounce I give you. That's like half of what I usually see from an ounce."

"That's cool."

"Aiight. Now, before we get to doin' our thing, is it anything that I need to know about'chu that'll get in the way of me doin' what I do?"

"What'chu see is what'chu get."

"Straight up," Slim said as he looked Peach up and down.

"I didn't mean it like that," Peach said with a laugh. "And I didn't mean that how you think I meant it." Peach made a sassy noise under her breath again before she took a sip from her drink. "So, what about'chu? Is it anything that I need to know about'chu?"

"Ain't nothin' goin' on wit' me that'll get in the way of what's goin' on wit' us."

"What about'cho lil' girlfriends? I ain't gotta worry about them comin' over and trippin' wit me, do I?" Peach took a fake sip from her drink as she was trying to hide her slick smile. Slim knew that she was fishing for information, so he took that as an opportunity to implement that he was anti-monogamous. It was for future references. "I don't do the boyfriend, girlfriend thing, so you ain't gotta worry 'bout no girls trippin' wit'chu over me."

"So, you a playa, huh," Peach asked with a feisty attitude.

"I just do what I do. That shouldn't effect what we got goin' on, right?"

"Right," Peach sarcastically agreed. "S'cuse me . I need to use the bathroom."

It was obvious to Slim that Peach was attracted to him. She was hot, so he was also attracted to her. However, he wasn't going to act on it until it was clear to her of what his main objective was.

When Peach came back into the living room, Slim decided to leave. He wanted to test her abilities with the ounce he gave her.

Slim woke up the next afternoon around 1PM with a hangover. Before he went to Sharon's house, he stopped to get something to eat. Peach was sitting on the porch steps when he got there. She had herself looking extra pretty in an outfit that was enticing.

"What's up," Slim spoke as he sat next to Peach and went through the bags.

"I'm good, but'chu look like you got a hangover," Peach said with a little laugh.

"I'm good," Slim said as he continued to fish through the bags. "Here. This yours, and I got this juice for you too."

"Thank you," Peach sweetly said as she was touched by Slim's thoughtfulness. "'Cause my mama ain't got nothin' good in there to eat."

"She woulda let'chu use her car," Slim teased.

"I see you got jokes," Peach said as she nudged Slim. "Trish and Val be comin' through tryin' to sell they food stamp cards. You should get 'em, so you don't have to go out to eat every time you get hungry.

"I'ma do that. But, how shit move last night?" Slim asked as he began to eat.

"It was fast. I haven't been to sleep yet. I just sold the last of that ounce right before you came. I made seventeen hundred and seventy-five from it," Peach proudly informed as she knew that Slim was testing her abilities.

"I'ma do somethin' else wit'chu when I re-up."

Slim and Peach were both hungry, so they ate with very little conversation as they enjoyed the weather. When they were done, she took their trash inside while he rolled a blunt.

While Peach was inside the house, Slim noticed the red Chevy that sped away yesterday. It parked behind his car. A skinny, dark skinned dude got out with a mouth full of gold. He had a frown on his face as he came up the steps. Slim put his hand on his lap where his pistol was tucked as he kept his eyes on the dude. The dude didn't make any threatening gestures with his hands, but Slim was still alert as he sat at the edge of the step.

"Peach in there?" the dude asked as he stopped at the bottom of the steps.

"She'll be out in a minute," Slim said as he held eye contact with the dude. He hadn't even thought about why this dude showed up. It was the fact that he showed up with hostility that had him on edge.

"Why you come over here?" Peach angrily asked as she came onto the porch.

Slim didn't bother to turn around to Peach. He kept his eyes on dude as he pulled on his blunt.

The dude's facial expressions softened as he looked up to Peach. "I just wanna talk to you. Can we go somewhere and do that?"

"Is you crazy? I'm not gettin' in that car wit'chu! I ain't got nothin' to say to you, and I don't wanna hear nothin' you gotta say!"

"It's like that?"

"I made that clear to you yesterday! Now, could you leave, and never come back over here?"

The dude stared at Peach for a few seconds before he shook his head up and down. He then turned to leave as he crossed eyes with Slim.

It was obvious to Slim that the dude had envy and hostility in his eyes. He watched him leave with his face twisted until he was in his car and gone. He sped off like he was in a rush to get back. Slim then turned to Peach with fury in his eyes.

"Get the fuck in the house," Slim ordered.

Peach immediately complied with Slim following behind her. "What the fuck is goin' on wit'chu and that nigga?" Slim asked as he slammed the door.

"Nothin'! Ain't nothin' goin' on wit' me and him. I told him yesterday, that I didn't want nothin' to do wit him."

"Why?" Slim demanded more information as he stood over Peach.

"He was into some things that I had to get away from."

"Like what?"

"He was snortin' dope!"

"Quit fuckin' playin' wit me! It's more to it than that," Slim said as he pushed Peach's head with his fingers.

Peach fell back to the couch and quickly sat back up with her face twisted at Slim.

"I will fuck you up in here," Slim threatened as he pointed his finger in Peach's face. "Now, you need to put me up on this clown-ass nigga! You brought this bullshit around me! And I asked you last night is it anything 'bout'chu that'll get in my way!"

Seeing Slim's point, Peach relaxed her face. "I was under the impression that it was over between us, so I didn't see no need for me to tell you about him."

"This shit ain't over, so you need to put me up on this nigga," Slim snarled as he sat on the table in front of Peach.

Peach took a deep breath and slowly exhaled. "I met Twan at the mall last year. Me and my sista was tryin' on these rings, and he came outta nowhere. He said some things I was feelin', and he ended up buyin' the rings I liked. And I ain't gon lie, that was the main reason I took his number. Any girl woulda loved the things he did for me after that. Slim, I didn't have nothin', and he gave me everything. So, as time went along, I grew feelings for him."

Slim smoked on his blunt, not caring about the love story, but he paid attention.

"We eventually got an apartment together, and that's when I found out that he was snortin' dope. I didn't think nothin' of it, 'cause I didn't know nothin' about heroin, and what it do to people. The more he did it, the more his tolerance level went up. He needed it to physically function, and snortin' it wasn't enough, so he started jackin' that shit in his veins. And I still didn't leave him when I found him passed out wit' a needle in his arm," Peach sighed before she shook her head from side to side, pausing momentarily before she continued on with a bitter tone.

"As soon as he was conscious, he checked his self outta the hospital. That's when I seen what that stuff really do to people. He fell off from his hustle and started sellin' all his stuff. His punk ass even sold the jewelry and the car he bought me. He started robbin' his homeboys, and now they tryin' to kill him. My cousin from his hood, and he the one who told me to get away from him. Now, he claimin' that I used him for his money. If that was the case, I woulda let him die and kept the lil' shit he still had."

Slim pulled on his blunt as he stared at Peach. Even though he wasn't looking for it, he got a definition of her character. He was impressed with her selfless commitment. However, compassion wasn't in his heart as he couldn't ignore the possible danger she brought.

"I'm sorry for bringin' this around you, but if you need me to do anything to help you feel comfortable just let me know," Peach softly said as she placed her hand on Slim's leg.

"Just fall back," Slim said as he removed Peach's hand from his leg.

Later on that night, Slim was sitting on the arm of the couch. He was watching the streets from the shadows with his pistol on his lap. Peach laid in a curl on the other end of the couch as she watched TV. He squinted his eyes as he focused on a car that was creeping up the street. It parked up the street, and on the same side as the house. He continued to watch as the lights on the car went out. When no one got out, his heart began to beat hard and slow. He could see a silhouette as it appeared that someone was looking back at the house.

"Who the fuck is this?" Slim asked as he looked to Peach, then back to the car.

Peach jumped up and came to the window. Slim watched her facial expressions as she studied the car. After a moment, her eyebrows went up as she slowly turned to him. It was the only confirmation he needed.

Slim pulled his t-shirt off and dropped it on the couch before he headed towards the back door. The door on the back porch was nailed shut by 2x4's, so he had to climb out of the window.

As Slim walked down the dark alley with his pistol out, he pulled his tank-top off and tucked it on his waist. None of the dogs barked as they could sense the danger. Not even his footsteps could be heard.

His father's question popped into his head. "*Is you prepared to put that iron on a nigga if he get in yo' way?*" He was prepared to do that with no hesitation.

When Slim got to the house where his presumed threat was parked in front, he jumped the fence into the backyard. He quickly made his way to the dark gangway with his pistol down to his side. At the head of the gangway, he knelt down in the shadows with his eyes on his target.

Slim could clearly see who was in the car. It was Twan. He'd just jumped from a nod and looked back to Sharon's house.

After a moment, the powerful heroin forced him back into a vulnerable nod. It's when Slim made his move.

Slim ran down the small hill holding his dick with his face twisted. When he stuck his pistol through the passenger side window, Twan was still in a nod. He had a mack-11 on his lap and a 12 gauge shotgun between the seats. They were useless as Slim caught him literally sleeping.

"Nigga, wake yo' stupid ass up," Slim aggressively spoke. Twan immediately jumped from his nod in confusion as he fumbled with the mack on his lap.

"Now, go back to sleep," Slim said as he pulled the trigger. Flames immediately jumped from the barrel with loud pops that came one after another. The first few slugs hit Twan's face, causing it to swell and buss open as he jerked into a slump. Slim slowly backed away from the mess as he continued to fill him up with hot lead. The pistol violently jerked, but he handled it with one hand as he emptied the clip into his upper body.

Slim left the scene the same way he came. When he got to the alley, he wiped the hot pistol down with his tank-top and dropped it into a sewer.

Back inside of Sharon's house, Slim stood at the entrance of the dark living room. Peach was sitting alone on the couch. His main objective was now clear to her as she became a witness to the lengths he'll go to, to secure his hustle. With that point being made, he was ready to put it on her.

"C'mere," Slim ordered.

With nothing needing to be said, Peach came to him as she was ready to submit herself to him. He looked her up and down with lust in his eyes before he took her up to her room. It's where she was pleased to submit herself to him.

Chapter 11: Her Submission

When Slim finished with Peach that night, he left her sleeping. He went downstairs and sat on the arm of the couch in the dark living room. From the shadows, he watched the irritated police and detectives clean up his mess. Things didn't clear up until 3AM. For that reason, he didn't leave until 6AM.

At his father's house, Slim stood under the shower water as he thought about what he needed to do to get back on track. There was no time for sleep. By 8:00 that morning, he was back at Sharon's house with two new pistols. He had a glock 40 for himself, and a chrome .380 for Peach. She was still sleeping while he waited for G-Will to return his page. He sat around for almost an hour before G-Will hit him back.

Nikki Pooh let Slim into the basement when he got to G-Will's house. She led him to the living room area where G-Will was slumped on the couch.

"This forty-five hundred," Slim said as he dumped rolls of money onto the table from a brown paper bag.

Nikki Pooh immediately began counting the money.

"I see you ain't bullshittin' over there," G-Will said as he sat up from his slump. "And I see you got Peach over there wit'chu, too."

"What'chu know 'bout Peach?" Slim asked.

"For all that matters, she's a solid bitch all around the board."

Slim shook his head up and down as G-Will confirmed his assumptions about Peach.

"But ay, I'm finna hit the Bahamas for two weeks or so, so I want'chu to put Nikki Pooh number in yo' beeper. She already know what's up wit'chu, so just hit her up when you ready to re-up."

"Aiight." Slim nodded.

"Sharon know what she doin' in the kitchen. She gave me the whip game. Just let her know, you want no mo' and no less than nine ounces from yo' shit."

After Slim put Nikki Pooh's number in his beeper, he clapped hands with G-Will. He then tucked the quarter key in his pants along with a digital scale G-Will gave him.

When Slim got back to Sharon's house, Peach was finally up. She was curled on the couch watching TV. He sat his things on the table before he slumped on the couch across from her.

"What's up? You cool?" Slim asked.

"I'm good. What's up wit'chu?"

"Waitin' on Sharon to get back. I sent her to get us somethin' to eat. Then I'ma have her whip up this dope. I want'chu to post up wit me so you can be on point, too."

Peach shook her head up and down as she kept her eyes on the TV.

"Can you handle this?" Slim asked as he pulled the .380 from under the couch.

"Yeah, I can handle that." Peach replied as she looked at the gun.

"I need you to get a phone, too."

"That was in my plans."

"Shit gon' move slow today. But tomorrow the first, so shit gon be movin' hella fast."

Just as Slim slumped back into the couch, Sharon came through the front door. He sat back up to the table as she put the bags of food there.

"I'ma need you in the kitchen when we finish eatin'," Slim said as he went through the bags of food.

Sharon looked at the quarter key on the table, then back to Slim. "I'ma go get everything ready," she said before she took off.

Sharon showed Slim how to rock up his dope in an old fashion way. She gave him the simplest whip game by using baking soda, a Pyrex jar, and the stove. Peach was right there with him, soaking up the game from her mother. When she was done, he gave her his last ten rocks.

Slim got exactly what he asked for. After breaking nine ounces from the quarter key, he and Peach sat at the table and broke three ounces down to twenty pieces. He gave her one to do her thing with while he kept two. After stashing three of them in his car, he took Peach up to her room. He pulled the bottom drawer from her dresser and stashed his other three ounces. His trusting gesture put a smile on her face.

With everything back on track, Slim decided to take advantage of the slow day and get some sleep. As soon as he pulled into the backyard of his father's house, he got a page from Vee. She was one of his prominent customers, so he couldn't put her off.

At Vee's apartment, Slim planned on dealing with her and leaving. But that wasn't the case. She had company, who sat in the back room and spent their money little by little. When their money was gone, the white couple went to an ATM machine and did it all over again.

While Slim was at Vee's apartment, other junkies knocked on the door for service. They knew what it was with him when they seen him coming into the building. Their small bills quickly added up in his pockets as he was unintentionally creating an establishment in the building.

By 5PM that evening, Slim ran through an ounce and a half. He left with $2,200 and more clientele. He also broke Vee off five rocks for bringing him the clientele, and allowing him to do his thing from her apartment.

At his father's house, Slim added his money to his stash. His stash was getting fat, so he moved it to under his dresser. He forgot all about sleep as he wanted to fill his bag of rocks back up.

Before Slim went to Sharon's house, he stopped to get something to eat. When he got there, Peach was curled on the couch with a sheet. He put his things on the table before he sat across from her. After giving her some food, he began to break down the two ounces he brought in from his car.

"Nothin' but two hundred came through while you was gone," Peach stated. Slim ignored Peach as he continued to break his dope down. "You haven't even been to sleep yet, huh?"

Slim looked up and stared at Peach with a blank expression before he continued with what he was doing.

Sensing that Slim was in no mood to answer frivolous questions, Peach left him alone. When he was done, he ate his food and stretched out on the couch with a blunt.

"Can I come and lay wit'chu?" Peach sweetly asked.

Slim stared at Peach for a moment before he made room for her. When Peach rose from the couch with her smile, she opened the sheet and let it blow behind her as she came to Slim. She had on a white tank-top and red cotton shorts. Her shorts were only big enough to cover her ass. She covered them with the sheet to their waist as she laid with her back towards him. She intentionally pressed her ass against him as she made herself comfortable.

"You comfortable wit' me like this?"

"I'm cool," Slim said as he passed Peach the blunt.

"Um, you told me to tell you anything about me that could get in the way of what we doin'."

Slim twisted his face as he thought about pushing Peach from the couch.

"Stop lookin' at me like that," Peach whined. "It ain't nothin' bad."

"What type of shit is you on?"

Peach pulled on the blunt before she responded." G-Will came over here yesterday mornin'. He told me that'chu was his homeboy. And I just wanted you to know I used to mess wit' him a long time ago."

Slim knew what Peach was doing. She was trying to get serious with him, and was clearing the path from anything that could have an effect on that.

"I don't see how that could get in the way of us doin' what we doin'."

"It shouldn't," Peach said with a smile.

Slim was confused by Peach's smile. Either she misunderstood him, or she wasn't trying to hear what he was talking about.

"Do we gotta understandin' as for as the page we on?"

"We gotta understandin' when you fucked me like that last night." Peach guided Slim's mind with her response. When he decided to put it on her last night, it was at a time when he made his objective clear to her. With her bringing last night up, he came to the conclusion that they were on the same page.

"I'm cool," Slim said as Peach tried to pass him the blunt. "So, you liked how I put it on you last night, huh," he asked as he slid his hand up her thigh.

"I'm feelin' you," Peach softly whispered as she cocked her leg.

Slim's hand found warmth between Peach's thighs. He slid his fingers under her shorts where they met her hot, naked lips. They quickly went from moist to juicy as he began to massage them. He watched her facial expressions with a slight smile as she aroused him. Her eyes were slightly closed as she moaned softly. She still held the blunt between her fingers as it hung loosely. When he eased his middle finger inside of her, she gasped for breath and let out a soft, trembling moan.

"I'm feelin' you," Peach whispered as she began to rock her hips.

"I'm tryin' to feel you too," Slim said as he pushed his clothes down to his knees.

"I'ma do whatever it takes to make that happen!"

"Take these shorts off!"

Peach immediately complied before she covered them back to their waist with the sheet. Slim positioned his dick to slide between her thighs as she pushed her hot ass against him. It parted her lips as she squeezed her thighs together. She squeezed his slippery dick with both hands as it came and went. He could see how hot he had her as she softly moaned with her heavy breathing.

"If y'all don't take y'all nasty ass upstairs," Sharon said as she came into the living room. Sharon startled Slim and Peach. They both froze up with guilty smiles as they stared up at her. She shook her head from side to side as she stood in the entrance of the living room. "Lemme get somethin' for this fifty," she finally said as she sat the money on the table.

Slim reached over Peach and pulled three rocks from his bag.

"And I hope y'all usin' condoms while y'all up here bein' grown," Sharon said as she took the dope and left.

"You wanna go upstairs," Peach softly asked.

"Nah. I wanna stay right here."

"Stop teasin' me then," Peach whined as she elbowed Slim.

"I showed you what I'm 'bout, so I'ma let'chu do yo' thing."

"I ain't got no problem wit' that," Peach happily said as she saddled Slim.

When Peach saddled Slim, the sheet fell behind her and exposed them. He grabbed her ass with one hand while she eased onto his hardness. He tightened his face and bit his bottom lip as her hot insides sucked him in.

"I want this to be yours," Peach cried out as she began to gracefully roll her hips.

Slim ignored Peach's submissive comment as she grabbed his hands and brought her chest to his. She held his hands over his head as she began to bounce on top of him. He twisted his face at her as he met her with his hard pushes. With the collision, her ass made loud clapping noises as it jiggled in all directions. With her moaning in his ear, she continued to tell him how she wanted to be his, and only his. He planned on setting her straight as soon as they were done. But when it was over, she found him sleeping like a baby when she came from the bathroom. She put it on him.

While Slim slept, Peach watched over him while she dealt with the light traffic. She brought the fan from her room and turned it on him with a fresh sheet. When traffic became too slow, she laid with him.

For a while, she stared at his peaceful face while she gently brushed the lining of his hair with her fingertips. After kissing his lips, she laid her head on his chest and went to sleep.

Slim was awaken the next morning by his face being caressed. When he opened his eyes, Peach was sitting in front of him. She stared down at him with a smile as she continued to caress his face. He stared into her eyes, inhaling the sweet smell of her before he looked her up and down. Two red balls held her ponytail together while two strands of hair spiraled loosely down the sides of her face. Her plump lips looked extra juicy with the peach lip gloss. She had her shiny jewelry on with a red, sleeveless blouse. A couple of buttons were undone and exposed her cleavage with her B-cups sitting up nicely. Her blouse stopped an inch from her waist, allowing her light-brown skin to peek out. A denim, blue jean mini-skirt fitted her tightly as it showed off her smooth legs. A red silk strand ran through the belt loops. It was tied in a knot on her side where two short strands dangled. Her red stilettos showed off her pretty toes while lace wrapped her legs.

"Baby, you hungry," Peach asked as she looked to the table, then back to Slim.

Slim stared at Peach's glowing face as he was touched by her sweet gesture. "What'chu doin'?"

"I'm feelin' you. But I wanna talk to you about that later on tonight wit' the things I said to you last night. I wanna cook somethin' for us, and we could talk then."

It was clear to Slim that Peach was feeling him beyond the understanding he thought they had. A talk with them opening up about it was exactly what he wanted. It would give him the opportunity to get things straight with her.

"That's cool," Slim said as her sat up.

"Now, c'mon and put somethin' in yo' stomach 'fore you get on the grind," Peach said as she turned to prepare Slim's food.

"How long you been up?"

"For about two hours. My mama was pacin' around, waitin' on her checks to come. I had her to bring us back somethin' to eat, and she came back wit Trish and Val. I'ma go to the grocery store wit' them when they finish doin' what they doin'. Is it anything specific you want?"

Slim shook his head from side to side as he continued to eat. It was after 10AM and the traffic was already moving. After he finished eating, he collected his things from the table.

"I need to go get this money. I'ma holla at'chu later."

"Can I have a kiss before you leave me?" Peach sweetly asked as she stood in front of Slim.

"You'll be aiight."

"No, I won't," Peach whined as she threw her arms around Slim's neck. "Kiss me!"

Slim stared into Peach's pretty, light brown eyes as she batted her lashes at him. He could smell her sweet lip gloss as she stuck her lips out. After a moment, she kissed his lips and left them wet. He could taste the lip gloss as he wiped it from his lips.

"Don't be wipin' my kiss off," Peach cried as she kissed Slim again. This time, Slim found himself participating in the kiss as it became passionate. He squeezed Peach's ass from the bottom and lifted her to her toes.

"Go on 'fore you start somethin'," Peach said as she pushed Slim away.

Slim shook his head in disbelief as he realized that Peach drew him out. He was attracted to her more than he realized. She watched him until he was in his car and gone.

When Slim got to Vee's apartment, she spent some money with him and introduced him to some of her friends. They all spent big with him as his personal clientele became longer. Her friend, Angie also came over and spent with him. While he was dealing with her, he got a weird vibe from her. It was as if she was ashamed to accept his dope. While he was there, other junkies who lived in the building came to see him. They all spent their government checks happily and irresponsibly.

By the time Slim left Vee's apartment, he ran through three ounces. That was with the help of those who paged him while he was there. He counted $5,235. Peach was also doing her thing. She ran through the ounce he gave her, and had to hit the stash for another one. He planned on seeing Nikki Pooh later on that night.

When Slim got back to Sharon's house, he was drawn to the kitchen by the mouth-watering aroma. It's where he found Peach over the stove. She ran him from the kitchen before he could see what she was putting together. He went back into the living room and broke down another ounce.

Just as Slim finished bagging his dope, Peach came into the living room for him.

"C'mon, baby. The food ready."

"Here I come."

"And wash yo' hands, too."

When Slim came from the bathroom, Peach led him to the kitchen by his hand. He became astonished as he stepped in.

"Daaamn!" Slim exclaimed as he looked to Peach, then back to what she put together.

Peach had that crack house kitchen looking like a five-star restaurant. Two lit candles sat in the middle of the table with a five-course meal prepared for them. Roast beef strips were on their plates with macaroni shells. Water and juice sat on one side of their plate. On the other side, improperly organized utensils sat on napkins. A salad sat on one side of the small table with a plate full of crispy croissants across from it. In between the candles was a store-bought cheesecake with slices of strawberries on top. Slim had never seen anything like this outside of TV.

He was expecting for Peach to fry some chicken and sit on his lap while they talked and ate from the same plate. She most definitely made him feel special with her ghetto classiness.

"C'mon, baby. Let's eat while it's still hot."

"I'm feelin' this," Slim said as he turned his hat backwards and sat at the table. "I'ma go on and do it like they do it on TV and put the napkin in my lap."

"You silly," Peach said with a laugh as she sat across from Slim. Just as Slim was about to dig into his plate, Peach stopped him.

"Wait a minute, baby! Gimme yo' hands," Peach said as she stretched her arms across the table and wiggled her fingers for Slim's hands.

Slim curiously stared at Peach before he put his fork back into its place. He then gave her his hands. Their arms stretched across the table with the candles between them.

The candles created a romantic glow around their face as they stared into each other's eyes.

"Baby, I just wanna um… I just wanna say grace and let'chu know how grateful I am to be here wit'chu like this. I think you deserve and would appreciate my commitment. And I want'chu to know, I can be all, and everything you need," Peach softly expressed.

Slim was feeling Peach's sincerity as he stared into her passionate eyes. She made it hard for him to express his opposition. She could feel the rejection as she watched his unenthused expressions. She released his hands and slid into a slump as she was hurt and disappointed.

"What we 'pose to eat first?"

"It don't matta," Peach mumbled as she fished around in her food with her fork.

"What the hell y'all got goin' on in here?" Sharon surprisingly asked as she came into the kitchen.

"Mama, what'chu want?" Peach asked with a bitchy attitude.

"I guess things ain't goin' yo' way. Well, I didn't come to see you anyway," Sharon said before she turned to Slim.

Slim looked to Sharon, then to Peach before he continued to eat. Peach rolled her eyes at Slim before she rose from the table and dealt with Sharon. When she came back to the table, she sat back in a slump and continued to play with her food.

"Holla at me," Slim said as he looked up to Peach.

"You already know that I'm tryin'to be wit'chu," Peach mumbled.

"Don't take this personal, but I ain't feelin' that wit'chu, or nobody else."

"So, I guess it's all about the money?"

Slim sat his fork down and sat up to the table. "We gettin' this money together, and doin' what we do along wit' that. Why can't that be enough? I mean, I'm feelin' how you get down wit' me. I just ain't feelin' that extra shit that's besides the point," he calmly spoke.

"It wouldn't be no point wit'out the extra shit," Peach said as she rolled her head. "What I mean is, the only reason I'm doin' what I do wit'chu is 'cause I'm feelin' you. I don't care about sellin' dope, and I damn sho don't need to do it to maintain my appearance. So, while you was so called analyzin' me, you failed to realize that I have other options. I agreed to be down wit'chu, 'cause it was an opportunity for me to show you that'chu can trust me while I make sacrifices to show you my sincerity. I guess you too caught up on gettin' money to identify and recognize a down ass bitch!"

"You can't be serious. You know I ain't no clueless nigga in the game. That's why you feelin' me. So, don't speak on what I can recognize and identify wit'. I know what's up wit'chu. Now, you fail to realize that this shit ain't all about'chu, and what'chu want. I been jammed up for over three years, and ain't been out two months yet.

I'm just tryin' to get this money and do what I do wit'out the extra obligations. If you can't accept that... you can keep it movin'," Slim said as he kept his cool composure.

Slim and Peach stared at each other, and kept the eye contact when Sharon came into the kitchen. She asked for service a few times before she became agitated.

"What'chu gon do?" Slim asked as he kept the eye contact with Peach.

After a moment, Peach rolled her eyes at Slim as she rose from the table. For a second, he thought she was about to leave the kitchen. Instead, she got up to deal with Sharon. He took that as a gesture of her acceptance and continued to eat.

Slim could feel Peach staring at him when she sat back at the table.

"I still can't change how I feel about'chu," Peach said in almost a mumble.

"I'm not askin' you to. I like how you feel about me, and I ain't got no problem wit'chu showin' it. I just ain't feelin' how you tryin' to press me wit that serious shit. I mean, if somethin' end up happenin' between us, we'll talk about it then," Slim said before he continued to eat.

"I can accept that," Peach said as a little smile appeared on her face.

Silence came in the kitchen as Slim could feel Peach staring at him again. When he looked up to her, curiosity was written all over her face.

"Why you lookin' at me like that?" Slim asked as he put his fork down and slumped into the chair.

"I'm jus curious about some things."

"So, you finna start harassin' me 'bout things that don't matter?"

"Ain't nobody finna harass you! I just wanna know yo' name and age."

"How is that important?"

"I can't believe you just asked me that," Peach whined.

"Lemme get somethin' for this fifty," Sharon asked as she came into the kitchen again.

"Get it from him. Whatever his name is. I ain't got no mo'," Peach said as she folded her arms across her chest.

When Slim finished dealing with Sharon, he turned to Peach. She still had her arms folded across her chest with a pouty expression.

"I like when you stick yo' lips out like that," Slim teased as he sat on Peach's lap.

"Don't say nothin' to me!"

"I thought'chu wanted to know my name and stuff," Slim said as he began to play with Peach's lips.

"Don't touch my lips! I don't know where yo' fingers been at," Peach whined as she swatted at Slim's hand.

"I guess you forgot about last night," Slim said with a laugh as he snatched his hand away. He then continued to play with Peach's lips.

"Why you playin' wit me?" Peach asked in frustration as she caught Slim's hand with a slap. It made a loud pop, and brought a little smile to her face.

"What's her name?" Slim asked as he pointed to Peach's smile.

"Peach Summers! I'm nineteen, and my birthday is December the 19th! Anything else you wanna know about me?"

"Nah. I know enough about'chu for the most important part."

"Slim, I ain't really trippin' off yo' age, but me knowin' yo name is important. Especially if we 'pose to be lookin' out for each other. What if you got locked up or somethin', and I needed to bond you out? I'll feel so stupid!"

"You right," Slim said with a smile.

A smile appeared on Peach's face as Slim agreed with her.

"My name King Daddy."

"Stop playin' wit me 'fore I slap you," Peach whined.

After one last laugh, Slim gave in. "My name, Jevon. Jevon Johnson."

"I like yo' naaame," Peach sweetly squealed. "Now, how old is you?"

"Sixteen."

"Boy, you ain't no damn sixteen! Quit playin' wit' me!"

"Two, twenty-seven eighty. You gotta problem wit' that?"

"Oh my god! You serious ain't chu," Peach said as she covered her mouth with surprise. "I can go to jail for messin' wit'chu," she added with a laugh.

"Nah, I can go to jail for how I be puttin' it on you," Slim said before he began to mimic Peach's cries.

"I don't sound like that," Peach said as she tapped Slim's stomach. "But I don't care how old you is, you still my King Daddy," she said before she kissed his lips.

"I need to go re-up again, so let me go do that."

"I got sixteen hundred for you. Do you need that?"

"Nah. Just put it in the stash, and do yo' thing wit' that other ounce. I'm glad we got a understandin', too," Slim said before he kissed Peach's lips.

It took Nikki Pooh less than five minutes to return Slim's page. She was next door, and told him to come over. Just like she said, the basement door was open. The only light in the basement came from the TV in the living room area. It's where he found her. She was laying on the couch under a sheet. He figured that she was about to go to sleep before he paged her.

"That's forty-five hundred," Slim said as he sat a stack of money on the table. He then picked up the quarter key.

"Nothin' against you, but do you mind if I count it before you leave?" Nikki Pooh kindly asked.

"It's cool. Do what'chu do," Slim said as he sat on the couch across from Nikki Pooh.

"Lemme turn this light on so I can see what I'm doin'," Nikki Pooh said as she came from under the sheet.

Slim hid his excitement as he slumped into the couch. The only thing Nikki Pooh had on was an extra small t-shirt and sky blue panties. Her every curve was revealed as her horse ass jiggled ridiculously. He shifted his eyes to the TV when she turned from the lamp.

"Can you roll that blunt up for me?" Nikki Pooh sweetly asked.

"I got'chu," Slim said as he sat up to the table.

Nikki Pooh was sitting directly across from Slim, so when he grabbed the blunt from the table, he could clearly see between her legs. Her fat lips sucked her panties in as her thick thighs were slightly parted. She caught his eyes, but didn't bother to adjust herself.

"Thank you," Nikki Pooh kindly said before she began to count the money.

When Slim finished rolling the blunt, Nikki Pooh was still counting the money. She appeared to be having problems with it.

"Damn!" Nikki Pooh exclaimed. "I'm sorry, but I just lost count again. Can you fire that blunt up for me?"

Slim twisted his face at Nikki Pooh as he sat up from his slump. "Fuck that blunt! What kinda games you playin' wit a nigga?"

"What'chu mean?" Nikki Pooh asked with a clueless expression.

"I don't know what's goin' on wit'chu, but'chu can't lil' boy me wit' the bullshit'chu on. I seen you count that lil' money in three minutes before. And you got'cho pussy in my face, tryin' to entice a nigga. I don't know what kinda nigga you think I am, but that's forty-five hundred," Slim said before he stood up and took the dope from the table.

"I heard what'chu had to say. Now, can you listen to me?"

Something in Nikki Pooh's calm tone made Slim stop and turn to her.

"Please, don't jump to conclusions on what'chu put together in yo' head. I do know what kinda nigga you is. And to make a long story short, ain't too many niggas in the game like you. Juts know as you elevate in the game, you'll see that everything ain't everything wit everybody. Just keep yo' eyes open," Nikki Pooh said before she lit her blunt.

Slim waved Nikki Pooh off as he left out. When he got outside of the door, he stood there in confusion. He was quite sure that Nikki Pooh was trying to seduce him. He figured that she was trying to test his loyalty, or for some reason, deceive G-Will. Then there was the, "everything ain't everything wit' everybody" statement she made. What she meant was, everything and everyone aren't always what they appear to be. He had no idea of what, or who she was implying that to, but he was going to keep his eyes open.

During the rest of the week, Slim spent majority of his time getting money. Peach was right by his side with her submissive attitude. That Friday morning, he went home and counted his money. He had $17,875 under his dresser, $2,500 in his top drawer, and $2,400 under Peach's dresser.

Chapter 12: She Got 'em

Weeks had gone by and money came easily to Slim with Peach's help. To her dismay, Slim continued with their arrangement as it was, showing no signs that he intended to make it more than what it was between them. But since her liking for him was so strong, she didn't stress him over it and decided to just roll with how things were going.

Slim slept until late one Friday afternoon. When he woke up, his intentions were to take a quick shower, and get back on the grind. When came from his room, he didn't notice Meka. She was sitting alone in the living room area. As soon as she noticed him, her face lit up.

"Jevon, C'mere," Meka whispered. Slim didn't notice Meka until he was at the bathroom door. "I thought we was gon try to figure somethin' out," Meka said as she got into Slim's face.

"I ain't forget about'chu. I just been on the move," Slim said as he looked Meka up and down with his eyes filled with lust.

"I like when you look at me like that. And if you woulda came home last night, you coulda got some." Meka teased.

"Straight up?"

"Yeah. I came down here when everybody was sleep."

"Do it again tonight and I'ma come and get it," Slim said as he pulled Meka closer to him by her ass.

"I'll be down here," Meka said before she hurried back to the couch.

When Slim got to Sharon's house, Peach was laying on the couch, still in her night clothes. Her hair was in a stringy ponytail, and she looked weak. It was a hot, sunny day, and she would usually have herself looking pretty for him.

"What's goin' on wit'chu?" Slim curiously asked as he sat next to Peach.

"I'm alright," Peach softly spoke.

"You don't look like it," Slim said as he gently brushed Peach's hair with his hand.

"I had mornin' sickness, and I'm still feelin' it."

"Mornin' sickness?! What the hell is that?"

"I was lightheaded, and I couldn't keep my food down."

"And you layin' here like it ain't nothin'. Get up and put some clothes on. I'm finna take you to the hospital. You probably got food poisonin' or somethin'," Slim said as he rose from the couch with Peach's hand.

"Baby, I know what's wrong wit' me. Sit down," Peach said as she pulled Slim back to the couch.

Slim curiously stared at Peach as she sat up and slid her feet into her house shoes. The seriousness in her face was starting to scare him.

"Baby… baby I'm pregnant," Peach said in almost a mumble.

"That's it? That's what's wrong wit'chu? You had me thinkin' you was finna die or somethin'," Slim said with a smile as he was relieved. "That ain't nothin'. Ain't it a clinic somewhere where we can take care of that?"

The grogginess instantly left Peach's face as she became furious. "Is you fuckin' serious?" she asked as she snatched her hand from Slim and stood up. "You ain't gon' even ask me how I feel about this? What if I don't believe in that?"

"First of all, you need to calm down and quit screamin' in my face," Slim calmly said as he stood up. "This ain't apart of our understandin', and…"

"Fuck an understandin ! You can't…"

Slim grabbed Peach's face before she could continue to interrupt him. He squeezed it as he covered her mouth. "You know what it is wit' me! I ain't feelin' this, and I ain't tryin' to get into this wit'chu, or nobody else! Don't play no games wit' me!"

Peach snatched herself away from Slim and grabbed her phone from the table. She then stomped away crying.

Slim sat on the arm of the couch and shook his head in disbelief. After a few minutes, he rolled himself a blunt. Slim had been sitting on the arm of the couch for about fifteen minutes when a dark pink jeep pulled in front of the house. A girl who sat inside began to blow its horn. He had no idea of who she was.

"You ain't gotta worry about takin' care of nothin' for me! I'll do it myself," Peach said as she came into the living room.

When Slim turned around, Peach was heading towards the door with a bag over her shoulder, and one in her hand. He shrugged his shoulders as he watched her leave. For some reason, that "everything ain't everything wit everybody" statement popped into his head. He wondered if Nikki Pooh was trying to tell him something about

Peach. His face became twisted as he rushed upstairs to check his stash.

When Slim checked his stash, his initial feelings about Peach were confirmed. His dope and his money were untouched. She was indeed trustworthy and not a vindictive girl. It was something he valued, but was willing to push her away to avoid the consuming obligations.

Slim stared at his stash, knowing that he had to move it. The three ounces wouldn't fit in his car where the other three were stashed. He shook his head from side to side as he thought about the only place where his dope would be safe. It was in a place where he would be breaking his honorable commitment.

Sharon was in the living room when Slim came back down. She was sitting on the couch waiting on him. His bag of rocks was on the table with the one Peach left. He looked at them, then back to Sharon with uncertainty.

"Slim, don't look at me like that! You do me too good for me to steal from you."

"What's up?" Slim asked as he began to collect his things from the table.

Sharon gave Slim a fifty-dollar bill with an attitude. "I'ma leave you somethin' to deal wit the traffic since you actin' all honest."

"I am honest! And where the hell Peach run off to?"

"She ain't feelin' too peachy right now, so I guess she went to get her head right."

Slim counted over $1,000 in rocks from Peach's bag. He told Sharon to give him $600 and keep the rest. When he got to the door, she called for him.

"I know my baby can be a handful at times, but she special," Sharon said before she turned to leave.

Slim stood at the door as he thought about Sharon's words. His heart agreed with her as he wished he hadn't been so insensitive with Peach.

After Slim stashed his dope under his dresser at his father's house, he left to deal with those who paged him. It was at Vee's apartment where he spent majority of his time.

After stashing his money that night, he went back to Sharon's house. He sat in the dark living room, slumped on the couch with a blunt and a fifth of Hennessy. He found himself thinking about Peach. He was already missing how she catered to his wants, needs and desires with pleasure.

"Slim… I didn't know you was up here," Sharon said as she came into the living room.

"What's up?"

"I got five hunnid for you," Sharon said as she sat across from Slim.

"That's cool," Slim said with a nonchalant attitude. Sharon stared at Slim as he appeared to be gloomy. "Boy, is you in love wit' my baby," she abruptly asked.

"What?" Slim asked as he twisted his face at Sharon.

"Nothin'… I didn't say nothin'," Sharon said as she left the living room with a smile.

Slim sat up from his slump as he thought about Sharon's question. After a moment, he dropped his head and shook it in disbelief. As much as he tried to avoid the uncontrollable feeling of love, he found himself falling for Peach. She got him!

Slim was awaken by his phone the next morning. He was still slumped on the couch with the empty bottle of Hennessy in his hand. When he opened his eyes, he squinted from the bright sun that beamed through the white curtains. He shifted his eyes to his things that were cluttered on the table. When he gained his focus, he grabbed his phone and looked at its caller ID. It was a call coming from home.

"What's up?" Slim answered his phone with a scratchy tone.

"I'ma slap you when you come home!" Jayla said in a furious tone before she hung up.

Slim looked at his phone in confusion as he had no idea of where Jayla's attitude came from. After a moment, he tossed his phone to the side and went to the bathroom.

When Slim came from the bathroom, his phone was ringing again. He looked at the unfamiliar number on its called ID before he answered it. "What's up? Who is this?"

"This Meka," she responded with a feisty attitude.

Slim forgot about his arrangement with Meka, and it still hadn't occurred to him. "Why the fuck everybody callin' me wit' these attitudes? And where you at?"

"I'm at home, 'cause me and Jay got into it this mornin'."

"What'chu mean, y'all got into it?"

"We just argued, and it's yo' fault! I was waitin' on you, and I fell asleep in yo' bed. When she woke me up this mornin', I didn't have nothin' on."

Slim shook his head in disbelief as he remembered. "My bad… Yesterday was hella crazy, and I forgot about'chu," he apologized.

"Whatever! I feel so stupid!"

"Don't feel like that, 'cause I still wanna see what's up wit'chu. Who you at home wit'?"

"Nobody. But'chu act like you too busy for me, so it don't matter."

"I got'cho numba in my phone, so when I finish doin' what I'm doin', I'ma come and see you."

"Whatever," Meka said with doubt.

"Aiight," Slim said before he clicked his phone off.

Slim ran straight into Jayla when he got home. She was sitting on the couch with Fe-Fe between her legs. She was French braiding the top of Fe Fe's head to where the braids would swirl into a ponytail. They both turned to him when he came through the door. Jayla frowned her face at him while Fe-Fe smiled. Jayla's frown only made her face cuter. It forced a smile on Slim's face.

"I don't know what'chu smilin' for! I'll snatch them things out'cho mouth," Jayla said as she got into Slim's face.

"What'chu trippin' wit me for, Jay?" Slim asked as he hunched his shoulders.

"Don't play stupid wit' me," Jayla said as she pushed Slim. "Why you have Meka waitin' on you like that?"

"I don't know what'chu talkin' 'bout."

"Why you standin' there lyin' wit' that stupid smirk? Just get outta my face 'fore I slap you!"

Jayla pushed Slim with excessive force before she went back to the couch. He followed her, and stood behind her as she continued to do Fe Fe's hair angrily.

"I'm sorry, Jay."

"It's too late for that! 'Cause I told you to leave her alone. I don't have company over here for you to do whatever you wanna do wit' them."

"For real, you don't need friends that be gettin' loose like that. I mean, I was tryin' to holla at her, but I didn't know she was waitin' on me wit' no clothes on."

"Don't tell me what I need! I'm smart enough to make my own decisions! And she musta called you, 'cause I didn't say nothin' about her not havin' clothes on! And you gon come in here like you didn't know nothin'," Jayla said before she rolled her eyes at Slim.

"Aiight Jay, I'm givin' you my word now. I ain't gon' mess wit' Meka if you don't want me to," Slim promised.

"I don't care what'chu do. You just bet'not bring her over here!"

"I still love you, Jay," Slim said before he stole a kiss from her cheek.

"Don't be puttin' yo' dog smellin', alcoholic lips on me," Jayla whined as she brushed her cheek with her shoulder. She then threw a comb at Slim as he left.

Meka heard the thunderous bass from Slim's car as he pulled in front of her house. She opened the door just as he was approaching her porch. She peeked outside, surprised that he actually came.

"It took you long enough," Meka smirked as she stepped back and opened the door for Slim.

Slim shook his head up and down as he came in. He stood behind Meka and looked her up and down, admiring her curvy body while she locked the door. She wore no socks or shoes with nylon shorts that fitted loosely and rode up her thighs. When she turned around, she smiled at him as he continued to check her out. It was obvious that she wore no bra with the white tank-top.

"I see you ready," Slim said as he came closer to Meka.

"You had me ready since the first day I seen you," Meka said as she threw her arms around Slim's neck.

"Take me to yo' room," Slim said as he gave Meka a fierce slap on her ass.

Slim's intentions were to put it on Meka, and get back on the grind. But his intentions changed once he began to put it on her. In the midst of him laying the pipe, she cried out some of the most submissive things to him. It was those cries that changed his intentions with her.

When Slim came from the bathroom, Meka was still laying on her back. He dropped a hot and soapy towel on her stomach before he got dressed. He then fired up a blunt and sat on the bed while she got dressed.

"You cool," Slim asked as Meka laid under him.

"You was tryin' to kill me, but I liked it," Meka said as she looked up to Slim with a smile.

"Who all stay here wit'chu?"

"Just me and my mama. She think she hip."

"She don't be trippin' off you havin' company?"

"No, but I don't be havin' nobody over here. Just my boyfriend."

"Yo' boyfriend, huh. What's up wit him?"

"He a pretty boy and a square. But I like him, 'cause he do whatever I tell him to do. But what's up wit'chu, why you questionin' me?"

"'Cause, I might want'chu to hold somethin' for me," Slim said before he passed Meka the blunt.

"I'll do it," Meka said excitedly as she sat up.

"You don't even know what it is," Slim said with a laugh.

"I don't care what it is. If I got somethin' of yours, that mean you'll have to always come and see me."

Slim shook his head from side to side as he realized just how much Meka was caught up on him. "So, how much you want for holdin' my stash?"

"I just want'chu to keep puttin' it on me," Meka said as she climbed into Slim's lap.

"I can do that. Lemme go get this shit, and I'll be right back."

"I'm finna take anotha shower, so leave the door unlocked."

When Slim came back to Meka's house, she was just coming from the bathroom as he was going into her room. He showed her what was what before he stashed four of his ounces under her dresser. He then waited for her on the porch while she got dressed. He'd just finished rolling a blunt when she sat next to him on the steps.

Slim and Meka talked for almost an hour. She was open and honest with him, and that made him feel comfortable about his spontaneous decision.

"Here come my mama," Meka said as a car parked behind Slim's.

Meka's mother surprised Slim when she got out of her car. She and Meka looked so much alike that they could easily pass for sisters. Her mother was only a few inches taller, thicker, and had shorter hair. The sun that twisted her face showed two solid golds on the sides of her two front teeth.

What really surprised him was the blue uniform she had on. It made him regret his spontaneous decision.

"Why you ain't tell me yo' mama was the police," Slim asked as he looked to Meka, then back to her mother.

"Boy, she ain't no police! She work at the City Jail," Meka said with a laugh.

As Meka's mother continued to approach the house, she shifted her eyes to the grass where Slim dumped the tobacco from his blunt. She stopped at the bottom of the steps as she continued to study it.

When she made out what it was, she looked up to Slim and Meka with a frown.

"Now, who dumped this shit in my grass?"

"My bad. I'll get it up," Slim calmly said as he was trying to conceal his nervousness.

"And who is you?"

"Slim… I'm Slim."

"Don't 'chu know Meka ain't nothin' but fifteen?"

"Yeah. But I ain't nothin' but sixteen."

"Sixteen! And is that'cho car parked in my space?"

"I'll move it," Slim said as he stood up and tried to leave.

"Don't try to run off now! Sit back down, 'cause I ain't through wit'chu," Meka's mother said as she stepped up closer to them..

Slim shook his head from side to side with a slight smile as he sat back down.

"Mama, leave him alone! This Jayla brotha," Meka intervened.

"You shut'cho fast ass up! And no wonder why you stay yo' hot ass around there!"

"No, it's not," Meka said as she rolled her eyes at her mother.

"Don't make me embarrass yo' pissy ass in front of yo' company," Meka's mother threatened before she turned to Slim. "Now, where you work at?"

Slim chuckled as he knew the indirect question was to expose what was obvious.

"Like I thought. You got'cho hands in out here."

Slim expected Meka's mother to run him off, but he was about to be surprised.

"Well, I'm Cocoa, and Meka don't run nothin' over here. This is my house," she said as she looked to Meka, then back to Slim. "It's all good though. Sell me some of that shit y'all been smokin' on. Wit ch'all high ass."

Slim stared at Cocoa for a moment with surprise. "Can we go in?"

"C'mon," Cocoa said as she led the way.

Slim followed Cocoa into the house with Meka behind him. "Gimme somethin' to put it in," Slim said as he sat at the counter.

Meka sat on the stool next to Slim with her head resting on her arm that stretched across the counter. Cocoa handed him a sandwich bag as she stood on the other side of the counter. He gave her a quarter of his last ounce of weed.

"This smell like summa that good," Cocoa said as she held the bag up to her nose. "How much you want for this?"

"You cool," Slim said as he snatched his vibrating beeper from his hip.

"Thank you, and I'll see you around," Cocoa said as she left the kitchen.

"I'ma holla at'chu later," Slim said.

"I know," Meka said with a smile before she walked Slim to the door.

Slim left feeling comfortable with leaving his dope there. It was Cocoa's cool character as she seemed to welcome him around.

A week had gone by and Slim still hadn't heard anything from Peach. When he got down to his last three ounces, he reached out to Nikki Pooh. It was strictly business between them with no riddles or metaphors. Early that next morning, he stashed nine ounces under Meka's dresser. As he was leaving, Cocoa came into the kitchen. He spoke to her, but she only responded with a nod before she went into the refrigerator.

That Saturday morning, he slept well into the afternoon. Before he left his father's house, Jayla made him promise to take her and Fe-Fe to the movies later on that night.

As Slim was pulling up at Sharon's house, he noticed that someone was sitting in his spot at the window. The sun created a glare on the window, so he couldn't see who it was. Whoever it was, they left the window as he was coming up the steps. He held onto his pistol that was tucked on his waist as he continued up the steps. When Slim got to the door, it came open. He relaxed when he saw who it was. It was Peach. She was dressed in a pink thermal, blue stretch pants and her house shoes. Her hair went behind her ears and laid on her back. Her appearance struck him as odd. Even though he was happy to see her, he showed no signs of it.

"Is you gon' let me in?" he smirked.

Peach stared at Slim as she held the door. She was looking for some type of reaction, or sign that gave away his feelings. She got nothing.

"I'm sorry," Peach said as she stepped back and opened the door.

When Slim came in, Sharon rose from the couch and left with a smile. He was quite sure that she shared her theory with her daughter about how he felt. He shook his head from side to side as he sat his things on the table.

After locking the door, Peach sat next to Slim facing him She stared at him with a sorrowful expression as she held her hands between her legs.

"What's up?" Slim asked as he looked at Peach.

"I did what'chu wanted me to do. And I'm sorry for runnin' off like that. My feelings was hurt, and I needed to get away to get my head together," Peach softly spoke.

"Did you?"

"I did. I mostly thought about how I feel about'chu, and I don't wanna force nothin' on you that'll bring conflict between us. I told you I just wanna be down wit'chu, and that means acceptin' things about'chu, even if I don't like 'em," Peach said as she brushed the lining of Slim's hair with her finger tips.

It was her soft touch that Slim missed. He wanted to kiss Peach's sweet lips and tell her how he felt about her while he wrapped her in his arms. Something he was unaware of was holding him back.

"Yeah, I ain't feelin' that conflict between us. And my bad, I could've handled things betta wit'chu."

Slim's apologetic response touched Peach as her face lit up with a smile. She then kissed his lips. When their kiss ended, he shifted his eyes to her thermal.

"Why you got that hot-ass thermal on?"

"'Cause you might be mad at me," Peach sweetly said with a guilty smile as she dropped her head.

Slim looked at Peach in confusion as he had no idea of what she was talking about.

"Stop lookin' at me like that," Peach whined.

"Why would I be mad 'cause you got that hot-ass thermal on? You must be tryin' to hide somethin'. What, you been lettin' some nigga suck on you?"

"Slim, don't play wit' me," Peach said as she pushed him. "I told you, ain't no other nigga gon' touch me but'chu."

"You know what, that's on you if you wanna burn up. You just look hella dumb," Slim said with a laugh as he reached for his blunt.

"So!"

Slim shrugged his shoulders before he lit his blunt.

"Umm You know how I feel about'chu, and it ain't no secret. Plus, you said you don't have a problem wit' me showin' it," Peach reminded Slim. "So, I hope you don't be mad when I show you this," she said before she pulled her thermal off.

Peach was topless as she stared at Slim with a smile. His eyes were instantly drawn to her left breast. His name was tatted in fancy cursive. He was astounded as he stared at it with his mouth open.

"Baby, do you like it?"

Slim shifted his eyes to Peach, then back to the tatt as he licked his two fingers. He then rubbed it.

"It's real," Peach said as she slapped Slim's hand.

"I see, and I could never be mad at that. I like it."

"I got anotha one," Peach proudly said as she turned her wrist over.

Slim shook his head in disbelief as he stared at the tatt with a smile. It was exactly like the one on her chest. before he could say anything, Peach surprised him with another tatt.

"I got anotha one," Peach said as she turned her back to Slim.

Slim wrinkled his forehead as he stared at the more alluring tatt. It was on her lower back, just above her ass. His name was boldly tatted in capital, English letters with dark ink. Her name was tatted in lower cased English letters with red ink. The first letter in her name was in front of the first letter in his name. Her name was spelled out through his name, and ended with the last letter in her name behind the last letter in his name. It was a perfect fit. Then there were fancy lines that swirled on the sides and the bottom of the tatt. It gave the tatt a classy look.

"Baby, see how my name playin' the background and on the sides of yo' name that's standin' out? That mean, I'ma always be on yo' side, even when you don't see me," Peach explained as she looked over her shoulder to Slim. "But wait a minute, I got one mo' to show you," she said as she sat on his lap. Peach gathered her hair to expose the back of her neck. There was another tatt there just like the ones on her wrist and neck.

Slim was past astounded. He was blown away from Peach's gesture showing that she worshipped him. But not even that could pull him away from what was restraining him from expressing his true feelings for her.

"I like how you representin' me," Slim said before he kissed Peach's lips. "Now, I want'chu to go put on some clothes that show off yo' tatts. I'm takin' you wit' me."

Peach looked at Slim side-ways as she was expecting a more intimate response from him. After a moment, she shook her head in disbelief as she knew that he was holding back. She tried to get up from his lap bu he held her there. When she turned to him, she got an unexpected passionate kiss. It was a kiss that expressed his true feelings for her. She could feel it, but she wanted to hear it from his mouth.

It took Peach almost two hours to get herself together, but it was worth the wait. She was stunningly beautiful and Slim was more than proud to have this vivacious diva by his side.

Before Slim picked up Jayla and Fe-Fe, he took care of those who paged him. He had Peach by his side, familiarizing her with everybody. His clientele spreads all over the city and county. Having Peach to take care of some of them would make things efficient. She needed her own car though.

When Slim finally got to his father's house, Jayla and Fe-Fe was sitting on the porch. They were both dressed in their designer clothes with their hair and nails done. Jayla had been calling him with her feisty attitude because he was late, so he knew that he was about to hear more of it. He took his pistol from his lap and slid it under his seat as they were approaching his car.

"Do you want me to get in the back?" Peach asked with a sly smile. She was trying to get Slim to expose how special she was to him. He knew what she was doing, but wasn't going to let her open him up like that. He shrugged his shoulders as he looked at her like it didn't matter. She rolled her eyes at him before she let the seat up for Jayla and Fe-Fe to get into the back. She just knew that she was special.

Jayla stood outside of the car with her hands on her hips as she stared at Peach. Peach looked for Slim to speak up, but he only sat there with a smile. After Fe-Fe said something to Jayla, they climbed into the back seat. Jayla rolled her eyes at Slim as he watched her in the rear-view mirror with a teasing smile. He turned the light on before he turned to her.

"You look nice, and I like yo' 'fit," Slim said as he looked Jayla up and down with a smile.

"Don't try to be friendly wit' me! I should punch you for hangin' up on me," Jayla said as she jumped at Slim with her fist.

Slim shook his head up and down with a smile as he turned to Fe-Fe. "You lookin' good too. What's up?"

"Thank you. And I'll look even betta when you fire somethin' up wit' me."

"I got'chu," Slim said before he introduced everyone. Peach spoke to them with politeness, and Fe-Fe greeted her with the same politeness. Jayla only gave an effortless wave.

"Is that'cho real hair," Fe-Fe curiously asked as she stared at Peach.

"It's real," Peach replied with a smile as she ran her fingers through her ponytail. "I like yo' hair. Where you get it done at?"

"My cousin did this."

"Where her shop at?" Peach asked with a lively interest.

"This my cousin right here," Fe-Fe said as she looked to Jayla, then back to Peach.

"How much you charge? Can we exchange numbers," Peach sweetly asked.

"I don't really do hair, but we can talk," Jayla said with a nonchalant attitude. She was actually flattered.

Slim had the door open, dumping the tobacco from the blunt onto the ground. He was aware of what was going on inside the car, and admired how Peach was working her charm on Jayla.

Jayla's eyes bubbled when Peach handed her the number. "Girl, why you let my brotha make you get his name on yo' wrist," she abruptly asked.

"He didn't make me do this," Peach said with a laugh. "I surprised him wit' this. I got three more. On my neck, my chest, and on my back," she proudly added.

"You shouldn't have did that, 'cause now he really finna think he somebody," Jayla said as she pushed the back of Slim's head.

"I want him to feel like that. That's why I got 'em."

Slim winked at Jayla, who was shaking her head at him.

When they got to the Northland Cinema, the parking lot was jammed packed. It was another hang out spot for the young crowd. They sat on cars, drinking and smoking weed while music blasted everywhere. Girls mingled around in flocks, gravitating towards the freshest, and ignored the unfortunate. Slim walked behind Peach, Jayla and Fe-Fe, who strutted as though they were the hottest on the planet. When they got inside, Slim went along with what they chose to see. They bought all kinds of junk food, and made him pay for everything.

The movie was just beginning when they made it into the theatre. Slim took his hat off and sat it in the empty seat next to him. He then sat in a slump and laid his head on Peach's chest. He made himself comfortable with his leg hanging over the arm rest. The movie that they were watching didn't interest him, so he eventually fell asleep.

It seemed like fifteen minutes later when Slim felt someone shaking him.

"Baby, wake up," Peach said as she continued to shake Slim. When Slim opened his eyes, the movie was just beginning to run its credits, and everyone was leaving. He got up and stretched before he followed Peach, Jayla and Fe-Fe out.

In the lobby, Slim caught the eyes of an older girl. She took in his appearance before she turned her head away. She had a pretty, thick face with a caramel skin complexion. Her hair was in a sagging ponytail that extended pass the middle of her back. She looked like she was mixed with something foreign. She wore a sophisticated outfit that revealed her sensual figure. Slim thought she looked out of place at Northland with its young and rowdy crowd.

When Slim got outside with Peach, Jayla and Fe-Fe, the night was still filled with its activities. It actually looked more crowded. When they got to his car, Peach noticed that he didn't have his hat. After a moment, he remembered where he left it and found it still in the empty seat he previously had been sitting int. As he was leaving the theatre, he was looking down at a page that came through his beeper. At the exit of the theatre, he came to a stop as some pretty toes stood in front of him. He slowly rose his head as he examined every curve on this breathtaking body. It was the out of place older girl who gave him the eye.

"What's up? You lose somethin' too?" Slim asked.

"No. I think I found something, but I don't know if I'll be able to keep it," she properly spoke with softness.

"What's yo' name?"

"Carmen."

"I'm Slim, and I can assist you wit gettin' yo' hands on what'chu found," he said as he stepped closer to Carmen.

"I like the sound of that. So, when will you be able to assist me?"

"I'ma put'cho number in my beeper, and get wit'chu ASAP," Slim said as he dialed his beeper number.

Slim put Carmen's number into his beeper as she called it out to him.

"I hope you can be available soon," Carmen said with a flirtatious smile before she turned to leave.

Slim shook his head up and down as he watched Carmen leave. When her sensual figure was out of his sight, he continued on. Slim was locking Carmen's number in his beeper as he headed to his car. When he looked up, he caught the scandalous eyes of two dudes. They were in front of him on his right.

He looked at them with suspicion as they walked in between the cars. When they met him at the end of the cars, he shifted his eyes to their hands, then back to them with his face twisted. One of the dudes held a .38 revolver down to his side.

"Yeah, derty. You already know what time it is! Take all that jewelry off, and empty yo' fuckin' pockets," the dude with the pistol ordered.

Slim couldn't believe the audacity of the clowns. They were robbing him with no regards to the crowded environment. It was ironic, because everyone appeared to be caught up in the excitement. After a few seconds, he slowly pulled a ring from his finger and dropped it to the ground. His robbers were agitated from his stalling, and ordered him to hurry up. He twisted his face at them before he began to take his other ring off. Soon after, several loud claps filled the air.

Slim stumbled backwards, feeling on his chest as he looked down to it with his face twisted. He then looked to his hands, expecting to see blood, but there was none. When he looked to the two dudes, they were curled on the ground, clutching their stomach.

"Baby c'mon!" Slim heard a familiar voice shout to him. When Slim looked to his side, he saw Peach. She was standing bare foot with her hot .380 down to her side. He moved quickly as he picked up his ring and made his way to his car. The parking lot was now in a disarray. Screams and screeching tires as people moved quickly to get away from the gun fire were all that was heard.

When Slim got into his car, he abruptly pulled off before he had the door closed. He carefully whipped his car around the jams before he made it to the busy street. His only concerns were to get away from the chaos, and get Jayla and Fe-Fe home safely. He kept his cool composure, making sure that he obeyed all traffic signs. They all rode in silence as they watched the police cars fly past them. When they got onto the highway, he began to relax and fully process everything.

"What's up? Y'all cool back there?" Slim asked.

"Yeah we cool. Fire somethin' up," Fe-Fe answered. Seeing someone shot up was nothing new to her.

Jayla only shook her head up and down as she continued to stare out of the window.

"I'm sorry y'all had to see that," Peach said as she looked back to Jayla and Fe-Fe.

Slim wasn't sorry for seeing Peach get down for him though. It made him think about everything she'd been expressing to him. It all coincided with her actions. He thought about the tatt on her lower back, and what she said it meant. She proved it to be true as she was by his side, even when he didn't notice her. It was her vigilance and her sacrifice that broke through whatever it was that was restraining him from letting himself go with her. She got him!

Slim looked over to Peach with a smile as he shook his head up and down. She rolled her eyes at him as she knew that he was about to come with it. She was a little disappointed that it took for her to shoot people for him to submit to what he felt for her.

After dropping Jayla and Fe-Fe off and making sure that they were safe inside, Slim continued on up to Sharon's house and parked. He turned the car off and leaned over to Peach with his arm resting on the headrest behind her.

"I shouldn't be surprised, huh," Slim softly spoke.

"No," Peach said as she rolled her head.

"I been knowin' what it was wit'chu, so I ain't surprised," Slim said before he grabbed Peach's hand. "You told me that'chu think I would deserve and appreciate yo' commitment. At that time, I was caught up on gettin' money, but'chu seen past that. You got me. Wit' everything you showed me, how can I not be serious about'chu. That's somethin' I said we was gon deal wit' if it ever came to this point. You told me that'chu accept everything about me, and I hope that don't change. I just want'chu to let me do me. Wit' me doin' me, I'ma always respect yo' feelings and make accommodations for you. Wit' us bein' serious, you got the authority to get in my face when I fuck up. I'm clamin' you as mine, and I want'chu to claim me as yours. Not only do I want'chu by my side, Peach, I need you by my side. I'm seriously feelin' you, and I don't wanna jump to conclusions, but'chu givin' me more than enough reasons for me to tell you, I'm in love wit'chu," he spoke with sincerity before he kissed her lips.

"I don't think you'll be jumpin' to conclusions. I feel it wit'chu. I was just waitin' on you to tell me, and you knew I was waitin'. Yo' words touched me. Slim, I will always accept everything about'chu, and have yo' best interest at the same time. I got'chu," Peach softly spoke before they shared a more passionate kiss.

"Let's go in, and I just want'chu to let me do me," Slim said as he looked into Peach's eyes with a passion like never before.

When they got inside, Slim led Peach to her room by her hand. He turned their phones off along with his beeper. This was an occasion where he was going to give her his undivided attention. He gently undressed her, and admired her body as if it was his first time seeing it. His touches were as if she was fragile and sacred. He then laid her on her back and undressed himself. His hands caressed her tender body with admiration as he licked and kissed his way down to her pelvis. It's where he stopped and savored the sweet heat that came from between her thighs. He looked to her with his passion in his eyes and moistened his lips. She bit one side of her bottom lip as she made herself more accessible for him. He was about to taste her sweet insides. He gently parted her hot, moist lips with his two fingers before he sent his tongue inside. He was an amateur guided by passion alone. She let him do him as she softly moaned with enjoyment. He then made love to her until the sun came up.

Before Slim went to sleep, Peach asked him about his reluctance to open his heart to her, even when he knew that she was the truth. She knew that it was more behind his opposition towards a serious relationship other than his focus on getting money. She was speaking as though he had issues. As they talked about it, the first girl he gave his heart to came to his mind. It was her who placed those restraints on his heart. Their abrupt separation affected him more than he realized. Peach understood when he told her about Angel.

Chapter 13:   Reunited

Slim woke up late that afternoon in Peach's bed. He laid naked and alone. He stared up at the ceiling as he thought about the day before. A slight smile spread across his face as he shook his head from side to side. He then thought about the day ahead of him, and what he needed to do.

Slim first turned his beeper back on. As soon as he turned his beeper on, it vibrated, making him aware of his missed pages. He flipped through the numerous pages before he called Pooch. While Slim was talking with Pooch, Peach came into the room. He was taken by her as he continued to talk. She was dressed in extra short, pink cotton shorts and a tank-top. She was carrying a plate with two burritos and a cup of juice. With her wild ponytail, she had a blunt behind her ear. It was her careless appearance that he was taken by as he thought it was sexy. He finished his conversation just as she sat next to him.

"What up, baby?" Peach softly spoke as she handed Slim the juice.

"I'm good. What's up wit'chu?" Slim responded before he took a sip from the juice. He then sat it on the night stand and took the plate from Peach.

"My mama gave me six hundred for you. She ran through whatever you gave her, so I got them three ounces from the car. I wiped that burna down and got rid of it too."

Slim shook his head up and down as he continued to eat. "Jay called me too. She was tryin' to call you. I asked her if she wanted me to wake you up, but she just told me to tell you to come home when you got up."

"I'ma go get'chu anotha burna, and I'ma go see what's up wit Jay. I need to go get some mo' dope too, but I'ma come back before I go holla at everybody that's been hittin' me. You can do yo' thing wit' them three ounces though."

Peach shook her head up and down as she put her arm around Slim. She wiped the sleep from his eyes with her wet fingertips while he continued to eat.

When Slim finished eating, Peach lit his blunt for him while he got dressed. He then collected his things from the night stand and took the blunt she held out to him.

"Love you," Peach said before she kissed Slim's lips.

"Love you too," Slim said before he returned Peach's kiss.

After Slim got another .380 and a quarter pound of weed from Pooch, he went home. From the unfamiliar car that was parked in front of the house, he figured that his father had company. When Slim came into the house, his father was sitting on the couch with his sister, Auntie Keda. He was explaining some real estate business to her from a piece of paper. His father looked to him followed by Auntie Keda. She still had a shiny, open faced gold on her front tooth, and looked as though she hadn't aged a bit. Slim stared at his favorite aunt with his glistening smile.

"Boy! Look at'chu," Auntie Keda excitedly said as she jumped up from the couch and rushed towards Slim. "I heard about'chu out here showin' yo' ass, but damn," she said as she hugged him.

Auntie Keda didn't even give Slim a chance to receive her with open arms. She wrapped him with her thick arms and squeezed as she rocked him from side to side.

"Look at'chu," Auntie Keda said as she stood back while holding Slim's hands.

Auntie Keda knew that her nephew was in the game from his appearance. He shrugged with a smile as he looked to himself.

"You still terrorizing shit?"

"I'm still me. How you been?"

"You still talk wit' them slurs wi' cho grown ass! I been alright Dealin' wit Fe-Fe's fast ass, and that Nut. He got his crazy ass downstairs."

As soon as Auntie Keda said that Nut was downstairs, Slim's face lit up with excitement. "Straight up! He out?"

"Yeah And y'all bet'not start no shit!"

"Aiigh, lemme go see what's up wit him," Slim said before he turned to his father. "What's up, old man?"

"You got it. Them plates came back. They on my bed wit' that driver's book. Get on top of that." Donnell told his son.

"I'ma get it togetha." Slim replied.

"And I still be havin' my card games, too. Come through and let me win summa that money. The fam gon' be there too," Auntie Keda said.

"I ain't got no money, but I'ma come and see what's up wit my peoples though," Slim said with a laugh as he continued on.

Auntie Keda shook her head from side to side as she watched Slim continue on. She knew that it was about to be some chaos now that the infamous two were reunited with no restraints.

"There he go right there," Fe-Fe said when she noticed Slim.

"Cuz!" Nut excitedly said as he jumped up from the couch. Slim stopped at the bottom of the steps and shook his head up and down while rubbing his hands together with a mischievous smirk. It was his and Nut's infamous trademark. They used to always do it when they were little. It meant, they did something, or they were about to do something. Nut did the same thing as he came towards Slim.

Nut had the same peanut butter complexion as Slim with a 5'11, natural gorilla build. His hands and arms were filled with tattoos that represented the streets. He and Slim also had the same sleepy brown eyes and talked with the same slurs.

They could easily pass as brothers with their hairless face and light mustache. Instead of the typical braids, Nut had thick waves with a fresh fade.

"What's up, nigga?" Slim greeted Nut with excitement. They did the hood clap and pulled each other in for a hug with excessive force.

"Nigga, you what's up! You got hella big, and I heard you been out here gettin' it," Nut said as he took a step back from Slim.

"We finna get it together! I'ma see what's up wit' Jay, and I'ma get in the water right quick. Just gimme a minute."

Jayla and Fe-Fe were watching Slim and Nut with smiles as they shook their heads from side to side.

"What's up, Jay," Slim asked as he sat next to her. "Peach said you told me to come home."

"I just wanted to tell you, Tehran was over here," Jayla said as she looked to Nut, then back to Slim.

"You cool?"

"Yeah, I'm cool."

"You sure?" Slim double checked.

"Yeah! Just stop turnin' yo' phone off," Jayla said as she pushed Slim. "And Auntie Keda musta been kissin' on you, 'cause you got lipstick all over yo' face," she added with a laugh.

"It's all good," Slim said as he rose from the couch.

After a quick shower, Slim got dressed in some of his flyest gear with his jewelry. Be then left the house with Nut. When they got outside, he switched plates and took the tops off of his car. Nut sat in on the passenger side, bobbing his head to the music. He was listening to, Tupac, "No More Pain", and smoking on a blunt that Slim had sitting in the ashtray. When Slim got into the car, Nut turned the music down, continuing to bob his head while he pulled on the blunt.

"That's two grand," Slim said as he handed Nut a thick roll of money. He then went under his seat and gave him one of the four ounces of weed.

"I'll feel hella crazy if I thanked you for this. Ain't shit changed wit' us. You made it there before me, but'chu know I'll play it the same way if I had yo' hands."

"I'm knowin' what it is, and I'm tryin' to see you wit'cho hands in, too. I know you ain't gon lemme do it by myself."

"C'mon, nigga! You know I'm wit'chu!"

"I got' chu," Slim said before he began to dial Meka's number. After only a few rings, he got an answer, but couldn't tell if it was Meka or Cocoa. "Can I speak to Meka?" he asked in confusion.

"This me," Meka sweetly said.

"I'm finna come through. Where Cocoa?"

"She just left. I'm on the porch wit' my cousin."

"Aiight," Slim said before he clicked his phone off.

When Slim pulled in front of Meka's house, she was sitting on the steps with her cousin. He squinted at her cousin, and became surprised when he made out who she was. It was a girl who he had something to prove to. She embarrassed him, and left him without the opportunity to redeem himself.

It was Kandi, but then, there was his thing with Meka. Even though his thing with Meka held no exclusive obligations, he had to be discreet with how he got at Kandi. He didn't want to create any conflict with Meka holding his stash. He turned the music down and turned to Nut when he parked.

"Ay Cuz, that's Kandi and Meka on the porch. I got Meka holdin' me down, but I need to get at Kandi. She the redbone, and I want'chu to get at her for me. I'm just tryin' to get her number, and get at her when I figure somethin' out."

"I got'chu," Nut said before he and Slim got out of the car. As Slim and Nut were approaching the house, Kandi looked Slim up and down astonished. The last time she saw him, he was just an ordinary dude. He was now stunning as he moved towards her. Meka rose from the steps as they came up.

"Jevon… I mean, Slim… this my cousin, Kandi," Meka said, taking her eyes from him.

Slim figured if Meka told Kandi about him, it was by Jevon, because Kandi was too surprised.

"What's up?" he spoke to Kandi.

Kandi was staring up at Slim, and only moved her lips with a squeak.

"This my peoples, Nut," Slim said before he looked at Meka. "Let's go in right quick," he said as he took the lead into the house. "I just came to grab somethin', but I'ma fuck wit'chu later."

"You always say that," Meka whined as she followed Slim up the steps.

Slim knew that he had to satisfy Meka, but his day was too busy. She took four of his nine ounces from his stash. He tried explaining to her why he couldn't stay but she wasn't trying to hear it though. She desperately wanted him to put it on her, but reluctantly accepted the rejection.

When Slim and Meka came back onto the porch, Nut and Kandi immediately stopped talking. Kandi shifted her eyes to Nut, then back to Slim as if she was trying to tell him something. He followed Nut to the car, figuring that it was all good.

"What's up?" Slim asked as he and Nut got into the car.

"It's all good. I ain't have to shoot shit at Kandi. She gave me her number for you, and said she ain't trippin' off yo' thing wit' Meka," Nut said as he gave Slim a small piece of paper. "She was on some shit like, she know you don't want things to end how they ended. What's up wit' that?"

Slim shook his head from side to side with a laugh before he pulled off. He then told Nut about that embarrassing incident with Kandi.

"Yeah cousin, you can't let her go," Nut said with a laugh.

When Slim parked in front of Sharon's house, he turned his car off and pulled his pistol from under his seat. He then sat in a slump with it on his lap. Nut shook his head up and down as he seen that his cousin was on point in the streets.

"I'ma give you two ounces to do yo' thing wit. after that, I'ma let'chu get 'em two for fifteen. That's all I can do right now. But when the homeboy get back, I can tie you wit' him on a quarter thang, plug for forty-five. He don't move nothin' less than that, so we gon get'chu there."

"I'm wit'chu, and I'll be through wit' them two zips by the morning"

"Aiight. This my spot right here, and we could break this shit down in here. I need to go get at everybody that's been hittin' me, then I'ma stop by yo' ol' bird spot and see what's up wit' the fam."

"Everybody 'pose to be over there. They gon' be fucked up when they see you, especially us together. But when we leave there, I'ma take you to the hood. That' s where I'ma be doin my thing at."

"You need a burna?" Slim checked.

"I got hella burnas."

"Aiight. Grab that weed and that burna from under yo' seat. That's for Peach."

"I heard about Peach."

"Yeah, that's me. But what's up wit' that static you was jammed up behind?"

"That's dead, "Nut simply implied with a blank expression.

When Slim and Nut came into the house, Peach was dealing with Sharon. Slim sat his things on the table before he pulled a tube sock from his shorts. He had four ounces of crack stacked inside of it. He gave two of them to Nut, who sat across from him. He immediately began to break his dope into all dimes with a safety pin he took from the table. Peach was just finishing up with Sharon, and came over to Slim counting money. She sat it on the table with other wads before she sat next to him.

"That's my peoples, Nut. He already know who you is," Slim said as he looked to Nut, then back to Peach.

Peach spoke to Nut with friendliness, and Nut did the same before he gave his attention back to his dope.

"That's yo burna on the table wit' a ounce of that weed. Leave one out for me, and put the other one up wit' that money."

"I was gon put it up after I counted it."

"We'll count it later, just put it up. I'm finna break this work down, then I'ma go get at everybody. I'ma catch up wit' my peoples after that, so I ain't gon be back 'til later on tonight."

"It's all good. I'ma hold it down for you," Peach said before she collected the things from the table and left.

"Cuz, you doin' yo' thing, and I like how you got Peach holdin' it down for you," Nut said as he continued to break his dope down.

"I'm feelin' her too, and that's why she my girl. I wasn't really feelin' that serious shit, but she let me do me. I respect her, though."

"I'm feelin' where you at. Wit' how we livin', we gotta have some type of honor and respect wit' those we eat and sleep wit. Especially wit' those who gon put it all on the line for us."

Slim shook his head up and down as he was happy to know that Nut had a sensible state of mind, at least for the most important part.

Vee's apartment was Slim's last stop where he got his money. He became more familiar with Nut as they talked. Nut was more experienced with the streets, which made him more knowledgeable than Slim on that issue. He most definitely wanted Nut by his side in the streets as he adamantly expressed that he would be there.

When Slim pulled in front of Auntie Keda's house with his disturbingly loud music, all heads turned. His peoples were packed on the front porch, and on the side walk leaning on cars. Kids ran around playing while one of his uncles barbecued on the side of the house. His father was also there with Jayla and Marcel.

Slim was familiar with most of his family and most of them were familiar with him. He wasn't very close to any of them, though. It was mostly because he was a problem child, and was always locked in his room. He was known as "Wild Child", and no one had seen him in years.

The first person who greeted Slim was a cute little girl. She ran up to him in her new outfit with her arms up while she wiggled her fingers.

"What's up cutie? What's yo' name?" Slim asked as he picked the little girl up.

The little girl was only interested in Slim's shiny jewelry and his sparkling smile. She stared at him for a moment before she began to fiddle with the anchor that dangled from his necklace. The crushed diamonds in it created a magic show that was fascinating to her.

"Cuz, that's Tish's baby, Tionna. That lil' girl hella mean, and I can't believe she all on you like that," Nut said with surprise.

"I guess bad asses do click," a girl said with a laugh as she approached Slim and Nut.

When Slim looked up, his older cousin was standing in front of him. Tish was five feet, petite, and could easily be mistaken for a teenager. He remembered her be the one who always let him out of his locked room.

"What's up, Tish?" Slim spoke with a smile.

"What's up wit'chu? You like sixteen now, right?" Tish asked as she took a step back and looked Slim up and down.

"Yeah, somethin' like that."

"And you and Nut togetha," Tish said as she shook her head in disbelief. "I'ma let'chu catch up wit' the rest of the fam. I'm finna go try to win me some money. I'ma holla at'chu though," she said as she took Tionna and left.

Slim shook his head up and down as he shifted his eyes to Jayla. She was coming from the house with their girl cousins. Neither one of them were older than fifteen, but didn't look like it.

"Here come the Fast Ass Click," Nut said with a laugh. "I'm finna go get me somethin' to eat and see what's poppin'."

Jayla had just approached Slim with their cousins. "Jevon, this Alisha, Niesha, and April."

"I know who they is." Slim remembered the twins for always dressing alike as they thought they were extra special, and April for always being scared of him.

"I never knew yo' name was Jevon. I thought'cho name was Wild Child, and I used to be scared of you," April said as she lightly pushed him.

"I guess you ain't scared no mo', huh," Slim stated with a laugh.

"No," April said as she rolled her eyes.

Slim's intrigued cousins held him there for almost twenty minutes with their questions. He then spoke to the rest of his family as he went into the house.

When Slim came into the loud house, it took him almost thirty minutes to get from the living room to the kitchen. His aunts hugged and kissed on him with their questions as they were all happy to see him. He didn't even get a chance to get a word in before he was passed to the next arms. The love was overwhelming. It was his grandmother that tore him away from everyone and took him into the kitchen.

On the way to the kitchen, Slim passed his brother in the crowded dining room. He was at the table with some of the family playing cards. They were playing deuces wild for three dollars a hand with side bets.

In the kitchen, Slim's grandmother fixed him a plate while she gave him a spiritual talk. When she finished, she kissed his cheek and went back to the card table. She was talking about winning her money back. He chuckled before he began to eat while he leaned against the counter. Slim looked up from his plate when his father came from the basement counting a stack of money.

"Jevon, don't go down there messin' wit'cho uncles on them dice. They some sharks," his father warned as he continued on.

Slim shook his head up and down as he continued to eat. He wasn't too familiar with shooting dice anyway. He was going to see what was going on though. He figured it's where Nut was.

As soon as Slim opened the door to the basement, he was hit by the strong smell of weed. UGK beat at a low tone in the sitting area where everyone mingled. His uncles Geno and Mike were kneeled down in a circle with a few of his older cousins. Nut was also there. His words to the circle were aggressive as he shook the dice with a stack of money in his hand. Beer bottles and bottles of hot cognac sat in the circle while joints were being smoked. He didn't recognize the three young girls who sat on the couch together. They sat quietly with their glasses filled with their favorite drink.

"Cuz, I'll be wit'chu in a minute! These washed up old heads tryin' to bring that penitentiary shit to the streets!

I'm finna shut this shit down," Nut spoke with confidence with his face twisted.

When everyone looked up to Slim, Nut manipulated the dice to roll in his favor. They all turned back to the game just as he was collecting money from the circle.

"Hold on lil' nigga! You need to shoot that shit again," Geno said as he stood over Nut.

"You got me fucked up! You see them dice," Nut barked back at Geno.

"Me and you heads up! I'm finna send yo' young ass back to the block," Geno said as he pushed several twenty dollar bills from a stack he held in his hand.

Nut twisted his face harder as he matched the money Geno put down.

"I see you Wild Child. I ain't surprised," Geno said before he got back into the game.

As Geno kneeled back into the game, he pulled a nickel plated .357 from his shoulder holster. He sat it at his feet and put more money into the game for a side bet. As long as Slim remembered, his uncle was always sharply dressed with a smooth swag. It was him who gave him the name, "Wild Child". He watched the intense game for a moment before he gave his attention to his ringing phone. Its caller ID told him that it was Peach.

Slim couldn't hear Peach's soft voice with the noise level in the basement. He went upstairs where it was just as noisy, so he continued on outside.

While Slim was leaning against his car with Peach on the phone, Tish came and leaned next to him. Peach told him that she "got around to doing *that*", and his next page was coming from her. He didn't understand until he looked at the four-digit number that popped into his beeper. It read, *2535*. She was telling him, she counted the money, and how much they had. After talking with her for a few more minutes, he turned to Tish.

"What's up? You still lookin' thirteen. What'chu been up to?"

"Just workin' and takin' care of my baby. I'm twenty-one though, and my baby three." Tish told him.

"She hella cute."

"She hella bad! And you know you surprised everybody wit'chu showin' up like this. I wasn't surprised, though. I knew you was gon' be a mess when you got loose," Tish said with a laugh.

"Straight up! You think I'ma mess?"

"You know what I mean," Tish said as she gave Slim a light push.

"You still stayin' here?"

"Hell naw! I had to get away from all these bad ass kids. I gotta spot on the south wit' my friend and her lil' boy."

"So, you doin' good?"

"Please! My lil' checks be gone before I get 'em."

"What's up wit'cho baby daddy?"

"He's cool. But he locked up though."

"Geno don't be lookin' out for you?"

"He be tryin' to, but I can't take nothin' from my daddy. Half of these bad ass kids runnin' around here is his. So, if I do take somethin' from him, I'll spend it on my lil' brothas and sistas."

"I wanna give you some money, but somethin' tellin' me that'chu won't take it," Slim said as he put his hands into his pockets.

"That's just how I am," Tish said as she folded her arms across her chest. "But'chu can front me some work. I know what I'm doin'."

"You just know I got my hands in, huh," Slim said with a laugh.

"C'mon nigga I know about the game. Don't let this pretty, innocent look throw you off," Tish said with a sassy attitude.

"Well, you gotta sit'cho stubborn attitude to the side, 'cause I ain't finna front'chu shit. You my peoples, and if I'm in a position to assist you, I'ma do it wit' no strings attached. Now, that's just how I am."

"I can't argue wit' that," Tish said with a smile.

"Get in right quick."

When Slim got into his car with Tish, he gave her a bag full of rocks. "That's all I got on me right now. That's like a lil' bit over a ounce. When you run through that, I can let'chu get two for fifteen "

"This hella cool. I can pop these off in my buildin'. And I'll be back to re-up wit'chu, so let me get'cho numba." While Tish was going into her purse, Slim noticed that she was packing a .38 snub nose. She could easily be underestimated from her childish look. It gave logic to why she carried the pistol. After she took his number, he locked hers in his beeper.

"I gotta go to work in the mornin', but keep yo' head up and we gon' get togetha." Tish told hime.

"Aiight."

Just as Tish was getting out of the car, Nut was getting in. He pulled a chrome .50 caliber from his pants and sat it on his lap before he looked over to Slim.

"Cuz, Geno got me," Nut said as he shook his head from side to side.

"What's up wit' Unc and 'nem?"

"They some penitentiary, cutthroat, dope jackin' ass killas! You can't take shit from 'em though, 'cause they 'bout what they 'bout. Them three hoes that's down there, Geno pimpin' 'em. He still gettin' it while he on parole. He don't give a fuck though. He just left my 'ol dude in the joint. He got all day in that bitch," Nut said before he lit his blunt.

Slim shook his head from side to side as he realized, he came from a family of hood people. It was in his blood.

"But ay, I'm tryin' to get it," Nut said before he directed Slim to his hood.

Chapter 14: Let's Get It

Nut directed Slim to some apartment complexes. The three-story buildings were spaced out with balconies, and had their own parking lot. A narrow road connected them and ran into a dead end. The night was filled with various types of illicit activities. Hustling, smoking weed and drinking hard liquor were some of the things that were happening under the dim street lights. The bright orange that majority of everyone wore lit up the night. Slim had never seen so many Six Duces and Kitchen Crips in one spot. This secluded area on the North Side was a part of Nut's hood. He pointed to the first parking lot where he wanted Slim to park.

"Before we slide up in here, I wanna put'chu up on somethin'. But let's step out right quick, 'cause everybody lookin', and wonderin' who we is," Nut said before he got out of the car. As Nut came around to where Slim was leaning on the car, he twisted his fingers into gang sings at his homeboys. Seeing that it was Nut, they twisted their fingers back at him and continued to do what they were doing.

"We finna post up at the homegirl Kiesha spot. She a solid bitch all around the board," Nut said as he passed Slim the blunt. "Her sista, Amil be over here, too. That's who I wanna put'chu up on. She don't fuck wit' nothin' but niggas who be gettin' it, and she gotta clique of young bad bitches under her wings. She be lacin' them hoes on how to trap niggas. I respect her game, though. I just wanna put'chu on point, 'cause I know them hoes gon' see the money." Slim shook his head up and down as he pulled on the blunt.

"Cuz, look how she ridin' off them niggas," Nut said as he shifted his eyes to an up-to-date, gray Benz coupe. "And that's only one of 'em. C'mon."

A 5'8, dark skinned girl who was standing on the first-floor balcony came for the door when she seen Nut coming with Slim. She had a fairly cute face with two French braids to the back. The blue San Diego hat that was pulled just above her cat eyes matched her jersey. Her orange, C-cup bra that could be seen through the jersey stopped at her waist. Blue jean shorts rode up her thick thighs and showed off her bubble booty. Her high top, blue Chucks had fat, orange laces in them. She was reppin' the hood to the fullest. She looked Slim up and down as she pulled on her cigarette.

"What's up, cuz? This my peoples, Slim. And this the home girl, Kiesha," Nut introduced them as he came into the building.

Slim and Kiesha spoke as they all went into the apartment. It opened up to a lavish living room where four girls sat on the leather couches. The three younger girls were listening to an exotically beautiful, older girl. Slim figured that she was Amil. She had sparkling diamonds in her ears, around her neck, and on her wrist and fingers. The red designer dress she wore showed off her thick, curvaceous figure. Her proteges were also hot, but they couldn't hold a candle to Amil.

Amil twisted her face at her proteges as they allowed themselves to be distracted by the appealing stranger. Her teachings were not exercised. Their curiosity put him in a dominant position. When Amil cleared her throat, they all took their eyes away from him. However, it was too late. The element of surprise showed their obvious attraction, and Slim was aware of it all.

"What's up, Nut? Who you got wit'chu," Amil asked as she looked to Slim, then back to Nut.

"My peoples," Nut simply replied.

"Do yo' peoples have a name?"

"I'm Slim. What's up?"

"I just wanted to know who was comin' up in here," Amil said before she turned back to her proteges.

As Slim followed Nut and Kiesha out to the balcony, the silence in the living room made him feel like all eyes were on him. When he came out to the balcony, Nut was calling junkies over to him. He kneeled down to their face and began to talk to them. He told them that he had some dope from Texas along with some more things that got them excited. After giving them all a free dime, he told them that they had to spend their money with him. He then threatened to run them from the hood if he found out that they spent somewhere else.

"I'm finna post up right here and Debo this mu-fucka all night," Nut said as he stood up and surveyed the night with his hungry eyes. After a moment, Nut looked back to Slim, then back to a dude who was approaching the building with a bouquet of roses. The dude was sharply dressed with expensive jewelry on. He didn't wear much of it, but the pieces he wore were extravagant. He was holding his waist as if he was carrying a pistol. Slim figured that he was there for Amil as Kiesha went for the door.

"And that's only one of 'em," Nut said as he sat in one of the chairs.

"Yeah. Ol' girl Amil on her shit," Slim said before he gave his attention to his vibrating beeper. "This my white girl out in Castle Point. I need to go get this money."

"Do what'chu do. Just get at me in the mornin'. I'ma be right here," Nut said as he and Slim clapped hands. When Slim came into the living room, he caught eye contact with Amil. She then shifted her eyes to one of her proteges before she gave her attention back to her dude. Her protege had her eyes on him as she rose from the couch. Amil was putting her on him. He hid his awareness as he continued on towards the door.

"Lemme get that door for you," the girl sweetly said as she came for the door.

Slim was at the door when he stopped and turned to the girl. Her 5'6, petite figure was in a Gucci outfit that showed off her curves. She had a pretty, banana skin complexion with her hair and nails freshly done. When she opened the door, he looked at another page that came through his beeper as he stepped out into the hall.

"You got some pretty hair," the girl said as she came out into the hall and closed the door behind herself.

Slim looked up to the girl as he slid his beeper back into its case.

"My sista gotta shop on Natural Bridge, and I wouldn't mind takin' care of you as one of my personal clients. I'm Fatimah."

Remembering what Nut told him, Slim figured that Fatimah was using her ability to do hair as a tactic to get up on him. He thought it was clever, but he was going to make her shoot harder as he was interested in what the impressive Amil was teaching the young girls.

"I got somebody takin' care of me on that note. Right on though," Slim politely rejected Fatimah.

Fatimah didn't hesitate to take her pursuit to the next level. "That's cool. But why don't we exchange numbers, and you can get at me if you ever wanna be handled wit' a more gentle touch," she softly spoke as she stepped closer to Slim.

"What's the name of yo' sista shop?"

"Diva's."

"Aiight. If I ever have that problem wit' how I'm bein' handled, I'ma come and see you."

"I'm sorry, but we don't accept walk-ins. I'm professional wit what I do, and I like to be prepared."

"In my book, professionals 'are always prepared wit' whatever they do. I see you missin' that page, so you can keep yo' number," Slim said before he left Fatimah speechless.

Later on that night, Slim took his last five ounces and dropped two of them off on Peach. He stashed two of them in his car for Nut, and used the other one to take care of his business with. After taking care of those who paged him, he got at Nikki Pooh.

Slim was up early that next morning to get at Nut. He was going to drop six ounces off at Meka's house first. He left three of them stashed under Peach's dresser to keep him from running in and out of Meka's house. She abruptly hung up on him after he told her that he was coming through. He figured that she was still mad at him for rejecting her yesterday.

He planned on adjusting her attitude with an early morning quickie.

As Slim was pulling up at Meka's house, he noticed that Cocoa's car was still parked there. When he parked, the front door came open. He was expecting Meka to come from the house, but it was Cocoa. He knew that she wasn't on her way to work from her attire. She was dressed in a quarter length robe with her house shoes as she approached his car. He dropped his head and shook it in disbelief as he realized that he was talking to Cocoa instead of Meka. He always got them confused as they sounded alike on the phone. When he looked up, she was reaching for his door handle. After he unlocked the door, she got inside.

"Where Meka?" Slim asked as he watched Cocoa make herself comfortable in the seat.

Cocoa looked at Slim and shook her head in disbelief.

"I know yo' daddy real good, and I can't believe you out here movin' sloppy like this. Did you ever ask yo'self, why I was so cool and welcomed you around? I gave you all the right reasons to feel comfortable, so I can see what was goin' on. Wit' me knowin' how you get down in the streets, do you really think I wasn't gon' watch you? Especially around my baby. Meka sleep, but I need you to tell me what'chu got goin' on wit' her that got'chu runnin' in and outta my house."

Slim was surprised as he recognized his flaws, but he wasn't going to give Cocoa any extra information. "You kinda puttin' me in a awkward position wit' askin' me to tell you 'bout Meka personal business."

"First of all, Meka don't have personal business under my roof. And it's kinda lame for you to insinuate that it's sex, 'cause you come and go in three minutes. Now, stop tryin' to be cute wit' me, 'cause I'm more experienced than you think I am," Cocoa spoke with a calm tone.

"I don't know what to tell you," Slim said as he shrugged his shoulders.

"I just want'cho respect. One of the things you learn in the game is, respect those who deserve it. I'm entitled to that respect, 'cause I respect you, and this is my house. Now, if you have any type of honor wit what'chu 'bout, you wouldn't leave me in the blind wit what'chu got goin' on where I lay my head at."

Slim knew that Cocoa was right. She reminded him of the honor and the respect he held with his father. It was the truth that touched him. He shook his head up and down before he responded. "I'm feelin' where you comin' from wit' the respect thing. I had Meka holdin' somethin' for me, but I'ma respect yo' house and keep it somewhere else."

"I knew that. I just wanted to see if you can recognize wit what's real and be honorable about it," Cocoa said before she took Slim's blunt from the ashtray. Slim shook his head from side to side with a slight smile as he was impressed with how Cocoa got to him. He intriguingly waited on what came next as she kept her cool composure.

"So, how much you givin' my baby to hold yo' dope?" Cocoa asked before she pulled on the blunt.

A slight smile appeared on Slim's face as he thought about what he was giving Meka to hold his dope.

"You know what, don't even answer that, 'cause I see you just workin' yo' lil' charm on my baby," Cocoa said as she passed Slim his blunt. "Like I told you, Meka don't run shit here. This is my house, and she ain't gon be holdin' nothin' for you. If you wanna stash somethin' here, you need to holla at me. Every Saturday, I'ma want two hundred, and a quarta ounce of that weed you gave me."

"That's cool," Slim said after a moment.

"I'ma need that up front, and make sure you keep callin' before you come through."

"I got'chu, but what if you or Meka ain't here?"

Cocoa thought for a moment. "I'ma give you a key, and only use it when ain't nobody here."

"Aiight. I actually came to put somethin' up though."

"That's cool, but lemme drop some game on you right quick," Cocoa said as she turned her body towards Slim. "Stop thinkin' wit'cho dick 'fore it get'chu in a jam. What I'm sayin' is, stop tryin' to capitalize off girls based on them likin' you. Base yo' decisions on their capabilities. My baby ain't ready for this, and I wanna keep it like that. Just think, if I was the police or somebody tryin' to get'chu in a jam, I coulda got up on you through her."

"Right on, I needed that," Slim said, accepting Cocoa's insight.

When they got inside, Slim stashed his dope under Cocoa's dresser. Before he left, she gave him a key, and he gave her what she asked for.

On Slim's way to see Nut, he wondered how Meka could be so gullible with having an experienced mother. He figured that Cocoa didn't see her baby falling for a street nigga. Meka said that her boyfriend was a pretty boy who she controlled. With Cocoa seeing that, she saw no need to lace her baby on how to deal with a street nigga. He knew that was about to change though. Before Slim got to Nut, He got a call from Meka. She apologized to him, and wanted to know if he was mad at her. He told her that it was all good and got her off the phone before she said the wrong things.

Nut was in the same spot with the same clothes on. When he saw Slim coming, he did their infamous trademark. Kiesha came for the door and led him inside. Amil was alone in the living room. She was sitting on the couch looking pretty while she talked on the phone. She put her index finger up for him to wait as she continued to talk. He stopped and looked at Kiesha, who shrugged her shoulders as she continued on out to the balcony. When he turned back to Amil, she was just clicking her phone off. He figured that she was intrigued by him rejecting one of her finest proteges.

"Can you sit down wit' me?" Amil kindly asked before she fired up her blunt.

"As much as I would like to sit down wit'chu, I can't do that. I'm on somethin' right now."

"Why would you like to sit down wit' me?"

"Don't read too much into that. I only meant that as a polite way to tell you, I ain't got time for you."

"I can make time to sit down wit'chu, why don't chu do the same for me."

"What's the point?"

"The purpose of us sittin' down togetha is to find a point."

"I found my point a long time ago."

"If you found yo' point a long time ago, why are you still in the game?"

"Findin' somethin' and gettin' yo' hands on it is two different things."

"I agree wit'chu on that. Now, if you find some time to sit down wit' me, you'll see that I can assist you wit' gettin' yo' hands on whatever it is you tryin' to get'cho hands on," Amil said before she pulled on her blunt.

"I ain't never modest when it comes to acceptin' assistance when I need it. It's who I accept it from that counts."

"I like you. Go see what's up wit' Nut," Amil said before she rose from the couch and left the apartment. When Amil left, Slim stood in confusion for a moment. He then thought about Nut doing their infamous trademark, and figured that it had something to do with her. Kiesha left when he came out to the balcony. Nut was slumped in the chair with his feet up on the rail. He thumped a cigarette butt away and blew the smoke in the air before he turned to Slim.

"What's up?" Slim asked as he sat in the chair next to Nut.

"What'chu think about Amil?"

"I like her, but I don't trust her. She shot one of her proteges at me last night."

"I heard how you shot her down. Fatimah a bad mu-fucka when it come to pullin' niggas, so you know you shook her image up behind that. It wasn't about shit though. Amil was just tryin' to see if you was a gullible nigga," Nut said before he shrugged his shoulders. "As far as what'chu said about Amil, I like the game, but I don't trust it neither. At the same time, I'm so far ahead wit' this street shit, I know how to make the game work for me."

"I'm feelin' that, but what's up," Slim asked before he lit his blunt.

"When you left last night, Amil shot her dude at me. I'ma tell you about this nigga Kerry 'fore I tell you about Amil," Nut said as he took his feet from the rail. "The nigga get to askin' me about my connect, and if it's secure. I'm knowin' where he goin', so I tell him, my connect shaky. He come wit' some shit like, he got quartas for forty-five, and halves for eighty-five. Cuz, the nigga get on some cocky shit and toss me his number like, get at me. I'm shakin' my head like, aiight bitch-ass nigga, I'ma get at'chu."

Slim was slumped in his chair, pulling on his blunt as he knew what Nut wanted to do. He only shook his head up and down as he was waiting to hear about the role Amil played.

"So, soon as the nigga leave, Amil come and sit down wit' me. And cuz, when Amil sit her pretty ass down wit' a nigga, she tryin' to get 'em, or get wit 'em. I'm knowin' what it is, so I open my ears. She come straight out and tell me, she shot the nigga at me. She say she put me in a position to assist her wit gettin' the nigga. She gave me some keys to his house, and claim she don't know where it's at. Amil a smart bitch, so I know she know more than what she puttin' on the table.

Wit' me knowin' how she get down, I'm knowin' that she lookin' for some hungry street niggas that know how to clean up her traps. She gave me the connect wit' the keys to see if I got the game to do the rest. I know she testin' me, 'cause all she want is ten grand. I'm finna get it, and I want'chu to get it wit' me."

Slim quickly realized that he could make this work for him as it would elevate him in the game. "How you wanna do this?"

"We need to find out where the nigga lay his head at first. I'ma tell the nigga, we ain't gon' do no transactions in the hood, 'cause it's too hot. Plus, I don't want the homeboys to jump down on him before we do. I'ma have him to pick a spot where he wanna meet me at. That'll keep him feelin' comfortable wit' thinkin' he in control. When I find out where he want me to meet him at, I'ma let'chu know, and you can take it from there. Once we find out where he lay his head at, we'll go from there."

"I'm wit'chu," Slim said as he slid his vibrating beeper from his hip. "What's up, though? Do you need these two ounces?"

"I just got this quarta thang money I'm finna get at dude wit."

"Aiight, I'm finna go get this money, and I'ma leave Keisha wit' my numba," Slim said as he stood up and clapped hands with Nut.

When Slim got to the parking lot, a light brown '86 Regal was parking next to his car. He thought about Peach when he seen the for-sale sign in the window. She needed a car to handle their business, and to take care of her business. He figured that the dude who got out of the car was from Nut's hood. He was boldly representing with his attire.

"What's up cuz? What'chu want for this?" Slim asked as he looked to the dude, then back to the car.

"Ain't chu Nut peoples?"

"Yeah. I'm Slim."

"I'm Scrap," he said as he did the hood clap with Slim. "Gimme fifteen hundred, and you can get it wit' the beats and the title."

Slim shook his head up and down before he continued to check out the car. The mint condition suede interior was a shade darker than the fresh paint job. After listening to the engine, he had his mind made up.

"Take that sign outta the window. I'll be right back."

When Slim came back with Peach, Scrap was sitting on the trunk of the Regal. He parked next to him and turned the music down before he turned to Peach with a smile.

"Baby, what is you doin'?" Peach curiously asked.

"I think you'll look good in that," Slim said as he looked to the Regal, then back to Peach. "What'chu think?"

Peach looked to the Regal and stretched her neck to get a better look at it. Slim watched her face light up as she covered her mouth with her fingers. Her eyes continuously blinked as her chest went in and out. He was touched to have made her happy and seeing that she was touched by his gift.

"I like it," Peach said as she tried to relax.

"It's yours. C'mon," Slim said before he got out of the car.

Peach stood at the trunk of the car with Slim while he counted out $1,500 to Scrap. After giving him the money, he gave him two sets of keys and the title. He relayed them to Peach, who couldn't wait to get in her new car. Slim talked with Scrap for a few minutes before he joined Peach. When he got into the car, she was bobbing her head to the music as she turned it down.

"Baby, I like this. And I love you for thinkin' about me, 'cause I really needed this."

"I know you did, 'cause I wasn't finna be sittin' in no beauty salons wit'chu all day," Slim said with a laugh.

"C'mere," Peach sweetly said, making a gesture with her finger.

Slim met Peach half of the way to where their lips met.

He teased her with his lips before he gave in to the passionate kiss. After breaking the kiss, his attention was grabbed by Kerry. He was coming towards the parking lot, unaware of Slim's eyes as he was talking on his phone. He figured that he just came from seeing Nut.

Peach's vigilance instantly kicked in as she noticed Slim's cutthroat mug. She shifted her eyes to Kerry, then back to Slim.

"You got'cho burna on you," Slim asked as he kept his eyes on Kerry.

"It's in my purse. What'chu want me to do?"

"I want'chu to follow that nigga, and find out where he lay his head wit'out him seein' you. I'ma meet'chu back at the spot," Slim said as he watched Kerry get into his SUV.

"I got'chu," Peach said with no questions asked. When Kerry turned the corner, Slim got out of Peach's car and watched her get on his trail. As he headed to his car, he noticed Nut on the balcony. He was aware of the move Slim just put down. They both did their infamous trademark as they were about to get it cracking once again.

Before Slim went to Sharon's house, he took care of those who paged him. He was expecting Peach to be there, but she wasn't.

More than an hour had gone by since he last saw her, and according to Sharon, she hadn't been back since she left with him. He called her phone, but he got no answer. He became extremely nervous, and started to regret sending her on that mission as he thought about the worst possibilities. He couldn't do nothing but sit down with his nerve wrecking thoughts and wait.

After a while, Slim dialed Peach's number again. When he put the phone to his ear, he could feel solid bass vibrating through the couch as it rumbled in the distance. It became more vigorous and louder before it stopped. He jumped up from the couch and rushed to the window. It was Peach. She was getting out of her car with bags of fast-food. Relief washed over him and left him frustrated as he met her at the door.

"Why you ain't answer yo' phone?" Slim asked with his face twisted at Peach.

"I'm sorry! I had the radio up, and it was in my purse," Peach said as she closed the door behind herself.

"How the fuck you 'pose to be followin' a nigga wit the radio beatin' like that?"

"Baby, I'm not stupid. I was through wit that like thirty minutes ago, then I went to get us somethin' to eat," Peach said as she sat the bags of food on the table with her things.

"I left you damn near two hours ago. What took you so long? You had me around here trippin'."

A smile appeared on Peach's face as she sat on Slim's lap. It was his concern for her that she was touched by. "Baby, I followed him out to this house in the county. I didn't wanna just leave, 'cause he coulda just been visitin' somebody. So, I sat at the end of the block to make sure. He came back out in like ten minutes. I followed him to the west, and a dude got in his truck for a minute. He made anotha drop on the west before I followed him to that same house in the county. I sat there for almost a hour before I left. That's where he lay his head at, and I wrote the address down for you," she informed before she reached for her purse.

"I'll get it later," Slim said as he pulled Peach back to him with a smile. "I like how you took care of that for me. That was some G-shit," he said before he kissed her lips.

"I'm always gon' be on some G-shit when it come to you," Peach said before she returned the kiss. "Now, let's eat 'fore this food get cold. And I still gotta go get my nails and stuff done."

Not once did Peach question Slim about why he had her follow Kerry. He got a call from Nut while they were eating. He told him that it was all good, and would see him in the morning.

Traffic was moving slow, so Slim decided to utilize that time to redeem himself with Kandi. There was one problem though; he lost her number. He knew that he didn't store it in his beeper like he should have, but he flipped through the numbers anyway. When he came across a number that was locked in his beeper, he forgot all about Kandi. It was a girl's number who he promised his assistance to. He shook his head up and down as he dialed her number.

"Can I speak to Carmen?" Slim asked when a soft voiced answered.

"Is this Slim," Carmen excitedly asked.

"This me. What's up?"

"I was so worried about you, and I'm so glad that you're okay! I don't know what happened that night, but some people were shot or something, and I'm so relieved that it wasn't you!"

"That's crazy. What's up wit'chu though? You sound like you was goin' crazy over me."

"I was! I'm really looking forward to that assistance you promised me."

"I ain't forget about'chu. That's actually why I called you. I'm available now. What's up wit'chu?"

"I'm so available for you!"

"Gimme 'bout a hour, and I'ma get at'chu. Where can I find you?"

After getting Carmen's address, Slim went home and took a quick shower.

Carmen lived in a luxurious, three-story house in the deep county. It was very quiet, and of the prominent. She shared the luxurious house with her older sister, Carmarella. Carmarella had two, five-year-old twins, Carmani and Carmello. Carmen was a twenty-one-year-old, Indian and Black woman. She was ambitious, and worked as a registered nurse while she went to medical school. She was only looking for excitement, and Slim was there to bring it into her boring life.

Carmen's lavish room was like a studio apartment. She welcomed Slim to make himself comfortable however he pleased. He wasn't modest about it. He made her feel more comfortable as she was fascinated by his cool composed, thuggish swag.

This preppy girl has never been affiliated with what was hood, and knew nothing about the streets. Their acquaintance was met on one of her sofa beds where they smoked on a blunt. It was the weed smoke that brought her sister up to her room. She was also curious and fascinated by the unusual company. When she became too friendly, Carmen sent her away. She was ready to get that assistance.

Despite Carmen's preppy mannerisms, Slim found that she was sexually impressive as she got obscenely loose with him. He put it on her like she had never had it before, giving her the excitement she'd been yearning for.

Before Slim left Carmen's house, she welcomed him back any time whether he wanted to get away for a while, or just for a brief visit, she welcomed him with expressing that she was excited by his presence alone. He was most definitely going to keep the peaceful environment and her sweet hospitality in mind.

It was 10PM on a Friday night and Slim and Nut were only a few hours away from moving on Kerry. Slim was at Sharon's house where Nut was going to meet him. His car was at Cocoa's house. He told her that he would be coming through later on that night to drop something off. If everything went as expected, he was going to spend the weekend at Carmen's house. It was in that peaceful environment where he wanted to reassess his hustle.

After Slim had Peach follow Kerry, he didn't involve her in anything else. She wasn't clueless though. She was very vigilant when it came to him, and even though she knew something was about to go down with him, she never asked questions.

She'd just came in from a shopping spree, and he was about to tell her about his weekend get-away.

"What's up, baby? You buy me somethin'?" Slim asked as he sat up on the couch.

"You know I did," Peach said as she dropped her bags and came to Slim. He met her lips as she leaned in to kiss him.

"Go put'cho bags up, and come sit down wit' me."

Peach stared at Slim as she could sense that something was up from his serious tone. After a moment, she took off. It was as if she threw her bags into her room, because she was back in a flash. He was pulling on his blunt when she sat next to him with her legs crossed.

"I need you to get that address for me."

When Peach went into her purse and gave Slim the piece of paper, he gave her the blunt.

"I'ma need you to hold it down on yo' own for the weekend. I'm leavin' you wit' the beepa and four ounces, and I'ma have my phone in case you need me."

Slim could see in Peach's face that she was already missing him. She took a deep breath and slowly exhaled as she gave him the blunt back.

"Is it anything else you need me to do?"

"Just hold it down, and I'ma holla at'chu when I get back."

"I got'chu."

Slim loved how Peach didn't question him, and was still willing to hold it down for him despite her feelings.

"Lemme put somethin' in yo' stomach before you leave me," Peach said as she rubbed on Slim.

"That's cool. And when we done I'ma put somethin' in yo' stomach."

Peach gave a little laugh before she got up and went into the kitchen. While she was cooking, Slim got a call from Tish. She wanted to re-up in the morning. He told her that he was tied up, but would send Peach at her. He gave her Peach's number, and told her that she would be expecting her call.

By the time he got off the phone, he was standing next to Peach. He told her about Tish while she fixed him a plate.

After Slim and Peach ate, they went up to her room and had amazing sex. They then laid together and smoked on a blunt. Not once did he think about the possibility of it being the last time he enjoyed the simple pleasures.

After a quick shower, Slim got dressed in all black. He had on his black Soulja Rees, black Girbaud jeans, and a black hoodie. He was in a monkey suit as he was prepared to act a fool. When he came down to the dark living room, Nut was there with Peach. Nut was sitting on the arm of the couch, looking out of the window while he smoked on a cigarette. He was keeping an eye on the car he stole. He was also dressed in a monkey suit. It was time to get it.

"Cuz," Slim said to get Nut's attention.

Nut was pulling on his cigarette as he looked over his shoulder to Slim. He looked like the Grim Reaper as the rim of his hoodie fell just above his eyes. He shook his head up and down as he rose from the couch. Peach stood up from the couch as Slim came towards her. With no words, they shared a brief kiss before he took off with Nut.

As they were heading towards the car, Nut gave Slim a pair of brown gloves. They both put on gloves before they got into the stolen car. Nut was a more experienced driver in case if they were pursued by the police, so he was doing the driving. He had a Mossberg pump on the back seat with two, reliable .44 revolvers. He also had a black ski-mask for himself and Slim. If they didn't wear them, Kerry would know his fate and refuse to cooperate. It was a psychological strategy.

They rode in silence, smoking on blunts of their own with their pistols in their lap.

When Slim and Nut got to Kerry's house, his truck was parked in the drive-way with another one behind it. They figured that it was his, or he had company. No lights were on in his house, and they took it as a good sign. Nut parked the car in front of the house next door and left it running. They covered their face before Nut reached into the back for the Mossberg.

"Let's get it," Nut said with aggression as he jacked the pump with one hand.

Slim and Nut looked around before they emerged into the late night/early morning. The sound of crickets filled the dimly lit street with the sound of buzzing in the street lights as the electricity flowed through them. They boldly marched towards Kerry's front door as if they owned the place.

At the front door, Nut faced the streets with his guns down to his side while Slim tried the keys. He had four keys, and kept his cool even after the first three didn't work. His heart was beating hard and slow as he tried the last one. He took a deep breath and exhaled slowly when the key turned with a soft click. He elbowed Nut to let him know that they were in. The door opened without a sound.

When Slim and Nut came into the house, they left the door ajar. They stood side by side in the living room, waving their guns in the air as their eyes adjusted to the darkness. Any little sound could trigger them as they were prepared to let off shots. When they gained their focus in the lavishly decorated living room, they quietly ventured through the downstairs. Their only guidance was from the moonlight that peeked through the satin curtains. The downstairs was clear.

As Slim and Nut crept upstairs, the plush carpet smothered any sound they could have made. When they made it upstairs, two long halls ran from the corridor that they were standing in. A room at the end of one of the halls immediately grabbed their attention. Light shined from a gap at the bottom of the door. They shook their head up and down at each other before they headed towards the door.

Nut aimed the Mossberg at the door with one hand, and the .44 with his other hand. Slim did the same thing as he walked beside him. As they got closer, they could hear soft moans from a woman. At the door, Slim put his hand in front of Nut for him to stop. He then brought his ear closer to the door for confirmation. He smiled slightly as he shook his head up and down. Nut nodded for him to move to the side. He then rose his guns as he took a step back. With one swift kick, he sent the door flying off its hinges.

Slim and Nut rushed into the room before the door hit the floor. A woman with a high yellow complexion jumped from Kerry's lap with a scream as she covered her naked body with a sheet. Kerry jumped as he held his trembling hands close to his face.

"Shut up, bitch 'fore I blow yo' face off," Nut threatened as he quickly moved to the edge of the bed with Slim.

The woman immediately complied as she shivered and scooted to the head of the bed. She was staring down the barrel of the Mossberg while Kerry had two .44's in his face. He didn't even think about reaching for the 9mm that was on his night stand.

"Who else in this rnu-fucka?" Nut growled at Kerry.

"Nobody," Kerry quickly responded.

"If you wanna see anotha day, I advise you not to play games wit me! I'ma ask you this one time; Where the money and the bricks at?"

"Under the mattress! It's all under the mattress!"

"Bitch-ass nigga! I don't want the shit'chu was finna move, or the shit'chu was finna count," Nut angrily said, doubting that the real stash wasn't under the mattress.

"It's four bricks and seventy-five grand! That's all I got here," Kerry claimed.

"Nigga, get the fuck on the floor," Nut ordered. "You too bitch! And leave that sheet!"

Kerry and the frightened woman immediately complied as they prayed that this overwhelming nightmare would end with a brighter day to look forward to. Nut made them lay their naked bodies face down on the floor and side by side. He stood over them with the destructive barrels aimed at the back of their heads. When they were in the submissive position, he nodded for Slim to check the mattress.

Slim flipped the mattress from the bed and got an instant rush. Four kilos of cocaine were heavily wrapped in s with three large zip-lock bags packed with money. All he saw was one hundred dollar bills that were neatly stacked. He shook his head up and down before he went to the closet. He came back with a duffel bag and quickly began to fill it.

Just as Slim zipped the duffel bag, two thunderous gunshots filled the room and left his ears ringing. The gunshots didn't startle him. The adrenaline that ran through him caused him to grab his pistol and look to Nut.

"We got it! Let's move," Nut said before he headed from the room.

Slim was right behind Nut, and couldn't help noticing the gruesome mess he made. He had no idea of which gun he hit them with, but there was a sloppy mess where their heads were supposed to be.

Slim and Nut didn't bother to look from the house before they stormed out. They came out ready to blaze their guns at anything that stood in their way. Fortunately, the street was still quiet, and the car was still running. They pulled their masks off and threw them into the back seat as they got inside. Just as Slim was closing the door, Nut was pulling away from the curb with ease. Still alert, they kept their pistol in their hand. It wasn't until they got to the middle of the next block when they encountered a problem.

"What the fuck?" Slim exclaimed as the car engine died.

Nut stopped the car in the middle of the street as he pulled a flathead screwdriver from under his seat. Slim's heart was pounding at a fast pace as he looked around with his finger on the trigger. Nut was calm as he tried to start the car from the left side of the steering column. He even remained calm when the engine refused to turn over. He then shifted his eyes to the rear-view mirror and twisted his face.

"Who the fuck is this?" Nut asked as he grabbed the Mossberg. He then jacked it as he got out of the car.

Slim got out on the other side with his pistol and watched as a car sped towards them with its lights out. He twisted his face with his eyes squinted as the car came closer. He then became relieved when he made out who it was.

"Hold on, Cuz. That's Peach," Slim said as he looked over to Nut.

Nut had the pump and the .44 aimed at Peach as he was prepared to shoot.

"C'mon," Slim said as he grabbed the duffel bag from the car. When Slim and Nut got into Peach's car, she whipped it around the car in front of her and continued on with ease. Slim hadn't even thought about her showing up out of nowhere yet. They rode in silence as they were all alert.

Far away from the scene, Slim began to relax as many questions filled his head. They all became self-explanatory as he thought about Peach's commitment and her vigilance. He looked over to her as she calmly drove with her pistol on her lap. The concept of the tatt on her lower back came to his mind. "always on yo' side even when you don't see me".

All along, she had her awareness up as she knew that he was about to get into something serious. She had a love for him that wouldn't allow her to sit back and do nothing while he was in jeopardy. She didn't come to interfere. She only wanted to put herself in a position to assist him if he needed her.

In this case, she was exactly where he needed her. It was another sacrifice that verified the sincerity in her commitment to him. He was proud of her vigilance, and had no room to be upset with her for going against his decision to exclude her.

"Cuz, my bad about the car," Nut broke the silence.

"It's all good. We got it," Slim said as he looked to Nut, then back to Peach with a smile.

Peach returned the smile before she gave her focus back to the road.

Slim directed Peach to Cocoa's house where they counted the money. Just as he expected, Cocoa and Meka was asleep. It took them twenty minutes as they carefully counted the money twice. Each time they added up $75,000. Nut took out $10,000 for Amil. That left him and Slim with $32,500 a piece.

After Slim stashed his two keys under Cocoa's dresser, he came back into the living room and told Peach to take Nut where ever he wanted to go. They shared a passionate kiss before they parted ways. When he got back from his weekend get-away, he was most definitely going to satisfy her.

Before Slim continued on with his plans, he went home to stash his money with the $27,000 he already had under his dresser.

Chapter 15: Get'cha Game Up

Slim was already woke when Carmen came into the room. He laid naked in her bed with the covers over his head. His eyes were closed as he listened to her. She was softly singing with her beautiful voice. He heard her sit something on the night stand before she sat on the bed. He kept his eyes closed as she slowly peeled the covers from his head.

"Maybe if I kissed him, he'll wake up," Carmen softly said as she caressed Slim's face.

"*What kinda fairy tale shit is she on?*" Slim thought to himself as he restrained himself from laughing.

Slim laid there, breathing in Carmen's sweet scent as he felt her coming closer to him. He could feel her warmth and hear her softly breathing. He figured that she was about to kiss him, and he was right. She gently rubbed her lips against his before she kissed them.

"Don't I 'pose to turn into a frog or somethin'?" Slim asked as his eyes popped open with a smile.

"You wasn't sleeping," Carmen grinned. "And it's a prince that you're supposed to turn into."

"I thought I was already a prince from how you treated me last night."

"You are, and that's why I brought you brunch in bed."

"It's smellin' good," Slim said as he sat up. "What'chu got for me?"

"I fried you two pork steaks, hash browns, eggs and toast. I even squeezed you some fresh orange juice," Carmen said before she went for the tray.

"Thank you."

"You're more than welcomed," Carmen said as she sat the tray over Slim's lap. "I was so excited when you told me that you wanted to spend the weekend with me."

"You sounded excited."

"I was so excited, I went out and bought you some things. Just some things for you to lounge around in. I also bought you some personal things. Let's see," Carmen paused as she looked off.

Slim sat his fork down and watched Carmen with a slight smile as she took a moment to recollect.

"I think those Polo boxers you wear are so cute. I bought you lots of those; Polo socks, tank-tops, and even those nylon basketball shorts with Polo slippers. I think you look sexy in your lounge around clothes," Carmen said before she paused, and continued on before Slim could say anything. "I know you didn't like my body wash on you, so I bought you your own soap. I see that you like Polo, so I bought you two Polo cosmetic sets. I even bought you a toothbrush."

Slim dropped his head and shook it in disbelief with a smile.

"I'm sorry! I didn't mean to confuse you! I enjoy your company, and I just want you to feel comfortable when you come over," Carmen said as she grabbed Slim's hand.

"I ain't confused. I was just lookin' for the right words to thank you."

"So, I guess I can continue to buy you things?"

"Don't break yo'self though," Slim said with a laugh.

"I don't think that's possible."

Slim shook his head up and down as he continued to eat. When he was done, Carmen took the tray and told him that his things were in the dresser.

Instead of a shower, Slim sat in the jacuzzi styled tub with a blunt stuffed with weed. It's where he began to reassess his hustle. With the amount of dope and money he had, he saw it as senseless to be hustling out of a crack house. It was time for him to get his game up. He was going to work off of his beeper, and cut nothing but boppas ($100 pieces) from his ounces. He wanted to see Peach with the same amount on her plate, so he was going to give her a quarter key and let her do her own thing with Sharon's house. He wasn't trying to re-up on nothing but a whole key from G-Will. With thirty-six ounces per key, he was also going to move ounces for $900. Most of his homeboys were locked up, and he wasn't going to be too quick to put anyone in his business. He had Tish doing her thing, and that was a start.

That weekend at Carmen's house was a very relaxing time for Slim. Not once did Peach call him. Other than Jayla, he got a call from G-Will. He was back. Early that Monday morning before Carmen went to work, Slim had breakfast with her. By that time, his mind was back on the streets. Before they parted ways, she reminded him that her doors will always be open for him.

When Slim got into his car, he pulled his pistol from under his seat and sat it on his lap. He was back in that street mode. He then called Nut to see what was going on in the city.

"What's up, Cuz? I'm on my way back. What's good?"

"It's all good. Ain't no bells ringin' behind that. Holla at me when you make yo' rounds though."

"Aiight," Slim said before he clicked his phone off. He then called Peach. "What's up, baby? Where you at?"

"At my mama house," Peach sweetly replied.

Slim could hear the excitement and the joy in Peach's voice. "Be still for me. I'm finna come through."

When Slim got to Sharon's house, Peach met him at the door. She didn't give him a chance to sit his things down before she greeted him with her affection. She threw her arms around him and planted several kisses on his face.

"You missed me," Slim asked as he kissed Peach's sweet lips.

"You know I did!"

"I missed you, too Let's sit down and catch up right quick," Slim said as he led Peach to the couch.

Slim sat his things on the table before he sat down with Peach on his lap. She looked him up and down with a smile while she brushed his fuzzy French braids with her hand. He was also checking her out, and noticed that she'd been with Jayla from her hair-do.

"I like yo' hair," Slim complimented Peach.

"Thank you! Jay did it for free," Peach proudly said. Slim shook his head up and down before he continued on.

"You know I can't be posted up in here no mo'. I'm jus finna pop off my beepa. I'ma give you a quarta thang and let'chu do yo' own thing wit' the spot. I want'chu to have yo' own money instead of keep breakin' me off."

Peach rolled her head back and stared at Slim with one side of her top lip curled. It was not the response he was looking for.

"What's wrong?" Slim cluelessly asked.

"I guess you forgot! I don't wanna do my own thing! It wouldn't be no purpose when I'm only doin' it for you. I love that'chu wanna see me wit' somethin', but I don't care about the money. I just wanna be wit'chu, so I'll feel outta place if I did my own thing."·

"My bad. I don't know what I was trippin' off of. And I could never forget where you stand wit' me," Slim said before he kissed Peach's lips.

"I understand why you don't wanna be up in here, and I gotta idea. I ran into my cousin Lil' Jo, and he asked me if I could tie him wit' somebody that'll sell him quarta thangs for forty• five. I didn't tell him about'chu, but I told him I'll get back wit' him on it. I was just thinkin', if you got at him and let him do his thing here, you can still get the money you got comin' through here. What'chu think?"

Slim thought for a moment. "I like that idea, but I don't wanna meet him. Since that's yo' peoples, I want'chu to get at him. And he gotta cook his own shit."

"He knows what he doin'. Now, if you wonderin' where I'ma be, lemme just tell you," Peach said before she saddled Slim and pushed him back to the couch. "I know you probably been over some lil' girl house," she said as she gave his face a light slap.

"You trippin'," Slim said with a guilty smile.

"I was so jealous, but that jealousy only made me do what I was 'pose to do in the first place. I shoulda been had a place for you to lay yo' head and get away from everything. Well, I found us an apartment. It's around there on Broadway," Peach said before she rolled her eyes at Slim.

"Get'cho game up then. I'm feelin' that," Slim said with a smile.

"I want my sista to live wit' us, too. She knows about'chu, but I didn't tell her about the apartment yet. I wanted to run it across you first," Peach said as she brushed the lining of Slim's hair.

"I remember you mentioning somethin' about'cho sister. What's up wit' her?"

"Her name, Kaliyah, and she a good girl. Even though we got different mamas, we real close. She's eighteen, and she work at a tele-marketing place. I want'chu to meet her."

"That's cool. I'ma give you ten grand to put our spot together. Would that be enough?"

"My sister holdin' sixty five for me, plus the two that's upstairs, so that should be enough. Me and her gon' put the apartment together by ourselves, 'cause I want it to be a surprise for you."

"Aiight. Did you holla at Tish?"

"Yeah! And I was confused, 'cause she kept callin' you Wild Child. Baby, why she call you that?"

"It's a long story, but remind me to tell you about it later. I'm finna go get this quarta for yo' peoples, then I'ma go catch up wit' Nut. When you done, I want'chu to call me so I can have you to meet me at my ol'dude house."

"I can just go over there," Peach proudly said.

"What'chu mean, you can just go over there?"

"I met'cho daddy and yo' brotha when Jay was doin' my hair, and she showed them my tatts. Yo' daddy invited me to dinner, we talked, and he told me that I was welcomed to come over anytime," Peach informed with her charming smile.

"I see you done just worked yo' way into my family," Slim said with a laugh.

"I am yo' family!"

"I'm feelin' that," Slim said before he kissed Peach's lips.

"Yo' daddy the one who rentin' us the apartment. I didn't tell him that'chu was gon be stayin' there, but I think he know."

"I'ma holla at him, but let me go get this shit right quick."

"Baby, I got somethin' else to tell you," Peach mumbled as she lowered her head.

"Don't do that wit me," Slim said as he gently lifted Peach's head. Peach took a deep breath and slowly exhaled. "Baby, I'm pregnant again, but I'ma go to the clinic. I'ma jus start takin' them pills or get that shot," she said before she began to bite her fingernails.

Slim stared at Peach with a slight smile as he shook his head from side to side. Even though she was serious about going to the clinic, she dreaded it. She made sure he knew it from her expressions. She didn't have to tell him about the pregnancy. She could've taken care of it discreetly instead of risking her feelings getting hurt again. She was trying to see if he felt the same way he felt before.

"You gon' run away again?"

"No," Peach mumbled.

"Tell me how you feel about this."

"Do it matter?"

"C'mon now, Peach. You know what it is wit' us. You showed me too much for me to disregard how you feel. So, what's up? Tell me how you feel."

Peach's face lit up with joy as Slim's sensitivity gave validity to her worthiness. "Jevon, I love you, and I feel like I deserve to have yo' baby," she cried.

"Peach, I love you too, and I feel like I deserve to be sharin' this wit'chu," Slim softly spoke before they engaged in a passionate kiss.

This was no ordinary kiss. It was one that connected their souls as they stared deep into each other's eyes. From that moment on, Slim would become extra protective over Peach.

After their kiss ended, they continued to gaze into each other's eyes as they caressed each other's face.

"I'm finna go get this shit for yo' peoples, and when you done, go straight to my ol' dude house and wait on me," Slim said firmly.

"I will." Peach replied in submission.

Cocoa was at work, and Meka was in the kitchen cooking herself breakfast when Slim got there. He was hoping that she was sleeping so he wouldn't have to hear her whining. She had a new attitude though.

"What's up, Slim? Do you want somethin' to eat?" Meka kindly asked.

"I'm cool."

"Alright. Make sure you lock the door behind you when you leave," Meka said as she left the kitchen.

Slim watched Meka leave with a slight smile. She didn't even look back to him as she continued on to her room. He figured that Cocoa had been talking with her about being conservative. When a girl is conservative as opposed to being loose, it challenges a dude as he becomes more interested. She had her game up.

Slim went to see Nut after he left Peach. He figured that Nut was going to get his game up after the heist, but he was not prepared for what he was about to encounter.

Slim found Nut leaning on a bright orange, '86 SS Monte Carlo. It was sitting on chrome, one hundred spokes that sparkled with the fresh candy paint job. His ears held 2 carat diamonds that glistened as the sun hit them. His neck, wrist, and pinkie fingers were also glistening. He was talking with Kiesha, who leaned across from him on a chocolate, '85 Cutlass. It was also sitting on chrome, one hundred spokes. Every time Nut opened his mouth, a blinding glare appeared. His top and bottom teeth were filled with crushed diamonds and golds. Even Kiesha had her top teeth shining with solid gold teeth.

When Slim got out of his car, stood at the trunk of Nut's and Kiesha's car. He looked back and forth to them before he dropped his head and shook it in disbelief.

"Cuz, I know you ain't surprised. I told you I was comin'," Nut said with a laugh as he clapped hands with Slim.

"I knew you was comin', but damn! You gon blind a nigga out here," Slim said before he turned to Kiesha. "I see you got'cho game up, too."

"You know my nigga wasn't gon leave me behind," Kiesha said as she clapped hands with Slim.

"Nut, I'm finna go take care of that, and I'ma put the numbers in yo' beeper."

Nut shook his head up and down as he watched Kiesha leave. He then turned to Slim. "I sat down wit' Amil when I gave her that money."

"What she on?"

"Exactly what I said she was on; tryin' to test a nigga. She's down in South Beach, and 'pose to get wit' me when she gets back."

"On some real shit, I ain't tryin' to fuck wit' her like that. The lie was cool. It got me where I wanted to be, and it got'chu good on yo' feet. I'm tryin' to tie you wit' the homeboy, and we could eat off these bricks."

"The same nigga that be gettin' at'chu wit' them quarta thangs? Cuz, that's love if you could tie that! Niggas just be playin' the game cold when it comes to movin' bricks."

While Nut was speaking as if Slim had something exclusive, he was dialing G-Will's number. When he got him on the line, he told him that he was on his way, and wanted to introduce him to someone. Nut followed Slim straight to G-Will's house. When they got there, Slim noticed a green Camaro parked in front of Sharon's house. He figured that it belonged to Peach's cousin. Nut was curiously looking at the car as he met Slim on the sidewalk.

"Cuz, what that nigga Lil' Jo doin' at'cho spot?"

"That's Peach peoples. You know that nigga?"

"Yeah. He's cool. He a Blood from Ghost Town. They fuck wit' the hood. Plus, I fuck wit' his sista."

Slim shook his head up and down before he led Nut to G-Will's basement door. On their way there, he told him about his new establishment, Peach's pregnancy, and his plans for her.

Nikki Pooh came to the door and led Slim and Nut over to the couches. G-Will was talking on his phone while he sat slumped on one of the couches. He had a quarter key on the table as he was expecting Slim to re-up. G-Will took a double take at Nut before he clapped hands with Slim. Nikki Pooh sat next to G-Will while Slim and Nut sat on the couch across from them.

"What's up, homie?" G-Will asked as he clicked his phone off.

"I'ma be good for a minute, but when I re-up, I'm tryin' to do a whole thang," Slim said as he sat up to the edge of the couch.

G-Will's eyebrows went up as he pulled on his blunt. "I can't do nothin' over a quarter thang," he dully said, losing the enthusiasm he greeted Slim with.

Slim stared at G-Will with a peculiar expression as some things began to run through his head. He knew that G-Will could sell him a brick from how fast Nikki Pooh was pushing quarters to him. Nut shook his head in disbelief as he flipped through the numbers in his beeper. He already knew what the problem was. When Slim shifted his eyes to Nikki Pooh, her words popped into his head. "as you elevate in the game, you'll see that everything ain't everything wit everybody." He realized that she was trying to tell him about G-Will. If he would've let his guards down and gave in to her enticement, she would've exposed her hand to him. "Ain't too many niggas in the game like you," he also remembered her saying. She knew some things about G-Will, and was still by his side for a reason. He figured that her deception came from his flaws, and from being unsatisfied.

"It's all good. I'ma holla at'chu," Slim finally said.

"Aiight, I need to make a move right quick," G-Will said before he began to dial numbers on his phone.

Without the usual departing hood clap with G-Will, Slim rose from the couch. Nut rose with him as he screwed his face at G-Will. When Slim caught Nikki Pooh's eyes, she gave him that, "I tried to tell you look". He was still processing everything as he headed to the front of the house with Nut.

"Cuz, that's a bitch-ass nigga you been dealin' wit," Nut angrily said as he punched the palm of his hand. "He don't wanna sell you nothin' over a quarta thang, so he can keep you under his wings. Fuck that nigga! If it get to the point where we ain't eatin' right out here, we comin' to get him. Please tell me you see this shit!"

"I'm on point. And I'm fucked up behind this, 'cause I looked up to this nigga like a big brotha. I see now, everything he did was for convenient purposes." Slim spat as he shook his head in disbelief.

"I'ma find us anotha plug."

"Do that. I'm finna go holla at Peach though. Her time up," Slim said as he clapped hands with Nut.

When Slim got to his father's house, he parked behind a dark pink jeep. It was the same jeep Peach ran off in when they had that disagreement about her pregnancy. She was on the porch with Jayla, FeFe, and another girl. As he approached the porch he figured that the other girl was her sister. She had the same light-brown skin complexion that matched her eyes. She was only a few inches shorter than Peach with long, curly hair.

"Jevon, you seen my brotha yet," Fe-Fe asked. "He came over here yesterday lookin' like a Christmas tree!"

Slim's head was somewhere else as he paid no attention to Fe-Fe. He stopped at the last step where Peach stood in front of him.

"Baby, this my sister, Kaliyah," Peach said with a smile as she looked to her sister, then back to Slim during the introduction.

Kaliyah waved at Slim with her pretty smile. He spoke to her, then to Jayla and Fe-Fe before he turned back to Peach.

"Let's go in so I can talk to you," Slim said as he led the way into the house.

Slim could feel Peach analyzing him as he led her to his room. Her vigilance was one of her qualities that got her into his heart. His heart now felt protective over her, and he had to set boundaries. When they got to his room, he opened the door and closed it behind them.

"Let's sit down," Slim said with a serious tone.

Peach stared at Slim with a puzzled expression as they sat on the bed together.

"Everything cool wit' me, so I want'chu to relax."

A slight smile appeared on Peach's face as she exhaled with relief.

"I like how you be on point wit' me, and how you be havin' yo' awareness up. But I need you to fall back and leave this street shit to me. I'm pullin' you away from the game. I just want'chu to focus on yo'self wit' the baby, and keep our spot together."

"Who gon' take care of things when you start school?"

"I'll think of somethin', but the only person I want'chu gettin' at is yo' peoples."

"I understand how you feel, 'cause I feel protective over you, too. So, it's gon be hard for me to play the sideline."

"I ain't puttin' you on the sideline. I'ma always need you. That's why I'm pullin' you away from the streets. I'm not askin' you to fall back, I'm tellin' you."

"Well, if that's what'chu want me to do, I won't fight wit'chu on it," Peach submitted.

"You ain't gon win anyway," Slim said with a laugh, breaking the seriousness with a little humor. Peach laughed with him before they shared a brief kiss. "What's up though? You touched yo' peoples?"

"Yeah. I got the money in my purse."

"Keep it, and I'ma put the rest of what I was gon' give you wit' it."

"I can't wait 'til we get settled in our apartment. Me and Kaliyah spendin' the next two days puttin' it togetha, so that mean we gon miss each other again."

"We'll be aiight. But'chu stayin' here wit' me tonight."

"You bet'not get me in trouble," Peach said with a smile as she pushed Slim.

"I'm finna go get this money. I'ma take yo' car and park it in the backyard when I'm finished doin' what I'm doin'," Slim said before he kissed Peach lips.

After dealing with those who paged him, Slim went to see Pooch for some weed. He could've sworn that he saw G-Will's Benz turning the corner as he pulled up. Pooch was someone who G-Will introduced him to, so he automatically questioned his loyalty. However, he didn't have a shallow mind that would cause him to jump to conclusions. Pooch had never displayed any type of selfishness towards him, so he wasn't going to let his ties with G-Will dictate how he would usually interact with him.

At the basement door, Pooch greeted Slim with the same love as usual before he came in. He took his usual spot on the couch while Pooch did his thing when he came to see him. He went to one of the rooms with Sha-Sha, who never left his side. She was a big head, solid black pit bull that was impressively trained. Slim always had the money on the table by the time Pooch came back with the quarter pound of weed.

"Cuz, you stay on the move. Lemme blow one wit'chu before you slide out," Pooch said as he sat across from Slim.

"I can be still for a minute," Slim said, sensing that Pooch had something on his mind.

Pooch shook his head up and down as he lit a blunt while pulling on the other end of it. "You been holdin' the hood down on yo' own, and I like how you move. You remind me of the homeboy, Sleep. He was quiet, gettin' that money and playin' the game how it go, too."

"I remember Sleep. What's up wit' the homeboy?"

"He got jammed up in that sweep wit' some mo' of the homeboys. All the other homeboys that didn't get jammed up scattered out to other hoods. From Five-Four to Ghost Town where the Dawgs at. I'm still here, though. I started Eight Duce, and I'ma clean up the bullshit that got the hood fucked up. It's a lot of coincidences circulatin' around how the homeboys got jammed up. I don't wanna expose my hand 'til I get the facts. But when I do, I got a mu-fucka right in my hands."

"Is it anything about the hood that I need to be up on?" Slim asked as he pulled on the blunt.

"Like I said, I don't wanna put nothin' out there 'til I get the facts. Just keep doin' yo' thing, and know that it's some sharks in the game. When they ain't eatin' right, or you start eatin' too much, you become a part of the food chain."

"I got'chu," Slim said with a good idea of who Pooch seen as a suspect.

"It is what it is wit' me," Pooch said, telling Slim that he was who he appeared to be.

"I'm wit'chu," Slim said feeling that his big homie was truly the big homie. They continued to talk for a short while before he left to deal with a few pages.

When Slim got home, Peach was in the living room with Marcel, Jayla and Fe-Fe. They were all laughing as they sat around Jayla. She was holding the family photo album in her lap. Peach was most definitely becoming a part of the family. The family's photo album ·held sentimental moments, and was only shared with family. Slim continued on with a smile as he was going to put his money away. When he got to the kitchen, he ran into his father. He was over the stove preparing dinner.

"Slow down, youngsta."

"What's up, old man?"

"Lemme get a word wit'chu."

Slim knew that his father wanted to talk with him about Peach. He leaned on the counter next to him.

"I met Peach, and I like her. We had some talks, and she really has your best interest at heart."

"Yeah, she do," Slim agreed.

"She made me think about that girl who used to call here for you. I think her name was Angel. She called here cryin' when you got locked up, and again before you went to that place. I told her that'chu was gon' be gone for a while, and that was the last time she called. So much was goin' on wit'chu around that time, I forgot to tell you. My bad."

"It's cool."

"I rented Peach one of my apartments, and I know wit' things bein' serious between y'all, you gon' be stayin' there wit' her, too. It's a nice and quiet place, and I want it to stay like that."

"If you tellin' me not to sell dope from the buildin', that's not my intentions. Peach want it to be a place where we can get away from everything, and that's how it's gon' be."

"You know, I never got the chance to talk to you about bein' wit' a girl. You just grew up on me so fast. I know you had that experience before. I just want'chu to wrap it up before you have a handful of Wild Childs runnin' around here."

Slim chuckled before he responded. "I already got one on the way. And the way I feel about Peach, I don't feel like not wrappin' it up was a mistake."

"So, you know what'chu need to do. You need to begin wit' separatin' yo' lifestyle from her. You also have to stop spendin' yo' money on bullshit and stack it. Wit' that, you have to think about more than yo'self. You bringin' an innocent child into this world who gon' be dependin' on you. And as long as you livin' that uncompromisin' lifestyle, you will always be unreliable. You got nine months or whatever to think about what's more important to you. I'm hopin' that this baby'll get'chu to look at things from another perspective. All you gotta do is go to school, and I got'chu. But I'ma continue to let'chu make yo' own decisions. Just allow me the opportunity to keep breathin' on you."

"Thank you, and you'll always have that opportunity."

"I invited Peach to eat wit' us. I want'chu to be here to welcome her into the family," Donnell said before he turned back to the stove.

"I'll be here."

After Slim put his money away, he took a quick shower and thought about his father's pep talk. When he came back to his room, Peach attacked him with a pillow.

"What'chu tell yo' daddy about me," Peach asked as she continued to hit Slim with the pillow.

Slim loved how Peach could go from being hood and a charming young lady to acting like a big kid. He laughed as he wrestled with her. She put up a fight, but he eventually restrained her on the bed. Her body hung halfway off the bed with him on top of her. He held her wrist over her head as he continued to kiss her face.

"I told him the same things you told him about me," Slim said as he released Peach.

"Well, he told me to come and get'chu so we can eat," Peach said as she put her ponytail back together.

Everyone was at the table when Slim joined them with Peach. He had a sly smile as he pulled out a chair for her. She looked at him with curiosity as he sat next to her. Jayla and Fe-Fe took over with starting a conversation with her. Slim quietly began to eat while his father gave him a look to break the news. Marcel looked back and forth to them, knowing that something was surfacing. Slim put his fork down and sat back for a moment until he came up with something.

"Peach, when you puttin' the apartment together, you have to remember to leave room for our baby," Slim said with a smile.

The kitchen became quiet and still as everyone stared at them in shock. Peach then looked to him as she didn't know what to say.

"Welcome to the fam," Slim said before he kissed Peach's lips.

Peach looked over to Slim's father with a tight smile as she tried to frown. Whatever he said to her now made sense to her as she realized that he knew about her pregnancy. He hunched his shoulders with a smile as Jayla and Fe-Fe began to question her. Marcel welcomed Peach into the family before he began to tease his father about becoming a grandfather.

After dinner, Peach helped Jayla and Fe-Fe clean the kitchen. Slim went down to his room where he found his vibrating beeper. He took it from his dresser along with his other things before he left. Slim was out getting money longer than he expected. When he finally got home, he found Peach in the basement with Jayla and Fe-Fe. He came in and went straight to his room.

Slim was exhausted. After stashing his money, he kicked his shoes off and laid across his bed. He stared up at the ceiling as he thought about how he was going to take care of his business when school started. His thoughts were interrupted by soft knocks on his door. They were followed by Peach coming into his room. She came in and closed the door

"Baby, you sleepy," Peach sweetly asked.

"Yeah. Turn that light off and come lay down wit' me," Slim said with a scratchy tone.

When Peach got into Slim's bed, she laid her head on his chest and rubbed his stomach. After a moment, she stopped rubbing his stomach and left her hand there.

"Baby, why Tish call you Wild Child?"

Slim thought about Peach's question and realized that his answer would lead to more questions, so he decided to give her the whole story.

"My uncle Geno gave me that name when I was little," he said before he paused. Slim went on to tell Peach about his troubled childhood up until he came home from D.Y.S. His story brought tears to her eyes as they discovered that they had more in common. They were both problematic children with lost mothers who they once shared a significant bond with. He learned that her father was murdered in front of her when she was only six years old. It's when her behavior problems began with her mother turning to the pipe for consolation.

After Slim and Peach talked, they consoled each other with their sweet love making. It was an expression of them becoming closer.

It was late night/early morning when Slim was awaken by his phone. He ignored it, hoping that whoever it was would hand up. It just continued to ring with desperation. He eventually got out of his bed and went for it with his face twisted. Frustrated from the interruption, he didn't bother to look at the caller ID before he answered.

"Who is this?"

"You got'cho game up?" a girl asked.

"Who the fuck is this?"

"Nikki Pooh."

Slim thought about Nikki Pooh's question for a moment before he figured out what it was she was asking him. She was asking him if he was aware of G-Will's flaws.

"Yeah, I got my game up."

"Just keep yo' hands closed and I'ma get at'chu. I can put'chu in a position where you can do yo' own thing. Jus lemme play it how it go, and I'ma give you the access."

Slim realized that Nikki Pooh was talking about knocking G-Will off and giving him the prosperous connect.

"It's all good. Do what'chu do," he said before he clicked his phone off.

"Baby, who was that?" Peach asked with a sleepy tone.

"Nobody. Go back to sleep," Slim said before he kissed Peach's lips and laid with her.

Chapter 16: Mama's Confessions

When Slim awakened the next morning, he was tortured by the sunlight that beamed through the small window above him. He pulled the covers over his head and reached for Peach. His hand fell to the bed before he felt around in the warm, empty spot. He was naked, and alone. The smell of breakfast food was in the air. He expected for his father and brother to be at work, so he figured that Peach was in the kitchen cooking.

After a quick shower, Slim got dressed in some of his new things with his jewelry. Despite everything that was going on in the streets, he was in a good mood. It was a beautiful day, and he was even going to ride with the tops off of his car. After putting $5,500 in Peach's purse, he headed up to the kitchen.

"What's up, sleepy head?" Peach spoke as she stood at the top of the steps. "I was just finna come and get'chu up," she said as she turned Slim's hat backwards and kissed his lips. "C'mon so you can eat wit' me."

Jayla and Fe-Fe were at the table eating, and looking like they were about to tease Slim.

"What's up, nappy head?" Jayla started at Slim with a laugh.

"Leave him alone! I like his fuzzy braids," Peach defended Slim as she sat on his lap.

"It's Peach's fault! She blew his head up, now he thinks he all that regardless," Fe-Fe said with a laugh.

"Baby, they must don't know, you was like this when I met'chu."

"They know what it is wit me. They just hatin'."

"Von-Von don't play wit' me! 'Cause if you think I'm hatin', I can do that," Jayla threatened with a teasing smile.

"So," Slim said as he shrugged his shoulders.

"What'chu mean, so?" Peach asked as she gave Slim a light slap.

"C'mon now, Peach. You know I ain't trippin' off no other girl but'chu," Slim said before he kissed her lips.

Jayla and Fe-Fe found Slim's submission to Peach sweet and amusing. They continued to watch them as they ate and talked about decorating their apartment.

Slim was too wrapped up in his debate with Peach about the kind of furniture for their apartment to notice Jayla get up from the table to answer the door. He wanted black leather while Peach opposed.

"Y'all should flip for it," a woman with a soft voice said as she came into the kitchen.

Slim and Peach turned to the woman at the same time. After a few seconds, she turned back to him. He was staring at the woman with his mouth partially open with his eyebrows up. He was surprised, but most of all, he was excited to see his mother.

Unlike majority of everyone else, Slim's mother showed no surprise to his appearance. She only smiled at him as she looked him up and down. She brought a sweet smell into the kitchen, and was dressed nicely with her narrow figure. Just as he remembered, her hair was still long and pretty. However, her once before beautiful face was tarnished from her destructive crack addiction.

"Can I have a hug?" Jenah softly asked as she held her arms out for him.

Jenah's voice was still soft and sweet, and he could see the longing in her eyes that reminded him of the bond they once shared. He couldn't reject her consoling arms, and Peach could see it in his eyes as she rose from his lap. His smile held compassion and a warm welcoming that brought tears from his mother's eyes. He was showing her his acceptance.

The kitchen went completely quiet and still as everyone watched Slim and his mother embrace each other. Her tender squeeze reminded him of how she used to console him when he was a child. Sentimental memories and emotions took over him as a tear ran from his eye.

"You're so handsome," Jenah said with a smile as she stood back while holding his hands.

"That's his problem now! He hears that too much. Wit' his big head," Jayla said with a laugh.

"I'm not surprised," Jenah said as she caressed his face. "And that must be yo' girlfriend."

"Yeah. That's Peach, and that's Fe-Fe." Jenah spoke to Peach and Fe-Fe with a smile and a wave, and received the same polite greeting from them.

"Mama, do you wanna eat wit' us," Jayla kindly asked.

"I'm okay, but thank you," she said before she turned to Slim. It's nice outside, so I'ma go sit on the porch. When you finish eatin', I was hopin' that'chu can come talk wit' me."

"We was done in here. We was just finna clean up," Peach said, encouraging Slim to go with his mother.

"I can go wit'chu," Slim said before he led his mother out to the porch.

On Slim's way out to the porch with his mother, his excitement from seeing her was wearing off as many questions came. However, he wasn't going to overwhelm her with questions that would make her feel any guiltier than she had already been feeling. He only wanted to show her that the bitterness was gone, and become reacquainted with her.

On the porch, Slim sat slumped on the bench while his mother sat with her body turned towards him. She shook her head from side to side with a smile as she was still taking in her grown baby.

"I ain't gon even ask what'chu been up to, 'cause I already heard. I ran into my old friend, Angie, and she told me how you been out here showin' yo' grown butt."

Slim shook his head in disbelief as he thought about Angie. It never occurred to him that she was the same woman who used to change his pampers and babysit him. It now made sense to him of why she was ashamed to accept his dope.

"I know I'm not in any position to tell you what to do, or what not to do, but baby, be careful. And listen to yo' daddy," Jenah expressed with deep concern.

"I do."

"I see you grew yo' hair back, and you got so big!"

"I gained a lot of weight in that place. I guess you can't call me Slim no mo', huh?"

"Baby, I didn't give you that name 'cause of yo' size!" Jenah chuckled.

"You didn't?" Slim asked feeling clueless.

Jenah shook her head from side to side as she recollected one of the most difficult periods in her life.

"I almost lost you when you was born," she said as she grabbed his hands.

A distressed expression appeared on Slim's mother's face as she continued to tell him about his unfortunate arrival, and where his name came from. By the time she finished, he was sitting up from his slump with one question.

"If you was so happy that I made it, why did you leave?"

"Baby, I'm regrettin' that decision every day of my life. I was under a lot of pressure, and I was weak. That's not an excuse, it's the truth."

Slim had already figured that it was some type of pressure that made his mother turn to the destructive habit. He wanted to ask her about that pressure, but the sorrowful sight of her was unbearable. He was only concerned with her well-being as he sympathized with her.

"I'm sorry for not bein' here, or never coming to see you in that place."

Slim understood how shame kept his mother away, but he was now curious of what gave her the courage to come around now. "So, what made you finally come and see us?"

"I been in and outta jail for writin' bad checks, and I'm finna go away for a while. I'm goin' to a six-month drug treatment program. I'm lookin' forward to gettin' myself together while I'm there. I don't know what type of restrictions I'll be on when I get there, so I just wanted to come and see my babies before I turn myself in," Jenah said before she wrapped her arms around him.

Slim stared at his mother with a smile as he was happy to see her taking the steps to find herself. She could sense his happiness and kissed his forehead.

"I'm not only doin' this for myself, but I owe it to y'all to become a betta person and make amends."

"You have my support, and when you come home, I wanna do whatever I can to help you get on yo' feet."

"I'ma be okay, baby," Jenah stated as she caressed his face. "Y'all haven't met them yet, but my mother, my daddy and my sister has been very supportive."

"That's somethin' I wanted to ask you about! Why we don't know nothin' about them?"

"Baby, I'm from a very prominent family, and… "

"You mean, you a rich girl?" Slim interjected.

"It all depends on what'chu call rich, but my family is considered to be upper class people. When I got wit'cho daddy, they didn't approve of it. I ended up havin' to choose between them, and it was one of the hardest things I had to do."

Slim figured that his grandparents disapproval came from his father's old lifestyle.

"I ended up stayin' wit'cho daddy, and I could never regret it when I have three beautiful babies. I only regret that I stopped tryin' to reach out to my family 'cause I really needed them when times got hard. But we made mistakes, and we all are tryin' to make amends."

"So, do I have any cousins?"

"You do. My sister has two daughters, Kelli and Bianca. They around yo' age, and when I come home, I'ma take y'all to meet them."

"When you 'pose to go to that place?"

"Later today."

"When you come home, Peach gon have a knot in her stomach," Slim proudly announced.

Jenah's face lit up with surprise as she covered her mouth with her hand. "Oh my God! I still feel like you my baby, so how you gon' be havin' a baby on me?"

"I can still be yo' baby," Slim said as he laid his head in his mother's lap.

"You gon' always be my baby, and I'm happy for you," Jenah smiled before she kissed his cheek.

"Jevon, I'm finna go get my sister so we can start puttin' the apartment together," Peach said as she came from the house.

"Black leather," Slim said as she sat up.

"And, why you not goin' to help her?"

"'Cause, he gon' jus be in the way, and I want it to be a surprise for him," Peach said before she kissed Slim. "It was nice meetin' you," she said as she looked to his mother.

"It was nice meetin' you too, and take care of yo'self," Jenah said as she waved at Peach. "Well baby, I'ma go in here and talk wit' Ms. Jay. I wanna let her know what's goin' on wit me, too, then I'ma go catch Marcel on his lunch break," she said as she rose from the bench.

Slim stood up with his mother and hugged her. She returned the affection with a more intense squeeze.

"I love you, and I can't wait 'til I get through this," Jenah said before she kissed his cheek.

"Love you too, and just take it one day at a time."

"You just make sure you be careful in these streets," Jenah urged her son as she grabbed his hands.

"I will." Slim promised.

"I'm serious!"

"I know."

Slim's mother stared at him with concern as she didn't want to let his hands go.

"Ma, I'ma be aiight," Slim assured her.

"Okay, baby."

Jenah stood at the top of the steps and watched him remove the tops from his car and leave with his loud music blasting from his stereo.

Chapter 17: Can't Let Her Go

Slim was heading to the gas station before he took care of those who paged him. When he came inside, his eyes were taken by a girl who was heading towards the counter. He could only see the back of her, but he could never forget this unique, pigeon-toed redbone. It was Kandi, and he was not about to let her get away from him. He approached her from behind just as she was about to pay for her things.

"Lemme take care of that for you," Slim said as he gave the cashier a twenty. "And put the rest on six."

Kandi twisted her face at Slim as she stood with her hand on her hip. He figured that she was mad because he never called her.

"I'll be out here. Come and see what's up wit me," Slim said before he turned to leave.

Slim had the pump in the tank of his car as he leaned next to it. He was flipping through the numbers in his beeper. He couldn't ignore his pages, nor was he trying to let Kandi get away from him.

"You must've lost my number! 'Cause I know you ain't been puttin' me off. Especially after what happened," Kandi said with a feisty attitude as she appeared next to Slim.

"And that's the only reason why I haven't got at'chu. Ride wit' me though, 'cause you know I ain't tryin' to let'chu get away from me," Slim said as he put the pump back into its place and got into his car.

"You could've at least asked me if I needed to be somewhere," Kandi said as she got into Slim's car.

"You 'pose to be wit' me," Slim said as he pulled off.

"Why do niggas get all cocky when they get to doin' they thing?"

"I can't speak for another nigga, but I'm still the same nigga you met in sweat pants and Rees. And when you finish doin' the math, you gon' come up wit' the same numbers."

"Well, if I'ma get the same results, you might as well keep yo' thing in yo' pants," Kandi teased.

Unaffected by Kandi's joke, Slim shook his head up and down as he focused on the road.

"And ain't chu too old to be messin' wit my lil' cousin?"

"You ain't gotta try to be slick wit' me. Just ask me what'chu tryin' to ask me." Slim smirked.

"If you know what I'm tryin' to ask you, just tell me." Kandi retorted as she rolled her neck.

"It don't work like that," Slim said with a laugh."

"Boy, how old is you?"

"Sixteen," Slim said as he looked at Kandi, then back to the road.

"No wonder why," Kandi teased as she turned her body towards Slim. She was intrigued.

Slim allowed Kandi to get her jokes off, but she had no idea that he was now a beast in the bed.

"Well, I just turned nineteen today," Kandi proudly stated.

"What'chu got planned?"

"Nothin'! My sister and Shay took me out to breakfast this mornin' before they went to work. They wanna hit the club tonight, but I just wanna kick it wit' my girls, smoke up they weed, and get drunk," Kandi said with no enthusiasm.

"That's who you stay wit'? Shay and yo' sister?"

"We stay together," Kandi clarified. "And I could've got'cho number from Meka, but I don't wanna mess up y'all relationship."

"You still tryin' to be slick wit' fishin' for information. You ain't gotta do that. Me and Meka just cool, though."

"So, you don't have a problem wit' me askin' you questions?"

"I ain't trippin', but that don't mean you gon' get the answer, or the response you lookin' for."

"I'm jus tryin' to get more familiar wit'chu, and I feel like I got the right to ask questions, 'cause I don't be just jumpin' in the car wit' anybody! Especially without them tellin' me where they takin' me."

"You good. Just lemme do what I do, and I'ma take you to yo' house where we gon' get that familiar thing taken care of," Slim said before he turned his music up.

Kandi rolled her head back as she stared at Slim with a smile. She admired his confidence.

Kandi sat inside of Slim's car while he dealt with those who paged him. He was in and out, then on to the next drop. When he got to Vee's apartment, he turned the car off.

"I'm finna post up in here for a minute. I ain't gon be long, but I want'chu to keep me company."

"That's cool," Kandi said as she put the strap of her purse over her shoulder.

Slim had Kandi put his weed into her purse before they went inside.

"What's up, Slim?" Vee spoke when she opened the door. "I see you got Peach wit'chu."

"You trippin', Vee. This Kandi," Slim sneered as they came into the apartment.

"My bad." Vee apologized.

Kandi shook her head from side to side with a slight smile as she sat on the couch. When Slim finished dealing with Vee, she went to the back room where her company was. He had the tops off of his car, so he was going to sit on the window ledge to keep an eye on it. He sat his things there before he answered his phone. It was Nut.

Nut was only touching bases with Slim. He split a blunt open with his fingernails while they were talking. When Kandi brought him his weed, she started to go back to the couch, but he pulled her back to him by the belt loop on her skirt.

She leaned next to him while he continued to talk. Before he got off the phone with Nut, he told him that he might have something lined up for them, and would talk with him about it later.

"What's up wit'chu,? Slim asked as he passed Kandi the blunt.

"So, is this Peach girl yo' girlfriend?" Kandi asked before she pulled on the blunt.

"You gotta problem wit' that?"

"Why should I? You just don't seem like the boyfriend-girlfriend type."

"I used to feel like that, but it's all good though. Especially when you come across that one person who gon' hold you down regardless. She's like fam, but let's shake that topic. It's all about the birthday girl, right now."

"I'm feelin' that," Kandi said with a smile.

"Hold that thought," Slim said as he grabbed his pistol from the ledge and went for the door.

At the door was a young woman who Slim came to know as Felicia. She lived in the building and looked to be in her mid-twenties. He was stunned when he found out that she was a crackhead. She had a pretty face and a beautiful body, and had the potential to be more than she was. Despite her addiction, she was a hustler. She came with a gold tennis bracelet and fifty dollars. He gave her a bopper for what she had. She was going to cut that boppa into twenty dimes, smoke some, and sell some to re-up with him.

"You like this?" Slim asked as he looked to the bracelet that dangled from his finger, then back to Kandi.

"Yeah, I like it, but I can't speak for yo' girl."

"I'm not askin' you to. Gimme yo' wrist, Birthday Girl," Slim said as he prepared the bracelet for Kandi's wrist.

Kandi was touched by the small gift. "Thank you!"

"It looks good on you," Slim said before he stepped off to deal with Vee. When he came back over to Kandi, she was pulling on the blunt with her eyes on her shiny, new bracelet. "Can I smoke wit'chu?"

"It got lip gloss on it," Kandi said with a guilty smile.

"You the birthday girl, so I'ma give you a free pass today."

"I like you," Kandi softly said.

"I like you too. C'mere," Slim said as he grabbed Kandi's hand and directed her in front of him.

Kandi stood in front of Slim with her soft ass pressed against him. He lovingly inhaled the mysteriously sweet smell of her as he gently squeezed her body.

"What'chu smell like?" Slim asked as he rubbed his nose back and forth across Kandi's neck. The gently strokes sent chills up her spine and caused her to shiver. "I got'chu," he said as he tightened his squeeze.

"Tommy Girl. I'm wearin' Tommy Girl," Kandi whispered as she looked to Slim.

Slim's and Kandi's face was so close, he could taste the cherry lip gloss on her lips as he inhaled her breath. He shifted his eyes to her luscious lips that he was crazy about, then back to her eyes. It only took for him to push his lips out to kiss them.

"You know what's goin' on wit me, so what's up wit'chu?" Slim asked.

Kandi took a deep breath and exhaled with a sigh.

"C'mon now, yo' life can't be that borin'," Slim said with a laugh.

"I wouldn't say it's borin', but it's nothin' to talk about."

"I still wanna know."

"Well, I would've been at work, but I got fired last week. Other than that, I be chillin' wit my sister and 'nem. We hit the club sometimes. Unlike you, I don't have anyone special. I talk to somebody, but it ain't nothin'."

While Kandi was talkin', Slim was rubbing her thighs while lovingly inhaling her with his eyes closed.

"You ain't even listenin' to me," Kandi whined.

"Yes I am. You said you got fired, 'cause you be shakin' yo' ass in the club wit'cho sister and 'nem all night. And you got a boyfriend, but he ain't talkin' 'bout shit."

"I didn't say all that," Kandi said with a laugh.

"Lemme fuck wit' her right quick," Slim said as Vee came into the living room.

After dealing with Vee, Slim came back over to Kandi. They talked and laughed together for over an hour before they left. She was hungry, and wanted to get Chinese food from the restaurant where they met.

When Slim and Kandi came into the Chinese restaurant, they were surprised by who they saw at the service window. It was Meka and her boyfriend. She gave him the bags as she turned from the window. She was just as surprised as Slim and Kandi. She rolled her head back as she stood with her hands on her hips.

"Wait on me in the car," Meka ordered her boyfriend as she kept her eyes on Slim and Kandi.

Meka's boyfriend walked off with nothing to say. Slim kept his cool as he stared up at the menu. He wasn't worried about the conflict between Meka and Kandi anymore. Cocoa governed his stash, and had an influence over Meka.

"What the hell is y'all doin' together?" Meka abruptly asked.

"Girl, I been knowin' Slim," Kandi said with a guilty smile.

"So, why was y'all actin' like y'all didn't know each other that day?"

"Meka, you know how you is about him, so I was tryin'… you know." Kandi vaguely explained.

"Girl please! You can never hurt my feelings! He gon' always have a spot at my house. Slim, let this bitch know what's up!"

"We ain't gotta get off into all that. You know what's up wit' me," Slim said before he turned to Kandi. "What's up? What'chu finna order?"

Kandi was looking for Slim to choose sides, but he was not about to get into their cat fight. She rolled her eyes at him before she placed her order.

"Bye, Slim," Meka said before she walked off with a smile. When she got to the door, she stopped and turned. "And happy birthday, slut," she said before she threw a fortune cookie at Kandi.

Kandi swatted the cookie away while Slim placed his order. After paying for their order, he joined Kandi at one of the tables. She had her lips poked out with her arms folded across her chest.

"I think we gotta understandin', so you can let that attitude go," Slim said just as Kandi was about to say something.

"You don't even know what I was about to say," Kandi said as she rolled her eyes at Slim.

"You ain't gotta say nothin', and we ain't gotta do no explainin' about what's goin' on between us. As long as we understand. Now, we can do what we do and go our seperate ways, or we can do what we do, and keep doin' what we do. It's all on you," Slim calmly said as he deleted unnecessary numbers from his beeper.

"I hope you makin' room for my number," Kandi said after stretching her neck to see what Slim was doing. She was telling him that she didn't want things to end after that day.

"We'll get to that later, 'cause you under investigation now." Slim smirked.

"I thought we had an understandin'?" Kandi asked, feeling perplexed.

"I thought we did, too."

"Just tell me what'chu lookin' for, and I might be able to help you find it."

In Kandi's eyes, Slim saw that she had a desire to please him. It made him think about the assistance he needed with his hustle when he started school. Cocoa's insightful words then popped into his head. *"stop thinkin' wit'cho dick 'fore it get'chu in a jam… stop tryin' to capitalize off girls based on them likin' you. Base yo' decisions on their capabilities"*.

"We'll talk… But right now, I'm tryin' to eat and get'chu in yo' birthday suit," Slim finally said.

"That's a good start," Kandi said with a smile before she went for their order.

Chapter 18: Her Capabilities

When Slim left the Chinese restaurant with Kandi, he was focused on her capabilities that would qualify her for the position he needed to fill. While she drove to her house, he recollected every little thing about her up until when he decided to analyze her. There was a lot that ruled in her favor, but he was far from making a decision. He thought about Nikki Pooh's deceit and how it came from being unsatisfied. If he was going to introduce Kandi into his circle, he was going to make sure that she was reasonably satisfied. He was going to play it how it go with her, even if she didn't know how the game was supposed to be played. That honor would most definitely help capture her loyalty. One thing that stuck out the most about her was, she wanted to be involved with him before he was doing his thing. It excluded an ulterior motive, and showed that she genuinely liked him.

When Kandi turned into an alley, Slim sat up and gripped the pistol on his lap. "Where the fuck is you takin' me" he asked as he twisted his face at her.

"You good. This how you get to my house." Kandi turned from the short alley and onto a narrow street. Slim passed that alley almost every day, and had no idea that it led to a street. The quiet street ran into a dead end where houses were lined in a hook. She lived in the core of the hook where she parked the car halfway on the side walk. Slim expected to be inside with Kandi for a while, so he put the tops back onto his car and chirped on the alarm. She led him up the driveway and took him into the small house from the side door. They came into the kitchen where she took him into the basement from there.

"So, this where you been hidin' at," Slim said as he observed the nicely decorated basement. It had two bedrooms on one end, a bathroom, and a living room area.

"Me and Shay share this space," Kandi said as she led Slim to the living room area.

As Slim sat on one of the couches with Kandi, he began to notice more things about her. This girl was a high maintenance diva. Every time he saw her, she was in designer clothes, and had her hair done with a fresh manicure and pedicure.

She also wore jewelry, but nothing too flashy. He then thought about her recent loss of employment that might interfere with her high maintenance status. It would give her motive to get down with him other than her liking him.

"How you get fired?" Slim asked with a laugh.

"I don't think it's funny! I needed my job," Kandi said with despair as she nudged Slim. That despair told him that she depended on herself.

"What happened? If you don't mind me askin'."

Kandi continued to eat, and took a moment to respond. "I was workin' at Famous wit my friend, Sheree, and she was stealin' all them people shit. They said if nobody don't come forward, they was gon' fire our whole shift. As much as I needed my job, I couldn't tell on my friend," she explained before she continued to eat.

Slim stared at Kandi with a slight smile as he was impressed by the sacrifice that showed her loyalty. It was one of the main qualities he was looking for.

"While you thinkin' this amusin', I got bills to pay! So, I wish you would take that stupid smile off your face!"

"I like how you get down, and how you don't just think about'cho self," Slim said as he sat his box of rice on the table. He then went into his pocket. "I ain't tryin' to reward you for keepin' it real, 'cause you 'pose to do that regardless, so happy b-day. That's like five hundred," he said as he put a wad of money on the table. He then picked up his food and continued to eat.

Kandi sat at the edge of the couch and stared back at Slim with a smile that stretched across her face. "Can I kiss you?" she sweetly asked.

"You know I'm in love wit'cho lips. C'mere," Slim said as he sat his food on the table and slumped into the couch.

Kandi's facial expressions became tender as she climbed into Slim's lap. He slid his hands up her thighs and under her skirt as she positioned herself. She wore thongs, which gave him the opportunity to squeeze her hot and loose, naked ass. Their first few kisses were modest as she teased him with her luscious lips. He squeezed her ass harder before she allowed him to suck on her lips during their passionate kissing. She grabbed the back of the couch as it became more intense.

"So, am I still under investigation?" Kandi softly asked as she chased her breath.

"I think we need to get a lil' more familiar, and I'm askin' for more than a taste."

Kandi kissed Slim's lips before she led him to her room by his hand. He closed the door behind them while she undressed herself on the way to the bed. He did the same thing, stripping down to nothing but his jewelry as he kept his eyes on her. Completely naked, she got on her knees in the middle of her bed and signaled for him to come to her. She held her head down with her seductive eyes on him as she moistened her lips with the tip of her tongue.

"You finna get it," Slim said as he came towards Kandi. He climbed onto the edge of the bed with his knees as she got down to her elbows and knees.

"Lemme take care of this for you," Kandi said as gently lifted Slim's dick to her mouth.

"It's all yours!"

Kandi wrapped her lips around the head of Slim's dick with her lips and massaged it with her tongue and jaws. She then ran her lips up and down the shaft of it as she was spreading the hot juices from her mouth. He sucked in air with his face tightened as he watched her do her thing with her eyes closed. Her hot mouth then gobbled his nuts with a slow slurp as she began to greedily enjoy them. He satisfyingly shook his head with one side of his face twisted while she slurped and smacked with her muffled moans. When she slowly pulled her mouth away, there was a loud smack. She then massaged his sack with one hand while her other hand stroked his dick. She continued to give it a gentle squeeze while the tight grip of her hot mouth worked the other end. It turns out that the birthday girl had some amazing capabilities. Her fire head had him ready to bust in three minutes.

"What's up? You gon' clean it up for me," Slim warned Kandi that he was about to explode.

Kandi became more excited as she began to twirl her head while her neck gracefully jerked back and forth. When Slim came, his growl was more like a roar. His head fell back with his eyes shut tight while he squeezed the back of her neck. When he looked back to her, she still had her mouth full, keeping him aroused and ready to put in work. After a moment, he shifted his eyes to her ass that was arched into a bubble.

"I'm good right here. I'm tryin' to get back there."

"You can have this birthday pussy however you want it," Kandi said with a sluttish attitude.

When Slim got behind Kandi, he grabbed onto her waist and watched her facial expressions as he slowly penetrated her. She gasped for breath as her tight insides snatched him inside. He pushed to the limit and rotated his hips as he pressed her ass against him. He bit his bottom lip with his eyes closed as the pleasurable tight grip took him away.

"Put it on me," Kandi softly whispered, taking Slim from his trance.

"I got it!" Slim's facial expressions became full of aggression as he remembered what he had to do. He started with ease and began to pound Kandi's ass with his fierce pushes from the bottom up. As he picked up his pace, he sent her ass waving back and forth with thunderous claps.

"Yes! Put it on me," Kandi cried out as she stood on her knees.

"Get'cho ass back down there," Slim growled in Kandi's ear as he grabbed her ponytail.

Slim wrapped Kandi's ponytail around his fist and forced her back to her hands and knees. He pulled her head back by her ponytail while he gripped her ass cheek. His pounding pushes were deep while she hysterically expressed the pleasure. Her moans came out in trembles as she took quick, deep breaths.

"Where yo' fuckin' jokes at now?" Slim growled in Kandi's face. "Turn over," he ordered.

Kandi was chasing her breath and trying to say something as she repositioned herself to her back. Before she could make herself clear, Slim put the tip of his two fingers into her mouth. She sucked and bit on them while he sucked and squeezed on her titties. He then stood on his knees while she made herself accessible for him. She opened her legs and brought the back of her calves to the back of her thighs with her back arched. Her arms were stretched over her head with her fingers entangled together. She looked at him with her sleepy eyes barely open as she bit one side of her bottom lip. As soon as he penetrated her, her bottom lip fumbled loose as she began to softly moan. Slim gripped Kandi's waist as he leaned forward with his deep plunges. She took deep breaths, and every time she exhaled, she cried out something that expressed her gratification.

All of a sudden, he found himself working his hot juices onto her chest. His head fell back with a vigorous growl while she continued to chase her breath. When he looked back to her, she was spreading his juices all over her hot titties as she squeezed them together.

"You a nasty bitch! I like that though," Slim said as he climbed from the bed.

"You brought it outta me," Kandi claimed.

Slim gave her a doubting smirk as he continued on to the bathroom.

After a quick and cold shower, Slim took a pink towel that was neatly folded across the rim of the tub and dried off with it. As he looked around, he realized that the towel was a part of the decorations. After a moment, he shrugged his shoulders and continued to dry off. He then put it into the dirty clothes hamper.

As Slim was about to leave the bathroom, he heard footsteps coming down to the basement. He stood there and held onto the door handle and listened.

"Kandi, who you got down here?" Slim heard a girl ask. It was obvious that Kandi had company from how Slim's car was boldly parked in front of the house. He remembered that his things were left on the table, including his pistol. He shook his head in disbelief as he went back for the pink towel. After wrapping it around his waist, he came from the bathroom.

Two girls were sitting on one of the couches in the living room area. Slim recognized one of them as Shay. He figured that the older girl was Kandi's sister. She was fairly cute, and shared no resemblance of Kandi. She looked at him with her forehead wrinkled while Shay squinted her eyes at him.

"S'cuse me," Kandi's sister tried to say politely.

"What's up?" Slim asked as he stopped.

"Can you come and get this thing?" Kandi's sister asked more politely as she shifted her eyes to the pistol, then back to Slim.

As Slim came over to the living room area, Kandi's sister looked him up and. Shay's eyes popped back open as if her study of him came to a conclusion.

"My bad," Slim said as he grabbed his pistol. His apology was sincerely expressed. If he was going to be doing his thing with Kandi, he had to make peace with her surroundings.

"Ain't cho name, Slim?" Shay asked with certainty.

"Yeah," Slim said before he turned to leave.

"And that towel you got wrapped around yo' naked ass 'pose to be for decorations," Shay complained with a feisty attitude.

"It is being… decorated," Kandi said as she came from her room.

Kandi had her naked body wrapped in a white sheet. Slim looked over his shoulder to Shay with a slight smile and shrugged his shoulders as he continued on.

"And you hoes bet'not mess wit' my birthday money," Kandi said before she went into the bathroom.

Slim slid his pistol under Kandi's bed before he got dressed. He thought about her authoritative attitude towards her sister and Shay. She showed no signs of embarrassment or guilt. It appeared that she had some control over what went on around the house. That built a little more trust as he felt more comfortable with pursuing his intentions with her.

Kandi was still in the bathroom when Slim came from her room. He could hear her singing in the shower when he passed it. Her sister and Shay was smoking on a blunt together when he came over to the living room area. He sat on the couch across from them and put the left-over food back into the bags. He could feel their eyes on him as he tidied up the table.

"You gave my lil' sister all that money?"

"It ain't nothin'," Slim said as he began to split a blunt with his fingernails.

"That's a lot of money to be givin' somebody you barely know. Unless you have some kinda strings attached," Kandi's sister said, playing her role as a big sister.

"It didn't take long for me to get to know the basic things about Kandi. I'm feelin' her, so whatever I do for her is based on that," Slim said as he reached for Kandi's purse.

"You hella bold! What if she got somethin' in there she don't want'chu to see?" Shay seen boldness in Slim going into Kandi's purse and became agitated as it reminded her of someone.

"Me and Kandi ain't caught up on the small shit," Slim calmly said. "And I'm hopin' you can find the difference between me and that other nigga."

"Fuck that nigga! You ain't have to bring that up!"

"You brought it up wit'cho attitude towards me, and I just wanna make things clear. Me and Kandi doin' our thing. Listen to her. Do it sound like she bein' mistreated? Like I said, we doin' our thing, so that should give you the opportunity to find the difference between me and that other nigga," he said as he sprinkled weed across his blunt.

Kandi's sister shook her head up and down while Shay twisted her face at Slim.

"So, what's yo' name? If you don't mind me askin'." Slim asked.

"You cool. I'm Samantha," she kindly said as she passed Shay the blunt.

Shay snatched the blunt from Samantha and rolled her eyes. She was mad at her for not sharing her hostility towards Slim. He began to wonder if she condemned him from her experience with G-Will, or was she mad for making the wrong choice.

"Girl, you need to stop it," Samantha said with a laugh as she knew where Shay's attitude came from. "So, what's up, Slim? You gon' kick it wit' us tonight for Kandi's b-day?"

"Is that an invitation?"

"No," Shay intervened.

"Don't trip off of her. She'll get over it. What'chu drink?" Samantha asked.

"Hennessy straight wit no ice." Slim replied as he sparked his blunt.

"I got'chu."

"Y'all bet'not be harassin' him," Kandi said as she came from the bathroom.

"Girl, please! Ain't nobody trippin' off of him," Shay became defensive.

"You bet'not be," Kandi said as she continued on to her room.

While Kandi was getting herself together, Slim was talking with Tish. She expressed her liking to Peach, and he invited her over to their apartment that Friday. She started to tell him something about Nut's appearance, but his attention was taken by Kandi as she sat next to him.

Kandi went from top model to hood with her appearance. She had on white and sky blue Jordans that looked perfect on her small, pigeon-toed feet. Her extra small, Polo shorts fit her tightly as they showed off her curves and plump booty. The sky-blue Polo halter top matched the Polo hat that she had pulled down above her eyes. She wore two French braids to the back with sky blue balls at the tips. She was imitating Slim with the same Jordans, black Polo shorts, sky blue Polo shirt, and the matching hat with two French braids.

When Slim got off the phone with Tish, he sat slumped in the couch and listened to Samantha and Shay tease Kandi about her appearance. Samantha's comments came from admiration, while

Shay's was to antagonize. There was no defending or explaining from Kandi. She just continued to roll her blunt with a smile on her face.

"You look like a lil' slut," Shay said with a laugh.

"So, my boo like it," Kandi said as she looked to Slim, then back to Shay.

"You wanna ride wit' me right quick," Slim asked as he slid his beeper from his hip. "We'll be right back."

"Of course," Kandi replied gladly.

Slim went into Kandi's room and got his pistol before they left the house. When they got into his car, she was quiet while she waited for him to say something.

"So, I'm yo' boo, huh?" Slim asked as he started the car.

"If that's cool wit'chu" Kandi blushed.

"I ain't trippin'."

"So, what would you introduce me as?"

"Kandi," Slim said with a laugh.

"That's cool. I can be yo' Kandi girl. I might spoil yo' appetite though."

"I can handle you," Slim said as he looked to Kandi, then back to the road.

"Yeah, you can."

Slim shook his head up and down as he turned his music up. He was out with Kandi longer than he expected to be. She didn't mind at all. She enjoyed being out with her new boo. When they finally made it back to her house, the day was just breaking. Cars lined in her driveway told them that her friends were there. As Slim walked up the driveway with Kandi, he noticed a tall, light skinned dude at the side door. When he looked to her, she had her face twisted at him. Her hostile expression set him off. Ever since that night at the movies, he became more alert as he was ready to blaze his pistol at any suspecting threat. He pulled it from his waist with his face screwed as they continued up the driveway.

"Hold on, boo. I know him," Kandi calmly said.

When the dude noticed Slim holding a pistol with an ignorant look, he jumped into a petrified stance. Slim continued to analyze him as he envisioned him pulling out a pistol of his own. He only stood there with his hands down to his side as he held a black box. Slim seen him as no threat, so he put his pistol back onto his waist.

"That's why you can't just be poppin' up over here! You know I don't play that shit," Kandi said as she stepped to the dude.

"My bad, I knew that it was yo' birthday, and I just wanted to surprise you wit' this," the dude said as he handed Kandi the box.

"Thank you. And I don't mean to be rude, but I have company," Kandi politely said.

"It's all good. Happy birthday," the dude said before he walked off.

"I'm sorry about that," Kandi said as she turned to Slim, who was leaning on the house. "But damn, you surprised me when you pulled that thing out," she said as she unlocked the door.

"Surprised! I guess you haven't realized what it is wit' me yet," Slim said as he followed Kandi into the house.

"I know what it is wit'chu. And don't no niggas be poppin' up over here on me, so you don't have to worry about that." Kandi was telling Slim that she could provide security, and that was another thing that gave her a plus with him.

"I wanna fuck wit'chu on some real shit, but right now, I'm tryin' to see the birthday girl shake her ass wit' her peoples."

"Okay," Kandi said as she carelessly tossed the box onto the table.

"Why you frontin'?" Slim asked with a laugh. "You know you wanna see what's in that box."

"I do wanna see what it is," Kandi said with a guilty smile. "But I'm more interested in showin' my boo off."

"I ain't trippin'. Open it."

"Well, if you insist," Kandi said as she went for the box. Her face became twisted when she opened it.

"What is it?"

"This is too much! I can't accept this," Kandi said as she lifted a gold necklace from the box with her finger. The thin rope held a heart pendant that was in the middle of an "I" and a "u".

"I see you spoiled somebody's appetite," Slim said with a laugh.

"Shut up! This is not funny," Kandi laughed with Slim as she put the necklace back into its box.

When Slim and Kandi stepped into the basement, they were hit by a thick cloud of funky weed smoke. Rap music played under the loud chatter of Samantha, Shay and Kandi's other three friends. They all sat around on the couches with their cups filled with Alize while three blunts were in rotation. The table was filled with their favorite drink, a fifth of Hennessy, along with a quarter pound of weed. They were too busy gossiping with their sassy hand gestures to notice Slim and Kandi at the bottom of the steps.

"You hoes betta recognize me," Kandi yelled over the noise level with her hands on her hips.

All at once, the chattering came to a stop as everyone gave Kandi the attention she demanded. Her friends became joyful as they rushed over to her with smiles. They were all dimes, and neither one of them out shined the other. After they greeted Kandi with hugs, kisses and happy birthday, they turned to Slim.

"Damn bitch! Introduce us," one of Kandi's friends said as she looked Slim up and down.

"This my boo, Slim. And Slim, this Jessica, Sheree, and Kim," Kandi proudly introduced them.

"Damn! You got her callin' you, boo already! You musta put it on her," Sheree surprisingly said. "What's up wit' that?"

"I'ma let Kandi answer that. It was nice meetin' y'all though," Slim said before he went to Kandi's room.

After Slim put his pistol under Kandi's bed, he joined the party. Kandi sat on one of the couches and opened her gifts as she was surrounded by her friends. They bought her everything from jewelry to lingerie. Slim sat on the couch across from them with Samantha and Shay. He rolled a blunt and watched Kandi's excitement as she opened her gifts.

Slim had been ignoring the pages that came through his beeper for the last thirty minutes. Kandi was sitting on his lap, sipping Alize with a stuffed blunt while he sipped his Hennessy from the bottle. They were watching her tipsy friends get loose to Master P's "Bounce That Ass" track. Even Shay got up to show off her fat, round booty. After he had the birthday girl to shut the show down with her seductive moves, it was time for him to go get his money. She was disappointed when he told her that he had to leave, but her face lit up when he told her that he wanted to come back and spend the night with her.

It wasn't until later on that night when Slim came back to Kandi's house. It was Samantha who let him into the quiet house. She came to the door groggy, wearing nothing but a tank-top and extra short shorts. Just as she was locking the door, Kandi came up from the basement. She was wearing a long t-shirt that stopped at the bottom of her ass cheeks.

Slim followed Kandi to her dim lit room and closed the door behind them. It looked as if she didn't have anything on under her t-shirt. Her loose ass jiggled with every step she took. And he was right. When she got to the edge of her bed, she pulled the shirt off over her head, revealing her naked body. She looked over her shoulder to him with a smile before she dropped it to the floor. She then crawled onto the bed as she kept her eyes on him. It was mesmerizing how the dim light made her reddish-brown skin glow. She laid on her back and sat up on her elbows with one knee up.

"It's yours, boo," Kandi whispered.

"And you know I'm finna get it!"

After Slim sat his things on the night stand, he got completely naked. He then got into the bed where Kandi welcomed him with her amazing head.

Slim was awakened the next morning by his vibrating beeper that rattled the glass night stand. He squinted his eyes as he opened them to the sun lit room. He laid on his back while Kandi slept with her head on his chest. She had her arm and leg across him as if she wasn't trying to let him get away from her. Her pretty face looked peaceful, and he could hear her softly breathing. He gazed over her beautiful body in admiration as he caressed it with his fingertips. Her skin was butter soft and tight with no stretch marks. When he got to her ass, he laid his hand there and gave it a gentle squeeze with his fingertips. He was ready to go another round, but his beeper demanded his attention. It was another check day, and a perfect time to introduce Kandi to the game.

"I'm hungry," Slim said after he fiercely smacked Kandi's ass.

Kandi's eyes slowly opened as she looked up to Slim, moistening her lips. "I'ma cook for you," she sweetly offered.

"I'ma take you up on that one day. But right now, I just want somethin' quick."

"Busy day, huh," Kandi predicted as she shifted her eyes to Slim's beeper, then back to him.

"Yeah, and I'm tryin' to include you in on it. Let's get up and talk about that."

Kandi liked the sound of that as she got up with a smile. She got dressed in a tank-top, pink cotton panties and white, fuzzy slippers while Slim got dressed and collected his things.

When they got to the kitchen, Slim sat slumped at the table while Kandi fixed him a big bowl of cereal. After fixing herself some, she sat across from him. He was already eating with the bowl between his arms and his face over it.

Kandi was still eating when Slim finished. He sat slumped in the chair while he flipped through the numbers in his beeper. He then called each one of them and promised generosity for their patience. When Kandi finished eating, she took the bowls from the table and washed them. She then rolled a blunt for Slim and lit it from the stove. He was just finishing his last phone call when she came back to the table.

"I'm feelin' you, and I want'chu to get this money wit' me," Slim said before he pulled on the blunt.

"I'm feelin' you too, and I'm open to whatever it is you tryin' to introduce to me."

"I'm tryin' to introduce you to somethin' I already got established," Slim said as he sat his beeper up on the table. "Believe it or not, but even though I'ma street nigga, I go to school. Plus, it's other things that be takin' up my time. So, I want'chu to be my right hand when I got my left hand full. If you get down wit' me, I'ma give you everything that'll help you be down wit' me. You seen how I move my work, so I ain't tryin' to have you posted on the block doin' nothin'. I run through two ounces at the most in two regular days, and see no less than thirty-five hundred from that. I'll give you a grand for every three you pick up for me."

Kandi thought for a moment as she shook her head up and down. "I like how you move. You got'cho thing set up simple, and you 'bout'cho business. That alone makes me feel comfortable wit' gettin' down wit'chu and acceptin' yo' guidance. So, yeah I wanna get down wit'chu," she said. "Plus, I need the money."

"I like that'chu wanna get down wit' me 'cause you need the money, and not all 'cause you feelin' me. You say I'm yo' boo, and that's cool. But let's not get the lines blurry that separates me as yo' boo, and you bein' my right hand."

"Business first. I got'chu."

"Aiight. Lemme go get this shit, and when I get back, I'ma give you the whip game and show you what's what."

When Slim got back to Kandi's house, he showed her everything she needed to know while he told her about the game. Before he hit the streets with her, he stashed four of the nine ounces he rocked up in her room. He wanted her to become familiar with the routes, so he let her do the driving. When they got to their destinations, he let her do the dealings while he stood on the side. Her response to the game impressed him as he seen that she was receptive to his insight.

On their way from making a drop, Slim directed Kandi to a car lot. It was a red and black, '87 S-10 Chevy Blazer that caught his attention.

They were shortly joined by the dealer who noticed their interest in the mint condition truck. He didn't have to do too much convincing. After the inspection, they all went into the dealer's office. Slim paid the total while Kandi did the paper work.

After dropping the truck off at Kandi's house, she and Slim were back on the move. In the midst of everything, he managed to pick up a phone and a pistol for her. It was at Vee's apartment where they spent most of their time. More pages came through while he was there. He left Kandi to deal with Vee, her company and Felicia. When he came back, he brought something to eat for them. Just as he expected, she was down to her last ounce. Through her cool composure, he could see the excitement as she counted stacks of money.

It wasn't until two in the morning when Slim and Kandi caught a break. They were in her room, counting everything they made. The money was piled in the middle of her bed while they sat across from each other. They smoked blunts of their own while they counted. They added up $7,400 twice before they fell to the bed. They stared at each other with neat stacks of money in between them.

"Shit be movin' hella fast on the first and the fifteenth," Slim said with grogginess.

"I can handle it."

"You did yo' thing for me today, and I'ma leave you wit' the beepa in the mornin'. I need to get situated wit somethin', so I'ma see you when I see you. You got my number though, and I'm just a phone call away."

"I got'chu."

"I know you do, but right now, I'm tryin' to get'chu to put me to sleep," Slim said as he brushed Kandi's lips with his fingertips.

"I can do that," Kandi said before she cleared the bed. She then granted Slim's request.

Chapter 19: Play It How It Go

Peach called Slim early that next morning, waking him from his deep sleep. It was actually Kandi who got him up for his phone. He'd only had a few hours of sleep. Peach was at his father's house, anxious and excited to show him their apartment. He forced himself out of bed and took a quick shower before he left.

When Slim got to his father's house, Peach was on the porch with Jayla and Fe-Fe. He didn't realize that he missed her up until that point, even though she called him those two days before she went to sleep. It was the fulfilling time with Kandi that occupied him. But as those charming, light brown eyes of Peach took him in, he was reminded of where his heart was.

Peach met Slim at the top of the steps with an affectionate smile that lifted her face. The chemistry between them overwhelmed his weariness. He returned the same amount of affection with a smile as he checked her out. After greeting each other, they all went to his room and helped him gather his things.

Slim left some of his clothes at his father's house with the $32,500 from the heist. He took a little over $23,000 to build a new stash at the apartment.

Slim followed Peach to some apartment buildings that were in the neighborhood. She had Jayla in the car with her while Fe-Fe rode with him. The two four family flats had a driveway between them that took them behind the buildings. There was a small, fenced parking lot behind the buildings. He passed those buildings every day, and had no idea that his father owned them.

As they entered through the front of the building, Slim noticed that the good maintenance matched the landscaping. After locking the door behind them, Peach led everyone upstairs. When she got to their door, she turned to Slim with a smile.

"Welcome home, baby," Peach said as she unlocked the door. The first thing Slim noticed when he came into the apartment was the black leather Peach opposed to. It had that brand-new smell along with mango air freshener that lingered in the air. He dropped his bags with a smile and sat in one of the recliners. From there, he could see most of the apartment.

Everything in the cozy living room sat on sky blue carpet. A full-sized sofa sat against the wall, facing an entertainment center. Glass end tables sat on each side of the sofa with touch lamps. The lamps were black and see through with sky blue shades. Another glass table sat in front of the sofa. Small, crystal animals decorated a corner of it. A love seat separated the living room from the dining room. The small dining room had a small table that seated four. A step away was the kitchen. A bar counter separated the two. Two rotating stools with cushioned arms and seats sat on each side of the counter. A carpeted hallway ran from the kitchen to the rest of the apartment.

Slim shook his head in approval while Peach watched him. Jayla and Fe-Fe looked around commenting on the lavish décor excitedly.

"C'mon, baby. Lemme show you our room," Peach said as she approached Slim.

"I seen enough," Slim teased. The comforting recliner put him back into his weary state. He reclined it and closed his eyes.

"C'mon," Peach whined as she pulled Slim's arm. It sounded as if Peach desperately wanted Slim to see their room. He kept his eyes closed with a smile while she continued to whine and pull on his dead weight.

"Von-Von get up, and quit playin'," Jayla ordered as she punched his arm.

"Yeah, lemme get up so I can put'chu out," Slim said as he rose with Peach's pull.

"I can get a key," Jayla said as she punched Slim again. Slim laughed at Jayla as Peach led him away by his hand.

She took him to the kitchen where the cabinets were full of food and kitchen accessories. Even the refrigerator was full. She then led him down the hall. He peeped into the bathroom and Kaliyah's fully furnished room on their way. The hall ran into the door of their room with the door that led to the back door on the left.

When Peach opened the door to their room, she stepped in and watched Slim's reaction as he came in behind her. He stepped into the light-brown carpeted room and got a heartwarming feeling. Coming from the wall on his right was a cherry wood, sleigh bed. The king-sized bed matched the chestnut night stands that sat on each side of it with lamps. A cherry wood dresser that came with the set sat against the wall in front of him. Directly from the foot of the bed was a small entertainment center. It sat against the wall with a love seat in front of it. The love seat was red suede, and sat on a red, plush rug.

"Baby, what'chu think," Peach sweetly asked.

"C'mere," Slim said as he pulled Peach closer to him. He wrapped his arms around her waist while she wrapped hers around his neck. "I like what'chu put together for us. I been runnin' the streets for two days straight, and to fall back to somethin' like this where I can do me at… I ain't surprised though. You always hold it down when it come to us, and I love you for that."

"Love you too," Peach said before she and Slim engaged in a passionate kiss.

During the intimacy, Jayla and Fe-Fe left the room giggling as they found Slim and Peach cute.

"Where's Kaliyah? I missed her the other day."

"She's at work. We gon' cook tonight, so y'all can talk then."

"That's cool. But right now, I'm finna get in that bed. I'm hella tired."

"You do that, and I'll put'cho stuff up," Peach said as she brushed Slim's weary face.

After kissing Peach, Slim headed towards the bed as he undressed himself. She watched him with a smile as he climbed into it. There was no need for him to make himself comfortable. The softness of the mattress relieved him of that. He laid on his stomach and quickly drifted into a deep sleep.

Slim peacefully slept until five that evening. He woke up in the same position he fell asleep in. It only took him a few seconds to remember that he was at home. He rolled over to his back and thought about it for a moment before he got up.

Slim found Peach over the stove when he came into the kitchen. Kaliyah was sitting at the counter, peeling potatoes while she held her phone to her ear with her shoulder. R&B played at a low volume in the living room. Neither one of them noticed him leaning at the entry of the kitchen. He was watching Peach. She was in fuzzy slippers, stretch pants, and a feminine tank-top with a stringy ponytail. She was happily singing to the music, not caring that she was off key with her notes. It was Kaliyah who noticed him after she clicked her phone off. He nodded his head at her, and when she spoke.

Peach turned to him with a bright smile.

"Hey, baby! How long you been standin there?"

"For a minute. I'ma go take a shower though."

"Okay. The food'll be ready in like thirty minutes," Peach said as she turned back to the stove, singing.

After his shower, the smell of fried chicken made his empty stomach growl. In his room, he got dressed in a tank-top, basketball shorts, and black leather slippers that Peach bought for him. Before he left the room, he called Nut and asked him to come over.

Peach had just finished fixing their plate when Slim came into the kitchen. She was heading towards the counter with them, where Kaliyah was already eating. After getting the juice and cups, he joined them.

"Baby, it's some more over there if that ain't enough," Peach said before she began to eat.

"This cool. Thank you," Slim said as he pulled his plate closer to him.

Kaliyah, who sat across from Slim and Peach stared at them in admiration.

"My bad for runnin' off on you the other day. I wanted to see what was up wit'chu, but'chu was gone when I came back," Slim apologized before he began to eat.

"I was about to 'pologize myself for runnin' off. I was on my lunch break, and I had to get back to work."

"It's all good. What's up, though? Peach said somethin' 'bout'chu bein' a good girl."

"I am a good girl," Kaliyah proudly said as she rolled her head at Peach.

"I never knew it was a such thing as a good girl. Do that mean you 'pose to be a saint or somethin'?"

"I'm far from a saint, but closer to it than the average girl my age. I don't think I'm betta than anybody. I just be into some different things."

"Like what? If you don't mind me askin'."

"I don't mind," Kaliyah replied with a smile as she was touched by Slim's interest. "I'm focused on gettin' myself established career wise, so I work and save my lil'money for college. My friend's sister own a beauty salon, and I work there sometimes to get familiar wit the business. Plus, my mama own a daycare center that I do volunteer work at some weekends. I love kids, so I wanna open up my own daycare centers too," she spoke with enthusiasm.

"Saint," Peach said with a laugh.

"She on her grind. I like that," Slim spoke with admiration. "So, I guess that's what makes you closer to a saint than the average girl yo' age. Now, what about the side that makes you far from it?"

"It ain't nothin'," Kaliyah said with a guilty smile.

"Uh-oh! I see horns comin' from yo' head," Slim said, giving Peach and Kaliyah a laugh.

"It ain't nothin'. I just smoke a lil' weed and other things that's too silly to mention."

"Tell me." Slim insisted.

Kaliyah gave a cute little laugh before she responded. "Well, like yesterday when me and Peach was at the grocery store shoppin', I was sneakin' and eatin' they grapes and gummy bears."

"Yeah, I agree wit' Peach. You is a saint," Slim said with a laugh. "It's all good though. I like you. So, what's up? I know you got a dude chasin' you."

"I'ma take that as a compliment, but I wouldnt say that I have people chasin' me. I do have a friend, but wit' me bein' serious about accomplishin' somethin' for myself, I choose not to become serious wit' anybody."

Slim shook his head up and down as they continued to eat, talk and laugh together. Kaliyah reminded him of Carmen in a sense. They both had career goals, were ambitious, and were levelheaded, but didn't claim to be innocent. She had a sweet and charming personality that he instantly became drawn to.

"What the hell?" Peach exclaimed as she looked around the apartment with her face twisted.

It was thunderous bass that sent vibrations through the apartment as it drowned the music that played in the living room.

"That's Nut," Slim said as he rose from the stool.

Nut was at the front door talking to two young women when Slim came down the steps. He stood close to them and used hand gestures with his words. Whatever he was saying to them, they found it impressive. They smiled from ear to ear as they were captivated by his cocky swag.

"What's up, Cuz? What'chu got goin' on down here?" Slim intervened.

"This Meko and Feenah. They stay next door to you, and as you can see, it's a lot goin' on wit' them. I'm just down here finna get involved," Nut said as he rubbed his hands together.

"And what's yo' name?" Meko asked with friendliness.

"Slim. But don't lemme interrupt. Y'all look like y'all was enjoyin' my peoples do what he do."

"Yeah, he is doin' what he do real good, but me and my girl might be too much for him to handle," Feenah said as she looked Nut up and down.

"Check this out," Nut said as he stepped closer to Meko and Feenah. "It's undastood that I'm feelin' y'all, and I know y'all feelin' me. So, let's wrap this up. I'm finna lock y'all number in my beeper, and we gon unwrap this and get loose when I get at y'all," he said as he dialed his beeper number. Meka and Feenah looked at each other with smiles before they shook their head up and down. After Meko call their number out to Nut, they left, anxiously waiting to get with this Hot Boy.

"I got 'em! All you gotta do is be there."

"As much as I wanna be involved wit' them gettin' down together, I gotta keep it movin'. They too close to home," Slim said as he shook his head from side to side.

"Cuz, I'm trippin'! You got Peach up there. And that's some real shit. Some niggas fail to realize, not playin' it how it go is why mu-fuckas get on some scandalous shit wit 'em."

"I'm glad you put that out there like that, 'cause you'll undastand what I'm 'bout to put in yo' ear," Slim said as he sat on the steps.

"What's up?" Nut asked as he sat with Slim.

From beginning to end, Slim told Nut about Nikki Pooh. He began with her enticement, and ended with the position she wanted to put him in. It all made sense to Nut as he was familiar with the game. He just listened, and shook his head up and down when Slim made his points.

"Cuz, you shoulda fucked her, but I understand where yo' head was at. And if you need my hands to play any part in this, I got'chu."

"I'm just layin' low right now, playin' it by ear wit my eyes open," Slim responded. "But ay, lemme show you how a boss live."

"I know you doin' it big up here!"

As Slim was going up the steps, he stopped and turned to Nut as he thought about something. "Ay Cuz! Lemme put'chu up on somethin' right quick."

"What's up?"

"Peach sister live up here too, and she hella bad. Her name Kaliyah, and when you see her, I know you gon shoot'cho shot. And that's cool, but check this out," Slim said before he paused. "I had a chance to sit down and vibe wit Kaliyah. I don't know how you play it, but I play it how it go all around the board. I respect things for what they worth, and stick to the script that comes wit every category. Everything has its place. I like Kaliyah to the point where I don't wanna see her head fucked up. If she give you that opportunity to get at her, I'm hopin' you'll play it how it go and treat her in accordance wit' what type of girl she is. I ain't tellin' you to step outside yo' character to get at her, 'cause you can do you wit' things still bein' all good. If you get at her, open yo' hand and let her know what's up wit'chu. If she accepts it, she'll know what to expect, and won't be misled. So, before anything, let her get to know you."

"Cuz, what's really goin' on wit ol'girl," Nut asked after a moment.

"She hella sweet, and she doin' her thing on some grown woman shit. I ain't tryin'a see her separated from that. Plus, I gotta live here wit' them, and I ain't tryin' to hear Peach mouth about, why I let'chu dog her sister. So at least on the strength of me, fuck wit' her right, or leave her alone."

"You rnakin' it seem like she can't think for herself."

"Her bein' able to think for herself is besides the point when it comes to dealin' wit' niggas like us. We gon' always find a way to do what we wanna do. I'm jus askin' you not to mistreat her."

"I can't do nothin' but respect what'chu on. And if I get at her, I'ma respect her mind and play it how it go. I got it in me."

"Jus keep yo' eyes open," Slim warned as he continued on up the steps.

When Slim and Nut came into the apartment, Peach was on the couch with Kaliyah. Kaliyah's poster and the attentive expression on her face said that she was being advised about something. Peach freezing up when Slim came in with Nut made it obvious. After locking the door, Slim formally introduced Nut and Kaliyah. Kaliyah spoke with modesty while Nut greeted her with a cool attitude.

"Yeah, Cuz. You doin' it big up here," Nut said as he kept his eyes on Kaliyah.

"Baby, c'mere," Peach sweetly said as she came to Slim and grabbed his hand.

Despite the sweetness in Peach's tone, Slim could hear the urgency. She took him to their room as he had a good idea of what was on her mind. He sat on their bed as she stood between his legs.

"Baby, I ain't got nothin' against Nut. He's cool and I like him," Peach said before she took a deep breath and slowly exhaled. "I know wit' him bein' around, he gon try to get at my sister. I ain't tryin' to make it seem like she too good for him. It's just that he is too much for her. She is too sweet, and she do not know how to deal wit a street nigga. She got all these things that she tryin' to accomplish, and I don't want her to get hurt. It could distract her. She do have a strong mind, but I know how a strong mind can be broken by a relentless street nigga. So, can you please tell him not to mess wit her?" Slim could hear the desperation Peach's sweet voice as she brushed his hair with her hand.

"Did you talk to her?"

"Yeah, but I still want 'chu to talk to Nut," Peach urged as she pushed Slim.

"I already did, and I understand yo' concerns. At the same time, we can't control what happens between them. I did tell Nut what kinda girl Kaliyah is. He knows how I feel about her, and if anything, his respect for me won't let him mistreat her."

"Okay. If she end up hurt, I'm holdin' you responsible," Peach said as she pushed Slim's head with her finger. He intentionally fell to the bed with a slight smile while she stared at him with her face tightened. After a moment, loosened up and smiled. "I like that'chu like my sister to where you'll look out for her. I love this soft side of you.

"Everything got its place. I jus respect everything and everybody for what they worth."

"So, I guess I don't have to worry about 'chu creepin' wit' these hoes that live in the buildin'."

"Do I really gotta explain myself to you?"

"No," Peach said before she kissed Slim. "C'mon. Let's go be nosy."

When Slim and Peach came into the living room, Nut was sitting next to Kaliyah, and had just clicked his phone off.

"Ay Cuz, I need to go take care of something right quick, but I'll be around," Nut said as he looked to Kaliyah, then back to Slim.

"It's all good. Do what'chu do," Slim said as he headed towards the door with Nut.

Before Slim and Nut left the apartment, Nut and Kaliyah gave each other friendly good-byes. As they were going down the steps, Nut was shaking his head from side to side with a smile.

"What's up? What'chu do," Slim asked.

"Jus that quick, I seen what'chu meant about Kaliyah. She hella sweet, and I'm finna get at her," Nut said with excitement.

"So, what about Meko and Feenah?"

"Damn! I forgot about them!"

"Play it how it go," Slim reminded Nut with a laugh

"And this is exactly why I don't get involved wit' this serious shit," Nut sadly said as he shook his head in disbelief. "But Kaliyah crushin' both of them hoes put togetha, so I ain't losin' shit."

"Do what'chu do."

"Me and summa the homeboys hittin' the club this weekend. You wit' me?"

"I'm wit'chu," Slim said as he and Nut clapped hands.

When Slim came back into the apartment, Peach was rolling a blunt while Kaliyah flipped through the channels. From the warm smile Kaliyah gave him, he figured that Peach told her about him having her best interest at heart. He sat between them, where they all began to talk and laugh together.

Kaliyah had to get up for work in the morning, so she went to her room after awhile. As soon as she was gone, Slim initiated the intimate touching with Peach. It wasn't long before they took it to their room. They weren't alone in the apartment, so they had to be respectful. Even though their love making was quiet, it didn't lack intensity or satisfaction.

When they were done, Slim smoked on a blunt and flipped through the channels while Peach laid with her head on his chest. She'd been rubbing his stomach, but suddenly stopped.

"Baby, I haven't been hearin' yo' beeper go off, and it ain't over there. Did you lose it?"

"I know where it's at," Slim said as he continued to channel surf.

Peach stared at Slim for a moment before she tightened her face. "Who is she?"

"What makes you so certain that it's a she?"

"'Cause I know you don't vibe wit' too many niggas, and these lil' girls will do anything just to fuck wit'chu."

"Her name Kandi, and she ain't pushin' for me 'cause she wanna fuck wit me."

"Do she know about me?"

"She knows about'chu, but we gotta understandin' where knowin' about'chu ain't necessary. Now, is you gon' trip off it bein' anotha girl, or is you gon' let me do what I do to make sure we eat."

"I was jus wonderin' if she knew what she was doin' wit'out chu holdin' her hand."

"Trust my judgment and let it go," Slim said before he pulled on his blunt.

"I do trust yo' judgment, but that has nothin' to do wit' how I feel about'chu. Just be patient wit me, 'cause it's hard for me to fall back."

"I can be patient wit'chu, and I'll always come to you about certain things."

A smile appeared on Peach's face as she was happy to know that Slim wasn't trying to shut her out completely.

Getting situated in the apartment came with ease for Slim, Peach and Kaliyah. Nut spent some time there. He was surprised to see how affectionate he was with Kaliyah. His gorilla built, ruthless cousin actually had a sensitive side. While he and Kaliyah were making a connection, Peach quietly held her reservations.

Slim hadn't left the apartment all week. It was now the weekend, and he was on the passenger side of Nut's car, ready to hit the club. Before Nut drove to his hood where everyone was going to meet, he stopped at the gas station.

Slim sat inside the car talking with Kandi while Nut went inside to pay for the gas. Everything was all good on her end, and he was going to get with her in the morning. Just as he clicked his phone off, Nikki Pooh was parking at the pump in front of him. When she caught his eyes, she fingered for him to come to her.

Nut was just coming from the gas station when Slim was heading towards Nikki Pooh's car. He shifted his eyes to her, then back to Slim as he continued on to his car. He kept his awareness up as Slim got into her car.

"What's up?" Slim asked before he pulled on his blunt.

"It's all good. I'm still doin' what I do on my end. I'm 'pose to pick up ten bricks in three weeks, and I'ma take care of him when I get back. Just be patient, and I promise you, it's gon be worth it."

"I ain't lookin' for no handouts, so why don't chu take care of him now, and we can go from there."

"I wanna end this wit' somethin' in my hands. I been holdin' it down for him, and I ain't got shit to show for it. He ain't been playin' it right wit me, and I jus been waitin' on the perfect time to get what I deserve."

"Aiight. Now, what I don't understand is, how you gon knock this nigga, and be gettin' at his connect?"

"I'm from Memphis, and these my peoples I'm gettin' at."

"I'm wit'chu. Now, tell me 'bout the position you tryin' to put me in."

"When I get back and do what I do, I'ma dump the bricks on you for the low. I'm hopin' that'chu fuck wit me on how you move 'em. I can move 'em myself, but I don't know too many people in the Lou. I'd rather put the shit in a nigga hands that's gon play the game how it go and give me security. I just wanna be satisfied and eat from my own plate," Nikki spoke with a mellow tone as she looked into Slim's eyes.

Slim shook his head up and down, pulling on his blunt as he thought about Nikki Pooh's appealing proposal. "Do what'chu do, and when you get done, you got my number."

"I'ma get wit'chu," Nikki Pooh promised. "But um, G-Will ain't expectin' me 'til a few hours. Can you get away wit' me. I keep a room at the "Ramada, or we can go where ever you wanna go."

Slim chuckled before he responded. "Is this yo' way of showin' me that'chu serious, or is it somethin' personal?"

"Both! But seein' you as a young nigga holdin' it down turns me on. You deserve this pussy, and I wanna let'chu have yo' way wit it," Nikki Pooh said as she looked Slim up and down.

"That sound hella good, but let's not jeopardize what we on by gettin' distracted by this extra shit. So look, when you get it together, we gon' get it together."

Nikki Pooh admired Slim's focus and how he made a logical decision instead of letting her sex appeal distract him. "I'm feelin' that."

"I'm waitin' on you," Slim said before he got out of the car.

On the way to Nut's hood, Slim filled him in on things with Nikki Pooh. He wanted him to be aware of the situation just in case things weren't what they appeared to be. Considering what was exposed about G-Will by Nikki Pooh, they didn't have much room to feel skeptical. They were both looking forward to the connection that would give them hood rich status.

The summer was almost over, and it was one that Slim would never forget. Things at home with Peach remained peaceful. If he wasn't in the streets, he was at the apartment with her and Kaliyah. It was her persistency that helped him get his driver's license. She also encouraged him to think beyond the dope game as they were preparing to share a child together.

Slim's hustle was prosperous with Kandi being worth the investment. She became familiar with his relationship with Cocoa, and Cocoa became familiar with his relationship with her niece. He was getting down to his last, but Nikki Pooh was only one week away from making her move.

Chapter 20: An Angel with Broken Wings

The night before Slim was supposed start school, he stayed out hustling with Kandi until 1AM. If it weren't for Peach, he would have overslept. When she woke him, he refused to get up. It wasn't until she reminded him that he had to pick up Jayla when he forced himself out of bed. He only had a few hours of sleep. Luckily for him, Peach had his clothes laid out for him. He lazily went to the bathroom and took care of the usual morning business while Peach cooked breakfast.

When Slim came from the bathroom, he got dressed in the clothes Peach laid out for him. He was careless with getting dressed, but was still coordinated with his thuggish swag.

After Slim ate breakfast with Peach and Kaliyah, Peach freshened his two French braids. He smoked on a blunt while she told him about her plans for the day. Before he left, she kissed his lips and told him to have a good day.

A slight smile appeared on Slim's face when Jayla came from the house. She was dressed in a blue jean designer outfit with black, heeled boots. Her hair and nails were freshly done, and she wore a few pieces of jewelry. A black leather bookbag hung across her shoulder with her purse. The bookbag looked as if it was already filled with books. She held a pastry in her hand with a napkin, and picked small pieces from it. He continued to stare at his adorable, grown little sister as she approached the car.

"Yeah, I know I'm cute," Jayla said as she got into the car.

"And I see I'ma have to bodyguard you."

"Please! You gon' be too busy chasin' them lil' girls." Jayla retorted.

"You know I ain't gotta chase nothin'," Slim said with a laugh as he pulled off.

"Von-Von, don't be doin' nothin' in front of me! You know how close me and Peach is, so I'm not finna lie for you."

"You won't have to, 'cause Peach won't put'chu in no type of awkward situations like that."

"You crazy anyway for messin' around on her. She pretty, and she everything you could want in a girlfriend. Now, how would you feel if she messed around on you?"

"You already know. I respect Peach though, and try not to let what I do become obvious. We got a understandin', and she know can't no other girl come close to what we got. I'ma settle down one day, and I'ma do it wit' Peach, 'cause she the one wit' me now, acceptin' me as I am."

"Well, I wish you hurry up," Jayla said with a smile. She was happy to hear Slim passionately talking about abandoning his player ways.

When Slim pulled up at Vashon High School, he and Jayla were stunned by the size of it. It was initially built as a factory.

He parked on the side of the school behind Nut's car. Nut was smoking on a blunt with Fe-Fe as they leaned on his car. Just like Slim and Jayla, they were dressed in their flyest gear. Nut showed no modesty with his flashy appearance. Small groups of students stood around socializing. The first day of school was like a fashion show.

Slim, Nut, Jayla and Fe-Fe all spoke to each other before Jayla and Fe-Fe went inside to meet with April and The Twins. Slim and Nut came in shortly after them. When Slim and Nut came into the school, they came under the scrutinizing eyes of two, young women security guards. They shook their head in disbelief as Slim and Nut got into the line that led through the metal detectors. The guards were allowing the students ahead of them to go through with little, or no inspection. They were very anxious to get to Slim and Nut. As soon as they put their keys in the basket and came through the metal detector, the guards stood in front of them.

"Now, this don't make no damn sense! This is a school, not no damn video shoot! And Nut, I know they didn't let'cho ass back in here," one of the guards said as she stood with her hands on her hips.

"And y'all smell like too much weed," the other guard said as she twitched her nose. "Do we need to strip search y'all?"

"I ain't got no problem wit that," Nut said as he stepped closer to the guards.

"You still got a nasty mouth! Wit'cho mannish ass! And this ain't the hood, so don't think y'all finna open up shop in this school."

"And y'all ain't finna be harassin' a nigga all year," Nut said as he twisted his face at the guards.

"You already know what's up," one of the guards said before she turned to Slim. "I'm Tammy, and this Rhonda. Don't nothin' pop off in this school wit'out us knowin' about it, so don't let this nut get'chu in trouble."

"C' mon, Cuz. They ain't talkin' 'bout shit," Nut said as he brushed past the guards.

On their way to the gym where they were going to get their schedules and have their ID's taken, Nut told Slim about Tammy and Rhonda. They weren't as righteous as their uniforms perceived them to be. They were from the hood. Last school year, they tried to get Nut to pay them for turning their head while he sold weed. Slim encouraged him to make some type of arrangements with them if he planned on doing his thing there.

After Slim and Nut had their ID's taken, they compared their schedules as they left the gym. They only had first period lunch together. Considering Slim's behavior and progress in the year-round school at D.Y.S., he was no longer in the B.D. class. He was a sophomore with two extra credits. It encouraged him to want to graduate. He left Nut talking with a girl as they planned on meeting up at lunch.

When Slim found his class, the first person he noticed was Meka. She was looking extra pretty with her new outfit on. She was surprised to see Slim in the school. He stopped at the teacher's desk to make his presence known and was issued a book. He then took a seat next to Meka in the back of the class. Still surprised, she shook her head in disbelief as she stared at him with a smile. He shrugged his shoulders as he slumped into the desk.

Slim was looking over his schedule when he heard a familiar name being called to the office over the intercom. Chills ran up his spine as he sat up from his slump and stared up at the intercom. When the name was repeated, he jumped up from his seat and shot towards the door. He ignored the teacher's question as he boldly left the classroom.

When Slim got to the first floor, he'd just missed the girl he was looking for. He only caught the back of her as she was going into the office. Even after over three years, she had that same catwalk. He didn't want to make a scene in the office, so he waited for her on the steps.

Underneath Slim's cool composure, he was extremely excited. He stood on the steps and leaned against the wall as he thought about old times with this girl. His slight smile left his face when he came to think about their abrupt departure. He still felt something for her, but was too excited to acknowledge it, or the dilemma it would put him in.

When the girl Slim was waiting for came through the double doors that led to the steps, she looked confused as she stared at a piece of paper. She stopped in the doorway, and was unaware of his eyes on her. She'd only grown a few inches. Her hair was in a long ponytail with big curls while bangs laid perfectly across her forehead. She wore a blue jean, designer outfit that showed her development. The red blouse under her jacket matched her heeled boots, belt, and the purse that hung from her shoulder. He only remembered her in tennis shoes with very little sex appeal. But he was now looking at a more developed, and a more feminine Angel.

"In trouble already?"

Angel could never forget the slurry speech of her first love. She looked up startled and dropped her things. Her eyes widened in surprise while her mouth fell open. She covered her mouth with her hand as a squeak came out. She was now looking at a more developed Jevon with a sparkling smile.

"Jevon?" Angel asked in a whiny tone.

"This me," Slim said as he came down the steps.

"Boy, look at' chu! "

"Nah, look at'chu. You lookin' good!"

Slim and Angel stood inches apart as they began to closely examine each other. She slowly rose her hand to his face and caressed it with her fingertips. Her facial expressions became tender as their touch confirmed that he was actually there. Something around her neck caught his attention. It was hidden under her blouse. His smile became brighter as he gently pulled it out. It was the necklace he gave her on Valentine's Day over three years ago. It still held the sparkling shine as it did when he first gave it to her. Slim held the heart pendant in the palm of his hand as he shifted his eyes to her.

"I see you still got my heart," Slim said, causing Angel to blush. "I missed you. Gimme a hug," he said as he wrapped his arms around her.

It took a moment for Angel to return Slim's embrace. When she did, she laid her head on his chest. Just like when they were in the sixth grade, he gently squeezed her tender body while lovingly inhaling the sweet smell of her. He had his eyes closed and ran his nose across her neck with his soft kisses. Their embrace was one that brought back a lot of sentimental memories. It was her sniffling that made him break the embrace. When he looked to her, she was crying.

"Angel, you aiight?"

Angel held her head down as she wiped the tears from her face. She then looked up to Slim with a weak smile. "When did you get out?"

"Right before the summer started."

"You was gone for a long time, but I see you didn't waste time wit gettin' back to doin' what'chu do."

"Regardless of what's goin' on wit me, I thought'chu would be excited to see me."

"I am. It's just that…" Angel softly said before she dropped her head.

"What? You got a boyfriend?"

"Yeah, but it's more to it than that."

"Aiight. Tell him go on 'bout his business, and we could fix whatever it is that's botherin' you."

"Jevon, I can't do him like that. And I don't think we can fix the problem," Angel said as she looked him up and down.

"Angel, just tell me what's goin' on wit'chu?" Slim insisted as he grabbed her hands.

Angel bowed her head and shook it from side to side. She then took a deep breath and slowly exhaled as she looked up to Slim. "Jevon, we need to talk. I don't wanna do it here, 'cause I'ma get all emotional and stuff. I'ma give you my number and I want'chu to call me tonight."

"I wanna talk wit'chu face to face, so let me take you home after school."

"Take me home? Why am I not surprised?"

"I don't know, but I'll be in two-thirteen my last period," Slim said after checking his schedule.

"Lemme see that," Angel said as she took Slim's schedule. After a moment of looking over it, a little smile appeared on her face. "I'll meet'chu there."

Slim was in class when the excitement from seeing Angel wore off. He realized that he still had feelings for her, and that put him in a dilemma. Those feelings were close to what he felt for Peach. What he told Jayla that morning about no other girl coming close to what he and Peach shared was now a lie. Choosing Angel over Peach was not one of his options, nor was ignoring what he felt for Angel. They both held significance to him, and there was nothing he was going to do that would make them despise him.

At lunch time, Slim sat at a table that was in the corner of the cafeteria. He sat in a slump with his foot resting in another chair. He sipped on his juice while he looked around for Angel. When he didn't see her, he figured that she had next lunch period.

"Damn Cuz," Nut said as he sat on the other side of the table, "Who you lookin' for?"

"You remember when I told you how I got jammed up at Yeatman wit' my girl, Angel? She go up here," Slim said after a moment.

"Straight up! I ain't know that was the Angel you was tellin' me 'bout. She went here last year, and it all make sense now."

"What'chu mean?"

"I tried to get at her last year, and she shot me down. She do not fuck wit' street niggas, and you the one who fucked her head up. Now, she got some square nigga that 'pose to be her boyfriend."

Slim shook his head in disbelief as he thought about Angel's strange behavior.

"Cuz, please tell me that'chu gon take her from that nigga."

"Even though I'm still feelin' Angel, you know where my heart at. I respect Angel and Peach, so I ain't gon' try to be a playa wit this. As for as me and Angel, it's gon' always be somethin' between us. No matter what type of nigga I am."

"I don't know what I'll do if I had yo' hands," Nut said before he went to the vendor machine.

Before lunch ended, Nut took Slim to one of the empty classrooms that was hidden behind a row of lockers. He jerked on the door before it came open. The abandoned classroom was dusty, and had scattered desk with empty file cabinets.

Blunt roaches were strewn across the floor with cigarette butts and tobacco from blunts. Nut opened up a window in the stuffy room before he rolled a blunt.

Slim and Nut were going to hide out in the empty classroom until second lunch period began. Within that time, Nut told Slim about a girl who he was going to have pushing weed at the school. He was going to have her selling quarter pounds to the dime sack and the five dollar blunt pushers.

On Slim's and Nut's way to the cafeteria, they just so happened to be walking behind Angel and her friends. Slim didn't want to make his presence known just yet. He wanted to see how everyone interacted with her.

In the cafeteria, Slim and Nut sat a few tables down from Angel and her friends. While she talked, her friends gave her their undivided attention. Whatever she was telling her friends had them surprised and fully into her. When she finished talking, they bombarded her with questions while she slumped in the chair and shook her head in disbelief.

"I bet'chu they down there talkin' 'bout'chu," Nut said with a laugh.

When a guy with a high yellow skin complexion approached Angel, her friends immediately stopped talking. He was sharply dressed with his shirt tucked inside of his khaki pants. His hair cut was fresh. He wore a curly box with waves that ran into his fade. After giving Angel a juice with her favorite snacks, he kissed her cheek.

"See what I mean? He the exact opposite of you," Nut said with a laugh, finding amusement in the situation.

Just as Angel's boyfriend left the table, she caught Slim's eyes on her. Her surprise caused her friends to become aware.

"Von-Von, y'all is not 'pose to be in here," Jayla said as she came to the table. She came with the Fast Ass Clique. They pulled up chairs and filled the table with their snacks.

"I'm followin' Slim. He chasin' Angel," Nut said as he looked to Angel, then back to Jayla.

Jayla looked to Angel, then back to Slim as she became surprised. "Von-Von, is that the same Angel?"

"That's her."

"We was talkin' this mornin' in class for awhile, 'cause we got on the same 'fit. It never crossed my mind that she was the same Angel that'chu used to lemme talk to."

Angel had the same realization as Jayla and was approaching the table with excitement. "Jay, girl, I didn't know that was you," she sweetly said as she opened her arms.

"I didn't know either," Jayla squeeled as she and Angel hugged. Slim had no idea of what Jayla and Angel used to talk about, but it was obvious that they established a bond. After they embraced, they exchanged numbers.

"We'll catch up," Angel said before she left with her friends.

When Jayla sat back at the table, she looked at Slim and shook her head in disbelief. With her knowing about the special history he and Angel shared, she was aware of his dilemma.

By the time Slim got to his last period class, he was well-known throughout the school. The gossip about he and Angel's history was everywhere. rt was a surprise to know that good girl Angel used to be with a thug.

When he came into his last period class, the teacher issued him a book. Their assignment was to read. He took a seat in the back of the class, slumped into the desk and opened his book. Just like the other assignments, he was very familiar with it. With him going to school year-round at D.Y.s., he was further advanced than the average sophomore.

Just as the bell rung to begin class, Angel strolled in. She gave Slim a weak smile before she turned to the teacher's desk. He then knew why she smiled when she looked at his schedule. After being issued a book, she took a seat in the front row of the class. During class, not once did she look back to Slim.

At the end of class, Slim approached Angel while she was gathering her things. "What's up••• You still gon let me take you home?"

"Can you gimme a minute," Angel asked as she looked to the door, then back to Slim.

When Slim looked to the door, Angel's boyfriend was there. "I'll be out here."

Slirn's locker wasn't far from his   last period class. After putting his book inside, he leaned there. From where he stood, he could see Angel down the hall with her boyfriend. After exchanging some words, he kissed her cheek and left in the opposite direction. A slight smile appeared on Slim's face as she was approaching him.

"Jevon, don't make this harder than it already is for me. And I know you don't have nothin' to say wit all these girls you got chasin' you."

"I ain't say nothin',"Slim   said with a laugh.

When Slim got outside with Angel, both sides of the street was crowded. It looked as if a parade was going on. The police and school security walked through the crowd as they were moving everyone along. Nut was already gone as he was anxious to get away from the authorities.

Jayla was leaning on Slim's car when he got there with Angel. She let Angel get into the front while she climbed into the back. After starting the car, Slim reached under his seat for his phone and looked at its caller ID. He was only interested in Kandi's number. After dialing her number, he pulled off.

"Could y'all hold it down for a minute," Slim politely asked. Jayla and A~gel were talking and laughing about something to where Slim couldn't hear Kandi. Despite his politeness, Jayla mumbled something under her breath.

"What's up? You tryin'a catch up wit me?"

"I1ma need to see you later," Kandi said, telling Slim that she was almost out of dope.

"I'ma get wit'chu. Is everything else good on yo' end?"

"Yeah, booh. Everything good."

"Aiight. I'ma get wit'chu later."

When Slim got to his father's house to drop Jayla off, he turned his music down as he stopped in the middle of the street.

"Von Von, make sure you call me tonight," Jayla said as she got out of the car.

"Aiight," Slim said, knowing that Jayla wanted to talk to him about the dilemma he was in.

Jayla and Angel wiggled their fingers at each other with smiles as Jayla headed towards the house. Slim waited until she was inside before he pulled off.

"Do you and Jay still talk a lot?"

"Not as much as we used to. But that's my heart, so I always get around to seein' what's up wit her."

"So, who do you stay wit," Angel asked as she turned her body towards Slim.

Slim chuckled as he realized that Angel's question came from her attentiveness.

"You live wit some girl, don't chu?"

"Where you live?"

"In the same house I been livin' in for years."

"I thought'chu moved, 'cause I tried to call you awhile back, but'cho phone was disconnected."

"Jevon, don't try to change the subject," Angel said as she tapped him.

"I ain't tryin'a change the subject. We gon get into that, and whatever it is that's botherin' you."

An uneasy expression appeared on Angel's face as she slowly turned her body away from Slim and stared out of the window.

"Angel, what's wrong," Slim asked as he gently pulled her ponytail from across her shoulder.

When Angel turned to Slim, he seen that she was about to cry as she looked him up and down with her eyes. They served as a window to her broken spirit. Compassion took over him as he pulled over to give her his undivided attention.

"Angel, talk to me," Slim softly spoke as he leaned over to her.

"This is so complicated for me, and seein1 you like this don't make things easier."

"Talk to me, and let's try to get some kinda undastandin1 so we can figure somethin1 out."

"I jus haven't been the same person since that day you left me. You know how I felt about'chu, but it was nothin1 compared to how I felt when they took you away from me. When you stepped up and told them people that that stuff was yours, it showed me how deep yo' feelin1s was for me. It was a sacrifice that showed me that my feelin1s were in the right place. My love for you became stronger, but it was like my heart was bein1 taken away from me at the same time. I cried, but that was only the beginnin' of the hurt. My mama had to come and get me," Angel said before a tear fell from her eye.

"Angel, I1m sorry for puttin1 you through that, and I was hurtin1 too."

"Jevon, I'm still goin1 through it in a way. My mama and counselors tried to help me get over you, but the only time I took this chain off was when I was cleanin' it. I never stopped hurtin1, and as I got older, I started to see how you affected me. I been wit one boy after you, and the most affection I've showed him was a kiss. I'll never be happy, 'cause the one thing that could make me happy is the same thing I'm scared of.

"Jevon, look at'chu••• wit'cho jewelry and them things in yo' mouth! You deep in the streets, and it's gon always be a possibility that'chu gon leave again. I told myself that I'll never be wit a thug, but at the same time, I can't control what I feel for you," Angel cried.

Slim fell back into his seat as he realized that there was nothing he could do, or say to console Angel. He was who he was, and unfortunately, what he felt for her wasn't stronger than his commitment to what he claimed to be.

"Jevon, these people in these streets don't care about' chu," Angel vigorously cried out.

Slim stared at Angel as her vigorous cry aroused his curiosity. "Is you tryin'a tell me somethin'?"

Angel shook her head from side to side as she dropped it with her eyes closed. After a moment, she took a deep breath and exhaled as she looked to Slim. "I know this won't change you, but it was J-Will who told on you. He got caught wit some weed, and told on you to save his self. I found out when my sista broke up wit him and didn't go to his funeral."

Slim's face tightened up as he thought about Det. Swanson's insightful words. "What you are committed to, and so called being loyal to, it holds deception that will eventually catch up with you." With everything he learned since that naive state of mind, what J-Will did didn't surprise him. Especially with G-Will being his big brother.

"I ain't surprised," he finally said as he shrugged his shoulders. "As for as me and you, you gon always be special to me. At the same time, I think we should take things one step at a time and jus be friends. If that's possible."

Angel shrugged her shoulders as she turned towards the window.

When Slim got to Angel's house, she had him to park his car so he can come inside to meet her mother. He was reluctant about it as he was uncertain about what he would encounter. Angel was adamant about it, and wasn't taking no for an answer.

Angel's sister was coming into the living room when Slim came into the house with Angel. She stopped and stared at him with her eyes squinted. She then looked to Angel, who folded her arms across her chest-   When she looked back to Slim, a big smile appeared on her face.

"Jevon," Teri said with excitement.

"What's up, Teri. I   see you still lookin' good."

"You got hella big! Lookin' like you jus jumped off a   t.v. screen! Gimme a hug," Teri said as she came towards Slim with her arms out. Her hug was tight as he could feel the love and the admiration she had for him. "Angel, where you find him at?"

"He go to the V wit me."

All of a sudden, Teri's eyes bubbled as she covered her mouth. Slim turned to Angel, who stood with her hands on her hips. "Mamaa! Look who Angel got in here," Teri yelled towards the kitchen as she kept her eyes on Slim.

Slim nervously stood in confusion as he looked back and forth to Angel and Teri. Before he could think of what to do, their beautiful mother came into the living room.

"Girl, what the••• ," their mother said before she paused and focused on Slim.

"Mama, this Jevon," Angel informed.

"Awww, okay. I finally get to meet the Jevon that got my baby head messed up," she said as she came and stood in front of him. "And yes, I know about everything that happened between y'all."

As a mother, it was logical for her to ask Angel certain questions from seeing how Slim affected her. He dropped his head and shied up as he was put on the spot.

"Un-uh! Look at me••• wit'cho grown ass," Angel's mother said as she lifted Slim's head with her finger. "Do you have any idea of what'chu did to my baby?"

"I loved Angel wit the bottom of my heart, and it was never my intentions to hurt her. We talked, and I 1pologized for how I affected her. It's still a lot of feelin1s between us that we can't ignore, and we jus tryin'a do what's right," Slim spoke with sincerity.

"You talk like you have some sense, and I respect·you for not lettin' my baby go down for that stuff. That told me a lot about'cho character, and it makes me feel a little comfortable wit'chu seein' her. I'ma let ch1all work things out, but I am her mother, so I will be involved in what goes on in her life."

"I can respect that," Slim humbly spoke.

"Now, how did y'all catch up wit each other?"

"School," Angel said with a smile.

"I'm glad you got'cho butt in school. But what'cho mama think about'chu runnin' the streets?"

"He live wit his girlfriend," Angel said as she nudged Slim.

"Well, I'm Ms. Pamela, and you welcomed to eat wit us, if you don't have any where to be."

"I ain't got nowhere to be. Thank you," Slim politely accepted Ms. Pamela's kindness.

"I'ma be right here in the kitchen, so y'all keep y'all hands to y'all self," Angel's mother said as she left the living room.

Slim rubbed his hands together as he looked Angel up and down with a smile.

"You gotta girlfriend," Angel said as she rolled her eyes at Slim and headed towards the couch.

"Well, I'ma go help mama in the kitchen and let'chu lovebirds get reacquainted," Teri said as she left the living room.

On Slim's way to the couch, his phone began to ring. He looked at its called ID as he sat next to Angel. It was Peach. "I don't wanna be rude, but I need to answer this."

"Answer it," Angel insisted.

Angel watched Slim and listened to him while he talked to Peach. She called to ask him about what he wanted to eat. After he told her that he wouldn't be home until later, she asked him about his day. He told her that it was cool, and would talk with her about it when he got there.

"Was that her," Angel asked when Slim clicked his phone off.

"Yeah••• Her name Peach."

"Tell me about her••• if you don't mind."

"It's cool. I wanna tell you about her, jus like I'ma tell her 'bout'chu again."

"Again!"

"It was kinda hard for me to open up to Peach and let myself go. Even after she gave me all the right reasons to. When I finally did, I realized that it was a affect from what happened between us. That's when I told her 'bout'chu, and she undastood. Angel, Peach is more than a girlfriend. She like family to me and my family."

"It's that serious, huh?"

"Yeah, and I respect her jus as much as I respect you," Slim said before he paused. Slim continued to tell Angel how his love and respect for Peach was basically formed. She was understanding, and shook her head affirmatively when he made his points. When he told her about the pregnancy, she dropped her head as if all hopes for them had died. He gently lifted her head before he began to recite the poem she gave him on Valentine's Day. He spoke softly as he looked into her eyes. By the time he was finished, tears were coming down her face.

"I cant believe you remembered it," Angel said as she was touched.

"I don't wanna confuse you. I jus want'chu to know, what we had is irreplaceable."

"I'm not confused," Angel said as she slid closer to Slim. Slim and Angel stared into each other's eyes where they rediscovered that undying chemistry. It was just as hot as it was when they first fell in love. The chemistry eventually brought their lips together. As they began to share a passionate kiss, their eyes closed slowly as her hand found its place on his cheek. It was the righteous of her that broke the kiss.

"I can't do this," Angel said as she pushed Slim away.

"My bad. I j us got••• "

"Jevon, I want'chu to leave! I need to do somethin' that I can't put off," Angel interrupted.

"That's cool. But can you at least tell me what got'chu all jumpy?"

"You gon hear about it anyway, and I want'chu to hear it from me first."

"What'chu finna do?"

"I'm finna break up wit my boyfriend. It's not right for me to be wit him when I got these feelin's for you," Angel said before she looked to the floor.

"You makin' me feel guilty about this."

"This ain't all about'chu. I have to do what I feel is right," Angel said before she went for the door.

When Slim got to the door, he stopped and stood in front of Angel. She was holding the door open for him as she looked to the floor. He gently lifted her head with his fingertips and looked into her eyes.

"Angel, I'm sorry for holdin' you back. I'm here wit'chu though, and we gon deal wit this togetha," he said as he felt responsible for her broken wings.

Chapter 21: Cold Game

On Slim's way home, he decided that he was going to talk with Peach in one of their most sentimental places. It was in the bath tub where they had a   lot of their sentimental talks.

On one occasion, she decorated the bathroom with scented candles and poured kiwi oil in the bath water. It's when she passionately expressed that she wanted to spend the rest of her life with him.

When Slim came into the apartment, Peach was cooking while Kaliyah sat at the counter on her phone. From her joyful expression, he figured that she was talking with Nut. When Peach noticed him, a big smile appeared on her face.

"Hey, baby," Peach enthusiastically greeted Slim. "I thought'chu wasn't gon be home 'til later."

"It looked that way, but'chu know how things always changin' wit me," Slim said as he hugged Peach from behind. "When we finish eatin', I'ma run us some water and tell you 'bout my day."

"It.-musta   been serious."

"It was."

"Well, whatever is goin' on wit'chu, you know I'm by yo' side."

"I know," Slim said before he kissed Peach's lips.

"Tehran comin' over," Kaliyah excitedly said when she clicked her phone off. "Is it enough for him?"

"It's enough."

"I'ma let'chu finish doin' what'chu doin' in here. I'ma go count this money and put it up, 'cause I know you ain't do it."

"I been gone all day," Peach said as she turned back to the stove.

After Slim counted the money he put in the top drawer last night, he added it to the stash under the dresser. It looked short, and that led him to counting it.

Slim stayed sitting on the floor after he counted the money. He expected it to be more than $28,600. Peach always told him what she took from the stash, and he kept track of what wen in and out. Even with what he spent school shopping, the cost of their living, and what they spent on things for the baby, it should be more. His hustle was very lucrative, especially with Lil' Jo doing his thing at Sharon's house. As he thought about it, Peach hasn't said anything about her cousin since he got that second package. It's been over two weeks, and that was odd, considering how fast things moved at Sharon's house•

After putting the drawer back into its place, he went into the kitchen with a confused expression.

"Baby, why you lookin' like that," Peach asked as she sat their plates on the table.

"What's up wit'cho peoples? He takin' too long to re-up."

"Can we talk about that later? I jus wanna eat wit'chu and let1chu tell me about'cho day."

Slim squinted his eyes at Peach as he could tell that she was keeping something from him. "Peach, you keepin' shit from me?"

"It's not like that! You know I'll never keep nothin' from you. I was gon tell you tonight, so we can figure this out togetha," Peach said as she grabbed Slim1s hands.

"Figure what out," Slim asked as he snatched his hands away from Peach.

"Baby, can we please talk about this when you calm down?" Peach's desperate plea only made Slim angrier as he was disappointed that she'd been keeping something from him.

"Peach, quit playin' games wit me, and tell me what's goin' on," he calmly demanded.

Peach knew that Slim's calmness was the last step from him erupting, so she submitted to his stubbornness. "Lil' ,Jo gettin' his dope from G-Will. But baby, it ain't nothin' to trip over. We don't need that money," she quickly said as she grabbed his hands.

"What," Slim furiously asked as he snatched his hands away from Peach.

"Baby, jus let it go!" Slim shook his head in disbelief as he headed towards his room.

"Jevon, where you goin'," Peach asked in a cry as she followed him.

Slim ignored Peach as he continued on to their room. When he got there, he got dressed in that monkey suit as he was prepared to act a fool. Peach continued to make desperate pleas for him to stay inside, but they fell on deaf ears.

"I'll be back," Slim said as he grabbed his pistol from under his pillow.

When Slim stood up from the bed, Peach stood in front of him. She wrapped her arms around him with a distressed expression.

"Jevon, our food gon get cold, and I wanna hear about'cho day. Baby, you ain't never put the streets over me. Please, don't leave like this," Peach sweetly said as one last attempt to keep him inside.

"I can't think straight 'til I handle this••• I'll be back." Peach gently brushed Slim's back as he walked away from her.

Slim parked his car in his father's backyard and walked up the dark alley with his pistol out. It wasn't about the money. It was about G-Will's vindictiveness as he put him in a position where he had to defend his street credibility. Then there was Lil' Jo, who benefited from an establishment he kept afloat, only to put the profits into the hands of an imposter. He was about to deal with the both of them, disregarding that Nikki Pooh was going to handle G-Will later on that night.

When Slim got to G-Will's backyard, he crept through the gangway to see if his car was parked in front of the house.

He was disappointed to find that he wasn't there, but luckily caught Lil' Jo. He was just going into Sharon's house.

It was nothing for Slim to discreetly get into Sharon's house. This was his old spot, so he knew the ends and outs of it. He remembered that the door on the back porch was nailed shut with 2x4's. It was because the kitchen door provided no security. He climbed through the same window on the back porch as he did before.

On the back porch, Slim listened for sound as his eyes adjusted to the darkness. He heard nothing but the refrigerator as he stood on the other side of the door. He took a deep breath and slowly exhaled as he opened the door to the. kitchen. It came open without a sound.

Slim stood with his back against the refrigerator. It was next to the entrance of the dining room. When he peeped from around the refrigerator, he could see straight into the living room. It was lit by the t.v. that gave a silhouette of Lil' Jo. He appeared to be counting money as he sat slumped on the couch with his head down.

Slim twisted his face as he came from around the refrigerator with his pistol pointed at Lil' Jo. He still had his head down, unaware of the approaching danger. Out of no where, the basement door swung open into the living room.

Lil' Jo looked up, but the door hid Slim before he could notice him. Slim slipped back into the kitchen and took his place back in front of the refrigerator. He stood there, listening to what was going on in the living room. Sharon was complaining about the dope Lil' Jo was serving. Her voice then grew louder as he could footsteps coming towards the kitchen. He prayed that she didn't come into the kitchen as his heart pounded his chest. He was relieved when he heard the basement door slam with her complaining dying•

After a moment, Slim peeped around the refrigerator. Lil' Jo had went back to counting his money. But this time, it was Slim that brought his awareness up. As soon as the wooden floor made a creak, he quickly rose his head. Unfortunately, it was too late. Slim had his pistol aimed at his head as he came into the living room. Lil' Jo remained in his slump, making no attempt to reach for his 9mm that was on the table.

"Nigga, who the fuck is you," Lil' Jo asked with hostility.

"I'm the nigga you 'pose to re-up wit," Slim calmly said as he moved closer to Lil' Jo.

"You mus be Slim."

"so, you know."

"You need to holla at'cho homeboy. He said, this his spot."

"I!ma holla at that rat ass nigga soons I finish hollin' at'chu," Slim said as he brought his other hand up to the pistol.

Just as Slim was about to squeeze shots off into Lil'Jo's head, the front door flew open. It was Peach who barged in with her pistol. That split second when Slim took his eyes away from Lil' Jo cost him. Lil' Jo had his pistol off the table and was filling his upper body with hot lead. Slim stumbled backwards with his face full of agony as he let out pointless shots.

"Noooo," Peach cried as she fired shots at Lil' Jo.

Peach continued to fire aimless shots at Lil' Jo as she jumped in front of Slim. Lil' Jo had no choice in turning the flames on his own cousin. Once she was in front of Slim, he could see her body jump with her arms flopping as the hot led hit her back. She lunged towards Slim and sent them crashing to the floor.

The living room went silent as Peach laid on top of Slim in a puddle of their own blood. Her arm was wrapped around him with her pistol still in her other hand. His arms were stretched out as he still gripped his pistol. His body was in shock while his senses were still functioning. He could hear tires peeling while the engine roared and faded into the night. The smell of guns smoke lingered in the air as he could also smell the sweet conditioner in Peach's hair. He could feel Peach's body as it began to violently shake. Her eyes blinked continuously as her mouth trembled. He couldn't talk. He could only helplessly witness as it was torturing. She began to choke on her blood as it filled her mouth and spilled onto his face. All of a sudden, she stopped shaking. Her eyes slowly closed as her head fell over his shoulder.

Peach died in the same place where she and Slim met, taking their unborn child along with her. It was a nightmare that he was unable to respond to. He could only witness it as it occurred. He could hear tires screeching as a car came to a stop in front of the house. Light began to fade from his vision as his grasp on his pistol became weak.

"Fuck! Cous, y'all can't go out like this!" Those were the last words Slim heard before he was abducted by the darkness.

Within the uncompromising street life, life can come to an abrupt end at any given moment. Being aware of that strong possibility doesn't include making preparations for that moment. Street niggas go on with life, creating dreams with plans to fulfill them. Dreams and plans aren't seen as hopeless when the essentials that makes them visible are present. For that reason, preparations for that unfortunate moment is disregarded. Life qoes on with doing what Ls ·necessary to lessen that detrimental moment from becoming a reality.

When a person is committed to a lifestyle that fulfills their intermost desires, there is nothing anyone can say or do to convert them. Sometimes, it takes experiences to create conversions. However, such touching experiences can cause a person to convert into many directions.

The street life can be brutally uncompromising, leaving some without the opportunity to find their true destiny. The dreams, plans, and the opportunity to make amends with those who were mentally and emotionally affected becomes forever lost. Love ones are left mourning with a reality that was put on ice. It's a cold game.

Chapter 22: I Am What I Am

Fortunately, Slim got another chance at life. He laid unconscious in a hospital bed while the physical, emotional, and the mental scars awaits him. Those scars are a development of consciousness that would either turn him away from the streets, or drive him deeper into them.

It was late that next afternoon when Slirn's eyes slowly opened. He stared up at the ceiling in the bright room as his eyes gained focus. The room was quiet and cold with a repeated beep. He shifted his eyes to someone who was sitting in a chair next to him. It was Jayla. She sat in a slump as she appeared to be sleeping. His forehead became wrinkled as he noticed dried up tear streaks of her face. He then shifted his eyes to his throbbing upper body. Two gauze pads were patched on his chest with two more on his left shoulder. On his stomach, there was another gauze pad from surgery. Within a blink of an eye, last nights' nightmare came back to him.

He let out an agonizing groan as he tried to get up, but his bodi was too weak.

"Von Von, don't try to get up," Jayla cried as she stood over him.

Slim let out a vigorous groan as tears ran down the sides of his face. His groan was a mixture of pain, rage and vengeance. He violently cussed as he found the strength to snatch the heart monitor from his chest. It left the machine making a flat beep. Before he could snatch the morphine and the IV from his veins, Jayla grabbed his wrist. She held them to the bed as tears fell from her face. There was nothing she could do, or say to console her brother. Doctors and nurses stormed into the room followed by his father and brother. One of the doctors took Jayla's place restraining Slim. It came to having to give him a sedative. After a couple minutes from the shot, he was out cold.

When Slim woke up that night, he was alone, and his body was weak. His vision was blurry, but he was thinking clearly. His clear thinking was to no consolation. It only brought him more in tune with the emotional pain and the mental anguish. Every time he closed his eyes, a piece of his life with Peach was envisioned. A single tear ran down the side of his face when he thought about the moment he accepted her pregnancy.

He could hear her joy and excitement. The emotional pain was nothing compared to the mental anguish when he thought about her desperate pleas to keep him inside. It was torturing to him to know that if he would've listened, she would still be with him. Especially with him knowing how vigilant, stubborn and protective she was when it came to him. It's why he excluded her from his street life. He became overwhelmed with guilt as he realized that he should have excluded her completely. However, his realization didn't pardon Lil' Jo and G-Will.

"Von Von," Jayla called out to him in a cry. It was the sound of Jayla's sorrow that brought Slim from his trance. She was standing in the door, holding a juice with her watery eyes. The sight of her sorrow was unbearable. He turned his head and looked to the floor as she approached him.

"I wanna hug you, but I don't wanna hurt'chu," Jayla said with sniffles as she pulled up a chair. "Von Von, I don't know how to deal wit this. I can't think or eat, and it feel like I'm suffocatin'. I'm tryin'a be strong, but it's hard when I feel like I'm the one layin' in this bed. I don't know exactly how you feel, but I can almost swear that I'm feelin' the same.

"I'm here wit'chu in every sense, and I hope I'm not makin' things harder wit me bein' here like this. I don't mean to be inconsiderate, but Von Von, you the only one who can help me get through this. I need you."

It took a tremendous amount of Slim's energy for him to vacate his distorted state of mind and sympathize with his innocent little sister. In all actuality, he was the cause of her grief. Despite everything he was going through, he was morally obligated to console her.

"Jay, I'm sorry for puttin' you through this," Slim weakly spoke as he opened his hand for hers.

"You don't have to 'pologize," Jayla said as she grabbed Slim's hand and sat on the bed.

Jayla's sweetness and strength was heartwarming, but there was nothing that could warm Slim's tormented soul. He gave her hand a gentle squeeze before he turned his head away from her.

"Daddy and Marcel out there wit that nurse lady. When she said you finna wake up, I went and got'cho favorite juice to take them pills wit."

Slim had already slipped back into his distorted state of mind, and was paying Jayla no attention. He didn't even notice the doctor when she came into the room with his father and brother.

"Hello Jevon••• I'm Dr. Ashley," she politely spoke as she stood over him.

Slim didn't bother to acknowledge the doctor. He kept his head turned as he stared at the floor.

"I must commend you on your strength. You are a very healthy young man. But at times, we all may need a little assistance with maintaining that healthiness. I took you off the morphine, and what I have for you are some ibuprofen and some antibiotics. They will reduce your pain and fight any infections from your wounds. I would like for you to take them, then I'll enlighten you on your condition."

Slim didn't want to take the pills as he felt that nothing could reduce his pain. He also didn't want the attention that came with refusing them. Dr. Ashley gave him a slight smile when he turned to her. After elevating his bed to a sitting position, she gave him the pills with Jayla giving him the juice. When he gave the juice back, he turned his head away from the sorrowful faces of his family.

"You'll have to take those pills three times a day, preferably after meals. It's important for you to do so. We successfully removed the bullets that were lodged in your chest through surgery. The wounds on your shoulder are only flesh wounds. The internal damage will heal on its own. To ensure proper healing on the outside, your bandages must be changed three times a day with applying the antibiotic cream that I'm providing you with. Resting is also important. It gives your body time to heal without too much energy fluctuating through your muscles. It's a simple, but important care that could be managed from your home. I'll be signing your release papers in two days. In the meantime, myself and the nurses will care for you, and answer any questions that you may have."

Slim didn't pay Dr. Ashley any attention. He stared at the floor while Jayla gently brushed his hair with her hand. It was her, who began to ask questions about how to care for him. She was unyielding with her questions until she had a clear understanding.

When Dr. Ashley left the room, it was taken over by complete silence. No one knew what to say in this difficult time, or was either searching for the correct words. Jayla was still brushing Slim's hair while his father and brother sat in chairs close to his bed. It was their father, who cleared his throat before he began to speak.

"I've never been at a lost for words, but I guess when words can't describe what we feel, it's hard for us to speak. It'll be insensitive for me to say, everything gon be aiight at a time like this. We all are hurtin' to the point where we don't know how we'll make it through the day. I can only assure you that, we as a family will get through this togetha. Let's jus take one day at a time, and pray for a betta one to come."

Marcel wrapped his arm around his father as he wiped a tear from his face. A tear ran down Slim's face as he thought about how Peach worked her way into his family with her gracious charm. Her death was a tragedy that scared all of their hearts. It felt like a sledge hammer hit his stomach when he thought about what Kaliyah must be going through. The more he processed, pain came piling on top of pain. It was suffocating him. He didn't even hear his brother expressing his sympathy. It was two white men that were dressed in dark blazers and jeans that grabbed his attention. They stood in the doorway, and came into the room after a moment.

"I'm Detective Grey, and this is my partner, Detective Peterson," he said as he looked to his partner, then back to everyone. "We're sorry to intrude as we know this is a difficult time for you all. But with all due respect, we have an obligation to apprehend those who are responsible for your grief. We would like to ask some questions, and your cooperation would be greatly appreciated."

Slim turned his head away from the detectives as he had no intentions on answering any of the detectives questions. Even within his distorted state of mind, he was keeping it hood. It was something he hadn't even considered.

"As you can see, my son is in no state of mind to answer any questions. Now wit all due respect, we would appreciate if y'all gave us some privacy," Slim's father humbly spoke as he looked over his shoulders to the detectives.

"As I   said, respects are in order, so I would like to leave you with my card," Det. Grey replied.

"I won't force my son to talk, nor will I encourage him to it," Slim's father clearly spoke before he turned away from the officers.

The detectives got the picture as they left with no more pressure on Slim's family.

"Jevon, I know yo' head is somewhere else, but I want'chu to get a grasp on what'chu goin' through right now. You have some decisions to make, and what you are going through will help you make those decisions," Slim's father spoke as he grabbed his hand. "You have to begin with askin' yo'self questions. Is this lifestyle worth the pain and the misery? I know you feelin' it, 'cause you can't even look at us. I jus want'chu to pay attention to what'chu goin' through. The risk in it will always be greater than the value. The money and everything else that come wit it becomes worthless. You'll never be able to trade it for what'chu came to lose. Those who love you go through the pain wit'chu. The streets don't deserve you, and I'm hopin' you see it when you question yo'self."

Slim was touched by his father's enlightenment. It's where he began to question his commitment to what he claimed to be. How could he remain faithful to something that has taken one of his greatest values?

"Von Von, do you wanna try to eat somethin'," Jayla sweetly asked.

Jayla had to call Slim a few times before he looked to her. Just the thought of eating turned his stomach. He shook his head from side to side before·he went back into his thoughts.

Before the nurse left with the food cart, she informed them of visiting hours as they were about to end. Within that thirty minutes, Jayla attentively watched as the nurse changed Slim's bandages. Before his family left, they all kissed his forehead as they planned on being there first thing in the morning.

Slim had been staring into the darkness for hours when a gorilla built figure appeared in the doorway. He elevated the bed to a sitting as he was drawn back to that moment before he lost consciousness. He dropped his head as he remembered that it was Nut who came to assist him. He felt the bed sink as Nut sat there.

"That nurse lady lemme slide up here. She say visitin' hours over, but I'm here. I- know you _ain't tryin'a talk to no mu-fucka, but I brought'cho phone in case you need me for anything," Nut said as he sat the phone next to Slim. "I wanna put'chu up on some shit, but lemme pay my respects to Peach. You know she was like fam to me too. I recognized the love and the honor wit her, so I couldn't do nothin' but give the same in return. If anybody deserves to be wit the gods, it's her. And I will always remember her as a goddess."

Slim shook his head up and down as he felt Nut's love for Peach. They both dropped their heads for a moment to give her a thought to honor her.

"What'chu wanna put me up on?"

Nut slumped into his chair with a lean. "Kaliyah told me everything when I got there. Peach had already slid off though. I immediately shot around there, and that's when I found y'all. I called the ambulance and called yo' ol'dude on the way to the hospital. Peach was already gone. When they said you was breathin', I was on the move. I told you I had ties to that nigga Lil' Jo. It was nothin' to for me to slide up on him wit the choppa. Now, I wasn't surprised when I came across G-Will. His basement doe was wide open. Some nigga stretched him and that bitch Nikki Pooh out. I got the fuck from outta there and parked Peach car in yo' ol' dude backyard."

Slim shook his head up and down as he thought about Pooh. Nikki Pooh was too slow with handling her business. "What's up wit "Kaliyah," he dreadfully asked.

"This tearin' her up, but I'ma help her keep it togetha." Slim dropped his head as Nut confirmed his thouqhts. They sat in silence as they knew the sorrow was a possibility that came with their lifestyle. It was Slim's phone that broke the silence. A reflex made him answer it.

"What's up," Slim mumbled.

"Everybody tryn'a eat, and I'm still waitin' on you."

It was Kandi, and she obviously hact no idea of what was going on with him. He held his phone to his ear as he thouaht about what she said. She needed more dope. Her request brought him to a very challenging decision. He had a choice to tell her that it was all over, or give her access to his stash that'll keep his lifestyle flourishing. His father's encouraging words came to his mind along with the mourning faces of his family. How could he choose a lifestyle that has brutally betrayed him?

"What'chu want me to do," Kandi asked.

"Holla at Cocoa.... She know what to do." He gave her access to his stash before he clicked off.